BURIED SECRETS

By Joseph Finder

Fiction:

The Moscow Club
Extraordinary Powers
The Zero Hour
High Crimes
Paranoia
Company Man
Killer Instinct
Power Play
Vanished
Buried Secrets

Non-Fiction:

Red Carpet: The Connection Between the Kremlin and
America's Most Powerful Businessmen

BURIED SECRETS

Joseph Finder

headline

First published in Great Britain in 2011 by
HEADLINE PUBLISHING GROUP

1

Cataloguing in Publication Data is available from the British Library

Hardback ISBN 978 0 7553 4211 2
Trade paperback ISBN 978 0 7553 4212 9

Typeset in Times by Avon DataSet Ltd,
Bidford-on-Avon, Warwickshire

Printed and bound in Great Britain by
Clays Ltd, St Ives plc

Headline's policy is to use papers that are natural, renewable and
recyclable products and made from wood grown in sustainable forests.
The logging and manufacturing processes are expected to conform
to the environmental regulations of the country of origin.

HEADLINE PUBLISHING GROUP
An Hachette UK Company
338 Euston Road
London NW1 3BH

www.headline.co.uk
www.hachette.co.uk

In grateful memory of Jack McGeorge and Ken Kooistra
– generous sources who became friends

And in loving memory of my dear cousin, Linda Gardner Segal
– way too early

Part One

There are some secrets which do not permit themselves to be told. Men die nightly in their beds, wringing the hands of ghostly confessors, and looking them piteously in the eyes, die with despair of heart and convulsion of throat, on account of the hideousness of mysteries which will not suffer themselves to be revealed. Now and then, alas, the conscience of man takes up a burden so heavy in horror that it can be thrown down only into the grave. And thus the essence of all crime is undivulged.

– Edgar Allan Poe, 'The Man of the Crowd' (1840)

ONE

If this was what a prison was like, Alexa Marcus thought, I could totally live here. Like, forever.

She and Taylor Armstrong, her best friend, were standing in a long line to get into the hottest bar in Boston. The bar was called Slammer, and it was in a luxury hotel that used to be a jail. They'd even kept the bars in the windows and the huge central rotunda ringed with catwalks, that whole cell-block effect.

She was checking out this bunch of guys behind her who looked like MIT frat boys trying too hard to be cool: the untucked shirts, the cheap blazers, all that product in their hair, the toxic fumes of their Axe body spray. They'd stumble home at two in the morning, puking on the bridge to Cambridge, bitching about how all the girls at Slammer were skanks.

'I'm loving the smoky eye,' Taylor said, studying Alexa's eye makeup. 'See? It looks amazing on you!'

'It took me like an hour,' Alexa said. The fake eyelashes, the black gel eyeliner and charcoal eye shadow: she looked like a hooker who'd been beat up by her pimp.

'Takes me like *thirty seconds*,' Taylor said. 'Now look at you – you're this totally hot babe instead of a suburban prepster.'

'I'm *so* not suburban,' Alexa protested. She glanced over at a couple of skinny Euro-looking guys smoking and talking on their mobile phones. Cute but maybe gay? 'Dad lives in Manchester.' She'd almost said, '*I* live in Manchester,' but she no longer thought of the great rambling house she grew up in as her home, not since Dad had married that gold-digger flight attendant, Belinda. She hadn't lived at home in almost four years, since going away to Exeter.

'Yeah, okay,' Taylor said. Alexa caught her tone. Taylor always had to let you know she was a city kid. She'd grown up in a town-house on Beacon Hill, in Louisburg Square – her dad was a United States senator – and considered herself urban and therefore cooler and more street-smart than anyone else. Plus, the last three years she'd been in rehab, attending the Marston-Lee Academy, the tough-love 'therapeutic boarding school' in Colorado where the senator had sent her to get cleaned up.

Good luck with that.

Every time Taylor came back to Boston on break, she was rocking some different Girls Gone Wild look. Last year she'd dyed her hair jet black and had bangs. Tonight it was the skin-tight black liquid leggings, the oversized gray sheer tee over the black lace bra, the studded booties. Whereas Alexa, less adventurous, was wearing her ink skinny jeans and her tan Tory Burch leather jacket over a tank top. Okay, not as fashion-forward as Taylor, but no way was it *suburban*.

'Oh God,' Alexa murmured as the line drew closer to the bouncer.

'Just relax, okay, *Lucia*?' Taylor said.

'Lucia—?' Alexa began, and then she remembered that 'Lucia' was the name on her fake ID. Actually, it was a real ID, just not hers – she was seventeen, and Taylor had just turned eighteen, and the drinking age was twenty-one, which was way stupid. Taylor had bought Alexa's fake ID off an older girl.

'Just look the bouncer in the eye and be casual,' Taylor said. 'You're *totally fine.*'

*   *   *

Taylor was right, of course.

The bouncer didn't even ask to see their IDs. When they entered the hotel lobby, Alexa followed Taylor to the old-fashioned elevator, the kind that had an arrow that pointed to the floor it was on. The elevator door opened, and an iron accordion gate slid aside. Taylor got in along with a bunch of others. Alexa hesitated, slipped in, shuddered – God, she hated elevators! – and just as the accordion gate was knifing closed, she blurted out, 'I'll take the stairs.'

They met up on the fourth floor and managed to snag a couple of big cushy chairs. A waitress in a halter top so skimpy you could see the flower tattoo below her armpit took their order: a couple of Ketel One vodka sodas.

'Check out the girls on the bar,' Taylor shouted. Models in black leather butt-baring shorts and black leather vests were parading around on top of the bar like it was a catwalk.

One of the MIT frat boys tried to mack on them, but Taylor blew the guy off: 'Yeah, I'll give you a call – next time I need tutoring in like *differential calculus.*'

Alexa felt Taylor's eyes on her.

'Hey, what's wrong, kid? You've been acting all depressed since you got here.'

'I'm fine.'

'You think maybe you need to change meds or something?'

Alexa shook her head. 'Dad's just, I don't know, being all weird.'

'Nothing new about that.'

'But like he's all paranoid all of a sudden? He just had these surveillance cameras put in, all around the house?'

'Well, he *is* like the richest guy in Boston. Or one of the richest—'

'I know, I know,' Alexa interrupted, not wanting to hear it. She'd spent her entire life dealing with being a rich kid: having to play down the money so her friends didn't feel jealous. 'But it's not his normal control-freak mode, you know? It's more like he's scared something's going to happen.'

'Try living with a father who's a friggin' United States senator.'

Taylor had started to look uncomfortable. She rolled her eyes, shook her head dismissively, looked around the now-crowded bar. 'I need another drink,' she said. She called the waitress over and asked for a dirty martini. 'How about you?' she asked Alexa.

'I'm good.' The truth was, she hated hard liquor, especially vodka. And gin was the worst. How could anyone voluntarily drink that stuff? It was like chugging turpentine.

Alexa's iPhone vibrated, so she took it out and read the text. A friend at some rager in Allston, telling her it was epic and she should come over. Alexa texted back sorry. Then, abruptly, she said, 'Oh my God, oh my God, did I ever show you this?' She flicked through her iPhone applications until she came to one she'd just downloaded, launched it, held the iPhone to her mouth. When she talked into it, her words came out high pitched and weird, like one of the Chipmunks: 'Hey, babe, wanna come back to my dorm and take off our clothes and do some algebra?'

Taylor squealed. 'What *is* that?' She tried to grab the phone, but Alexa yanked it away, swiped the screen and started speaking in the creepy voice of Gollum from *The Lord of the Rings*: 'Must have preciousssss!'

Taylor shrieked, and they both laughed so hard that tears came to their eyes. 'See – you're feeling better already, right?' said Taylor.

'May I join you?' A male voice.

Alexa looked up, saw a guy standing there. Not one of the frat boys, though. *Definitely* not. This one had dark hair and brown eyes, a day's growth of beard, and he was totally a babe. Black shirt with white pinstripes, narrow waist, broad shoulders.

Alexa smiled, blushed – she couldn't help it – and looked at Taylor.

'Do we know you?' Taylor said.

'Not yet,' the guy said, flashing a dazzling smile. Late twenties, early thirties, maybe? Hard to tell. 'My friends ditched me. They went to a party in the South End I don't feel like going to.' He had some kind of Spanish accent.

'There's only two chairs,' Taylor said.

He said something to a couple seated next to them, slid a vacant chair over. Extended a hand to shake Taylor's, then Alexa's.

'I'm Lorenzo,' he said.

TWO

The bathroom had Molton Brown hand soap (Thai Vert) and real towels, folded into perfect squares. Alexa reapplied her lip gloss while Taylor touched up her eyes.

'He's totally into you,' Taylor said.

'What are you talking about?'

'Like you don't know it.' Taylor was outlining her eyes with a kohl pencil.

'How old do you think he is?'

'I don't know, thirties?'

'*Thirties?* I thought maybe thirty at the oldest. Do you think he knows we're only . . .' but another couple of girls entered the bathroom, and she let her sentence trail off.

'Go for it,' Taylor said. 'It's totally cool. I promise.'

When they finally succeeded in elbowing their way back to their chairs, the Black Eyed Peas blasting so loud her ears hurt, Alexa half-expected Lorenzo to be gone.

But he was still there, slouching a little in his chair, sipping his vodka. Alexa reached for her drink – a Peartini, at Lorenzo's suggestion – and was surprised it was half gone. *Man*, she thought, *I am truly wasted.*

Lorenzo smiled that awesome smile. His eyes weren't just brown, she noticed. They were light brown. *Tiger's eye*, she thought. She had a tiger's eye choker her mom had given her a couple months before she died. She couldn't bring herself to wear it, but she loved looking at the stones.

'If you kids'll excuse me,' Taylor said, 'I really need to get going.'

'Taylor!' Alexa said.

'Why?' said Lorenzo. 'Please stay.'

'Can't,' Taylor said. 'My dad's waiting up for me.' With a conspiratorial sparkle in her eye, Taylor gave a little wave and disappeared into the crowd.

Lorenzo moved to Taylor's chair, next to Alexa's. 'That's okay. Tell me about you, Lucia. How come I never see you here before?'

For a moment she forgot who 'Lucia' was.

Now she was definitely drunk.

She felt like she was floating above the clouds, singing along to Rihanna, smiling like an idiot, while Lorenzo was saying something to her. The room swam. She was finding it hard to separate his voice from everyone else's, a cacophony of a thousand individual conversations, little snatches, layer upon layer upon layer, none of them making any sense. Her mouth was dry. She reached for her glass of Pellegrino, knocked it over. Smiled sheepishly. She just stared at the spill open-mouthed, amazed that the water glass hadn't broken, gave Lorenzo a goofy smile, and he gave that spectacular smile back, his brown eyes soft and sexy. He reached over and dropped his napkin over the puddle to blot it up.

She said, 'I think I need to go home.'

'I take you,' he said.

He tossed a bunch of twenties on the table, stood, reached for her hand. She tried to stand but it felt like her knees were hinged. He took her hand again, his other hand around her waist, half-lifted her up.

'My car . . .'

'You shouldn't drive,' he said. 'I drive you home. You can get your car back tomorrow.'

'But . . .'

'It's not a problem. Come, Lucia.' He steered her through the crowd, his arms strong. People were staring at her, leering, laughter echoing, the lights streaky rainbow and glittery, like being underwater and looking up at the sky, everything so distant.

Now she felt the pleasant clear coolness of the late-night air on her face.

Traffic noise, the bleat of car horns, smearing by.

She was lying down on the back seat of a strange car, her cheek pressed against the cold hard cracked leather. The car smelled like stale cigarette smoke and beer. A few beer bottles rolled around on the floor. A Jag, she was pretty sure, but old and skeezy and filthy inside. Definitely not what she imagined a guy like Lorenzo driving.

'Do you know how to get there?' she tried to say. But the words came out slurred.

She felt seasick, hoped she wasn't going to vomit in the back seat of Lorenzo's Jaguar. That would be nasty.

She wondered: How did he know where to go?

Now she heard the car door open and close. The engine had been shut off. Why was he stopping so soon?

When she opened her eyes, she noticed it was dark. No streetlights. No traffic sounds, either. Her sluggish brain registered a faint, distant alarm. Was he leaving her here? Where were they? What was he doing?

Someone was walking toward the Jaguar. It was too dark to make out his face. A lean, powerful build, that was all she could see.

The door opened, and the light came on, illuminating the man's face. Shaved head, piercing blue eyes, sharp jaw, unshaven.

Handsome, until he smiled and showed brown rodent's teeth.

'Come with me, please,' the new man said.

She awoke in the back seat of a big new SUV. An Escalade, maybe, or a Navigator.

Very warm in here, almost hot. A smell like cheap air freshener.

She looked at the back of the driver's head. He had shaved black hair. On the back of his neck, a strange tattoo crawled up from beneath his sweatshirt. Her first thought was: angry eyes. A bird?

'What happened to Lorenzo?' she tried to say, but she wasn't sure what came out.

'Just stretch out and have yourself a nice rest, Alexa,' the man said. He had an accent too, but harsher, more guttural.

That sounded like a good idea. She felt herself drifting off, but then her heart started to race, as if her body realized even before her mind did.

He knew her real name.

THREE

'Here's the thing,' the short guy said. 'I always like to know who I'm doing business with.'

I nodded, smiled.

What a jerk.

If Short Man's Disease were recognized by modern medicine as the serious syndrome it is, all the textbooks would use Philip Curtis's picture, along with those of Mussolini, Stalin, Attila the Hun, and of course the patron saint of all miniature tyrants, Napoléon Bonaparte. Granted, I'm over six feet, but I know tall guys with Short Man's Disease too.

Philip Curtis, as he called himself, was so small and compact that I was convinced I could pick him up in one hand and hurl him through my office window, and by now I was sorely tempted to. He was maybe an inch or two above five feet, shiny bald, and wore enormous black-framed glasses, which he probably thought made him look more imposing, instead of like a turtle who'd lost his shell and was pissed off about it.

The vintage Patek Philippe watch on his wrist had to be sixty years old. That told me a lot. It was the only flashy object he wore, and it said 'inherited money'. His Patek Philippe had been passed down, probably from his dad.

'I checked you out.' His brow arched significantly. 'Did the whole due-diligence thing. Gotta say, you don't leave a lot of tracks.'

'So I'm told.'

'You don't have a website.'

'Don't need one.'

'You're not on Facebook.'

'My teenage nephew's on it. Does that count?'

'Barely anything turned up on Google. So I asked around. Seems you've got an unusual background. Went to Yale but never graduated. Did a couple of summer internships at McKinsey, huh?'

'I was young. I didn't know any better.'

His smile was reptilian. But a small reptile. A gecko, maybe. 'I worked there myself.'

'And I was almost starting to respect you,' I said.

'The part I don't get is, you dropped out of Yale to join the army. What was *that* all about? Guys like us don't do that.'

'Go to Yale?'

He shook his head, annoyed. 'You know, I thought the name "Heller" sounded familiar. Your dad's Victor Heller, right?'

I shrugged as if to say, *You got me.*

'Your father was a true legend.'

'Is,' I said.

'Excuse me?'

'Is,' I repeated. 'He's still alive. Doing twenty-some years in prison.'

'Right, right. Well, he sure got the shaft, didn't he?'

'So he tells people.' My father, Victor Heller, the so-called Dark Prince of Wall Street, was currently serving a twenty-eight-year sentence for securities fraud. 'Legend' was a polite way of referring to him.

'I was always a big admirer of your dad's. He was a real pioneer. Then again, I bet some potential clients, they hear you're Victor Heller's son, they're gonna think twice about hiring you, huh?'

'You think?'

'You know what I mean, the whole . . .' He faltered, then probably decided he didn't have to. He figured he'd made his point.

But I wasn't going to let him off so easily. 'You mean the apple doesn't fall far from the tree, right? Like father, like son?'

'Well, yeah, sort of. That might bother some guys, but not me. Uh-uh. Way I figure it, that means you're probably not going to be too finicky about the gray areas.'

'The gray areas.'

'All the fussy legal stuff, know what I'm saying?'

'Ah, gotcha,' I said. For a long moment I found myself looking out the window. I'd been doing that a lot lately. I liked the view. You could see right down High Street to the ocean, the waterfront at Rowes Wharf framed by a grand Italianate marble arch.

I'd moved to Boston from Washington a few months ago and was lucky enough to find an office in an old brick-and-beam building in the financial district, a rehabbed nineteenth-century lead-pipe factory. From the outside it looked like a Victorian poor-house out of Dickens. But on the inside, with its bare brick walls and tall arched windows and exposed ductwork and factory-floor open spaces, you couldn't forget it was a place where they used to actually make stuff. And I liked that. It had a sort of steampunk vibe. The other tenants in the building were consulting firms, an accounting firm, and several small real-estate offices. On the first floor was an 'exotic sushi and tapas' place that had gone out of business, and the showroom for Derderian Fine Oriental Rugs.

My office had belonged to some high-flying dot-com that made nothing, including money. They'd gone bust suddenly, so I caught a nice break on the price. They'd absconded so quickly they left all their fancy hanging metal-and-glass light fixtures and even some very expensive office chairs.

'So you say someone on your board of directors is leaking derogatory information about your company,' I said, turning around

slowly, 'and you want us to – how'd you put it? – "plug the leak".
Right?'

'Exactly.'

I gave him my finest conspiratorial grin. 'Meaning you want
their phones tapped and their e-mails accessed.'

'Hey, you're a pro,' he said with a quick, smarmy wink. 'I'd
never tell you how to do your job.'

'Better not to know the details, right? How we work our
magic?'

He nodded, a couple of sharp up-and-downs. 'Plausible deniability
and all that. You got it.'

'Of course. Obviously you know that what you're asking me to
do is basically illegal.'

'We're both big boys,' he said.

I had to bite my lip. One of us was, anyway.

Just then my phone buzzed – an internal line – and I picked it
up. 'Yeah?'

'Okay, you were right.' The smoky voice of my forensic data
tech, Dorothy Duval. 'His name isn't Philip Curtis.'

'Of course,' I said.

'Don't rub it in.'

'Not at all,' I said. 'It's a teachable moment. You should know
by now not to question me.'

'Yeah, yeah. Well, I'm stuck. If you have any ideas, just IM me,
and I'll check them out.'

'Thanks,' I said, and I hung up.

The man who wasn't Philip Curtis had a strong Chicago accent.
Wherever he lived now, he was raised in Chicago. He had a rich
dad: the hand-me-down Patek Philippe confirmed that.

Then there was the black luggage tag on his Louis Vuitton
briefcase. A fractional jet card. He leased a private jet for some
limited number of hours per year. Which meant he wanted a private
jet but couldn't afford one.

I had a vague recollection of an item I'd seen on BizWire about troubles in a family-held business in Chicago. 'Will you excuse me for just one more minute?' I said. 'I have to put out a fire.' Then I typed out an instant message and sent it to Dorothy.

The answer came back less than a minute later: a *Wall Street Journal* article she'd pulled up on ProQuest. I skimmed it, and I knew I'd guessed right. I remembered hearing the whole sordid story not too long ago.

Then I leaned back in my chair. 'So here's the problem,' I said.

'Problem?'

'I'm not interested in your business.'

Stunned, he whirled around to look at me. 'What did you just say?'

'If you really did your homework, you know that I do intelligence work for private clients. I'm not a private investigator, I don't tap phones, and I don't do divorces. And I'm sure as hell not a family therapist.'

'Family . . . ?'

'This is clearly a family squabble, Sam.'

Small round pink spots had formed high on his cheeks. 'I told you my name is—'

'Don't even bother,' I said wearily. 'This has nothing to do with plugging a leak. Your family troubles aren't exactly a secret. You were supposed to take over Daddy's company until he heard you were talking to the private equity guys about taking Richter private and cashing out.'

'I have no idea what you're referring to.'

His father, Jacob Richter, had gone from owning a parking lot in Chicago to creating the largest luxury hotel chain in the world. Over a hundred five-star hotels in forty countries, plus a couple of cruise lines, shopping malls, office buildings, and a hell of a lot of real estate. A company valued at ten billion dollars.

'So Dad gets pissed off,' I went on, 'and squeezes you out and appoints Big Sis chief executive officer and heir apparent instead of you. Didn't expect that, did you? You figured you were a shoo-in.

But you're not gonna put up with that, are you? Since you know all of Dad's dirty laundry, you figure you'll get him on tape making one of his shady real estate deals, offering kickbacks and bribes, and you'll be able to blackmail your way back in. I guess that's called winning ugly, right?'

Sam Richter's face had gone dark red, almost purple. A couple of bulging veins on top of his scalp were throbbing so hard I thought he was going to have a coronary right in the middle of my office. 'Who did you talk to?' he demanded.

'Nobody. Just did the whole due-diligence thing. I always like to know who I'm doing business with. And I really don't like being lied to.'

As Richter lurched to his feet, he shoved the chair – one of the expensive Humanscale office chairs left by the dot-com – and it crashed to the floor, leaving a visible dent in the old wood. From the doorway, he said, 'You know, for a guy whose father's in prison for fraud, you sure act all high and mighty.'

'You've got a point,' I conceded. 'Sorry to waste your time. Mind showing yourself out?' Behind him Dorothy was standing, arms folded.

'Victor Heller was . . . the *scum of the earth*!' he sputtered.

'Is,' I corrected him.

FOUR

'You don't tap phones,' Dorothy said, arms folded, moving into my office.

I smiled, shrugged. 'I always forget you can hear. Someday that's gonna get me in trouble.' Our standard arrangement was for her to listen in on all client meetings via the IP video camera built into the huge desktop monitor on my desk.

'You don't tap phones,' she said again. Her lips were pressed into a smirk. 'Mm-hmm.'

'As a general rule,' I said.

'Please,' she said. 'You *hire* guys to do it.'

'Exactly.'

'What the *hell* was that all about?' she snapped with a fierce glare.

Dorothy and I had worked together at Stoddard Associates in DC before I moved to Boston and stole her away. She wasn't really a computer genius – there were certainly more knowledgeable ones around – but she knew digital forensics inside and out. She'd worked at the National Security Agency for nine years, and they don't hire just anyone. As much as she detested working there, they'd trained her well. More important, no one was as stubborn as Dorothy. She simply did not give up. And there was no one more loyal.

She was feisty and blunt-spoken and didn't play well with others, which was why she and the NSA were a lousy fit, but it was one of the things I liked about her. She never held back. She loved telling me off and showing me up and proving me wrong, and I enjoyed that too. You did not want to mess with her.

'You heard me. I don't like liars.'

'Get over it. We need the business, and you've turned down more work than you've taken on.'

'I appreciate your concern,' I said, 'but you don't need to worry about the firm's cash flow. Your salary's guaranteed.'

'Until Heller Associates goes bust because the overhead's too high and you got no income. I am not slinking back to Jay Stoddard, and I am not moving back to Washington.'

'Don't worry about it.'

I'd worked closely with Dorothy, even intimately, but I knew almost nothing about her. She never talked about her love life, and I never asked. I wasn't even sure whether she preferred men or women. Everyone's entitled to their zone of privacy.

She was an attractive, striking woman with mocha skin, liquid brown eyes, and an incandescent smile. She always dressed elegantly, even though she didn't need to, since she rarely met with clients. Today she was wearing a shimmering lilac silk blouse and a black pencil skirt and some kind of strappy heels. She wore her hair extremely short – almost bald, in fact. On most women that might look bizarre, but on her it somehow worked. Attached to her earlobes were turquoise copper-enamel discs the size of Frisbees.

Dorothy was a mass of contradictions, which was another thing I liked about her. She was a regular churchgoer – even before she'd found an apartment, she'd joined an AME Zion church in the South End – but she was no church lady. The opposite, in fact: she had an almost profane sense of humor about her faith. She'd put a plaque on her cubicle wall that said JESUS LOVES YOU – EVERYONE ELSE THINKS YOU'RE AN ASSHOLE, right next to one that said I LOVE MARY'S BABYDADDY.

'I think we need to have regular status-update meetings like we used to do at Stoddard,' she said. 'I want to go over the Entronics case and the Garrison case.'

'I need coffee first,' I said. 'And not that swill that Jillian makes.'

Jillian Alperin, our receptionist and office manager, was a strict vegan. (Veganism is apparently the paramilitary wing of vegetarianism.) She had multiple piercings, including one on her lip, and several tattoos. One was of a butterfly, on her right shoulder. I'd caught a glimpse of another one on her lower back too one day.

She was also a 'green' fanatic who had banned all foam and paper cups in the office. Everything had to be organic, ethical, free-range, fair-trade, and cruelty-free. The coffee she ordered for the office machine was organic fair-trade ethical beans shade-grown using sustainable cultivation methods by a small co-op of indigenous peasant farmers in resistance in Chiapas, Mexico. It cost as much as Bolivian cocaine and probably would have been rejected by a death-row inmate.

'Well, aren't you fussy,' Dorothy said. 'There's a Starbucks across the street.'

'There's a Dunkin' Donuts down the block,' I said.

'That better not be a hint. I don't do coffee.'

'I know better than to ask,' I said, getting up.

The phone rang: the muted internal ringtone. Jillian's voice came over the intercom: 'A Marshall Marcus for you?'

'*The* Marshall Marcus?' Dorothy said. 'As in the richest guy in Boston?'

I nodded.

'You turn this one down, Nick, and I'm gonna whip your butt.'

'I doubt it's a job,' I said. 'Probably personal.' I picked up and said, 'Marshall. Long time.'

'Nick,' he said. 'I need your help. Alexa's gone.'

FIVE

Marshall Marcus lived on the North Shore, about a forty-minute drive from Boston, in the impossibly quaint town of Manchester-by-the-Sea, once a summer colony for rich Bostonians. His house was enormous and handsome, a rambling shingle-and-stone residence perched on a promontory above the jagged coastline. It had a wrap-around porch and too many rooms to count. There were probably rooms seen only by a maid. Marcus lived there with his fourth wife, Belinda. His only child, a daughter named Alexa, was away at boarding school, would soon be away at college, and – from what she'd once told me about her home life – wasn't likely to be around much after that.

Even after you'd pulled off the main road and could see Marcus's house off in the distance, it took a good ten minutes to get there, winding your way along a twisting narrow coastal lane, past immense 'cottages' and modest suburban houses built in the last half-century on small lots sold off by old-money Brahmins whose fortunes had dwindled away. A few of the grand old homes remained in the hands of the shabby gentry, the descendants of proper Bostonians, but they'd mostly fallen into disrepair. Many of the big houses had been snatched up by the hedge-fund honchos and the titans of tech.

Marshall Marcus was the richest of the nouveau riche, though not the most nouveau. He'd grown up poor on Blue Hill Avenue in Mattapan, in the old Jewish working-class enclave. Apparently his uncle owned a casino out west and Marshall had learned to play blackjack as a kid. He figured out pretty early that the house always has an advantage, so he started coming up with all sorts of card-counting schemes. He got a full scholarship to MIT, where he taught himself Fortran on those big old IBM 704 mainframes the size of ranch houses. He came up with a clever way to use Big Iron, as they called the early computers, to improve his odds at blackjack.

According to legend, one weekend he won ten thousand bucks in Reno. It didn't take him long to see that if he put this to use in the financial markets he could really clean up. So he opened a brokerage account with his tuition money and was a millionaire by the time he graduated, having devised some immensely complicated investment formula involving options arbitrage and derivatives. Eventually he perfected this proprietary algorithm and started a hedge fund and became a billionaire many times over.

My mother, who worked for him for years, once tried to explain it to me, but I didn't quite get it. I was never good at math. All I needed to know about Marshall Marcus was that he was good to my mother when things were bad.

When we moved to Boston after my father disappeared – Dad had gotten tipped off that he was about to be arrested, and he chose to go fugitive instead – we had no money, no house, nothing. We had to move in with my grandmother, Mom's mother, in Malden, outside of Boston. Mom, desperate for money, took a job as an office manager to Marshall Marcus, who was a friend of my father's. She ended up becoming his personal assistant. She loved working for him, and he always treated her well. He paid her a lot. Even after she retired, he continued to send her extremely generous Christmas presents.

Despite the fact that he'd been a friend of my father's, I liked him a lot. You couldn't help it. He was gregarious and affectionate and funny, a man of large appetites – he loved food, wine, cigars, and women, and all to excess. There was something immensely appealing about the guy.

His house looked exactly the same as the last time I'd visited: the Har-Tru tennis court, the Olympic-size swimming pool overlooking the ocean, the carriage house down the hill. The only thing new was a guard booth. A drop-arm beam barricade blocked the narrow roadway. A guard came out of the booth and asked my name, even asked to see my driver's license.

This surprised me. Marcus, despite his enormous wealth, had never lived like a prisoner, the way a lot of very rich people do, in gated communities behind high fences with bodyguards. Something had changed.

Once the guard let me through, I drove up to the semicircular driveway and parked right in front of the house. When I got out of the car I glanced around and spotted an array of security cameras mounted discreetly around the house and property.

I crossed the broad porch and rang the bell. A minute or so later the door opened and Marshall Marcus emerged, his short arms extended, face lit up.

'Nickeleh!' he said, his customary term of endearment for me. He bumped the screen door aside and engulfed me in a bear hug. He was even fatter, and his hair was different. When I last saw him, he was mostly bald on top and wore his gray hair down to his shirt collar. Now he was coloring it brown, with an orange tint, and the hair on the top of his head had magically grown back. I couldn't tell if it was a toupee or very good implants.

He was wearing a navy blue robe over pajamas, and he had deep circles under his eyes. He looked exhausted.

He released me, then pushed against my chest and leaned back to examine my face. 'Look at you – you get more and more handsome each time I see you. Enough, already! You don't age. You make a deal with the devil, Nicky? Is there a portrait of you looking like an *alter kaker* in your attic?'

'I live in the city,' I said. 'No attic.'

He laughed. 'You're not married, are you?'

'I've avoided that so far.'

He put a palm on my cheek and slapped gently. '*Punim* like this, I bet you gotta beat off the girls with a stick.' He was trying valiantly to feign his customary high spirits, but I wasn't convinced. He put a pudgy arm around my lower back. He couldn't reach as high as my shoulders. 'Thank you for coming, Nickeleh, my friend. Thank you.'

'Of course.'

'This new?' he said, jerking his head toward my car.

'I've had it for a while.'

I drive a Land Rover Defender 110, which is boxy and Jeep-like and virtually indestructible. Hand-cranked windows. Rock-hard seats. Not a very comfortable ride, and pretty noisy inside when you exceed thirty miles an hour. But it's the best car I've ever owned.

'Love it. *Love it.* I drove one of those around the Serengeti once on safari. Ten days. Annelise and Alexa and me. Of course, the girls hated Africa. Spent the whole time complaining about the insects, and how much the animals stank, and . . .' His smile disappeared abruptly, his face drooping as if worn out by the effort of keeping up the façade. 'Ahhh, Nick,' he whispered, a look of pain contorting his face, 'I'm scared out of my mind.'

SIX

'When did you last hear from her?' I said.

We sat in the only room downstairs that looked like it got any use, a big L-shaped eat-in kitchen/sitting room, in comfortable chairs covered in slouchy off-white slipcovers. The view was spectacular: the steely gray waves of Cape Ann lapping against the rocky coastline.

'Last night she drove down to Boston – she told Belinda she'd be back later, which Belinda assumed meant, you know, midnight or something. One or two in the morning, if she was having a good time.'

'When was this – what time did she leave the house?'

'Early evening, I think. I was on my way back from work.' Marcus Capital Management had an entire floor in one of the new buildings on Rowes Wharf, which I could see from a corner of my own office. He always worked long hours when Mom was his assistant, and he probably still did. A town car would take him into Boston every morning and take him home to Manchester every night. 'She was gone by the time I got home.'

'What was she doing in Boston?'

He heaved a long sigh, more like a moan. 'Oh, you know, she's always partying, that one. Always going out, to discos or what have you.'

Disco. I couldn't remember when I last heard that word. 'She drove herself? Or did she get a ride with a friend?'

'She drove. Loves to drive. She got her permit on the day she turned sixteen.'

'Was she meeting friends? Or was this a date? Or what?'

'Meeting a friend, I think. Alexa's not dating, thank God. Not yet, anyway. I mean, not as far as I know.'

I wondered how much Alexa told her father about her social life. Not much, I suspected. 'Did she say where she was going?'

'She just told Belinda she was meeting someone.'

'But not a guy.'

'No, not a man.' He sounded annoyed. 'Friends. Or a friend. She told Belinda . . .' Marcus shook his head, his cheeks quivering. Then he put a hand over his eyes, squeezing hard, and gave another long sigh.

After a few seconds I asked softly, 'Where's Belinda?'

'She's upstairs, lying down,' Marcus said, his pudgy hand still covering his eyes. 'She's just sick about it. She's taking this really hard, Nick. She didn't sleep all night. She's a wreck. She blames herself.'

'For what?'

'For letting Alexa go out. Not asking enough questions, I don't know. It's not Belinda's fault. It's not easy being the stepmother. Any time she tries to, you know, lay down the law, Alexa bites her head off. Calls her the "stepmonster" and all that – it's not fair. She cares about Alexa like she was her own, she really does. She loves that girl.'

I nodded. Waited half a minute or so. Then I said, 'Obviously you tried her cell.'

'A million times. I even called your mom – I figured maybe it got late and she didn't want to drive and she didn't want to call us, so maybe she decided to spend the night at Frankie's. She loves

Francine.' My mother's condo was in Newton, which was a lot closer to downtown Boston than Manchester-by-the-Sea.

'Do you have reason to believe something happened to her?' I asked.

'Of *course* something happened to her. She wouldn't just run off without telling anybody!'

'Marshall,' I said, 'I can't blame you for being scared. But don't forget, she does have a track record for acting out.'

'That's all behind her,' he said. 'She's a good kid now. That's the past.'

'Maybe,' I said. 'But maybe not.'

SEVEN

Some years back, as a kid, Alexa had been abducted in the Chestnut Hill Mall parking lot, right in front of her mother, Annelise, Marcus's third wife.

She hadn't been harmed, though. She'd been taken for a ride, driven around, and a few hours later dropped off at another parking lot across town. She insisted she hadn't been sexually assaulted, and an examination by a doctor confirmed it. She hadn't been threatened. They hadn't even spoken to her, she said.

So the whole thing remained a mystery. Did her abductors get scared off? Did they change their minds? It happened. Marcus was known to be very rich; maybe it had been an aborted kidnapping-for-ransom attempt. That was my assumption, anyway. Then her mother left, telling Marcus she couldn't bear to live with him anymore. Maybe it was precipitated by her daughter's kidnapping.

Who knows what the real reason was. She'd died of breast cancer last year, so she wasn't around to ask. But Alexa was never the same after that, and she wasn't exactly an easygoing, well-adjusted kid before the incident took place. She got even more rebellious, smoking at school, breaking curfew, doing whatever she could to get into trouble.

So one day a few months after it happened, my mother called

me – I was working in Washington at the time, at the Defense Department – and asked me to drive up to New Hampshire and have a talk with Alexa at Exeter.

I tracked her down on the stadium field and watched her play field hockey for a while. Even though she didn't consider herself a jock, she moved with a sinewy grace. She played with immense concentration. She had the rare ability to completely lose herself in the flow of the game.

She wasn't easy to talk to, but since I was Frankie Heller's son, and she loved my mom unambivalently, and since I wasn't her dad, eventually I broke through. She still hadn't metabolized the terror of the abduction. I told her that was normal, and that I'd worry about her if she hadn't been so deeply frightened by that day. I said it was great she was being so defiant.

She looked at me with disbelief, then suspicion. What kind of mind game was I playing?

I said I was serious. Defiance is great. That is how you learn to resist. I told her that fear is a tremendously useful instinct, since it's a warning signal. Fear tells us we're facing danger. We have to listen to it, use it. I even gave her a book about 'the gift of fear', though I doubt she ever read it.

I told her that she was not only a girl but a beautiful girl *and* a rich girl, and that those were three strikes against her. I taught her how to look for danger signals, and then I showed her some rudimentary self-defense techniques, a few basic martial-arts moves. Nothing fancy, but enough. I'd hate to be a drunken Exeter boy who tried to push her too far.

I took her to a dojo outside Boston and introduced her to Bujinkan self-defense techniques. I knew it would be great discipline for her, instill some self-confidence, be a healthy outlet for some of the aggression that had been building up inside her. Whenever I came to Boston and she was home from school, we'd make a point of getting together and practicing. And even, after a while, talking.

It wasn't the solution I'd hoped it would be, though. She continued doing stuff she knew would get her in trouble – smoking, drinking, whatever – and Marcus had to send her to some kind of reform school for a year. Who knows why she went through such a difficult period. It might have been the trauma of the abduction. But it might just as well have been a reaction to her mother's running off.

Or maybe it was just being a teenager.

'What's with all the security?' I asked. 'It wasn't here last time I visited.'

Marcus paused. 'Times have changed. More crazies out there. I have more money. *Newsweek* did a story about me. *Forbes*, *Fortune*, the cable news – I mean, it's not like I'm a shrinking violet.'

'Have you received any threats?'

'Threats? Like, did someone come up to me on State Street with a gun and threaten to blow my brains out or something? No. But I'm not going to wait.'

'So it's just a precaution.'

'What, you don't think I should be taking precautions?'

'Of course you should. I just want to know if you had any specific warning, a break-in, whatever – anything that inspired you to tighten your security.'

'I made him do it,' a female voice said.

Belinda Marcus had entered the kitchen. She was a tall, slender blonde, extremely beautiful. But icy. Maybe forty, but a well-cared-for forty. A forty that got regular Botox and collagen fillers and the occasional well-timed mini-facelift. A woman whose idea of 'work' was something you had done at a plastic surgeon's office.

She was all in white: skinny white ankle-slit pants, a white silk top with wide shoulder straps that looked like they were made out of origami, a low neckline with seamed cups that drew your eye to her small but pert breasts. She was barefoot. Her toenails were painted coral.

'I thought it was absolutely *mad* that Marshall didn't have any guards. A man who's worth as much as Marshall Marcus? As prominent as he is? We're just sitting ducks out here at the end of the point. And after what happened to Alexa?'

'They were out *shopping*, Belinda. A movie, whatever. That coulda happened even if we had a . . . an armed battalion surrounding the house. They were in the Chestnut Hill Mall, for Christ's sake!'

'You haven't introduced me to Mr Heller,' Belinda said. She approached, offered me her hand. It was bony and cool. Her fingernails were painted coral too. She had the vacant beauty of your classic trophy-wife bimbo, and she spoke with a sugary Georgia accent, all mint juleps and sweet iced tea.

I stood up. 'Nick,' I said. All I knew about her was what I'd heard from my mother. Belinda Jackson Marcus had been a flight attendant with Delta and met Marcus in the bar at the Ritz-Carlton Buckhead, in Atlanta.

'Pardon my manners,' Marcus said but remained slouched in his chair. 'Nick, Belinda. Belinda, Nick,' he added perfunctorily. 'Is she not a gorgeous creature, this girl?' A wide, pleased smile: he'd gotten his teeth capped too. That and the new hair: Marcus had never been vain, so I assumed he'd done all this work out of insecurity at having a wife so much younger and so beautiful. Or maybe she'd been pushing him to renovate.

Belinda tipped her head and rolled her eyes, a coy, fawnlike gesture. 'Have you offered Mr Heller some lunch?'

'I'm fine,' I said.

'Now, what's *wrong* with you, sugar?' Belinda said.

'What kind of lousy host am I?' he said. 'See? What would I do without Belinda? I'm an animal. An uncivilized beast. How about a sandwich, Nickeleh?'

'I'm good,' I said.

'Nothing?'

'I'm fine.'

Belinda said, 'How about I fix y'all some coffee?'

'Sure.'

She glided over to the long black soapstone-topped island and clicked on an electric kettle. Her tight white pants emphasized the curves of her tight butt. She clearly spent most of her time working out, probably with a trainer, with a special focus on the glutes. 'I'm not really much for making coffee,' she said, 'but we have instant. It's quite good, actually.' She held up a little foil packet.

'You know, I've changed my mind,' I said. 'I've had too much coffee this morning already.'

Belinda turned around suddenly. 'Nick,' she said. 'You have to find her.' She approached slowly. 'Please. You have to find her.'

She was freshly made up, I noticed. She didn't look like she'd been up all night. Unlike her husband, she looked refreshed, as if she'd just awakened from a long restorative nap. She wore pink lip gloss, her lips perfectly lined. I knew enough about women and their makeup to know that you didn't roll out of bed looking like that.

'Did Alexa tell you who she was meeting?' I asked.

'I didn't . . . she doesn't exactly tell me everything. Me being the stepmother and all.'

'She loves you,' Marcus said. 'She just doesn't realize it yet.'

'But you asked her, right?' I said.

Belinda's glossy lips parted half an inch. 'Of course I asked!' she said, indignant.

'She didn't tell you what time she'd be back?'

'Well, I assumed by midnight, maybe a little later, but you know, she doesn't take it too well when I ask her that sort of thing. She says she doesn't like to be treated like a child.'

'Still, that's pretty late.'

'For these kids? That's when the night begins.'

'That's not what I mean,' I said. 'I thought kids under eighteen aren't allowed to drive after midnight – twelve thirty, maybe – unless a parent or a guardian is in the car with them. If they get caught, they can have their license suspended for sixty days.'

'Is that right?' Belinda said. 'She didn't tell me anything of the kind.'

I found that strange. Alexa would never have planned to do something that might jeopardize her driver's license, and all the autonomy it represented. Also, it seemed out of character for Belinda not to have stayed on top of all the rules. Not a woman like that, attentive to every detail, who lined her lips before meeting me at a time when she should have been a mental wreck over her missing stepdaughter.

'So what do you think might have happened to her?' I said.

Her hands flew up, palms open. 'I don't know.' She looked at Marcus in bewilderment. 'We don't know. We just want you to find her!'

'Have you called the police?' I said.

'Of course not,' Marcus said.

'Of course *not*?' I said.

Belinda said, 'The police aren't going to do anything. They'll come and take a report and tell us to wait until twenty-four hours is up, and then it's just gonna be file-and-forget.'

'She's under eighteen,' I said. 'They take missing-teenager cases pretty seriously. I suggest you call them right now.'

'Nick,' Marcus said, 'I need *you* to look for her. Not the cops. Have I ever asked for your help before?'

'Please,' Belinda said. 'I love that girl so much. I don't know what I'd do if anything happened to her.'

Marcus waved a hand and said something like 'Poo-poo-poo.' I think that was meant to ward away the evil eye. 'Don't talk like that, baby,' he said.

'Have you called any of the hospitals?' I said.

The two exchanged a quick, anxious look before Belinda replied, shaking her head, 'If anything had happened to her, we'd have heard by now, right?'

'Not necessarily,' I said. 'That's the first thing you want to do. Let's start there.'

'I think it may be something else,' Marcus said. 'I don't think my little girl got hurt. I think . . .'

'We don't know *what* happened,' Belinda interrupted.

'Something bad,' Marcus said. 'Oh, dear God.'

'Well, let's start by calling the hospitals,' I said. 'Just to rule that out. I want her cell phone number. Maybe my tech person can locate her that way.'

'Of course,' Marcus said.

'And I want you to call the police. Okay?'

Belinda nodded and Marcus shrugged. 'They won't do *bupkes*,' he said, 'but if you insist.'

None of the hospitals between Manchester and Boston had admitted anyone fitting Alexa's description, which didn't seem to give Marcus and his wife the sense of relief you might expect.

Instead it seemed that the two of them were harboring some deep-seated dread that they refused to divulge to me, that they were holding back something important, something dire. I think that gut instinct was the reason I took Marcus's request seriously. Something was very wrong here. It was a bad feeling, and it only got worse.

Call it the gift of fear.

EIGHT

Alexa stirred and shifted in her bed.

It was the throbbing in her forehead that had awakened her, a rhythmic pulsing that had steadily grown stronger and stronger, tugging her into consciousness.

Knife-stabs of pain pierced the backs of her eyeballs.

It felt like someone was pounding an ice pick into the top of her skull and had just broken through the fragile shell, sending cracks throughout the lobes of her brain right behind her forehead.

Her mouth was terribly dry. Her tongue cleaved to the roof of her mouth. She tried to swallow.

Where was she?

She couldn't see anything.

The darkness was absolute. She wondered whether she'd gone blind.

But maybe she was dreaming.

It didn't feel like a dream, though. She remembered . . . drinking at Slammer with Taylor Armstrong. Something about her iPhone. Laughing about something. Everything else was blurry, clouded.

She had no recollection of how she'd gotten home, to her dad's house, how she'd ended up in her bed with the shades drawn.

She inhaled a strange musty odor. Unfamiliar. *Was* she at home in bed? It didn't smell like her room in the Manchester house. The sheets didn't have that fabric-softener fragrance she liked.

Had she crashed at someone's house? Not Taylor's, she didn't think. Her house smelled like lemon furniture polish, and her sheets were always too crisp. But where else could she be? She had no memory of . . . of *anything*, really, after laughing with Taylor about something on her iPhone . . .

She only knew that she was sleeping on top of a bed. No sheets covering her. They must have slid off her during the night. She preferred being under a sheet, even on the hottest days when there wasn't any air-conditioning. Like that awful year at Marston-Lee in Colorado, where there was no air-conditioning in the summer and they made you sleep in bunk beds and she had to bribe her bitch of a roommate for the top one. The bottom bunk made her feel trapped and anxious.

Her hands were at her sides. She fluttered her fingers, feeling for the hem of a sheet, and then the back of her right hand brushed against something smooth and solid. With her fingertips she felt some kind of satiny material over something hard, like the slatted wooden safety rails on the sides of her bunk bed at Marston-Lee that kept you from falling out of bed and crashing to the floor.

Was she back at Marston-Lee, or just dreaming that she was?

Yet if she were dreaming, would she have such an incredible headache?

She knew she was awake. She just knew it.

But she could still see nothing. Total perfect darkness, not even a glimmer of light.

She could smell the stale air and feel the soft yielding mattress below her and the soft pajamas on her legs . . . her fingertips scuttled over the soft fabric on her thighs, which didn't feel like the sweatpants she usually wore to bed. She was wearing something different. Not sweatpants, not pajamas. Hospital scrubs, maybe?

Was she in a hospital?

Had she gotten hurt, maybe been in an accident?

The ice pick was driving deeper and deeper into the gray matter of her brain, and the pain was indescribable, and she just wanted to roll over and put a pillow over her head. She raised her knees to gently torque her body and flip over, slowly and gently so her head didn't crack apart . . .

And her knees hit something.

Something hard.

Startled, she lifted her head, almost an involuntary reflex, and her forehead and the bridge of her nose collided with something hard too.

Both hands flew outward, striking hard walls. A few inches on either side. Her knees came up again, maybe three inches, and once again they struck a solid wall.

No.

Fingers skittering up the sides and then the top, satin-covered walls barely three inches from her lips.

Even before her brain was able to make sense of it, some animal instinct within her realized, with a dread that crept over her and turned her numb and ice-cold.

She was in a box.

She could touch the end of the box with her toes.

She started breathing fast. Short, panicked gasps.

Her heart raced.

She shuddered, but the shuddering didn't stop.

She gasped for air, but couldn't get more than a few inches of air into the very top of her lungs.

She tried to sit up, but her forehead struck the ceiling once again. Couldn't move. Couldn't change positions.

She panted faster and faster, heart juddering, sweat breaking out all over her body, hot and cold at the same time.

This couldn't be real. She *had* to be in some kind of nightmare: the worst nightmare she'd ever had. Trapped in a box. Like a . . .

Satin lining. Walls of wood, maybe steel.

Like being in a coffin.

Her hands twitched, kept knocking against the hard walls, as she gasped over and over again: 'No . . . no . . . no . . .'

She'd forgotten all about her headache.

That light-headed feeling that accompanied the hardness in her stomach and the coldness throughout her body, which she always felt before she passed out.

And she was gone.

NINE

By the time I got back into the Defender headed down 128 South toward Boston it was after noon. I couldn't shake the feeling that Marshall Marcus really did have a serious reason to fear that something had happened to his daughter. Something he'd actually anticipated.

In other words, not an accident. Even if it had nothing to do with the brief abduction a few years back. Maybe it was nothing more than a fight between Alexa and her stepmother, which ended with Alexa making a threat – *I'm leaving, and I'm never coming back!* – and then taking off.

Though it didn't really make sense that Marcus would withhold that sort of thing from me. Even if he was being chivalrous and wanted to shield his wife from the embarrassment of airing the family's dirty laundry, it wasn't like Marcus to be discreet. This was a guy who happily discussed his constipation, his difficulty urinating, and how Viagra had improved his sex life even more than JDate. He was the king of 'TMI', as my nephew Gabe would say: Too Much Information.

Just as I was about to call Dorothy and ask her how we might be able to locate Alexa's phone, my BlackBerry rang. Jillian, the office manager.

'Your son's here,' she said.

'Uh, I don't have a son.'

'He says you two were supposed to have lunch?' In the background I could hear cacophonous music playing way too loud. She'd turned my office into a dorm room.

'Whoops. Right. He's my nephew. Not my son.' I'd promised Gabe I'd take him to lunch, but I'd forgotten to put it on the calendar.

'That's funny,' she said. 'We just had a long talk, Gabe and me, and I just assumed he was your son, and he never corrected me.'

'Yeah, well.' *He wishes*, I thought. 'Thanks. Tell him I'll be there soon.'

'Cool kid.'

'Yeah. That your music?'

There was a click, and the music stopped. 'Music?'

'Could you put me through to Dorothy?' I said.

TEN

Gabe Heller was my brother Roger's stepson. He was sixteen, a very smart kid but definitely a misfit. He had hardly any friends at the private boys' school he attended in Washington. He dressed all in black: black jeans, black hoodies, black Chuck Taylors. Recently he'd even started dying his hair black too. It's not easy being sixteen, but it must have been particularly hard to be Gabe Heller.

Roger, my estranged brother, was a jerk, not to put too fine a point on it. He was also, like our father, in prison. Luckily, Gabe was genetically unrelated to his father, or he'd probably be in juvie. I seemed to be the only adult he could talk to. I don't know what it is about me and troubled kids. Maybe, the way dogs can smell fear, they can sense that I'll never be a parent, and so I'm safe. I don't know.

Gabe was spending the summer at my mother's condo in Newton. He was taking art classes in a summer program for high school students at the Museum School. He loved his Nana and wanted to get away from his mother, Lauren – who was no doubt relieved not to have to deal with him after school was out. My mother was hardly strict, so he was able to hop on the T and go into town and hang out in Harvard Square when he wasn't in school, and I'm sure he enjoyed feeling like a grown-up.

But I think the main reason he wanted to be in Boston was that it gave him an excuse to see me, though he'd never admit it. I loved the kid and enjoyed spending time with him. It wasn't always easy. Not everything worthwhile is easy.

He was sitting at my desk, drawing in his sketch pad. Gabe was a scarily talented artist.

'Working on your comic book?' I said as I entered.

'Graphic novel,' he said stiffly.

'Right, sorry, I forgot.'

'And hey, way to remember our lunch.' He was wearing a black hoodie, zipped up, with straps and D-rings and grommets on it. I noticed a tiny gold stud earring in his left ear but decided not to call attention to it. Yet.

'Sorry about that, too. How's the summer going for you?'

'Boring.'

For Gabe, that was a rave. 'Wanna grab some lunch?' I said.

'I'm only about to pass out from hunger.'

'I'll take that as a yes.'

I noticed Dorothy hovering at the threshold. 'Listen, Nick,' she said. 'That number you gave me? I'm not going to be able to locate her phone.'

'That doesn't sound like you. That sounds . . . defeatist,' I said.

'Ain't got nothing to do with defeatism,' she said. 'Nothing to do with my ability. It's a matter of law.'

'Like that ever stopped you?'

'It's not – oh, hello, Gabriel.' Her tone cooled.

Gabe grunted. He and Dorothy had a history of clashing. Gabe thought he was smarter than she, which was probably true, since he was an alarmingly brainy kid – and better at computers, which wasn't true. Not yet, anyway. Still, he was sixteen, which meant that he *thought* he was better at everything. And that just pissed Dorothy off.

'Here's the deal,' she said. 'The person whose phone you want me to locate . . .' She glanced at Gabe in annoyance. She was always discreet about the work she did for me, but she was being particularly careful.

'Can we speak in private, Nick?'

'Gabe, give me two minutes,' I said.

'Fine,' he snapped, and left my office.

'Sounds like you're actually taking the case,' Dorothy said. 'Will wonders never cease.'

I nodded.

'Couldn't pass up the money?'

I replied with sarcasm, 'Yeah, it's all about the money.'

'You got a problem with money?'

'No, it's . . . it's complicated. This is not about Marshall Marcus. I happen to like his daughter. I'm worried about her.'

'Why is he freaking out? I mean, she's seventeen, right? Drives into town, probably to some club, hooks up with a guy. That's what these kids do.'

'You sleep around a lot when you were her age, Dorothy?'

She gave me a stern look and held up a warning forefinger with a long lilac fingernail. I didn't understand how she could type with nails that long.

I smiled. As little as I knew about her sex life, I knew she was hardly the promiscuous type.

'I don't get it either,' I admitted.

'I mean, I understand why the dad could be losing it if this was right after she got snatched in that parking lot. But that was years ago, right?'

'Right. I think he knows more than he's telling me.'

'Like what?'

'I don't know.'

'Maybe you need to ask him some direct questions.'

'I will. So tell me about Facebook.'

'Tell you about Facebook? All you need to know, Nick, is it's not for you.'

'I mean Alexa. She must be on Facebook, right?'

'I think it's a legal requirement for all teenagers,' she said. 'Like the draft, back in the day.'

'Maybe there's something on her Facebook page. Don't kids post everything they do every second?'

'What makes you think I know the first thing about teenagers?'

'See what she has on Facebook, okay?'

'You can't do that unless you're one of her "friends".'

'Can't you just hack her password?'

She shrugged. 'I'll look into it.'

'So what's the problem with locating her iPhone?'

'It's just about impossible unless you're law enforcement.'

'I thought there was some way for iPhone owners to track down their lost phones.'

'We'd need her Mac user name and password. And I'm guessing she doesn't share things like passwords with Daddy.'

'You can't crack it, or hack it, or whatever you do?'

'Yeah, I can just snap my fingers and I'm in, just like magic. No, Nick, that takes time. I'd have to make a list of her pets' names and any important dates, and try the ten most common passwords, and that's a crapshoot. Even if I do succeed, odds are we won't get anything, because she'd have had to activate the MobileMe finder on her phone, and I doubt she did. She's seventeen and probably not real big into the technology.'

'Probably not.'

'Fastest way is ask AT&T to ping the phone through their network.'

'Which they'll only do for law enforcement,' I said. 'There's got to be some other way to find this girl's phone.'

'Not that I know of.'

'So you're giving up.'

'I said not that I know of. I didn't say I'm giving up. I never give up.' She looked up and noticed Gabe lurking outside my office door. 'Anyway, I think your son is getting hungry,' she said with a wink.

ELEVEN

I took Gabe to Mojo's, a bar down the street that served lunch. This was a typical Boston bar – five flat screens all showing sports or sports news shows, lots of Red Sox and Celtics memorabilia, a foosball table in the back, pub food like wings and nachos and burgers, a sticky wooden-plank floor. They served good cold beer as well as the infamous local brew, Brubaker's, which even I had to admit was pretty bad. The patrons were a democratic mix of stockbrokers and cabdrivers. A local reviewer once compared Mojo's regulars to the cantina scene in *Star Wars*: that collection of weird-looking intergalactic creatures. Herb, the owner, liked that so much he had the article framed and put on the wall.

'I like that new girl you hired,' Gabe said.

'Jillian?'

'Yeah, she's cool.'

'She's different, that's for sure. Now, tell me: is Nana abusing you?'

'Nah, she's cool.'

'How about Lilly? How's Lilly treating you?'

Lilly was my mother's dog, a shar-pei/English mastiff mix she'd rescued from the pound. Lilly was not only the ugliest dog in the world but also the worst-tempered. She'd been abandoned multiple times and I could see why.

'I'm really trying to like her,' Gabe said, 'but she's . . . I mean, I hate that dog. Plus, she stinks.'

'She's the hound from hell. Don't look into her eyes.'

'Why not?'

'The last person who did dropped dead on the spot. They say it was a heart attack, but . . .' I shrugged.

'Yeah, right.'

'You miss being home?'

'Miss it? Are you kidding?'

'Life at home not so good these days?'

'It sucks.'

'Can I ask you something?'

'What?'

'What's with the earring?'

He said, defensively, 'What about it?'

'Does your mom know you got your ear pierced?'

He shrugged. Asked and answered.

'I forget,' I said. 'Does the left side mean you're gay?'

He blushed, which turned his acne scarlet. 'No. Left is right and right is wrong, ever hear that?'

'Aha,' I said. 'So being gay is wrong?'

'That's not what I meant.'

I smiled. Gabe could be insufferable in that know-it-all teenage way, so I considered it my civic duty to keep him off balance.

Herb took our order. Normally he was stationed behind the bar, but lunchtimes were always slow. He was a large-framed potbellied guy with a heavy Southie accent. 'Yo Nicky,' he said. 'How's the accounting business? You got any tips for me, like how to stop paying taxes?'

'Easy.'

'Yeah?'

'Do what I do. Just don't pay 'em.'

He paused, then laughed loudly. It didn't take much to amuse him.

'Truth is, I'm an actuary.' The sign on our office door said HELLER ASSOCIATES – ACTUARIAL CONSULTING SERVICES. This was an excellent cover. As soon as I told people I was an actuary, they stopped asking questions.

'Right, right,' he said. 'What's an actuary, again?'

'Damned if I know.'

He laughed again. 'Gotta hand it to you, man,' he said kindly, 'I don't know how you do it. Crunching numbers all day? I'd go out of my mind.' Gabe gave me a quick, knowing smile. I ordered a burger and fries and asked him to make sure they weren't the 'curry fries', which were inedible. Gabe looked up from the menu. 'Do you have veggie burgers?' he asked.

'We have turkey burgers, young fella,' Herb said.

Gabe furrowed his brow and tipped his head to the side. I recognized that look. It was the supercilious expression that got him beat up at school on a regular basis and sometimes even thrown out of classes. 'Oh,' he said, 'I didn't realize turkey was a vegetable.'

Herb gave me a sideways glance as if to say, *Who the hell is this kid?* But he liked me too much to give it back to my guest. 'How about a Cobb salad?' he said blandly.

'Yuck,' Gabe said. 'I'll just have a plate of fries and ketchup. And a Coke.'

When Herb left, I said, 'Looks like Jillian has a new recruit.'

'Jillian says that eating red meat makes you aggressive,' Gabe said.

'And that's a bad thing?'

He refused to take the bait. 'Whatever. Hey, Uncle Nick, you know, that was a good idea you had about Alexa's Facebook.'

'What are you talking about?'

'Alexa Marcus? Her dad is scared something might've happened to her?'

I looked at him for a few seconds, then slowly smiled. 'You son of a bitch. You were eavesdropping.'

'No.'

'Come on.'

'Did you know Dorothy has an audio feed on her computer that lets her listen in to everything you say in your office?'

'Yes, Gabe. That's our arrangement. The real question is, does Dorothy know you were snooping around on her computer?'

'Please don't tell her. Please, Uncle Nick.'

'So what were you thinking about her Facebook page?'

'You're not going to tell her, are you?'

'Of course not.'

'Okay. I'm pretty sure I know where Alexa went last night.'

'How so?'

'It was on her Facebook wall.'

'How were you able to see that?'

'We're Facebook friends.'

'Really?'

'Well, I mean, like,' he stammered, his face flushing again, 'she has like eleven hundred Facebook friends, but she let me friend her.'

'Very cool,' I said, only because he sounded so proud.

'She came over to Nana's a couple of times since I've been there. I like her. She's cool. And it's not like she has to be nice to me, you know?'

I nodded. Beautiful rich girls like Alexa Marcus usually weren't nice to annoying, nerdy boys like Gabe Heller.

'So where'd she go?'

'She and her friend Taylor went to Slammer.'

'Which is what?'

'Some fancy bar in that hotel that used to be a jail? I think it's called the Graybar?'

'Taylor – is that a boy or a girl?'

'A girl. Taylor Armstrong? She's the daughter of Senator Richard

Armstrong. Taylor and Alexa went to school together.'

I glanced at my watch, put my hand on his shoulder. 'How about we ask them to pack up our food to go?' I said.

'You're going to talk to Taylor?'

I nodded.

'She's at home today,' Gabe said. 'Probably sleeping it off. I bet you find Alexa there too. Uncle Nick?'

'What?'

'Don't tell Alexa I told you. She'll think I'm like a stalker or something.'

TWELVE

I found the junior senator from Massachusetts picking up his dog's poop.

Senator Richard Armstrong's large white standard poodle was trimmed in a full Continental clip: shaven body, white pom-poms on his feet and tail, and a big white Afro perched atop his head. The senator, in a crisp blue shirt and impeccably knotted tie, was groomed just as carefully. His silver hair was perfectly coiffed, with a sharp part on one side. He leaned over, his hand inside a plastic bag, grabbed the dog's excrement, and deftly turned the bag inside out. He stood upright, face red, and noticed me standing there.

'Senator,' I said.

'Yes?' A wary look. As a well-known, highly recognizable figure, he had to worry about lunatics. Even in this very posh neighborhood.

We stood in a long oval park, enclosed by a wrought-iron picket fence, in the middle of Louisburg Square on Beacon Hill. Louisburg Square is a private enclave of long red-brick row houses built in the nineteenth century, considered one of the most elegant neighborhoods in Boston.

'Nick Heller,' I said.

'Ah, yes,' he said, and gave a big, relieved smile. 'Sheesh, I thought you were with the association. Technically, you're not supposed to walk your dog here, and some of my neighbors get quite upset.'

'I won't tell,' I said. 'Anyway, I've always thought that dogs should be trained to pick up *our* poop.'

'Yes, well . . . I'd shake your hand, but . . .'

'That's all right,' I said. 'Is this a good time?' I'd reached out to him through a mutual friend, told him what was going on, and asked if I could come by.

'Walk with me,' he said. I followed him to a historic-looking trash bin, where he dropped his little bundle. 'So, I'm sorry to hear about the Marcus girl. Any news? I'm sure it's just a family quarrel.'

Armstrong had a Boston Brahmin accent, which is nothing like what most people think of as a Boston accent. It's very upper-crust WASP, mid-Atlantic, and it's dying out. Hardly anyone speaks that way anymore except maybe a few old walruses at the Somerset Club. He sounded like a cross between William F. Buckley and Thurston Howell III from *Gilligan's Island*. Someone once told me that if you listened to recordings of Armstrong when he was a young man, he sounded entirely different. Somewhere along the way he'd acquired the patina. But he really was descended from an old Boston family. 'My family didn't come over on the *Mayflower*,' he'd once said. 'We sent the servants over on the *Mayflower*.'

We stood before his house – bow front, freshly painted black shutters, glossy black door, big American flag waving – and he began to climb the gray-painted concrete steps. 'Well, if there's anything in the world I can do to help, just ask,' he said. 'I do have friends.'

He gave me his famous smile, which had gotten him, a moderate Republican, elected to the Senate four times. A journalist once compared the Armstrong smile to a warm fire. Up close, though, it seemed more like an artificial fireplace, with faux ceramic 'logs' painted red to simulate glowing embers.

'Excellent,' I said. 'I'd like to talk to your daughter.'

'My daughter? You'd be wasting your time. I doubt Taylor has seen the Marcus girl in months.'

'They saw each other last night.'

The senator shifted his weight from one foot to another. His poodle whined, and Armstrong gave the leash an abrupt yank. 'News to me,' he finally said. 'Anyway, I'm afraid Taylor's out shopping. That girl likes to shop.' He gave me the sort of beleaguered smile guys often give other guys, as if to say, *Women – can't live with 'em, can't live without 'em.*

'You might want to check again,' I said. 'She's upstairs right now.'

Gabe was monitoring her incessant Facebook postings and texting me updates. I didn't know how, since he wasn't a Facebook friend of Taylor's, but he'd found some way.

Taylor Armstrong, he'd texted me a few minutes ago, had told her 1372 friends that she was watching an old *Gilmore Girls* rerun and was bored out of her skull.

'I'm sure she and her mother—'

'Senator,' I said. 'Please get her for me. This is important. Or should I just call her cell?'

Of course, I didn't actually have Taylor Armstrong's cell phone number, but it turned out I didn't need it. Armstrong invited me in, no longer bothering to conceal his annoyance. The poodle whined again, and Armstrong snapped the leash. No more election-winning smile. The electric fireplace had been switched off.

THIRTEEN

Taylor Armstrong entered her father's study like a kid summoned to the principal's office, trying to mask her apprehension with sullenness. She sat down in a big overstuffed kilim-covered chair and crossed her legs doubly, the top leg tucked tightly under the lower. Her arms were folded, her shoulders hunched. If she were a turtle, she'd be deep inside her shell.

I sat in a facing chair while Senator Armstrong skimmed papers through half-frame glasses at his simple mahogany desk. He was pretending to ignore us.

The girl was pretty – quite pretty, in fact. Her hair was black, obviously dyed, and she wore heavy eye makeup. She dressed like a rich girl gone bad, which apparently she was: she went to the same rich-girls' reform school out west where Alexa had spent a year. She was wearing a brown suede tank top with a chunky turquoise necklace, skinny jeans, and short brown leather boots.

I introduced myself and said, 'I'd like to ask you a few questions about Alexa.'

She examined the old Persian carpet and said nothing.

'Alexa's missing,' I said. 'Her parents are extremely worried.'

She looked up, petulant. For a moment it looked like she

was about to say something, but then she apparently changed her mind.

'Have you heard from her?' I said.

She shook her head. 'No.'

'When did you last see her?'

'Last night. We went out.'

I was glad she didn't try to lie about it. Or maybe her father had briefed her when he'd gone upstairs to fetch her.

'How about we go for a walk?' I said.

'A walk?' she said with distaste, as if I'd just asked her to eat a live bat, head first.

'Sure. Get some fresh air.'

She hesitated, and her father said, without even looking up from his papers, 'You two can talk right here.'

For a few seconds she looked trapped. Then, to my surprise, she said, 'I wouldn't mind getting out of the house.'

From Louisburg Square we crossed Mount Vernon Street and made our way down the steep slope of Willow Street. 'I figured you could use a cigarette.'

'I don't smoke.'

But I could smell it on her when she first came downstairs. 'Go ahead, I'm not going to report back to Daddy.'

Her expression softened almost imperceptibly. She shrugged, took a pack of Marlboros and a gold S. T. Dupont cigarette lighter from her little black handbag.

'I won't even tell Daddy about the fake IDs,' I said.

She gave me a quick sidelong glance as she opened the lighter, making that distinctive ping. She flicked it crisply, lighted a cigarette, and drew a lungful of smoke.

'Drinking age is twenty-one,' I said. 'How else are you going to get a drink around here?'

She exhaled twin plumes from her nostrils like a movie star from the old days and said nothing.

I went on, 'I used to forge fake IDs for my friends and me when I was a kid. I used the darkroom at school. Some of my friends sent away for "international student IDs".'

'That's fascinating.'

'Gotta be easier today, with scanners and Photoshop and all that.'

'I wouldn't know. You just buy one from a friend.'

We crossed over to West Cedar down a tiny alley called Acorn Street, paved in cobblestones dredged from the Charles River a long time ago. This was a real street, and it was charming, but I doubted the Defender could fit through it. Also, the cobblestones would have done a number on the suspension.

'So why didn't your dad want you to talk to me?'

She shrugged.

'No idea?'

'Why do you think?' she said bitterly. 'Because he's the *senator*. It's all about his career.'

'Senators' daughters aren't allowed to have a good time?'

A mirthless laugh. 'From what I've heard, he did nothing *but* have a good time before he met my mom.' She paused for dramatic effect. 'And plenty after too.'

I ignored that. I'm sure the rumors were true. Richard Armstrong had a reputation, and not for his legislative work. 'You two went to Slammer together,' I said. I waited a long time for her response – five, ten seconds.

'We just had a couple of drinks,' she said finally.

'Did she seem upset? Pissed off at her parents?'

'No more than usual.'

'Did she say anything about getting out of the house, just taking off somewhere?'

'No.'

'Does she have a boyfriend?'

'No.' She sounded hostile, like it was none of my business.

'Did she say she was scared of something? Or someone? She was once grabbed in a parking lot—'

55

'I know,' she said scornfully. 'I'm like her best friend.'

'Well, was she afraid that something like that might happen again?'

She shook her head. 'But she said her dad was acting weird.'

'Weird how?'

'Like maybe he was in trouble? I really don't remember. I was moderately lit at that point.'

'Where'd she go after Slammer?'

'How should I know? I assume she went home.'

'Did you two leave the bar together?'

She hesitated. 'Yeah.'

She was so obviously lying that I hesitated to call her on it outright for fear of losing any chance of her cooperation.

Suddenly she blurted out, 'Did something happen to Lexie? Do you *know* something? Did she get hurt?'

We'd stopped at the corner of Mount Vernon Street, waited for a couple to pass out of hearing range. 'Maybe,' I said.

'*Maybe?* What's that supposed to mean?'

'It means I need you to tell me everything.'

She threw down her cigarette on the buckled brick sidewalk, stubbed it out, pulled another from her handbag. 'Look, she met a guy, okay?'

'Do you remember his name?'

She shook her head, lighted the cigarette, clearly avoiding my eyes. 'Some Spanish guy, maybe. I don't remember. Their names all sound the same to me. Marco. Alfredo. Something.'

'Were you with her when she met this guy?'

I could see her running through a series of mental calculations. If this, then that. If she said she wasn't with Alexa, why not? Where was she? Two girls go to a bar, they almost always stay together. They don't divide and conquer. They protect each other, signal to each other, vet prospects for each other. And compete for a guy sometimes, sure. But for the most part they work as a team.

'Yeah,' she said. 'But it was loud, and I didn't really catch his name. And I was definitely sideways by then and I just wanted to go home.'

'The guy didn't try to hit on you?'

Her eyes narrowed. Now it was a point of pride. 'The guy was so lame,' she said. 'I totally blew him off.'

'Did they leave together?' I said.

I waited so long I thought she might not have heard me. When I was about to repeat the question, she said, 'I guess. I don't really know.'

'How could you not know?'

'Because I left first.'

I didn't bother to point out the contradiction. 'You went straight home?'

She nodded.

'You walked?' Louisburg Square was directly up the hill, a fairly short walk unless you were hammered and wearing stilettos.

'Cab.'

'Did you hear anything from Alexa later on that night?'

'Why would I?'

'Come on, Taylor. You girls document every minute of your lives with text messages or on Facebook or whatever. You post something when you brush your teeth. You mean to tell me she didn't text you to say "OMG I'm at this guy's apartment" or whatever?'

She looked contemptuous, did the eye-roll thing again.

'You haven't heard from her since you left Slammer last night?'

'Right.'

'Have you tried to call her?'

She shook her head.

'Text her?'

She shook her head again.

'You didn't check in with her for an update on how the night went? I thought you guys are, like, BFFs.' Somehow I knew that was chat-speak for Best Friends Forever.

She shrugged.

'Do you understand that if you're lying to me, if you're covering something up, you might be endangering your best friend's life?'

She shook her head, started walking down the street, away from me. 'I haven't heard anything,' she said without turning back.

My gut instinct told me she wasn't lying about that. Obviously, though, she was lying about something. Her guilt flashed like a neon sign. Maybe she didn't want to come off as a bad friend. Maybe she'd ditched Alexa for some hot guy herself.

I called Dorothy and said, 'Any progress in locating Alexa's phone?'

'No change. We're going to need the assistance of someone in law enforcement, Nick. No way around it.'

'I have an idea,' I said.

FOURTEEN

When your job involves working with the clandestine, as mine does, you learn the power of a secret. Knowing one can give you leverage, even control, over another, whether in the halls of Congress or the halls of high school, in the boardroom or the faculty lounge or at the racetrack.

Most secrets are kept to conceal crimes, abuses, or failures. They can destroy a career or undermine an enemy, and they've brought down quite a few world leaders. In Washington, where you're only as important as the secrets you know, secrets are truly the coin of the realm.

It was time to spend some of that coin.

When I worked at Stoddard Associates in DC, I did a project for a freshman congressman from Florida who was fighting a nasty re-election battle. His opponent had got hold of a copy of the lease on an apartment in Sarasota he'd rented for his girlfriend, a hostess at Hooters. This was news to his wife, the mother of his six children, and definitely inconvenient for the congressman, given his strong family-values platform. I did some cleanup work and the whole paper trail disappeared. The waitress found new employment in Pensacola. Her landlord had no recollection of renting to the congressman and declared the deed a forgery. The congressman won the election in a squeaker.

It wasn't a job I was proud of. But now the congressman was the ranking member on the House Judiciary Committee, which oversees the FBI. He didn't owe me any favors, since he'd paid well for Stoddard's 'research services', but I knew certain things about him, which was even worse. I reached him on his private line and asked him to make a call for me to the Boston field office of the FBI.

I told him I needed to talk to someone senior. Now.

A parking space was about to open up on Cambridge Street directly in front of the FBI, which is roughly as common as a solar eclipse. I double-parked and waited for the woman in the Buick, who'd just switched on her engine, to pull out.

But she was taking her time. First she had to touch up her lipstick; then she had to make a phone call. I allowed her ten more seconds before I gave up.

In the meantime, I called Marcus. 'Marshall, what did the police tell you?'

'The police? Oh, you know, the usual nothing. If she hasn't turned up by tonight, I can file a missing-persons report.'

'Well, we're not waiting.'

'Do you know anything?'

'No,' I said flatly. 'I'll tell you as soon as I do.'

I gave up on the woman in the Buick and drove on.

FIFTEEN

The FBI's Boston field office is located in One Center Plaza, part of the hideous Government Center complex, which some architects praise as 'imposing' but most Bostonians consider a blight, a concrete scar on the face of our beautiful city. The only positive thing I can say about Government Center is that it once inspired a decent song by the proto-punk band the Modern Lovers.

When I got out of the elevator on the sixth floor, I saw a huge gold FBI seal on the wall and a Ten Most Wanted poster. In a small waiting area were a metal detector gate and a portable baggage X-ray machine, neither in use. A couple of receptionists sat behind bulletproof glass.

I pushed my driver's license into a slot like a bank teller's, and they made me surrender my BlackBerry. In exchange they gave me a badge that said ESCORT REQUIRED in red.

One of the women behind the glass spoke into a phone and told me someone would be out in a few minutes.

I waited. There was nothing to look at but a photo of the president, in a frame that hung askew on the wall, and an array of pamphlets advertising careers in the FBI. No magazines or newspapers. Without my BlackBerry I couldn't check my e-mail or call anyone.

I waited some more.

After half an hour I went back to the lady behind the glass and asked her whether I'd been forgotten. She apologized, assured me I hadn't been, but gave no explanation.

When they make you wait ten or fifteen minutes, it's probably because a meeting is running late. When you're past the forty-five-minute mark, they're sending you a message.

It was close to an hour before the FBI guy emerged.

He wasn't what I expected. He was a hulking guy who looked like he spent a lot of time pumping iron. He was entirely bald, the kind of shiny bald that takes work, requires a lot of shaving and waxing or whatever. He wore a knockoff Rolex, a gray suit that was too short in the sleeves, a white shirt too tight at the neck, and a regimental striped tie.

'Mr Heller?' he said in a deep and rumbling voice. 'Gordon Snyder.'

He offered me a hand as huge and leathery as an old baseball mitt, and shook way too hard. 'Assistant Special Agent in Charge,' he added.

That meant he was one of the top guys in the FBI's Boston office, reporting directly to the Special Agent in Charge. I had to give credit to my philandering congressman from Sarasota.

Snyder pushed the door open, then led me down a blank white corridor to his outer office, where a weary-looking secretary didn't even look up from her computer as we passed. His office was large and overlooked Cambridge Street. A long desk, two computer monitors, a large flat-screen TV with the sound off, set to CNN. A round glass-topped conference table and a red leatherette couch. Two flags behind his desk on either side, the US flag and the FBI's light blue one. By government standards, this was an *Architectural Digest* spread.

He sat behind his perfectly clean glass-topped desk and hunched his shoulders. 'I understand you work in the private sector these days, Mr Heller.'

'Right.' I suppose that was his not-so-subtle way of letting me know he'd read a dossier on me.

'So what can I do for you?'

'I'm helping a friend look for his daughter,' I said.

He furrowed his brows sympathetically. 'What's the girl's name?'

'Alexa Marcus.'

He nodded. The name didn't seem to mean anything to him.

'Her father is Marshall Marcus. Hedge-fund guy in Boston.'

'How old is she?'

'Seventeen.'

He nodded again, shrugged. 'And why's this a matter for the FBI?'

'Given her father's wealth and prominence—'

'She's been kidnapped?'

'Possibly.'

'Well, is there a ransom demand?'

'Not yet. But given the circumstances and her own history—'

'So you're saying the father's concerned his daughter *might* have been kidnapped.'

There was something strange about Snyder's expression. A look of confusion so exaggerated it was almost comic. Or maybe sardonic. 'Huh. See, what baffles me, Mr Heller, is why the Boston police never reached out to us.'

'They sure should have.'

'I know, right? Normally that's the first thing they'd do, in a case like this. Kidnappings are FBI business. Gotta wonder why not.'

I shrugged. 'Well, whatever the reason, if you could arrange to ping her phone—'

But Snyder wasn't finished yet. 'I wonder if the *reason* they never reached out to us,' he said with careful emphasis, 'is that no one notified them about the missing girl in the first place. You think that might explain it?' He clasped his hands, looked down at his desk and then up at me. 'See, Marshall Marcus never called it in to them. Interesting, isn't it? You'd think he'd be all *over* the police and the FBI to locate his daughter, wouldn't you? If it was *my* daughter, I wouldn't wait two seconds. Would you?' His eyes pierced mine, his upper lip curled in disgust.

'He called the police,' I said again. 'A couple of hours ago. Might not even be logged in yet.'

He shook his head and said firmly, 'Never happened.'

'You have bad information.'

'We have *excellent* information on Marcus,' he said. 'We know for a fact that neither he nor his wife placed a call to the police. Not from any of his four home landlines. Neither of his two cell phones. Nor his wife's cell phone. Nor any landline at Marcus Capital.'

I said nothing.

He gave me a long, grave look. 'That's right. We've had Marshall Marcus under court-ordered surveillance for quite some time now. As I'm sure he knows. Did he send you here, Mr Heller?'

Gordon Snyder's eyes were small and deep-set, which made them look beady and insectlike. 'Please don't bother trying to deny the fact that you met with Marcus at his house in Manchester this morning, Heller. Is this why you're here? Acting as his agent? Trying to check up on us, see what we've got on him?'

'I came here because a girl's life may be in danger.'

'This is the same girl who had to be sent away to a special disciplinary school because of repeated behavior problems at her private school?'

I tried to keep my voice controlled, but it was all I could do not to lose it. 'That's right. After she was abducted. Stuff like that can really screw with your head. You don't get it, do you? We're on the same side here.'

'You're working for Marcus, right?'

'Yeah, but—'

'Then we're on opposite sides. We clear?'

SIXTEEN

Alexa felt her heart thud faster and faster. She could hear it. In the terrible silence, where she could even hear her own eyelids blink shut, her heartbeat was like a kettledrum. She felt a prickly heat and a bone-deep chill at the same time, and she began to shiver uncontrollably.

'You can hear me, Alexa, yes?' said the tinny voice.

A wash of acid scalded her esophagus. She gagged, retched, felt as if she were going to expel her stomach through her mouth. A little vomit splashed on her damp shirt, settled back down her throat.

She needed to sit upright to empty her mouth, but she couldn't sit up. She couldn't raise her head more than a few inches. She couldn't even turn to the side. She was trapped here.

She couldn't move.

Now she was gagging from the vomit that had backwashed down her throat.

'Please take care of yourself,' the voice said. 'We cannot open your coffin if something happens to you.'

'Coffin . . .' she gasped.

'There is no reason for you to die. We don't want you to die. We only want you to convince your father to cooperate with us.'

'How much money do you want?' she whispered. 'Just tell me what you want and my father will give it to you.'

'Why do you think we want money, Alexa? And even if we did want money, your father has nothing.'

'My father is . . . he has an obscene amount of money, okay? He can pay you anything you want. He'll give it all to you, everything he has, if you please please please let me out now.'

'Alexa, now you must listen to me very, very carefully, because your survival depends on it.'

She swallowed. A lump had lodged in her throat.

'I'm listening,' she whispered.

'I can't hear you.'

She tried to speak louder. 'I'm – I'm listening.'

'Good. Now, Alexa? I have already told you how to relieve yourself. Now we must talk about your breathing. Okay? You are listening?'

She shuddered and moaned, 'Please . . .'

'I want you to know that you have air in your coffin, but it is not so much.'

'*Not . . . so much*?' she whispered.

'Listen closely. If we just put you in the casket and sealed it and put it in the ground you would not last half of an hour. But we know this is not enough time for you.'

She heard 'in the ground' and she bit her lower lip so hard she felt the blood start to trickle. '*The ground?*' she whispered.

'Yes. You are in a steel casket far below the ground. You are buried under ten feet of earth. Alexa, you have been buried alive. But I'm sure you already know this.'

Something exploded in her brain: bright sparkles of light. She screamed with vocal cords so raw that the only sound that came out was a wheezing gasp, but in the darkness and the absolute silence it was thunderously loud.

SEVENTEEN

A fluorescent orange parking ticket was tucked under the Defender's windshield wipers. Damn Snyder. If he hadn't been playing his power games and kept me waiting so long, the time on the meter wouldn't have run out. I felt like sending him the bill.

I had my BlackBerry out, about to call Marcus, when I heard a female voice behind me: 'Nico?'

The nickname that hardly anyone used anymore except a few people I knew in DC a long time ago.

I sensed her, maybe even smelled her, before she touched my shoulder. Without even looking around, I said, 'Diana?'

'You still have the Defender, I see,' she said. 'I like that. You don't change much, do you?'

'Hey,' I said, and I gave her a hug. For a moment I didn't know whether to kiss her on the mouth – those days were long gone, after all – but she offered me her cheek. 'You look great.'

I wasn't lying. Diana Madigan had on tight jeans and worn brown cowboy boots and an emerald green top that emphasized the swell of her breasts and brought out her amazing pale green eyes. Statistically, it turns out that green eyes occur in less than two per cent of the global population.

But that wasn't the only thing about her that was rare. I'd never met a woman quite like her. She was tough and empathic and elegant. And beautiful. She had a taut, lithe body with a head of crazy wavy hair that obeyed its own laws of physics. It was light honey brown with auburn highlights. Her nose was strong yet delicate, with slightly flared nostrils. The only sign of the years that had passed were the faint laugh lines etched around her eyes.

We hadn't seen each other in five or six years, since she was transferred from the FBI's Washington Field Office to Seattle and declared she didn't want a long-distance relationship. Ours had been casual – not Friends With Benefits, exactly, but no pressure, no expectations. Not a gateway drug that would lead inexorably to a long-term addiction. This was the way she wanted it, and given how long my work hours were and how much I traveled, I was fine with the arrangement. I enjoyed her company and she enjoyed mine.

Still, when I got a call from Diana telling me that she'd moved to Seattle, I quickly went from baffled to wounded. I cared for her deeply, and I was surprised she didn't feel the same. I'm not used to women walking away from me, but this wasn't just a male ego thing. I was disappointed in myself for having misread her so badly. Until then I'd always considered my ability to read others one of my natural talents.

She wasn't the type to insist on a Deep Talk, like so many women. In that way, her emotional architecture resembled mine. So the end of my relationship with Diana Madigan went into my mental cold-case file.

But I've always found unsolved cases irresistible.

'I look like a wreck, and you know it,' she said. 'I'm just getting off the night shift, and on my way home.'

'Since when do you work nights?'

'I've been up all night texting predators, pretending to be a fourteen-year-old girl.'

'Yeah? What a coincidence. Me too.'

'This one sicko is fifty-one,' she said, ignoring me. Her work was something she never joked about. 'We arranged to meet at a motel in Everett. Will *he* be surprised.'

'So you're still working CARD?'

'Believe it or not.'

CARD stood for the FBI's Child Abduction Rapid Deployment unit. It was heart-wrenching work. The things she saw: I never knew how she could keep doing it. I thought by now she'd have burned out.

She wasn't wearing a wedding ring, and I could only assume she didn't have kids either. I wondered whether she ever would, having seen what could happen to them.

'Why don't I give you a lift home,' I said.

'How do you know I don't have my car here?'

'Because you'd have parked in the underground garage like all FBI employees do. Plus, you'd be carrying your car keys in your left hand. Don't forget, I know you.'

She looked away. Embarrassed? Unreadable, in any case. As always, the emotional equivalent of Kryptonite. 'My apartment's in the South End. I was going to take the T.'

I opened the passenger-side door for her.

EIGHTEEN

'So now the next shift takes over texting your predators?' I said.

'We can't do that,' Diana said. 'Perps can sometimes sense a change in respondents. Even in short message texts there can be subtle nuances in tone and rhythm.'

As I drove I caught the faintest whiff of her perfume. It was something I'd never smelled on another woman: rose and violet and cedar, sophisticated and haunting and unforgettable.

Neuroscientists tell us that nothing brings back the past as quickly and powerfully as a smell. Apparently the olfactory nerve arouses something in the limbic center of your brain where you store long-term memories on your mental hard drive.

Diana's perfume brought back a rush of memories. Mostly happy ones.

'How long have you been in Boston?' I asked.

'A little over a year. I heard through the grapevine you might be here. Did Stoddard send you here to open a satellite office or something?'

'No, I'm on my own now.' I wondered whether she'd been asking around about me, and I suppressed a smile.

'You like it?'

'It would be perfect if the boss weren't such a hard-ass.'

She laughed ruefully. 'Nick Heller, company man.'

'You said Pembroke Street, right?'

'Right. Off Columbus Ave. Thanks for doing this.'

'My pleasure.'

'Listen, I'm sorry about Spike,' she said.

'Spike?'

'Gordon Snyder. Spike's his childhood nickname. He's spent his entire life trying to make people forget it.'

'Spike?'

'Don't ever tell him I told you. You promise?'

'I can think of some better nicknames for him than Spike,' I said. 'None of them very nice. So how did you know I met with him?'

She shrugged. 'I saw you storm out. Looked like it didn't go too well.'

'Did he tell you what we talked about?'

'Sure.'

I wondered whether she'd followed me out too. Maybe this meeting wasn't a coincidence. Maybe she heard I was in the building and wanted to say hi.

Maybe that was all she wanted.

I dropped another note into the cold-case file marked MADIGAN, DIANA.

'So what's with his fixation on Marshall Marcus?'

'Marcus is his great white whale.'

'But why?'

'Guys like that, the more elusive the target, the more obsessed they become. That may sound familiar, Nico.'

Tell me about it, I thought. 'Well, he seemed a whole lot more interested in taking down Marcus than finding his daughter.'

'Maybe because he's in charge of financial crimes.'

'Aha.'

'I have to say, I don't understand why you were meeting with the head of the financial crimes unit if you were looking for a missing girl.'

I was beginning to wonder the same thing. 'That was the name I was given.'

'Is Marshall Marcus a friend of yours?'

'Friend of the family.'

'Friend of your father's?'

'My mother worked for him,' I said. 'And I like his kid.'

'How much do you know about him?'

'Not enough, I guess. Apparently you guys are investigating him for something. What can *you* tell me about him?'

'Not much.'

'Not much because you don't know? Or because he's the subject of an FBI probe?'

'Because it's a sealed investigation. And I'm on the other side of the firewall.'

I pulled up in front of her narrow bow-front brownstone, double-parking in front of a space easily big enough for the Defender to fit.

'Well, thanks again,' she said, opening the door.

'Hold on. I need to ask you a favor.'

'What's that?'

'You think you can put in a request to locate Alexa Marcus's cell phone?'

'I – that's a little complicated. It's not so easy to do an end run around Snyder. What makes you think something happened to her?'

I was about to answer when she looked around and said, 'Look, if you want, you can come up for a sec, explain this all to me.'

I shrugged, playing it cool. 'Hell, seems a shame to waste a perfectly good parking space,' I said.

NINETEEN

Her apartment, on the second floor, wasn't very big. It couldn't have been much more than seven or eight hundred square feet. Yet it didn't feel small. It felt lush and rich and textured. The walls were painted various shades of chocolate brown and earth tones. It was furnished with what looked like stuff from flea markets. But every single piece of furniture, every object, every strange iron lamp or tapestry-covered pillow or copper picture frame, had been carefully selected.

She pointed me to a big overstuffed corner sofa while she made coffee for me – freshly ground beans, a French press – and served it in a big mug that looked hand-painted. It was dark and strong and perfect. She didn't have any, though, because she needed to sleep. She fixed herself a glass of sparkling water with some lime squeezed into it.

She had music playing softly in the background, a simple and infectious tune, a gentle guitar, highly syncopated. A smoky female voice singing in Portuguese and then English, a lilting song about a stick and a stone and a sliver of glass, the end of despair, the joy in your heart.

The lilting voice was singing in Portuguese now: *É pau, é pedra, é o fim do caminho . . . um pouco sozinho*. I didn't know what the words meant, but I liked the way they sounded.

'Who's singing?' I said. She'd always loved female vocalists – Ella Fitzgerald and Billie Holiday, Nina Simone and Judy Collins. All the greats, all of them different.

'Susannah McCorkle. "The Waters of March." It's an amazing rendition, isn't it? The more you listen to it, the more its layers unfold. It's casual and easygoing and then it just gets deeper and deeper and more soulful.'

I grunted agreement.

A woman invites you up to her apartment, you usually know what to expect. But not in this case. We'd both moved on. We'd gone from Friends With Benefits to Just Friends.

I had plenty of friends. But there was only one Diana.

And being Just Friends didn't change the way I felt about her. It didn't make her any less attractive to me. It didn't keep me from watching her from behind, appreciating the curve of her waist as it met her shapely butt. It didn't make me admire her less or find her any less fascinating. It didn't diminish the strength of her magnetic field.

The damn woman had some kind of built-in tractor beam. It wasn't fair.

But we were here to talk about Alexa Marcus, and I was determined to respect the implicit boundaries. I told her what little I knew about what had happened to Alexa, and about Taylor Armstrong, her Best Friend Forever.

'I hate to say it, but Snyder has a point,' she said. 'It hasn't even been twelve hours, right? So she met a guy and went home with him and she's sleeping it off in some BU dorm. That's entirely possible, right?'

'Possible, sure. Not likely.'

'Why not?'

'For one thing, it's not like a girl her age to go dark, go off the grid. She'd have checked in with her friends. These girls are constantly texting each other. They work their little mobile phones like speed typists.'

'She's an overprotected girl with a troubled home life, and she's testing the limits,' Diana said. She was sitting in an easy chair set at a right angle to the matching couch, her legs crossed. She'd removed her cowboy boots. Her toenails were painted deep oxblood red. The only makeup she had on was lip gloss. Her skin was translucent. She took a long drink of sparkling water, from a funky hand-blown blue glass tumbler.

'I don't think you really believe that,' I said. 'With the kind of work you do.'

The shape of her mouth gradually changed, so subtly that you'd have to know her well to see it. 'You're right,' she said. 'I'm sorry. I was playing devil's advocate. Maybe trying to see it the way Snyder sees it. Given what the girl's gone through – that attempted abduction a few years ago – she's not likely to go home with a strange guy no matter how much she's drunk. She's always going to be nervous.'

'It wasn't an *attempted* abduction,' I said. 'She was abducted. Then released.'

'And they never found out who did it?'

'Right.'

'Strange, isn't it?'

'Very.'

'No ransom demand.'

'None.'

'They just . . . grabbed her, drove her around for a few hours, and then released her? All that risk of exposure with no payoff?'

'Apparently so.'

'And you believe this?'

'I have no reason not to. I've spent a lot of time talking with Alexa about it.'

She leaned back in her chair, looked up at the ceiling. Her jawline was sharp, her neck swanlike. 'If her father secretly paid a ransom and didn't want to tell anyone, would she really know?'

She was smart. I'd forgotten how smart. 'If he had a reason to keep it secret, maybe not. But that was never the sense I got.'

'Maybe he doesn't tell you everything.'

'Maybe there's something *you're* not telling.'

She looked away. There was something. After a moment she said, 'I have to tread really carefully here.'

'I understand.' I took another sip and set the mug down on the coffee table, which was old and ornately carved from weathered teak.

'I know I can trust your discretion.'

'Always.'

Her eyes seemed to be focused on some middle distance. They kept moving down and to the right, which meant that she was internally debating something. I waited. If I pushed too hard, she'd close right up.

She turned to me. 'You know I'd never divulge confidential details of an ongoing investigation, and I'm not going to start now. No leaks, no favors. I've never worked that way.'

'I know.'

'So the speculation seems to be that Marshall Marcus is laundering money for some very bad guys.'

'Laundering money? That's ridiculous. The guy's a billionaire. He doesn't need to launder money. Maybe he's managing money for some questionable clients. But that's not the same thing as laundering it.'

She shrugged. 'I'm just telling you what I hear. And I should also warn you: Gordon Snyder is not a guy you want for an enemy.'

'Some people say that about me.'

'That's also true. But just . . . watch out for the guy. If he thinks you're working against him, against his case, he'll come gunning for you.'

'Oh?'

'He won't break the law. But he'll go right up to the edge. He'll use every legal tool he has. Nothing gets in his way.'

'Consider me warned.'

'Okay. Now, do you have a picture of Alexa?'

'Sure,' I said, reaching into my breast pocket for one of the photos Marcus had given me. 'But why?'

'I need to see her face.'

She came over and sat next to me on the couch, and I felt my heart speed up a little and I could feel the heat from her body. Another song was playing now: Judy Collins's haunting ballad 'My Father'. I handed her a picture of Alexa in her field hockey uniform, her blond hair pulled back in a headband, cheeks rosy and healthy, blue eyes sparkling.

'Pretty,' she said. 'She looks like she's got fight.'

'She does. She's had a rough patch, last few years.'

'Not an easy age. I hated being seventeen.'

Diana never talked much about growing up, besides the fact that she was raised in Scottsdale, Arizona, where her father was with the US Marshals Service and was killed in the line of duty when she was a teenager. After that her mother moved them to Sedona and opened a New Age jewelry and crystal shop.

I noticed her body shifting slightly toward me. 'You know, I recognize that shirt,' she said. 'Didn't I give it to you?'

'You did. I haven't taken it off since.'

'Good old Nico. You're the one fixed point in a changing age.'

'Sherlock Holmes, right?'

She gave me one of her inscrutable smiles. 'All right, I'll put in a request to AT&T. I'll find a way to push it through.'

'I appreciate it.'

'Look, it's not about you. Or us. It's about the girl. As far as I'm concerned, Alexa Marcus is legally a minor, and she may be in some kind of trouble, and that's all I need to hear.'

'So does this make it officially an FBI matter?'

'Not necessarily. Not yet, anyway. But if I can help out on this, you know where to find me.'

'Thanks.' A long, awkward silence followed. Neither one of us was the type to mull over every slight, to pick at emotional scabs. Yet at the same time we were both blunt-spoken. And there we were, sitting in her apartment, just the two of us, and if ever there was a time to talk about the elephant in the room, this was it.

'So how come—' I began, but stopped. *How come you never told me you were posted to Boston?* I wanted to say. But I didn't want it to sound like a reproach. Instead, I told her: 'Well, same here. You ever need anything, I'll be there. Right on your doorstep. Like a box from Zappos.'

She smiled and turned to look at me, but as soon as I met those green eyes and felt her breath on my face, my lips were on hers. They were warm and soft and her mouth tasted of lime, and I couldn't resist exploring it.

A phone started ringing.

With my hands drifting to her hips, almost involuntarily, I was probably the first to notice her vibrating BlackBerry.

Diana pulled away. 'Hold on, Nico,' she said, drawing her BlackBerry from the holster on her belt.

She listened. 'Okay,' she said. 'I'll be right in.'

'What is it?'

'My predator,' she said. 'He's been texting me again. I think he's getting a little suspicious. He wants to change our meeting time. They need me back at work. I'm – I'm sorry.'

'Me too,' I said.

She was on her feet, looking for her keycard and her house keys. 'What the hell did we just do?' she said, not looking at me.

'What we just did – I don't know, but—'

'I'll let you know if I get anything back on that iPhone,' she said.

'Let me drive you back.'

Suddenly she was all business. She shook her head and said firmly, 'My car's right here.'

It felt like jumping out of a sauna into four feet of snow.

TWENTY

Next, I drove over to the foot of Beacon Hill and pulled into the circular drive in front of the Graybar Hotel, the last place I knew Alexa had been.

You'd think most people would feel uneasy about spending the night in a hotel that used to be a prison. But the developers of the Graybar had done a remarkable job of converting the old Boston House of Corrections. It was once a grim, hulking, black monstrosity, filthy and overcrowded, the riots legendary. When Roger and I were kids and Mom drove us on Storrow Drive past the prison, we used to try to catch a glimpse of the inmates in their cell windows.

Personally, I don't believe that buildings store negative energy, but the developers wanted to be safe, so they brought in a group of Buddhist monks to burn sage and chant prayers and cleanse the place of any bad karma.

The monks seemed to have missed a spot, though. The negative energy at the front desk was so thick I felt like pointing a nine-millimeter semiautomatic pistol at the supercilious front-desk clerk just to get his attention. He seemed to be caught up in a conversation about *Jersey Shore* with a female desk clerk. Plus the music in the lobby was ear-splittingly loud. Fortunately, my weapon was in my gun safe at the office.

I cleared my throat. 'Can someone call Naji, please? Tell him it's Nick Heller.' Naji was the hotel's security director.

The guy sullenly picked up his phone and spoke softly into it. 'He'll be up soon,' he said. He had artfully messy hair with a lot of gel in it. His hair half covered his eyes. He had groovy day-old facial stubble. He wore a black suit that was too tight and too short in the arms, with high armholes and lapels about half an inch wide, like he'd borrowed it from Pee-wee Herman.

I stood at the desk, waiting. He went back to arguing about Snooki and The Situation. He noticed me out of the corner of his eye and turned around again, saying with annoyance, 'Um, it might be a while?'

So I strolled through the lobby. I saw a sign for Slammer in a brass standing frame holder in front of an ancient-looking elevator. I took the elevator to the fourth floor and looked around. Flat-screen TVs mounted on the brick walls, all tuned to the same Fox News show. Celebrity mug shots on the walls, too – Jim Morrison, Michael Jackson, O. J. Simpson, Janis Joplin, Eminem, even Bill Gates when he was a teenager. Everyone but my father, it seemed.

Leather couches and banquettes. A very long bar. Lights in the floors. A black iron railing around an atrium three stories high. At night this place was probably impressive, but in the unforgiving light of day it was drab and disappointing, like a magician's stage props seen up close.

There were a fair number of security cameras, mostly the standard low-profile shiny black domes mounted on the ceiling. A few were camouflaged as spotlights – you could tell because the 'bulbs', actually camera lenses, were a different color. The ones behind the bar were there to discourage employees from pilfering cash or stealing bottles. The cameras in the lounge area were more discreetly concealed, probably because the bar patrons might have gotten uncomfortable if they knew their every embarrassing move was being recorded. Though it occurred to me that closed-circuit cameras worked perfectly with the prison décor.

When I returned to the front desk, a very good-looking dark-haired guy was waiting for me. Classic Arab facial features: olive complexion, dark eyes, a prominent nose. He wore the same Pee-wee Herman suit, but he'd shaved and combed his hair.

He smiled as I approached. 'Mr Heller?'

'Thanks for meeting me, Naji,' I said.

'Mr Marcus is a very good friend of the Graybar,' he said. 'Anything I can do, please, I am at your service.' Marshall Marcus was not just a 'friend' of the hotel's but one of the original, and biggest, investors. He'd called ahead, as I'd asked.

Naji produced an oblong key fob with a BMW logo at the center: the keyless entry fob to Marcus's four-year-old M3. This was the 'junker' he'd given Alexa to drive. Attached to the keychain was a valet ticket stub.

'Her car was left in our underground parking garage. If you wish, I will take you there myself.'

'So she never claimed the car?'

'Apparently not. I made sure no one touched the vehicle, in case you needed to run prints.'

The guy was clearly experienced. 'The police might,' I said. 'Any idea what time she valeted the car?'

'Of course, sir,' Naji said, and he took out a valet ticket. This was a typical five-part perforated form. The bottom two sections were gone, one presumably handed to Alexa when she'd dropped the car off. Each remaining section was time-stamped 9:37. That was the time Alexa had arrived at the Graybar and given her dad's BMW to the valet.

'I'd like to look at the surveillance video,' I said.

'In the parking garage, do you mean? Or at the valet station?'

'Everywhere,' I said.

The Graybar's security command center was a small room in the business offices in the back. It was outfitted with twenty or so wall-mounted monitors showing views of the exterior, the lobby, the kitchen, the halls outside the restrooms. A chunky guy with a goatee was sitting there, watching the screens. Actually, he was reading the *Boston Herald*, but he hastily put it down when Naji entered.

'Leo,' Naji said, 'can you pull up last night's video feeds from cameras three through five?'

Naji and I stood behind Leo as he clicked a mouse and opened several windows on a computer screen.

'Start from around nine thirty,' I said.

There seemed to be at least three cameras positioned in the valet area in front of the hotel. The video footage was digital and sharp. As Leo advanced the frames at double and triple speed, the cars pulled up faster and faster. Guests zipped out of their cars at a Keystone Kops pace, touching their hair, patting their jackets. At nine thirty-five a black BMW parked and Alexa got out.

The valet handed her a ticket, and Alexa joined a long line waiting to get into the lobby as the valet drove off with her car.

'Can we zoom in?' I said.

I often enjoy looking at surveillance video. It's like being in an episode of *CSI*. Unfortunately, in real life, when you enlarge part of a video on a computer monitor, you don't hear any whooshing sounds or high-pitched beeping.

On TV and in the movies, all techies have an amazing ability to zoom in on a fuzzy image and magically sharpen it using some mythical digital enhancement 'algorithm' so they can read the label on a prescription bottle reflected in someone's eye or something.

Leo wasn't that good.

He moved the mouse, clicked a few keys. I saw Alexa hugging another girl who was already in line.

Taylor Armstrong.

They began talking animatedly, touching each other's sleeves the way girls do, occasionally glancing around, maybe scoping out some guy.

'Can we follow her into the hotel?' I asked.

'Of course. Leo, pull up nine and twelve,' Naji said.

From another angle, just inside the lobby, I could see the girls approach the elevator. The image was fairly smooth. Probably the standard thirty frames per second.

Then the elevator doors came open and the two girls got in. Abruptly, Alexa got out. Taylor remained.

Alexa was claustrophobic. She couldn't bear to be in enclosed spaces, especially elevators.

'Ah,' I said. 'I want to see where that one's going, the one who didn't get in the elevator.'

From another camera, probably mounted in the ceiling of the second floor, I watched Alexa climb the stairs.

Another camera showed her arriving at the fourth-floor bar, where she met up with Taylor.

'I like to take the stairs too,' Naji said helpfully. 'It's good exercise.'

We continued watching as they found some chairs. For a long stretch, nothing much happened. The bar got increasingly crowded. A waitress in a skimpy outfit, her boobs almost popping out of her low-cut bra, took their order. The girls talked.

A guy approached.

'Move in on this,' Naji said to Leo. Now he was joining the effort.

The guy had his shirttails untucked. He looked to be in his early twenties. Blond, ruddy face, an overbite. He sure didn't look Spanish. Alexa smiled, but Taylor didn't look at him.

After a few seconds, he left. I actually felt sorry for the kid.

The girls kept talking. They laughed, and I surmised it was about the guy with the untucked shirt.

'You can fast-forward,' I said.

Leo clicked on 3x mode, and the video sped up. Fast, jerky movements like in an old silent film. Laugh, drink, laugh, drink, smile. Alexa took out something and held it up. A phone, maybe? An iPhone, I realized. Taking a picture, probably.

No: she held it near her mouth. Taylor laughed. They were

playing around. Taylor grabbed it, and she too put it to her mouth. They laughed again. Taylor handed it back, and Alexa put the phone into a front pocket of her leather blazer. I made a mental note of that.

Another guy approached. This one was dark-haired. Mediterranean, maybe Italian, maybe Spanish. This time the girls both smiled. Their body language was open; they looked at him, smiled. They were more receptive. This was a side to Taylor I hadn't seen – no sullen pout. Lively and animated.

'Is there a different angle on this?' I said.

Leo opened another window on his monitor, and then I could see the man's face in profile. He zoomed in for a close-up.

Spanish or Portuguese. Maybe South American. In any case, a handsome guy. He appeared to be in his early to mid thirties. Well groomed, expensively dressed.

The guy pulled a chair over and sat down, apparently having been invited. He signaled for a waitress.

'This man, he comes here often,' Naji said.

I turned to him. 'Oh?'

'I recognize him. The regular patrons, I get to know their faces.'

'What's his name?'

He shook his head. 'I don't know.'

He was withholding something.

I turned back to the monitor. The guy and the two girls were talking and laughing. The waitress came, took their drink orders. They talked and laughed some more. The girls seemed to be enjoying his company.

The man was sitting next to Taylor, but didn't pay her much attention. He was much more interested in Alexa. He kept leaning toward her, conversing with her, barely giving Taylor a glance.

Interesting, I thought. Taylor was at least as pretty as Alexa, if sluttier-looking; Alexa seemed somehow more elegant, pure.

But Alexa's father was a billionaire.

Yet how would he know that – unless he'd picked out his target in advance?

The drinks came, served in big martini glasses.

They drank some more, and after a while both girls got up. The man remained at the table by himself. He looked around the bar idly.

'Can we follow the girls?' I said.

Leo switched to an already open window, made it bigger. The girls were walking together, holding on to each other, both looking a little tipsy.

'Keep on them,' I said.

Leo made the window on the computer screen bigger still. I watched them enter the ladies' room.

'No cameras inside the restrooms?' I asked.

Naji smiled. 'That's illegal, sir.'

'I know. But I had to ask.'

Then something in the other computer window caught my eye. The camera in which you could see the Latin man sitting alone.

He was doing something.

In one quick motion, he reached out a hand and slid Alexa's half-full martini glass across the table toward himself.

'What the hell?' I said. 'Enlarge this window, could you?'

Once Leo did so, we could see everything he was doing. The man slipped his right hand into his jacket. He glanced around. Then, nonchalantly, he dropped something into Alexa's martini glass.

He took the swizzle stick from his own drink and stirred hers, apparently dissolving whatever he'd just put in. Then he pushed her cocktail back in front of Alexa's place.

The whole process took around ten seconds, maybe fifteen.

'Oh, God,' I said.

TWENTY-ONE

'He put something in her drink,' Naji said.

I guess someone had to speak the obvious.

'Betcha it's Special K,' Leo said. 'Or Liquid X.'

In the other window on the monitor, the girls emerged from the restroom, walked down the hall, and returned to their table.

Alexa took a drink.

More laughter, more conversation. A few minutes later, Taylor stood up, said something. Alexa looked upset, but the guy didn't. Taylor left.

Alexa stayed.

She drank some more, and the two of them laughed and talked.

It was only a few minutes before Alexa began to exhibit signs of serious intoxication. It wasn't just the alcohol. She slumped back in her chair, her head lolled to one side, smiling gamely. But she looked sick.

The man signaled again for the waitress, then seemed to think better of it. Instead, he pulled out a billfold, put down some cash, then helped Alexa to her feet. She looked as if she could barely stand on her own.

'Cash,' I said, mostly to myself.

But Naji understood. 'He always pays in cash.'

'That's why you don't know his name?'

He nodded, started to speak, but hesitated.

'You know something.'

'I can't say for sure, but I think he may be a dealer.'

'Drugs.'

Naji nodded. He quickly added, 'But he never deals here. Never. If he ever did, we would ban him.'

'Of course.'

This wasn't good.

Now the Spanish guy turned back, took Alexa's handbag from the floor, then walked her toward the elevator. He pushed the button. She hung on his arm. A minute later the elevator arrived and they got in.

She had an elevator phobia, but I doubted she knew where she was.

The lobby camera captured the guy escorting Alexa toward the front door, almost dragging her. In his left hand he held her handbag. She was stumbling. People entering the hotel saw this and smiled. They probably figured the guy's girlfriend had had too much to drink.

In one of the exterior cameras, Alexa appeared to be almost asleep standing up in front of the hotel's entrance. The man handed a claim check to the valet.

Five minutes later, an older black Jaguar arrived: a 911, it looked like, from the 1980s. A classic, but not in very good shape. The rear quarter panel was dented, and there were dings and scrapes all over.

The dealer helped Alexa into the back seat, where she lay flat.

My stomach clenched. The car pulled away and out of the circular drive.

'I need another angle,' I said.

'Certainly, sir,' Naji said. 'His face?'

'No,' I said. 'His license plate.'

Of course, the plate number would be recorded on the man's valet ticket, but I wanted to be absolutely certain. A camera directly in front of the valet station had captured his license plate with perfect clarity.

The name on the ticket was Costa. He'd arrived at 9:08, before the girls did.

Naji burned a bunch of still frames of Alexa and Taylor with the guy, including close-ups of his face from several different angles, to a CD. I had him make me a couple of copies. Then I borrowed his computer and e-mailed a few of the stills of Costa to Dorothy.

The Defender was parked in one of the short-term spaces out front. I got in and called Dorothy. When she answered, I gave her a quick recap of what I'd seen. Then I read her the license plate number, a Massachusetts tag, and asked her to pull up the vehicle owner's name and address and anything else she could get. I gave her the name Costa, warned her it was probably fake, and asked her to check her e-mail. She already had. I told her that the hotel's security director suspected he was a narcotics dealer.

Then I pulled out of the hotel's front lot. About three blocks away I suddenly had another thought, and I drove back to the hotel. This time I didn't bother with the groovy kid with the stubble at the reception desk. I walked straight back and found Naji in the hall.

'Sorry,' I said. 'One more thing.'

'Of course.'

'The Jaguar,' I said. 'The valet records show an arrival time of nine oh eight.'

'Yes?'

'I'd like to see all video from the valet station around that time.'

It took Leo no more than a minute to call up the video I wanted: the banged-up Jaguar pulling up to the curb earlier in the evening, and Costa getting out.

Then I saw something I didn't expect.

Someone getting out of the passenger's side. A woman.

Taylor Armstrong.

TWENTY-TWO

'Alexa,' the voice said, 'please do not scream. No one can hear. Do you understand this?'

She tried to swallow.

'You see, when you panic or scream, you hyperventilate, and this only uses up your air supply much quicker.' His accent was thick and crude but his voice was bland and matter-of-fact, and all the more terrifying because of it.

'*No no no no no no*,' she chanted in a little voice, a child's voice. And she thought: *This is not happening to me. I am not here. This is not real.*

'Carbon dioxide poisoning is not pleasant, Alexa. You feel like you are drowning. You will die slowly and painfully and you will go into convulsions as your organs fail one by one. This is not a peaceful death, Alexa. I promise, you do not want to die this way.'

The top of the casket was two or three inches from her face. That was the most horrible thing of all, how close it was.

She gasped desperately for air, but she could only take shallow little breaths. She imagined the tiny space at the very top of her lungs. She thought of the air in her lungs as if it were water steadily rising in some sealed room in a horror movie, the air pocket shrinking to just an inch or two.

She felt her entire body wracked by violent shudders.

She was trapped ten feet underground, under tons of dirt, in this little tiny box in which she could barely move, and the air would soon run out.

Frantically she clawed at the silky fabric directly above her face. Her throbbing bloody fingertips touched the bare cold metal and tore off strips. They hung down and tickled her eyes and cheeks.

Her shuddering was uncontrollable.

'You are listening to me, Alexa?'

'Please,' she whispered. 'Please don't do this. Please.'

'Alexa?' the voice said. 'I can see you. A video camera is mounted right over your head. It gives infrared light you cannot see. I can also hear you through the microphone. Everything comes to us over the Internet. And when you speak to your father, he will see and hear you too.'

'Please, let me talk to him!'

'Yes, of course. Very soon. But first let us make sure you know what you must say and how to say it.'

'Why are you doing this?' she cried, barely able to talk through the sobs. 'You don't *need* to do this.'

'If you say your lines correctly and your father gives us what we want, you will be free in a matter of hours. You will be free, Alexa.'

'He'll give you anything – please let me out now, oh God, please, what can I possibly do to *you*?'

'Alexa, you must listen.'

'You can lock me up in a room or a closet if you want. You don't need to do this, please oh God, please don't do this . . .'

'If you do exactly as we ask you will be out of there right away.'

'You are a goddamned *monster*! Do you know what's going to happen to you when they catch you? Do you have any idea, you sick goddamned *psychopath*?'

There was a long silence. She could hear her own breathing, shallow and labored and quick.

She said, 'Do you *hear* me, you creep? Do you know what they'll do to you?'

More silence.

She waited tensely for his reply.

Had he decided to stop talking?

Only then did she understand how much she depended on the Owl.

The man with the owl tattoo on the back of his head. The Owl was her one and only lifeline to the world. Its power over her was absolute.

She must never again offend the Owl.

'I'm sorry,' she said.

More silence.

She said, 'Please, I'm so sorry, I shouldn't have said that. *Please talk to me.*'

Nothing.

Oh, God, now she understood that phrase 'the silence of the grave'. Absolute silence wasn't peaceful at all. It was the worst thing in the world.

It was hell.

She shuddered and moaned and cried softly, 'I'm sorry. Come back.'

'Alexa,' the voice said finally, and she felt such sweet relief.

'Do you want to cooperate with us?'

She began to weep.

'Oh, I do, I do, please, tell me what you want me to say.'

'Do you understand that it is my decision whether you live or die?'

'Yes,' she said. 'Yes. Please, I *do*. Anything. If you let me out of here I will do anything you want. Anything at all. Anything you want.'

But why was he now saying 'I' instead of 'we'? What did that mean?

'Alexa, I want you to reach under your mattress. Can you do this?'

'Yes.'

Obediently she lowered both hands to the thin mattress and discovered that it rested on a series of metal bands that ran crosswise, spaced a few inches apart and probably running down the length of the casket. Her hands found a space between the bands and plunged into an open area below. How far down did this space go? Her left hand touched an object, a cluster of objects, and she grasped the cap and narrow neck of what felt like a plastic bottle. There were many. She grabbed one in her left hand and pulled it up and through the space between the bands. A water bottle.

'Yes, very good,' said the voice. 'You see I have given you some water. You must be thirsty.'

'Yes, oh God, yes, I am.'

Now that she thought about it, her mouth was completely dry.

'Please to drink,' he said.

She twisted the cap with her other hand, and it came off with a satisfying snap and she put it to her parched lips and drank greedily, spilling some on her face and her shirt, but she didn't care.

'There is water enough to last you a few days,' the voice said. 'Perhaps a week. There are protein bars too, but not so many. Enough for a few days. When the food and water run out, that is all. Then you will starve to death. But before that you will suffocate.'

She kept drinking, swallowing down gulps of air along with the water, quenching a deep thirst she hadn't been aware of until now.

'Now you must listen to me, Alexa.'

She pulled the bottle away from her mouth, terrified that the Owl would abandon her again. She gasped, '*Yes*.'

'If you say exactly what I tell you, and your father does exactly what I ask, you will be free from this torture.'

'He'll give you whatever you want,' she said.

'But are you sure he loves you enough to set you free? Does he love you enough?'

'Yes!' she said.

'Does he love you at all, really? A mother will do anything for her child, but your mother is dead. A child never really knows about his father.'

'He *loves* me,' she said piteously.

'I guess you will now learn if this is true,' the voice said. 'You will learn the answer very quickly. Because if your father does not love you, you will die terribly down there. You will run out of air and you will be dizzy and confused and you will vomit and you will have convulsions and I will watch you die, Alexa. And I will enjoy it.'

'Please don't please don't please don't . . .'

'I will watch the last minutes of your life, and you know what, Alexa?'

He paused for a long time, and she whimpered like a baby, a small animal.

'Your father will watch the last minutes of your life too. He will try to look away or turn it off but it is human nature – whether he loves you or not, he will not be able to stop watching his only child's last minutes on this earth.'

TWENTY-THREE

After a brief visit to a great old tobacco shop on Park Square, I made a pit stop at home to do some tinkering. I called a friend of mine and asked him to do a very quick job for me. A little while later, my BlackBerry rang.

Without preface, Dorothy said: 'The Jaguar is registered to a Richard Campisi of Dunstable Street in Charlestown.'

'Bingo,' I said.

'No bingo. He reported his car stolen over a week ago.'

'I take it you've looked at his photo.'

'Of course. And he's not Costa. Not even close.'

'So our guy stole the car.'

'Looks that way.'

'So he couldn't be traced, I assume. This isn't good, Dorothy. It's been more than twelve hours since she disappeared. No one's heard from her. No one can reach her. It's like what happened to her a few years ago, only this time it's for real.'

'A kidnap for ransom, you think?'

'I hope that's all it is.'

'You hope it's a kidnapping?'

'I hope it's a kidnap for ransom. Because that means she's alive, and all her dad has to do is pay money. The other possibility . . .'

'Yeah,' I said. 'I know what the other possibility is.'

I called Diana and asked her to put a rush on her request to locate Alexa Marcus's phone.

This time the door to Senator Armstrong's Louisburg Square town-house was opened by a housekeeper, a plump Filipina in a black dress with white trim and a white apron.

'The senator not here,' she said.

'I'm here to see Taylor, actually.'

'Miss Taylor . . . she is expecting you?'

'Please tell her it's Nick Heller.'

She looked uncertain whether to show me in. In the end she closed the front door and asked me to wait outside.

The door opened again five minutes later.

It was Taylor. She looked dressed to go out, her small black handbag slung over her shoulder.

'What?' She said it the way you might talk to some neighborhood kid who'd rung your doorbell as a prank.

'Time for a walk,' I said.

'Is this going to take long?' she said.

'Not long at all.'

Halfway down Mount Vernon Street I said, 'The guy Alexa left Slammer with last night – what's his name?'

'I told you, I don't remember.'

'He never told you his name?'

'If he did, I couldn't hear it. Anyway, he wasn't interested in me. He was, like, hitting on Alexa the whole time.'

'So you have no idea what his name is.'

'How many times are you going to ask me? Is that what you came back for? I thought you said you found something.'

'I just wanted to be sure I understood you right. Does your daddy know you got a ride with some guy whose name you don't even know?'

For a split second I could see the panic in her eyes, but she covered smoothly with a scowl of disbelief. 'I didn't get a ride with him. I got a cab home.'

'I'm not talking about how you got *home*. I'm talking about how you got to the bar in the first place.'

'I took a cab.' Then she must have remembered about things like taxicab company call records and the like, and she added, 'I hailed one on Charles Street.'

'No,' I said softly, 'you arrived with him in his Jaguar.'

She did the disbelief-scowl again, but before she could dig herself in deeper, I said, 'It's all on the surveillance video at the hotel. You sure you want to keep lying to me?'

The look of desperation returned to her face, and she didn't try to conceal it. 'Look, I didn't . . .' She started off prickly, defiant, but seemed to crumple in front of me. Her voice was suddenly small and high and plaintive. 'I swear, I was just trying to help her out.'

TWENTY-FOUR

'I met this guy at a Starbucks, okay?' Taylor said. 'Yesterday afternoon. And he really, like, came on to me.'

She looked at me, waiting for a reaction, but I kept my face unreadable.

'We just started talking, and he seemed like a cool guy. He asked if I wanted to go to Slammer with him, and I . . . I was sort of nervous, 'cause I'd just met him, you know? I said, okay, sure, but I wanted my friend to join us. So it wouldn't be so intense. Like not really a date, you know?'

'Alexa knew all this?'

She nodded.

'His name?'

A beat. 'Lorenzo.'

'Last name?'

'He might have told me, but I don't remember.'

'So you two came to the Graybar together, and Alexa met you – where? Upstairs in the bar? Or in front of the hotel?'

'In line, in front. There's always a line there like a mile long.'

'I see.' I let her continue spinning her tale for a while longer. The surveillance video was fresh in my mind: Alexa joining Taylor in line, no guy with her. The guy had approached the two of them in the bar an hour later. Acting as if he'd never met either one of them before.

So: a total setup. He'd pretended to introduce himself to both girls. Taylor had been part of the arrangement.

'You got a smoke?' I said.

She shrugged, took the pack of Marlboros from her handbag.

'Light?' I said.

She shook her head in annoyance, fished around in her handbag, and pulled out the gold Dupont lighter. As I took it from her it slipped out of my hand and clattered to the cobblestones.

'Jesus!' she said.

I picked it up, lighted a cigarette, handed the lighter back. 'Thank you. Now, tell me about Lorenzo.'

'What about him?'

'How old?'

'Thirty, thirty-five.'

'What kind of accent?'

'Spanish.'

'Did he give you his cell phone number?'

'No,' she said.

'How'd you feel when he went home with your best friend instead of you?' I said.

She fell silent for a few seconds. I had a feeling she was thinking about how, if there were cameras outside the hotel, there might be cameras inside too. She said, unconvincingly, 'He wasn't my type.'

I'd deliberately led her down Mount Vernon across Charles Street, then left on River Street. I didn't want to walk down Charles. Not yet.

'Huh. When you met him at Starbucks earlier in the day, you must have been at least intrigued enough to agree to see him again.'

'Yeah, well, he turned out to be kind of, I don't know, sleazy? Anyway, he was definitely more into Alexa, and I figured, *Hey, you go, girl.*'

'Very nice of you,' I said acidly. 'A good friend.'

'I wasn't being nice. Just . . .'

'Reasonable,' I offered.

'Whatever.'

'So when you met Lorenzo at Starbucks, were you sitting at one of those big soft chairs in the window?'

She nodded.

'He just came and sat down next to you?'

She nodded again.

'Which Starbucks was this?'

'The one on Charles Street.' She gave a wave in the direction of Charles, about half a block away.

'Aren't there two of them on Charles?'

'The one on the corner of Beacon.'

'And you were just sitting alone?' I said. 'Sitting by yourself in one of those big soft chairs by the window?'

Her eyes narrowed. She didn't like the way I repeated the bit about the big soft chairs. 'Yeah. Just sitting there, reading a magazine. What's your point?'

'Well, what do . . . What do you know,' I said. 'Here we are.'

'What?'

We'd stopped at the corner of Beacon and Charles. Directly across the street was the Starbucks she was talking about. 'Take a look,' I said.

'What?'

'No big soft chairs.'

'Well, but—'

'And see? There sure as hell aren't any chairs in the window. Right?'

She stared, but only for show, because she knew she'd just been caught in another lie. 'Look, he was just going to show her a good time,' she said in a flat, emotionless voice. She took out a cigarette and lighted it. She inhaled. 'I was doing her a favor. I mean, she's never even had a serious relationship.'

'Man, what a friend you are,' I said. 'I'd hate to be your enemy.

You knew Alexa had been abducted once before and was still traumatized by it. Then you meet a guy, or maybe you already knew him, and you set him up with your so-called best friend. A guy you thought was sleazy. A guy who put a date-rape drug in your best friend's drink, probably with your full knowledge. And abducted her. Maybe killed her.'

A long black limousine pulled up to the red light next to us.

I was pushing her hard, and I knew it would get a reaction out of her.

I just didn't expect the reaction I got.

She blew out a plume of smoke, then flipped her hair back. 'All you can prove is that I went to Graybar with some guy. All that other crap – you're just guessing.'

The rear passenger's window in the limousine rolled smoothly down. A man I recognized stared at me, a natty fellow in a tweed jacket with a bow tie and round horn-rimmed glasses. His name was David Schechter. He was a well-known Boston attorney and power broker, a guy who knew all the players, knew which strings to pull to make things happen. He was utterly ruthless. You did not want to get on David Schechter's bad side.

Next to him in the back seat was Senator Richard Armstrong.

'Taylor,' the senator said, 'get in.'

'Senator,' I said, 'your daughter is implicated in Alexa Marcus's disappearance.'

Armstrong's face didn't register surprise or dismay. He turned to his attorney, as if deferring.

Taylor Armstrong opened the limo door and got in. I made one last attempt to get through to her. 'And I thought you were her best friend,' I said.

'I don't think I'm going to have a problem finding a new one,' she said with a smile, and I felt a chill.

The limousine had a large spacious interior. Taylor sat in a seat facing her father. Then David Schechter leaned forward and gestured for me to come closer.

'Mr Heller,' said Schechter, speaking so softly I could barely hear him. A powerful man who was accustomed to getting what he wanted without ever having to raise his voice. 'The senator and his daughter do not wish to speak to you again.'

Then he slammed the door and the limo pulled away from the curb and into traffic.

I pinched out my cigarette and tossed it into a trashcan. I'd given up smoking a long time ago and didn't want to start again.

My BlackBerry started ringing. I pulled it out, saw Marcus's number. 'Nick,' he said. 'Oh, thank God.' There was panic in his voice.

'What is it?' I said.

'They have her – they—'

He broke off. Silence. I could hear him breathing.

'Marshall?'

'It's my baby. My Lexie. They have her.'

'You got a ransom demand?'

'No.'

'Then how do you know—'

'It's just an e-mail with a link to some – oh, please God, Nick, get out here now.'

I looked at my watch. Soon it would be rush hour. The drive to Manchester would take even longer than usual.

'Did you click on the link?'

'Not yet.'

'Don't open it until we get there.'

'Oh, Jesus, Nick, come out here now. *Please.*'

'I'm on my way,' I said.

TWENTY-FIVE

There was no day or night. There was no time. There was only the trickle of her sweat down her face and neck. Her rapid breathing, that agonizing shortness of breath, the cold terror that she could never again fill her lungs with air.

The blank nothingness in which her mind raced like a hamster on a wheel.

The wanting to die.

She'd decided she had to kill herself.

This was the first time in her seventeen years that the thought of suicide had ever seriously occurred to her. But now she knew that death was the only way out for her.

When you hyperventilate you will increase the carbon dioxide.

She began panting, breathing as deep and fast as she could. Trying to use up the limited supply of air inside the casket. Panting. She could feel her exhalations settling around her, a warm, humid blanket of carbon dioxide. Keep at it, and maybe she'd pass out.

She began to feel woozy, light-headed. Faint and dizzy.

It was working.

And then she felt something different. A cool ripple of air.

Fresh air. It smelled of pine forest, of distant fires, of diesel and wet leaves.

Seeping in from somewhere. Her right hand felt for the source of the air flow. It was coming from the bottom of the coffin, beneath the metal support bands under the mattress, down where the bottles of water and the protein bars were. She touched the floor of the casket, her fingers tracing the outline of a round perforated metal disc maybe an inch in diameter.

An air intake.

She could hear a distant hum. No, not a hum, really. The far-off sound of a . . . a garbage disposal? Then something that sounded like a car engine. The regular chugging of pistons pumping. Very fast, far away.

She didn't know what it was, but she knew it had something to do with this new influx of air. A fan? But more mechanical and sort of *bumpy* than that.

Air was being circulated.

The Owl had been watching her pathetic efforts. Saw what she was trying to do. And was defeating her.

She couldn't help herself: she gasped deeply, drank down the cool fresh air as gratefully as she'd swallowed the water from the bottle. The fresh air was keeping her alive.

She couldn't asphyxiate herself. She couldn't kill herself.

He'd deprived her of the only power she had.

TWENTY-SIX

I picked up Dorothy at the office. We made better time than I expected and got to the security booth at the perimeter of Marcus's property just before six.

'Whoa,' she said softly as we walked up the porch steps, goggle-eyed at the spread. 'And I was just starting to be happy with my apartment.'

Marcus met us at the door. Ashen-faced, he thanked us somberly and showed us in. Belinda rushed up to me in the dimly lit hallway and threw her arms around me, a display of affection I'd never have expected. Her back was bony. I introduced Dorothy. Belinda thanked me profusely, and Marcus just nodded and led us to his study. His house slippers scuffed against the oak floor.

His study was a large, comfortable room, not at all showy. The shades were drawn. The only illumination was a circle of light cast by a banker's lamp with a green glass shade. It sat in the middle of a massive refectory table that served as his desk, carved from ancient oak. The only other objects on the table were a large flat-screen computer monitor and a wireless keyboard, which looked out of place.

He sat in a high-backed tufted black leather chair and tapped a few keys. His hands were trembling. Belinda stood behind him.

Dorothy and I stood on either side and watched him open an e-mail message.

'As soon as this came in, I told him to call you,' Belinda said. 'I also told him not to do *anything* until y'all got here.'

'This is my personal e-mail account,' he said quietly. 'Not many people have it. That's the weird thing – how'd they get it?'

Dorothy, wearing red-framed reading glasses on an ornate beaded chain, noticed something else.

'They used a nym,' she said.

'A who?' I said.

'An anonymizer. A disposable anonymous e-mail address. Untraceable.'

The subject heading read 'Your Daughter.' The message was brief:

> Mr Marcus:
> If you want to see your daughter again, click here:
> www.CamFriendz.com
> Click on: Private Chat Rooms
> Enter in search box: Alexa M.
> User name: Marcus
> Password: LiveOrDie?
> Note: case-sensitive.
> You may log in only from your home or office. No other
> location. We monitor everyone who signs in. If we detect
> any other incoming IP addresses, including any law
> enforcement agencies, local or national, all communications
> will be severed and your daughter will be terminated.

He turned around to look at us. There were deep hollows under his eyes. 'Belinda wouldn't let me click on the link.' He sounded depleted and resigned.

'What's CamFriendz-dot-com?' Belinda said.

'It's a live video site,' Dorothy said. 'Social networking. Mostly for teens.'

Marcus said, 'What should I do?'

'Don't touch the keyboard,' Belinda said.

'Wait a minute,' Dorothy said. She took out her laptop and hooked in the back of his computer. 'Okay.'

'What are you doing?' Belinda said.

'A couple things,' she said. 'Screen-capture software so we can record anything they send you. Also, packet-sniffing software so I can log network activity remotely.'

'Are you *mad*?' Belinda cried. 'They say if anyone else tries to look at this, they're going to cut off all communication! Are you trying to get her killed?'

'No,' Dorothy said, patiently. 'All I'm doing is setting up in effect a clone of this computer. I'm not logging in. No one's going to detect it.'

'Well, you can just look at Marshall's computer,' Belinda said. 'I will not have you compromise Alexa's safety in any way.'

'They have no way to know what I'm doing,' Dorothy said. I could see her patience was beginning to run out. 'Also, we need to make sure they're not trying to infect this computer with malicious code.'

'What's the point of that?' Marshall said.

'To take control of your computer,' Dorothy said. 'May I?' Her fingers were poised over his keyboard. He nodded, wheeled his chair back to let her at it.

'Don't touch that!' Belinda said, alarmed.

'Can I talk to you for a moment?' I said to her, and I took her out into the hall. In a low voice, I continued, 'I'm worried about your husband.'

'You are?'

'He'd be panicking by now if it weren't for you. You're his rock. You did the right thing by telling him to call me and by not letting him click on that link.'

She looked pleased.

'And I hate to impose on you further at a time like this,' I said, 'but I need you to go into another room and make an evidentiary compilation for me.'

'An . . . evidentiary . . . ?'

'Sorry, that's the technical term for an exhaustive description of all potential evidence that might help lead to her whereabouts,' I said. I'd made it up on the spot, but it sounded plausible.

'What sort of evidence?'

'Everything. I mean, what was Alexa wearing when she left. The make and size of her shoes and each item of clothing, her purse, anything she might have been carrying in her purse. You're far more observant than Marshall, and men never pay attention to that kind of thing anyway. I know it seems tedious, but it's extremely important, there's no one else who can do it. And we need it right away. Within the next hour, if at all possible.'

'Y'all want me to use a computer or a typewriter?'

'Whatever's fastest for you,' I said.

I went back in. Dorothy had positioned herself in front of Marshall's computer, standing. She tapped, moved the mouse, and after a minute she said, 'Okay, open the hyperlink.'

In a few seconds a new window had opened. It showed a cheesy-looking website with a banner across the top: CAMFRIENDZ – THE LIVE COMMUNITY!

Within it were lots of moving video windows. In some of them were second-tier celebs. In others, teenage girls wearing low-cut tank tops and a lot of eye makeup were making provocative poses, and doing suggestive things with their tongues. Some of them had pierced lips.

'What *is* this?' Marcus said. 'Some kind of pornography site?'

'Teenage girls and guys sit in front of the camera on their computer and talk to each other,' Dorothy said. 'Sometimes more than talk.'

Dorothy tapped and moused again, entered some text, scrolled down, clicked and clicked some more.

And then a still photo of Alexa popped up.

A school portrait, it looked like, from when she was younger. Her blond hair cut into bangs, a white headband, wearing a plaid jumper, probably a school uniform. Very sweet and innocent. Before the trouble started.

'Oh, my God,' Marcus moaned. 'Oh, my God. They put her picture up here where anyone can see it? What – what are they trying to do?'

Green letters at the top of Alexa's photo said ENTER CHAT.

'Chat?' Marcus said. 'What's this – who am I chatting with? What the hell?'

Dorothy clicked on it, and a log-in window appeared. She entered the user name and password they'd supplied. For a while nothing happened. She sidled over to her laptop, and Marshall and I came closer to the screen to watch.

Then a big window popped up with another still photo of Alexa.

Only this looked like it had been taken recently.

She appeared to be sleeping. Her eyes were closed, with dark smudges of eye makeup that made her look like a raccoon. Her hair was scraggly. She looked terrible.

Then I realized this wasn't a still photo at all. It was live video.

You could see slight motion as she shifted in her sleep. The streaming video had all the production values of a snuff film: the camera too close to her face, the image grainy and the focus tight, and the light strange, green-saturated, as if taken with an infrared camera.

Indicating that she was in the dark.

A loud metallic voice: 'Alexa, wake up! It's time to say hello to your father.' A man's voice. A pronounced accent: Eastern European, maybe.

Alexa's eyes came open, her eyes staring wide, her mouth agape.

Marcus gasped. 'That's her!' he said, probably because he

couldn't think of anything else. Then: 'She's alive. God almighty, she's *alive.*'

Alexa's eyes were shifting back and forth.

Unsettled. Panicky.

Something about her face looked different, though I couldn't quite put my finger on it.

She said, 'Dad?'

Marcus stood up, shouted, 'Lexie. Baby! I'm here!'

'She can't hear you,' Dorothy said.

'Dad?' Alexa said again.

The amplified voice said, 'You may speak, Alexa.'

Her words came all in a rush, a high-pitched shriek. 'Dad, oh God, please, they've got me in this—'

The sound of her voice abruptly cut out and the accented voice said, 'Follow the script exactly, Alexa, or you will never talk to your father, or anyone else, again.'

Now she was screaming, her eyes bulging, face flushed, head moving side to side, but there was no sound, and after ten more seconds the window went black.

Marcus said, '*No!*' and he catapulted himself out of his chair, touching the screen with his stubby fingers. 'My baby! My baby!'

'The link's gone down,' Dorothy said. The video image had once again become Alexa's school portrait. The sweet little girl with headband and bangs. 'She didn't cooperate. She was trying to tell us something – maybe her location.'

Marcus seemed to bob and weave, unsteady on his feet. Terror rilled his forehead.

'I doubt it,' I said. 'Everything about this says professional. They'd never have let her see where they took her.' I glanced over at Dorothy's laptop, saw a column of white numbers whizzing by on a black background, way too fast to read. 'What'd you get?' I asked her. 'Can you tell where the signal's coming from?'

She shook her head. 'Looks like CamFriendz is based in the Philippines, believe it or not. That's where the video feed originated. So that's a dead end too. These guys probably have a free account. They could be anywhere in the world.'

Marcus began to teeter, and I caught him before he sank to the floor. He hadn't passed out, not quite. I set him down gently in the chair.

'They killed her,' he said. He stared dully into some middle distance.

'No,' I said. 'That's not in their interest. They need her for ransom.'

He moaned, covered his face with his hands.

Dorothy got up and excused herself and said she wanted to give us some privacy to talk. She took a second laptop from her Gucci bag and went to work in the sitting area off the kitchen to try tracing the IP address.

'You were expecting something like this, weren't you?' I said.

'Every day, Nick,' he said sadly.

'After what happened to Alexa at the Chestnut Hill Mall that time.'

'Right,' he said softly.

'What do you think they want?'

He didn't reply.

'You'd pay any amount of money to get her back, wouldn't you?'

Now he just stared straight ahead, and I couldn't tell what he was thinking.

I leaned forward in my chair and spoke quietly to him. 'Don't. If they contact you and demand money wired to some offshore account, I know you'd do it in a heartbeat. I know you. But I need you to promise me you won't. Not until you consult with me and we make sure it's done the right way. If you want to get your daughter back alive.'

He kept staring, his eyes focusing on something that wasn't in the room.

'Marshall?' I said. 'I want your word on this.'

'Fine.'

'You never did call the police, did you?' I said.

'I—'

I interrupted him before he could go on. 'You need to know something about me,' I said. 'I don't like being lied to by my clients. I took this job because of Alexa, but if I find out you're lying, or holding anything back, I'll walk away. Simple as that. Got it?'

He looked at me for a long time, blinking fast.

'I'll give you amnesty for anything you did or said up till now,' I said. 'But from here on out, any lie, and I'm off the case. So let's try again: Did you call the police?'

He paused. Then, eyes closed, he shook his head. 'No.'

'Okay. This is a start. Why not?'

'Because I knew they'd just bring in the FBI.'

'So?'

'All the FBI cares about is putting me in prison. Making an example of me.'

'And why's that? Do they have a case?'

He hesitated. Then: 'Yes.'

I looked at him. 'They do?'

He just looked back.

'If you don't tell me everything now, I'll walk.'

'You wouldn't do that to Alexa.'

'*I* haven't done anything to Alexa.' I stood up. 'And I'm sure the FBI will do everything possible to find her.'

'Nick,' he said. 'You can't do this.'

'Watch me.'

I walked toward his office door.

'Wait!' Marcus called after me. 'Nick, listen to me.'

I turned back.

'Yes?'

'Even if they asked for ransom, I couldn't pay it.'

'What's that supposed to mean?'

His face was full of humiliation and anger and deep sadness all at once. A terrible, vulnerable expression.

'I have nothing,' he said. 'Completely wiped out. I'm ruined.'

Part Two

Why does man not see things? He is himself
standing in the way: he conceals things.
                    – Friedrich Nietzsche, *Daybreak*

TWENTY-SEVEN

'It's all gone,' Marcus said. He spoke without affect, like he'd been anaesthetized.

'You have ten billion dollars under management.'

'Had. It's all gone.'

'Ten *billion* dollars is gone?'

He nodded.

'That's not possible.' Then I had a terrible thought. 'My God, you never had it in the first place, did you? Right? It was never real, was it?'

Marcus stiffened. 'I'm no Bernie Madoff,' he said, offended.

I looked at him, cocked my head. He looked gutted, defeated. 'So what happened?'

He looked down. For the first time I noticed the age spots mottling his face. The network of lines and wrinkles suddenly seemed to have gotten deeper and more pronounced. He looked pale and his eyes were sunken. 'About six or seven months ago my CFO noticed something so bizarre he thought we'd accidentally gotten the wrong statements. He saw that all of our stock holdings had been sold. All the proceeds were wired out, along with all the rest of our cash on hand.'

'Wired where?'

'I don't know.'

'By who?'

'If I knew, I'd have it back.'

'Well, you have a prime broker, don't you, that does all your trading?'

'Sure.'

'So if they screwed up, they have to unwind it.'

Slowly he shook his head. 'All the trades were authorized, using our codes and passwords. Our broker says they're not responsible – there's nothing they can do about it.'

'Isn't there one guy there who's in charge of your account?'

'Of course. But by the time we discovered what had happened, he'd left the bank. A few days later he was found in Venezuela. Dead. He and his entire family had been killed in a car accident in Caracas.'

'What brokerage firm do you use?' I was expecting to hear Goldman Sachs or Morgan Stanley or Credit Suisse, one of the major players, and I was surprised when he answered, 'Banco Transnacional de Panamá.'

'*Panama*?' I said. 'Why?'

He shrugged. 'Half of our funds are offshore, you know. Arabs and the like – those are the ones with the real money.'

But I was dubious. Panama was the Switzerland of Latin America: the land of bank secrecy, an excellent place to stash money with no questions asked. Even more secretive, actually.

Panama meant you had something to hide.

'Suddenly Marcus Capital Management had no capital to manage. We had nothing. *Nothing*.' A vein throbbed along the ridge of his forehead. I was afraid he might have a coronary right there in front of me.

'I think I see where this is going. You couldn't tell your investors they'd lost all their money. Right?'

'Some of them had hundreds of millions of dollars invested

with me. What was I going to tell them, I screwed up? I couldn't face that. You know I never had a single losing quarter, all those decades? No one's ever had a record like that. I mean, the sainted Warren *Buffett* lost almost ten per cent a few years back.'

'So what'd you do, Marshall? Dummy up statements like Bernie Madoff?'

'No! I needed cash. Lots and lots of it. Massive infusions. And no bank in the world would lend me money.'

'Ah, gotcha. You took in new money. So you could make it look like you hadn't lost anything.'

He nodded, shrugged.

'That's still fraud,' I said.

'That wasn't my intent!'

'No, of course not. So who'd you take money from?'

'You don't want to know, Nickeleh. Believe me, you don't want to know. The less you know, the better.'

'At this point I think you better tell me.'

'Let's just say you're not going to run into any of these guys at the Union League Club, okay? These are bad men, Nicky.' A twitch had started in his left eye.

'Let me hear some names.'

'You ever hear of Joost Van Zandt?'

'Are you out of your mind?' Van Zandt was a Dutch arms dealer whose private militia had supported Liberia's murderous dictator, Charles Taylor.

'Desperate, more like,' he said. 'How about Agim Grazdani? Or Juan Carlos Santiago Guzman?'

Agim Grazdani was the head of the Albanian mafia. His portfolio included gunrunning, human trafficking, and counterfeiting. When Italy's top prosecutor issued a warrant for his arrest a couple of years ago, the prosecutor and his entire family turned up in the meat locker of the justice minister's favorite restaurant in Rome, their bodies dismembered and frozen.

Since then Italian prosecutors have been too busy with other cases to go after him.

Juan Carlos Santiago Guzman, the leader of Colombia's Norte del Valle cartel, was one of the most violent narcotics traffickers in the world. He'd altered his appearance through repeated plastic surgeries, was believed to be living somewhere in Brazil, and basically made Pablo Escobar look like Mister Rogers.

'And the damned Russians,' he said. 'Stanislav Luzhin and Roman Navrozov and Oleg Uspensky.'

'My God, Marshall, what the hell was the idea?' I said.

'I thought I could get the ship righted with all the new cash and I'd be back on my feet. But it wasn't enough to meet all the margin calls. My whole firm went down the crapper anyway.'

'The new money with the old.'

He nodded.

'Guzman and Van Zandt and Grazdani and the Russians,' I said.

'Right.'

'You lost all their money too.'

He winced.

'You know, when Bernie Madoff's investors lost everything the most they could do was cry in front of a judge. These guys aren't the crying type. So which one of them took your daughter?'

'I have no idea.'

'I'm going to need a list of all of your investors.'

'You're not walking away? Thank you.' Tears sprang to Marcus's eyes. He gripped my forearms in his bear paws. 'Thank you, Nick.'

'A complete list,' I said. 'Every single name. No omissions.'

'Yes,' he said. 'Of course.'

'I also want a list of all your employees, past and present. Including household staff, past and present. Personnel files too.'

There was a knock on the door.

'I'm sorry to interrupt,' Dorothy said, 'but the live feed's back up.'

'The feed?' Marcus said, confused.

'It's Alexa,' she said. 'The video stream is back online.'

TWENTY-EIGHT

We crowded around the monitor. Marcus hunched forward in his chair while Dorothy worked the keyboard.

'It just started up,' Dorothy said.

The same still photo of Alexa as a girl. Superimposed over it, in green letters: LIVE and ENTER CHAT. Dorothy moved the mouse and clicked.

Then Alexa's face appeared again. That same extreme close-up. Eyes brimming with tears.

'Dad?' she said. She wasn't looking straight at the camera but slightly off to the side, as if she didn't know for sure where the lens was. 'Dad?'

Marcus said, 'Lexie? Daddy's right here.'

'She still can't hear you,' Dorothy said.

'Daddy, they're not going to let me go unless you give them something, okay?'

The picture was sort of stuttery and jittery. Not very high quality. Like TV reception used to be in the days before cable.

'Um . . . first, they say if you contact the police or anything they're just going to . . .'

She blinked rapidly, tears streaming down her cheeks. She shuddered.

'I'm so cold and afraid, I'm too weak,' she said suddenly, almost in a monotone. Then, as her voice got fainter, I could make out something about twisting and turning, she said she was in the darkest space.

'Oh, Lord,' Dorothy said.

'Shhh!' Marcus said. 'Please!'

There was a low rumble, and suddenly the image pixelated: it froze, turned into thousands of tiny squares that broke apart, and then the screen went dark.

'No!' Marcus said. 'Not again! Why is this happening?'

But then the video was back. Alexa was saying, 'They want *Mercury*, Daddy, okay? You have to give them Mercury in the raw. I – I don't know what that means. They said you will. Please, Daddy, I don't think I can hold out any longer.'

And the image went dark once again. We waited a few seconds, but this time it didn't come back.

'Is that it?' Marcus said, looking wildly from me to Dorothy and back. 'That's the end of the video?'

'I'm sure it's not the last,' I said.

'IR camera for sure,' Dorothy said. Infrared, she meant. The reason for the video's monochrome, greenish cast. A video camera like that would have its own built-in infrared light source, invisible to the human eye.

'They're holding her in total darkness,' I said.

Marcus shouted, 'My little Lexie! What are they doing to her? Where is she?'

'They don't want us to know yet,' I said. 'It's part of the pressure, the . . . cruelty. The not-knowing.'

Marcus put a hand over his eyes. His lower lip was trembling, his face was flushed. He was sobbing noiselessly.

'I really do think she's lying down,' Dorothy said. 'Just based on the appearance of her face.'

'So what happened to the image at the end?' I said. 'What caused it to break up?'

'Some kind of transmission error, maybe.'

'I'm not so sure. You notice that low-pitched sound? Sounded like a car or a truck nearby.'

Dorothy nodded. 'A big old truck, maybe. They're probably near traffic. Probably right off a main road or a highway or something.'

'Nope,' I said. 'Not a main road. Not a busy street. That was the first vehicle we heard. So that tells us she's near a road but not a busy one.' I turned to Marcus. 'What's Mercury?'

He lifted his hand from his eyes. They were scrunched and red and flooded with tears. 'No idea.'

'And what was all that about being too weak and twisting and turning in the darkest space?'

'Who the hell knows,' he said, his voice phlegmy. He cleared his throat. 'She's scared out of her mind.'

'But it's not the way she normally talks, is it?'

'She's terrified. She was just . . . babbling!'

'Was she quoting a poem, maybe?'

Marcus looked blank.

'It sounds like a reference to something. Like she was reciting something. Doesn't sound familiar at all?'

He shook his head.

'A book?' I suggested. 'Maybe something you used to read to her when she was a little kid?'

'I, you know . . .' He faltered. 'You know, her mother read to her. And your mother. I – I never did. I really wasn't around very much.'

And he put a hand over his eyes again.

As we drove away from Marcus's house into the gloom of a starless night – away from what I now thought of as Marshall Marcus's compound, defended as it was by armed guards – I told Dorothy about how Marshall Marcus had lost it all.

She reacted with the same kind of slack-jawed disbelief that I had. 'You telling me this guy lost ten billion dollars like it dropped behind the sofa cushions?'

'Basically.'

'That can happen?'

'Easy.'

She shook her head. 'See, this is why I'm glad I never went into finance. I'm always losing my keys and my glasses. If you can lose something, I'll lose it.'

She was multitasking, tapping away at her BlackBerry as she talked.

'Remind me not to give you any money to manage,' I said.

'You have any idea what Mercury is?'

'Marshall doesn't know. Why should I?'

'Marshall *says* he doesn't know.'

'True.'

'Maybe it's, like, one of his offshore funds or something. Money he's stashed somewhere.'

'No.'

'Why not?'

'If the kidnappers know they lost their whole investment, they also know he's broke. So "Mercury" *can't* refer to money.'

'Maybe they figure he's got something stashed away somewhere. All these guys hide chunky nuts of money away. They're like squirrels. Evil squirrels.'

'But why not just say it straight? Why not just say, wire three hundred million dollars into such-and-such an offshore account or we kill the kid?'

'I don't know,' she admitted.

'Well, what's more valuable than money?'

'A virtuous woman.' Dorothy pursed her lips.

'Some proprietary trading algorithm, maybe. Some investment formula he invented.'

She shook her head, kept tapping away. 'A trading algorithm? Guy's busted flat. Whatever secret sauce the guy's got I ain't buying.'

I smiled.

'You think he knows but he's not telling us?' she said.

'Yep.'

'Even if it gets his daughter killed?'

For a long time I said nothing. 'Hard to believe, isn't it?'

'You know him,' she said. 'I don't.'

'No,' I said. 'I thought I knew him. Now I'm not so sure.'

'Hmph,' she said.

'What?'

'Oh, man, this can't be true.'

'What?'

'Oh, dear God, please don't let this be true.'

'What are you talking about?'

For a quick second I took my eyes off the road to glance at Dorothy. She was staring at her BlackBerry. 'That crazy stuff Alexa was saying? You thought it might be a music quote?'

'Yeah?'

'I Googled it and I think I've found it. I think it's a lyric from a song by a rock group called Alter Bridge.'

'Okay.'

'The song's called "Buried Alive".'

TWENTY-NINE

By the time I'd dropped Dorothy off at her apartment in Mission Hill, it was almost nine at night.

My apartment was a loft in the leather district, which may sound kinky, but actually refers to the six-square-block area of downtown Boston between Chinatown and the financial district, where the old red-brick buildings used to be shoe factories and leather tanneries and warehouses.

I found a parking space a few blocks away, cut through the alley into the grim service entrance and up the steel-treaded back stairwell to the back door on the fifth floor.

The loft was one large open space with a fifteen-foot ceiling. The bedroom was in an alcove, on the opposite side of the apartment from the bathroom. Bad design. In another alcove was a kitchen equipped with high-end appliances, none of which I'd ever used, except the refrigerator. There were a lot of cast-iron support columns and exposed brick and of course the obligatory exposed ductwork. The place was spare and functional and unadorned. Uncluttered.

I'm sure a psychiatrist would say that I was reacting against my upbringing in an immense mansion in Bedford, New York, stuffed with precious antiques. My brother and I couldn't run around inside without knocking over some priceless Etruscan vase or a John Townsend highboy.

But maybe I just hate clutter.

The comedian George Carlin used to do a great routine about 'stuff', the crap we all go through life accumulating and shuffling around from place to place. A house is just a pile of stuff with a cover on it, he said, a place to put your stuff while you go out and get more stuff. I have as little stuff as possible, but what I have is simple and good.

I went straight to the bathroom, stripped, and jumped in the shower. For a long time I stood there, feeling the hot water pound my head, my neck, my back.

Unable to get the image of poor Alexa Marcus out of my head. The raccoon eyes, the abject terror. It reminded me of one of the most harrowing Web videos I've ever seen: the beheading of a brave *Wall Street Journal* reporter some years ago by monsters in black hoods.

And that association filled me with dread.

I wondered what she meant by 'buried alive'. Maybe she was locked in an underground bunker or vault of some kind.

When I shut off the water and reached for the towel I thought I heard a noise.

A snap or a click.

Or nothing.

I stopped, listened a moment longer, then began toweling myself off.

And heard it again. Definitely something.

Inside the apartment.

THIRTY

I stared out through the halfway-open bathroom door, saw nothing.

In such an old building in the middle of a city at night, there were all sorts of sounds. Delivery trucks and garbage compactors and screeching brakes and car doors slamming and buses belching diesel. Car alarms, night and day.

But this was coming from inside my apartment for sure.

A scritch scritch scritch from the front of the loft.

Naked, still wet, I let the towel drop and nudged the bathroom door open a bit wider. Stepped out, dripping on the hardwood floor.

Listened harder.

The *scritch scritch scritch* even more distinct. It was definitely inside the loft, at the front.

Both of my firearms were out of reach. The SIG-Sauer P250 semiautomatic pistol was under my bed. But to reach the bedroom alcove I'd have to pass them first. I cursed the idiotic layout of the place, putting the bathroom so far from the bedroom. The other weapon, a Smith & Wesson M&P nine-millimeter, was in a floor safe under the kitchen floor.

Closer to them than to me.

The wooden floors, once scarred and dented, had been recently refinished. They were solid and silky-smooth and they didn't squeak when you walked on them. Barefoot, I was able to take a few noiseless steps into the room.

Two men in black ambush jackets. One was large and heavily muscled with a Neanderthal forehead and a black brush cut. He was sitting at my desk, doing something to my keyboard, even though he didn't look like the computer-savvy type. The other was small and slender with short mouse-brown hair, sallow complexion, and cheeks deeply pitted with acne scars. He sat on the floor beneath my huge wall-mounted flat-screen TV. He was holding my cable modem and doing something with a screwdriver.

Both of them wore latex gloves. They were also wearing new-looking jeans and dark jackets. Most people wouldn't notice anything special about the way they were dressed. But if you've ever worked undercover, their clothing was as conspicuous as an electronic Times Square billboard. It was carry-conceal attire, with hidden pistol pockets and magazine pouches.

I had no idea who they were or why they were here, but I knew immediately they were armed.

And I wasn't.

I wasn't even dressed.

THIRTY-ONE

I wasn't scared, either. I was pissed off, outraged at the audacity of these two intruding into my living space. Messing with my computer and my new flat-screen TV.

Most people feel a jolt of adrenaline and their heart starts to race. Mine slows. I breathe more deeply, see more clearly. My senses are heightened.

If I simply wanted them to leave, I'd only have to make a sound, and they'd abandon their black-bag job and slip out. But I didn't want them gone.

I wanted them dead. After we'd had a conversation, of course. I wanted to know who'd sent them, and why.

So I backed into the bathroom and stood there for a moment, still dripping on the floor, considering my options, thinking.

Somehow they'd gotten in without setting off the alarm. They'd managed to defeat my security system, which wasn't easy. The front door was ajar, I noticed, and one of the big old factory windows was open. I doubted they'd entered through the window, on that busy street. That would have attracted all kinds of attention, even at night: I was on the fifth floor. But to have gotten in through my front door meant knowing the code to disarm the system.

Obviously they hadn't expected me to be home. Nor did they see or hear me come in through the service entrance at the back of the loft, which I seldom used. They hadn't heard me showering at the other end of the apartment: in this old building, water constantly flowed through the pipes.

My only advantage was that they didn't know I was here.

Looking down at my pants, heaped on the bathroom floor, I ran through a quick mental catalogue. Just the usual objects that can be used as improvised weapons, like keys or pens, but only at close range.

This was a time when a little clutter might have been useful. At first glance, I saw nothing promising. Toothbrush and toothpaste, water glass, mouthwash. Hand towels and shower towels.

A towel can be an effective makeshift weapon if you use it like a *kusari-fundo*, a Japanese weighted chain. But only if you're close enough.

Then I saw my electric razor. I'm normally a blade guy, but in a rush, electric is faster. Its coil cord was about two feet long. Stretched to its full length it would probably reach six feet.

I slipped on my pants, unplugged the razor, then padded silently, stealthily, into the main room.

I had to go for the muscle first. The computer guy wasn't likely to be much of a threat. Once Mongo was out of the way, I'd find out whatever I could from Gigabyte.

My bare feet were still damp and a little sticky and made a slight sucking noise as I lifted them off the floor. So I approached slowly, tried to minimize the sound.

In a few seconds I was ten feet away from the intruders, hidden behind a column. I inhaled slowly and deeply. Holding the shaver in my right hand and the plug in my left, I pulled my right hand back, stretching out the coiled cord like a slingshot.

Then hurled it, hard, at the side of the bigger man's head.

It made an audible crack. His hands flew up to protect his face, a second too late. He screamed, tipped back in the chair, and crashed to the floor. I jerked at the cord, and the shaver ricocheted back to me.

Meanwhile the computer guy was scrambling to his feet. But I wanted to make sure the big one stayed down. I launched myself at the guy, landing on top of him, and jammed my right knee into his solar plexus. The wind came out of him. He tried to rear up, flinging his fists at me without much success. He gasped for breath. He did manage to land a few punches on my ears and one particularly hard one on my left jaw, painful but not disabling. I aimed a drive at his face with everything I had. It connected with a wet crunch. I felt something sharp and hard give way.

He screamed, writhed in agony. His nose was broken, maybe a few teeth as well. Blood spattered my face.

In my peripheral vision I noticed that the weedy computer guy had clambered to his feet and was pulling what appeared to be a weapon from his jacket.

During the brief struggle, I'd dropped the electric razor, so I reached for the heavy weighted Scotch-tape dispenser on my desk. In one smooth sharp arc, I hurled it at him. He ducked, and it clipped him on the shoulder, the roll of tape flying out as it thunked to the floor.

A miss, but it gave me a couple of seconds. The weapon in his right hand, I saw now, was a black pistol with a fat oblong barrel. A Taser.

Tasers are meant to incapacitate, not kill, but take my word for it, you don't want to get zapped with one. Each Taser cartridge shoots out two barbed probes, tethered to the weapon by thin filaments. They send fifty thousand volts and a few amps coursing through your body, paralyzing you, disrupting your central nervous system.

He hunched forward, Taser extended, and took aim like an expert. He was less than fifteen feet from me, which indicated he knew what he was doing. Fired from twenty feet away, the electrical darts spread too far apart to hit the body and make a circuit.

I leaped to one side and something grabbed my ankle, causing me to stumble. It was the beefy guy. His face was a bloody mess. He was groaning and pawing the air, arms swarming, bellowing like a wounded boar.

The thin sallow-faced one smiled at me.

I heard the click of the Taser being armed.

Sweeping the big black Maglite flashlight from the edge of my desk, I swung it at his knees, but he was quick. He dodged just in time. The Maglite missed his kneecaps, struck his legs just below with a satisfying crack. He made an *ooof* sound, his knees buckling, and roared in pain and fury.

I reached up to grab the Taser from his hands, but instead I got hold of the black canvas tool bag on his shoulder. He spun away, aimed the Taser again, and fired.

The pain was unbelievable.

Every single muscle in my body cramped tighter and tighter, something I'd never experienced before and just about impossible to describe. I was no longer in control of my body. My muscles seemed to seize. My body went rigid as a board, and I toppled to the floor.

By the time I could move, two minutes or so later, both men were gone. Far too late to attempt to give chase, even if I were able to run. Which I certainly wasn't.

I got up gingerly, forced myself to remain standing, though I wanted only to sink back to the floor. I surveyed the mess in my apartment, my anger building, wondering who had sent the two.

And then I realized they'd been considerate enough to leave some evidence behind.

THIRTY-TWO

The SIG was still under the bed.

The Smith & Wesson nine-millimeter was locked away, as a precaution, in case someone found the SIG. Concealed beneath the bluestone tiles of the kitchen was a floor safe. I popped the touch latch to lift one of the tiles, dialed open the safe, found the contents – a lot of cash, various identity documents, some papers, and the pistol – intact.

They hadn't found it.

They probably hadn't even looked for it. That wasn't what they were here for.

I gathered the things the intruders had left behind in their haste to leave, including a black canvas tool bag and my dismantled cable modem. And one thing more: a little white device connected between one of the USB ports on the back of my computer tower and the cable to my keyboard. The color matched exactly. It almost looked like it belonged there. If you weren't looking for it, you'd never notice it.

I'm no computer expert, by any means, but you don't have to be an auto mechanic to know how to drive a car. This little doohickey was called a keylogger. It contained a miniature USB drive that captured every single keystroke you typed and stored it on a memory chip. Sure, you can grab the same data with a software package. But that's a whole lot trickier now that most people use antivirus software. Had I not had reason to look for it, I'd never have found it.

Inside the case to my cable modem I found a little black device that I recognized as a flash drive. I had a feeling it didn't belong there either.

I called Dorothy.

'They knew you were meeting with Marcus,' she said. 'And they didn't think you'd be home.'

'Well, if so, that means they weren't watching us.'

'You'd have detected physical surveillance, Nick. They're not stupid.'

'So who are they?'

'I want you to put that keylogger back in the USB drive, okay?' I did.

'Do you know how to open a text editor?'

'I do if you tell me how.'

She did, and I opened a window on my computer and read off a long series of numbers. Then I took the keylogger out of the USB port and inserted the little device from the cable modem. And repeated the process, reading off more numbers.

'Hang on,' she said.

I waited. The two spots where the Taser prongs had sunk in, on my right shoulder and my left lower back, were still twitching and were starting to get itchy.

I heard keyboard tapping and mumbling and the occasional grunt.

'Huh,' she said.

'Yeah?'

'Oh, now, this is interesting.'

'Okay.'

'The electronic serial numbers you just gave me? That's law-enforcement-grade equipment. Whoever broke in was working for the US government.'

'Or using government equipment,' I pointed out. 'They weren't necessarily government operatives themselves.'

'Fair enough.'

Though now I had a fairly good idea who might have sent them.

Even before I arrived at the Boston field office of the FBI, Gordon Snyder had figured out who I was. He knew why I wanted to talk with him, and he knew I was working for Marshall Marcus.

Who was the target of a major high-level FBI investigation. And I, as someone employed by Marcus, was probably an accomplice.

Which made me a target too.

Snyder had flat-out told me that the FBI was tapping Marcus's phones. They were probably monitoring his e-mail as well. Which meant he knew I'd driven up to Manchester. He knew I wasn't home, that it was safe to send his black-bag boys.

I recalled Diana's warning: *Watch out for the guy. If he thinks you're working against him, against his case, he'll come gunning for you.*

'Can you pull up the video for my home cameras?' I said. 'I want to see how they got in.'

When I moved in, I'd had a security firm put in a couple of high-resolution digital surveillance cameras outside the doors to my loft. Two of them were hidden dummy smoke detectors, and a couple of Misumi ultra-mini snake IP cameras were concealed in dummy air vents. They were all motion-activated and networked into a video server at the office.

How this worked exactly, I had no idea. That wasn't in my skill set. But the surveillance video was stored on the office network.

She said she'd get back to me. While I waited, I searched the apartment for more equipment, or even just traces, left by Gordon Snyder's team.

When Dorothy called back, she said, 'I'm afraid I don't have the answer for you.'

'Why not?'

'Take a look at your computer.'

I walked back to my desk and saw what looked like four photographs on my screen, still photos of the stairwells outside the front and back doors to my loft. Each, I saw, was the video feed from a different camera. Beneath each window were date and time and a jumble of other numbers that didn't seem important.

Somehow she'd put them on my computer remotely.

'How'd you do that?' I said.

'A good magician never reveals her secrets.' The cursor began moving on its own, circling the first two windows. 'These first two didn't get any action, so forget them.' They disappeared. 'Now watch.'

The remaining two windows grew bigger so that they now took up most of the monitor. 'They entered your apartment at 8:22 P.M.'

I glanced at my watch. 'Okay.'

'So here we are, 8:21 and . . . thirty seconds.' Both windows advanced a few frames, and suddenly a red starburst appeared in the middle of each one, blooming into a red cloud that obliterated the entire image.

'Laser zapper,' I said.

'Exactly.'

After a minute the picture returned to normal.

Then there was nothing to see but an empty stairwell.

'So we still don't know how they got in,' I said. 'But this tells us something useful.'

'What, they knew how to dazzle the cameras? It's all over the Internet.'

'No. They knew where the cameras were.'

'Why do you say that?'

'No fumbling around. Quick and efficient. You can't blind the cameras if you can't find them. They knew exactly where to look.'

'So?'

'The cameras are concealed,' I said. 'One in a smoke detector, and one in an air vent. The smoke-detector camera isn't all that original, if you're familiar with what's on the market. But the air-vent one – that's custom. It's a fiber-optic camera that's like a quarter inch thick. Takes some serious skill to hit that one first time.'

'So what's your point?'

'They got hold of the schematics. As well as my password.'

'Maybe from the security company that put them in.'

'Possibly. Or maybe from my own files. Right there in the office.'

'Not possible,' she said. 'I'd have detected the intrusion, Nick.'

'Maybe.'

'Not maybe,' she said, defensive. 'For sure.'

'Put it this way,' I said. 'Not only did they know exactly where my cameras are, but they were able to disarm the system. Meaning they knew the code.'

'From your security company.'

'The company doesn't know my code.'

'Who does?'

'Just me.'

'You don't keep your code written down anywhere?'

'Just in my personal files at the office,' I said.

'In your file drawers?'

'On my computer. Stored on our server.'

'Oh.'

'You see?' I said.

'Yeah,' she said, and the other line rang. I saw from the caller ID it was Diana. 'Someone's gotten into the office network.'

'Or else we've got a leak,' I said. 'Let me take this.'

I clicked over to Diana's call.

'Nick,' she said, her voice tight. 'I just heard from AT&T. I think we've found our girl.'

THIRTY-THREE

Not until Alexa went away to boarding school did she learn that other kids, normal kids, didn't have the kind of dreams she did. Others dreamed of flying, like she sometimes did, but they also dreamed about their teeth falling out. They dreamed of getting lost in mazes or realizing, with immense embarrassment, that they were walking around school naked. They all had anxiety dreams about having to take a final exam in a class they'd forgotten to attend.

Not Alexa.

She dreamed over and over about crawling on her belly through an endless network of caves and getting stuck in one of the narrow tunnels, thousands of feet underground. She'd always wake up sweating and trembling.

The thing about phobias, she'd learned, was that once you had one, some small part of your brain was always working to justify its existence. To show you why your phobia made perfect sense.

Wasn't it logical to be afraid of snakes? Who could argue with that? Why wasn't it logical to fear germs or spiders or flying in an airplane? You could die any of these ways, right? It wasn't like your brain had to work very hard to justify any of these phobias.

Being in an enclosed space was the most deeply terrifying thing she could imagine. She didn't require logic. She just *knew*.

Like a magpie forever gathering shiny little scraps, her mind collected the most horrifying tales, things she'd read about or heard from friends, stories that proved her fears were legitimate. Things most people barely noticed, she filed away obsessively.

Stories from history books of people who'd fallen ill during the Plague, gone into comas, declared dead. Stories she wished she could unread.

Coffin lids with scratch marks on the inside. Skeletons found with fistfuls of human hair clenched in their bony hands.

She'd never forget reading about the Ohio girl in the late nineteenth century who got sick and her doctor thought she'd died, and for some reason her body was placed in a temporary vault, maybe because the ground was too frozen to bury her, and when they opened the vault in the spring to put the body in the ground, they found that the girl's hair had been pulled out. And that some of her fingers had been chewed off.

The girl had eaten her own fingers to stay alive.

Her English teacher at Exeter had made them read Poe. It was hard enough just trying to understand the guy's writing, the strange words she'd never heard of. But his stories – she couldn't bear to read them. Because he was one of the very few who actually got it. He understood the terror. Her classmates would say things like 'That's one sick dude', but she knew that Edgar Allan Poe saw the truth. 'The Fall of the House of Usher' and 'The Cask of Amontillado' – all those stories about people being buried alive – she couldn't bring herself to finish them. How could anyone?

Why was her fevered magpie mind dwelling on all those awful stories?

After all, she was living her own worst nightmare.

THIRTY-FOUR

'Her phone's on and transmitting,' Diana said.

'Where is she?' I said.

'Leominster.' She said it wrong, like most people new to the state. It's supposed to rhyme with 'lemming', almost.

'That's an hour away.' I looked at my watch. 'Maybe less, this time of night. How precise a location did they give you?'

'They're e-mailing me lat-and-long coordinates, in degrees and minutes.'

'Okay,' I said. 'That could be as big an area as a thousand square meters, the way these things work. But once I'm there I can start searching for likely locations.'

'Give me ten minutes.'

'Go back to bed. Otherwise, you'll be a wreck tomorrow. I got this.'

'Technically, I put in the request. I'm not allowed to pass on the information to someone outside the Bureau.'

'Okay,' I said. 'I'll drive, you navigate.'

I quickly gathered some equipment, including the Smith & Wesson and a handheld GPS unit, a ruggedized yellow Garmin eTrex.

As we drove, I told her what had happened in the hours since

I'd seen her last: the surveillance tape at the Graybar Hotel, the guy who'd spiked Alexa's drink and driven her away. Her 'friend' Taylor Armstrong, the senator's daughter, who'd cooperated in the abduction for some reason I didn't yet understand. The streaming video. Marshall Marcus's admission that he'd taken money from some dangerous people in a last-ditch attempt to save his fund, though he lost it all anyway.

Diana furrowed her brow. 'Let me check the phone detail records.' She began scrolling through her BlackBerry.

'Yeah, I'd like to know when the last phone call was, in or out.'

'The last outgoing call hit the tower in Leominster at two thirty-seven A.M.'

'Almost twenty-four hours ago,' I said. 'How long did it last?'

More scrolling. 'About ten seconds.'

'Ten seconds?' I said. 'That's pretty short.'

I heard her scroll some more, and then she said, 'The last call was to nine-one-one. Emergency. But it doesn't look like the call ever went through. It hit the tower, but it must have been cut off.'

'I'm impressed. She must have been pretty spaced-out from the drugs, but she had the wherewithal to try to call for help. What calls did she receive around then?'

'A bunch of incoming, between three in the morning to around noon today.'

'Can you see who they're from?'

'Yeah. Four different numbers. Two landlines in Manchester-by-the-Sea.'

'Her dad.'

'One mobile phone, also Marcus's. The fourth is another mobile phone registered to Taylor Armstrong.'

'So Taylor did try to call. Interesting.'

'Why?'

'If she was trying to reach Alexa, that may indicate she was actually worried about her friend. Which indicates she might not have known what happened to her.'

'Or that she was feeling guilty about what she'd done and wanted to make sure Alexa was okay.'

'Right,' I said. For a long time we didn't talk. There was no quick way to Leominster. No shortcut. I had to take the Mass Turnpike to 95 North and then onto Route 2. Leominster is on Route 2, an east-west highway that winds through Lincoln and Concord and then keeps going west to New York State.

But I wasn't too concerned about the speed limit. I had a federal law-enforcement officer in the front seat next to me. If ever I had a chance of beating a speeding ticket, this was it.

It had started to rain. I switched on the wipers. The only vehicles on the road at this time of night were trucks. An old tractor-trailer was just ahead of me, rubber mudguards flapping, sheeting water onto my windshield. I clicked the wipers faster and changed lanes.

I began to sense her looking at me.

'What?' I said.

'Why is there blood on your collar? And please don't tell me you cut yourself shaving.'

I explained about the break-in at my loft. Gave her my theory that Gordon Snyder was behind it. As I talked, she shook her head slowly, and when I was done, she said, 'That's not FBI. That's not how we work. We don't do that kind of stuff.'

'Not officially.'

'If Snyder wanted to monitor your e-mail, he'd do it remotely. He wouldn't send a couple of guys in to do a black-bag job.'

I thought for a moment. 'You may have a point.'

We went quiet again. I was about to ask her about what had happened between us – or almost happened between us – earlier in the day, when she said abruptly, 'Why is her phone still on?'

'Good question. They should have turned it off. Taken out the battery. Better yet, destroyed it. Anyone who watches crime shows on TV knows a cell phone can give up your location.'

'Maybe they didn't find it on her.'

'Doubt it. She had it in the front pocket of her jacket.'

'Then maybe she hid it somewhere. Like in the vehicle she was abducted in.'

'Maybe.'

A black Silverado was weaving between lanes without signaling.

'I'm glad we reconnected,' I said. It came out a little stiff, a little formal.

She didn't say anything.

I tried again. 'Funny to think we've both been in Boston all these months.'

'I meant to call.'

'Nah, where's the fun in that? Keep the guy guessing. That's way more fun.' I wondered if that sounded resentful. I hoped not.

She was silent for a long moment. 'Did I ever tell you about my dad?'

'A bit.' I knew he'd been killed while tracking down a fugitive, but I waited to see what she'd say.

'You know he was a US Marshal, right? I remember how my mom always lived with that knot in her stomach, you know – when he left for work in the morning, would he come home safe?'

'Yet you risk your own safety every day,' I said gently, not sure what she was getting at.

'Well, that's the life I signed up for. But always having to worry about someone else? That's more than I can stand, Nico.'

'What are you saying?'

'I'm saying we had an understanding, and I knew I wasn't abiding by it.'

'An understanding?'

'We were supposed to be casual, no strings, no pressure, no commitment, right? But I was starting to get in a little too deep, and I knew that wasn't going to be good for either one of us.'

'Is that what you told yourself?'

'Do we really have to do this?'

I couldn't help thinking about all that had been left unsaid between us, but all I managed was 'You never said a word about it.'

She shrugged, went quiet.

We were driving along an endless, monotonous flat stretch of three-lane highway somewhere west of Chelmsford, through miles and miles of scraggly evergreen forest, steeply banked on either side. The broken white lane markers were worn. The only sound was the highway hum, a faint rhythmic thrumming.

'They didn't ask me to go to Seattle,' she said softly. 'I put in for a transfer.'

'Okay,' I said. It could have been a cool breeze from the window that was numbing my face.

'I had to pull myself out. I thought I saw my future and it scared me. Because I saw what my mom went through. I should probably marry a CPA, you know?'

For a long time no one spoke.

Now we were zooming along Route 12 North, which seemed to be the main commercial thoroughfare. On the other side of the street was a Staples and a Marshalls. A Bickford's restaurant that advertised 'breakfast any time', except apparently at two in the morning. A Friendly's restaurant, closed and dark too. I pulled over to the shoulder and put on the flashers.

She looked up from the GPS. 'This is it,' she said. 'We're within a thousand feet of her phone right now.'

THIRTY-FIVE

'Right there.' Diana pointed. 'That's 482 North Main Street.'

Behind the Friendly's was a four-story motel built of stucco and brick in the classic American architectural style best described as Motel Ugly. A tall pole-mounted road sign out front with a yellow-and-red Motel 12 logo brightly illuminated. It looked like the local kids had been using it for target practice, because there were a couple of holes and cracks in it where white light shone through. Mounted below that was a marquee sign board that said in black plastic letters COMPLEMENTARY HI SPED.

I pulled into the motel parking lot. There were maybe a dozen cars parked here. None of them was the Jaguar I'd seen on the surveillance video, not that I expected to see it here. On the other side of the motel loomed a tall self-storage building.

'Dammit,' I said, 'we need more precise coordinates. Can you call AT&T back and ask them to ping the phone again? I want the GPS coordinates in decimal format.'

While she called, I walked back toward the road. A few cars passed. A sign across the street said SHERATON FOUR POINTS. No construction lots that I could see, no fields or private homes.

'Got it,' Diana called out, running toward me. She held the Garmin out, and I took it. She'd already programmed the new coordinates in. A flashing arrow represented us. A dot indicated Alexa's iPhone, and it was quite near. I walked closer to the road and the flashing arrow moved with me.

Closer to Alexa's iPhone.

I crossed the street, glancing at the GPS screen as I did, to a scrubby shoulder beside a guardrail. Now the arrow and the dot were almost aligned. Her phone had to be right around here.

I stepped over the guardrail and onto a steep downward grade that rolled into a drainage ditch, then rose sharply. I scrambled down the hill, lost my footing, and slid part of the way.

As I got to my feet at the bottom, I looked again at the GPS. The arrow was precisely on top of the dot. I looked up, then to my right, and to my left.

And there, in the yellow light of the streetlamp, I saw it. Lying in the ditch, a few feet away. An iPhone in a pink rubber case.

Alexa's iPhone.

Discarded by the side of the road.

THIRTY-SIX

'Alexa?'

The Owl's voice startled her.

She'd been trying to remember the lyrics to 'Lose Yourself' by Eminem. She'd been singing songs dredged up from memory, jingles from TV commercials, anything she could think of. Anything to keep her mind off where she was. She'd managed to recall all of the words to 'American Pie'. That took a long time. She didn't know how long, since she'd lost all sense of time.

'You deviated from the script, Alexa.'

She didn't reply. She didn't know what he was talking about.

Then she remembered. The way she'd sneaked in those song lyrics to tell her father what they'd done to her.

'Do you understand that your life is entirely in my hands?'

'Oh – God – *kill me*!' she screamed, though it came out as a strangled croak. 'Just do it. I don't care!'

'Why would I want to kill you, Alexa? It is much worse for you to be buried so deep under the ground in your coffin.'

'Oh God, kill me, *please*!'

'Oh, no,' said the voice. 'I want you to stay alive for a very long time. Knowing that no one will ever find you. No one.'

She moaned, screamed, felt light-headed, nauseous.

'There you are, ten feet underground, and no one has any idea where you are. Maybe I go for a ride. Maybe I go for a trip for some days. I will keep the ventilation on, of course, so you won't run out of air. You will scream and no one can hear you, and you will beat your fists and claw against the steel walls of your casket, and no one knows you are there.'

'Please, I'll do anything,' she said. 'Anything.' She paused, swallowed hard, thought she might be sick again. 'You're very strong. I think you're a very attractive man.'

A chuckle came from the speaker overhead. 'Nothing you can do to me can excite me more than watching you beg. This is very *very* exciting to me, Alexa.'

'My father will give you anything you want. Anything!'

'No. You are wrong. He gives nothing to free you.'

'Maybe he doesn't know what Mercury is.'

'Your father knows. He understands very well. Do you know why he doesn't give what we ask?'

'He doesn't know what you want!'

'You are not important to him, Alexa. He loves his wife and his money more than he loves you. Maybe he never loves you. You are trapped like a rat and your father knows you are there and he doesn't even care.'

'*That's not true!*'

No reply.

Just silence.

'It's not true,' Alexa repeated. 'Let me talk to him again. I'll tell him he has to do it now.'

Nothing. Silence.

'Please, let me talk to him.'

Not a sound.

In the dreadful silence she began to hear distant sounds that at first she thought were just hallucinations, squeaking from the hamster wheel of her terrified mind.

But no, these really were voices. Murmured, indistinct, but

definitely voices. The way she'd sometimes hear her parents' voices coming through the heating grates in the floor of the big old house, even though they were two floors below.

There were people up there. Probably the Owl and the others he was working with. Their voices were coming through the tube or pipe or duct that let in the fresh air. Were they with him? What if they weren't and they knew nothing about her?

She yelled as loudly as she could: 'HELP ME HELP ME HELP ME PLEASE SOMEBODY HELP ME I'M DOWN HERE HELP ME!'

Only silence in reply.

Then the distant murmuring started up again, and she was sure she could hear someone laughing.

THIRTY-SEVEN

Instead of finding Alexa, we'd found her discarded phone.

A huge disappointment, sure. But the more I thought about it, the more it told us.

It told us she was probably within a hundred miles of Boston.

We knew from the hotel's surveillance tape what time she'd been abducted. We knew from the 911 call that she'd passed through Leominster, north of Boston, less than an hour later.

Once Diana had made a few calls, we concluded that Alexa had probably been driven, not put on a plane. The only airfield nearby was the Fitchburg Municipal Airport, which had two runways and was used by a couple of small charter companies. But no flights had left between midnight the night before and six that morning.

Only fourteen hours had elapsed between her abduction and the first time her kidnappers had contacted Marshall Marcus. That included transporting her and then – if her clues were to be taken literally – burying her in some sort of crypt or vault. And setting up cameras that could broadcast over the Internet. An arrangement like that was complicated and time-intensive and must have taken several hours. So they couldn't have gone too far.

But that didn't narrow it down much.

* * *

I dropped Diana off at FBI headquarters. It was barely six in the morning, but she thought she might as well get a very early start on the day. She'd grab the techs as soon as they got in and ask them for a complete workup of Alexa's phone.

After she got out I sat in the Defender for a while, idling in front of One Center Plaza, and thought about going home to catch a few hours' sleep, since it was likely to be a very long day.

Until I checked my e-mail.

I found a long series of e-mails not from a name but from a number I didn't recognize. It took me a few seconds to realize that they'd been sent automatically by the miniature GPS tracker concealed in Taylor Armstrong's gold S. T. Dupont lighter.

Well, not *her* lighter, but the one I'd switched with hers when I'd 'accidentally' dropped it on the cobblestones of Beacon Hill. I'd bought it at the tobacco shop in Park Square, the exact same S. T. Dupont Ligne 2 Gold Diamond Head lighter. A classic, and ridiculously expensive. But a lot cheaper, and more reliable, than hiring someone to tail her.

The tiny tracking device had been installed by an old Special Forces buddy of mine we used to call Romeo who had his own business in TSCM, or technical surveillance countermeasures. He complained bitterly about how small the lighter was. He wasn't sure he had a tracker small enough. He wanted me to steal her cell phone: that would have been a breeze.

It would have been easier to remove one of her kidneys.

But Romeo figured out how to wedge a nano GPS device inside the lighter's fluid reservoir. Complaining all the while, of course. Romeo, whose real name was George Devlin, was not an easy man to deal with, but he did great work.

He programmed the thing to start sending out location signals only when it was moved more than a thousand feet. Now I could see that, immediately after Taylor and I had our little talk on the corner of Charles and Beacon, she went home – or was driven home in

David Schechter's limousine – and then she drove to Medford, five miles northwest.

So who might she be meeting so urgently?

I had a pretty good idea.

THIRTY-EIGHT

Twenty minutes later I was driving down Oldfield Road in Medford, a pleasant street lined with graceful old trees and clapboard houses. Some were two-family houses, some apartment buildings. Most of them were well maintained, regularly painted, their lawns neatly mowed and shrubs perfectly clipped, their driveways polished ebony. A few looked like they'd been all but abandoned by absentee landlords who'd thrown up their hands in despair at the squalor of their student tenants. The Tufts University campus was a short walk away.

The house where Taylor Armstrong had spent forty-three minutes last night was a white-painted three-story wooden house, one of the nicer ones. At six thirty in the morning, there wasn't much going on in the neighborhood. A woman running in black-and-turquoise spandex. A car pulling out of a driveway at the other end of the block. I waited and watched the house.

Then I got out and walked past the house as if I were a neighbor out for a morning stroll. With a quick glance around, I climbed the front porch quietly, but casually, and saw a stack of five buzzers with a stack of matching names. Five apartments. One was probably the owner. Two apartments each on the upper two floors.

Five surnames. Schiff, Murdoch, Perreira, O'Connor, and Unger.

I memorized them, went back to the car, hit a speed-dial button on my BlackBerry, and woke Dorothy up.

She called back five minutes later.

'Margaret O'Connor is seventy-nine years old, a widow for fifteen years, and has owned the house since 1974. The other four rent. One's a recent graduate of the college who works for Amnesty International. Two of them are Tufts graduate students. The fourth is our guy.'

'Which one?'

'Perreira. His full name is Mauricio da Silva Cordeiro-Perreira, and yes, I pulled up his pic. It's the same guy from the hotel surveillance tape.'

'Taylor called him Lorenzo.'

'He gave her a fake name.'

'His surname's on his doorbell. So even if she didn't know his true first name, she knew his last name. What's his connection to her?'

'Here's what I found out: thirty-two years old. Born in São Paulo, Brazil. Rich family – we're talking major money. Daddy's with the UN in New York.'

'Huh. What does his father do?'

'Probably not much. He's a member of Brazil's permanent mission, and those guys don't do anything, far as I can tell. Mauricio grew up in a gated compound in Morumbi, on the outskirts of São Paulo. Our boy went to a bilingual school – Saint Paul's, then Universidade de São Paulo. A member of the Harmonia tennis club and the Helvetia polo club—'

'So how'd a rich boy like that end up living in a crappy walk-up apartment in Medford?'

'Looks like he did a few lazy years as a grad student at the Fletcher School of Law and Diplomacy at Tufts. But he didn't spend much time at Tisch Library. He's a dealer – mostly coke and weed, some meth.'

'Now it gets interesting. What do you have on that?'

'A couple years ago there was this joint DEA/ICE investigation on the theory that the kid was using his father's diplomatic pouch to bring in controlled substances.'

'Dad must not have been too pleased with that,' I said.

'Wouldn't surprise me if Daddy disowned him. He's been busted a couple of times, but nothing sticks. Sounds like the kid knows how to game the system.'

'If his dad's at the UN, he's protected by diplomatic immunity.'

'That covers a diplomat's grown kids?'

'All family,' I said.

'They can't get arrested for drugs?'

'They can't get arrested for murder,' I said.

'Man, I picked the wrong life. I shoulda been a diplomat. What I'd give for a loaded gun and ten minutes of diplomatic immunity.'

'Now this is starting to come together,' I said. 'Taylor has a record of drug problems, and Mauricio is probably her dealer.' His wealthy family background gave him entrée to the right social circles. It probably lent him an air of panache, an ease with well-off college kids, who'd never be caught dead associating with some clocker from Revere.

Not just college students. Also prep school kids like Taylor Armstrong, the senator's daughter.

'Daddy disowns him, there goes the trust fund,' Dorothy said. 'And the diplomatic pouch. Supply drops, money stops gushing in, it gets hard to pay the rent. Or keep up the car payments. Guy like that might get desperate for money. Take on a high-risk job like kidnapping a rich girl.'

'Or maybe he was hired because he was Taylor's dealer,' I said. 'Made it easy.'

'Hired by who?'

'Well, Mauricio is from Brazil, from a rich, well-connected family. One of Marcus Capital's unhappy investors is Juan Carlos Guzman.'

'Who is . . . ?'

'Colombian drug lord who lives in Brazil.'

'Oh God,' she said. 'Oh, sweet Jesus. A drug cartel has that girl? And you think you're gonna get her back?'

'With your help I have a chance.'

'Nick, there's no way I or anyone else is gonna trace that video feed. I've talked to everyone I know, including some people who've been at this a whole lot longer.'

'You told people what we're working on?'

'Of course not. We were talking IP traces and algorithms. Digital forensics. We're not going to find them that way.'

'They went to a lot of trouble to send Marcus a ransom demand,' I said.

'You think our guy's still in that apartment, or do you think he took off after Taylor warned him?'

'I don't know. If he's in there, he was just the courier – he just picked Alexa up and handed her off to someone else. He wouldn't have driven her out to Leominster and back here.'

'Maybe he dumped her phone there to set up a fake trail. So people would think she's out there instead of right near Boston.'

'That's too complex. Much smarter to just destroy her phone and have no trail at all. Also, he was driving a stolen car. Not worth the risk of getting caught with a broken taillight or an out-of-date registration sticker. Or just having some ambitious local cop run the plates.'

'What if he's not there?'

'I'll ransack his apartment and see what I can find that might lead me to Alexa. Bills, scraps of papers, computer files, anything.'

'Well, if he is there? Don't forget, rich boy or not, he's a dealer. He's gonna be armed. Please don't get yourself killed before our ten o'clock.'

'Ten o'clock?'

'The governor? Hello? You wanted me around in case they had technical questions you couldn't answer because you're only the "big picture" guy?'

She was talking about a long-scheduled meeting with a former governor of a large state who'd been forced to resign over a bribery scandal. Everyone on the inside knew he'd been set up.

'Tell Jillian to cancel it,' I said.

'Cancel it?' she said incredulously. 'These lawyers flew up from New York for this meeting. You can't just cancel it.'

'Last I checked, I'm still the boss. Tell Jillian to cancel it. And ask her to clear my calendar for the rest of the week. Everything. I'm not doing anything else until I get this girl home.'

'The rest of the week?' she said. 'You think this is only gonna take you a couple of days, you got your head up your butt. Anyway—'

'Talk later,' I interrupted, and I clicked off and got out of the car. Walked around to the side of the apartment building where Mauricio Perreira lived.

Drug dealers tend to live in a state of permanent paranoia. He probably had a gun close to the bed. Not under the pillow, which isn't very comfortable. But under the bed or behind the headboard.

The only workable plan was to take him by surprise.

THIRTY-NINE

Unless you pick locks for a living, knowing how doesn't mean doing it well. I once hired a professional locksmith to give me lessons, though I'd already learned the basics from a repo man I'd met as a teenager, hanging out at the body shop of Norman Lang Motors in Malden.

I also kept an assortment of tools in my car's glove box, including a professional locksmith's set of lock picks and tension wrenches. But an old-fashioned lock-pick set requires finesse, time, and patience. And I was short on all three. I grabbed my SouthOrd electric pick gun, a sleek stainless-steel instrument the size of an electric toothbrush, which is quicker and easier, though noisier, than any hand tool. But the batteries were dead. So I reached for the EZ snap gun, a good old manual lock pick, originally developed for police officers who didn't have time to learn the fine, slow art of lockpicking.

Unfortunately, lock-pick guns aren't particularly quiet. They make a fairly loud snap. But they're quick.

I mounted the apartment building's side stairs, which provided exterior entry to the separate units. A short cement flight of steps led to a narrow porch with a gray-painted wooden railing. From there on up, the stairs were painted wood. Keeping my tread light, I ascended to the top level, sidled along the railing for a few feet, and assessed.

A small window, curtains drawn, next to the apartment door. A simple pin tumbler lock. Not Schlage or some high-security brand, which would have been a challenge. Some no-name brand. That was a relief.

And a pinpoint LED light: a security system.

But the light was dark. He probably disarmed the system when he was at home.

So maybe he was here. Good.

I didn't even look around. In case one of the neighbors was up early and happened to see me, I wanted to look like I was supposed to be there.

I worked quickly but casually. First I inserted the tension tool, roughly the size of a straightened paper clip, into the keyhole and worked it a bit. Grasping the snap gun in my right hand, I poked its needle into the keyhole beside the tension tool, careful not to touch the pins, and squeezed the handle.

A loud *snap*.

I had to snap it ten or eleven more times. The sound echoed in the gulley between the houses. Unless Perreira was a sound sleeper, he must have heard it.

Finally I felt the lock turn.

And I was in.

FORTY

The air was cold. An air conditioner was on somewhere, in another room. I was hit at once by the fetid, festering-swamp stench of old bong water.

Someone was here.

All the curtains were closed. The front room was almost completely dark. In a few seconds, though, my eyes became accustomed, and I was able to make my way through the cluttered room, weaving between an enormous flat-screen TV and an outsize leather couch, the path strewn with discarded beer and wine bottles. Somehow managing not to knock anything over, I approached the loud snoring that came from an open bedroom door. At the threshold I stopped. A lump in the bed, I saw. No, two lumps.

Long blond hair lay atop a pillow as if a lion had coughed up a hairball. I saw the nape of a woman's neck, her well-defined shoulders. Next to her, mouth gaping, snoring like a buzz saw, was the man I recognized as Lorenzo. The guy from the security video at Slammer. The guy who'd abducted Alexa. No question about it.

I thought for just a second. Ran through my options.

Decided on the simplest one.

I came around to the side of the bed where Perreira lay under the rumpled sheet, half under the blanket. My footsteps were muffled by the wall-to-wall carpet. An old air conditioner rattled and roared like a jet engine. The room was ice-cold and smelled of rancid sweat. His face was turned away, toward the blond girl, the sheet pulled up to his chin.

In my left fist I grabbed the end of the sheet. With a swift jerk I yanked it up and over his head, then under, trapping his head. He began to flail. He cursed and shouted and thrashed his arms and legs. But he was wrapped as tight as a mummy. My right hand gripped his throat and squeezed. His struggles grew more frenzied, his screams muffled by the sheet.

The blond girl in the bed next to him screamed too and scrambled out of the bed, the screams strangely deep and masculine. As I clambered on top of Mauricio's writhing body, pinning him down with my knees, I saw that the long-haired blond was in fact a skinny, delicate-looking young man.

'I don't have anything to do with anything!' the boy shouted. 'Dude, I barely *know* this guy!'

He backed away, as if he expected me to lunge at him too, but I turned and let him go.

I was afraid Perreira might pass out, so I eased up a bit on his throat. He gasped, then said hoarsely: '*O que você quer? O que diabos você quer?*'

I had no idea what he was saying. I don't speak Portuguese. 'Where is she?' I said.

'*Entreguei o pacote!*'

'Where is she?'

'*Eu entreguei a menina!*'

'Speak English.'

'*O pacote! Entreguei o pacote!*'

One of the words sounded sort of familiar. 'The package?'

'I deliver' – he gasped – 'the package. I *deliver* the package!'

'*Package?*' A white-hot anger crackled in my blood like a live wire. It took great restraint to keep from crushing his windpipe.

Clearly he thought I was connected to the kidnapping. Someone he worked for. So he *was* just the delivery boy. The first link in the chain. He'd been hired to abduct Alexa and hand her over to someone else.

And since he thought I was one of his employers, that meant he probably didn't know them, hadn't met them. This could be useful. I relaxed my grip on his throat, and he croaked, '*Entreguei a cadela, qual é?*'

Though I don't speak Portuguese, I do know a few obscenities in several languages, and I was pretty sure he'd just used one in reference to Alexa. This displeased me. I squeezed his throat until I felt the soft cartilage start to give way, and then I made myself stop. Killing this cockroach was pointless. He was useful to me only alive.

'I'm going to let you go so you can answer a few questions,' I said. 'If you lie about anything at all, no matter how trivial, I'm going to slice your ear off and send it to your father at the UN. For his office wall. The second lie, you lose the other ear. That one goes—'

'No! *No!* I tell you everything! What do you want? I do what you say! I do everything you say! I gave you this girl and I shut my mouth.'

'Where is she?'

'Why you asking me this? You tell me to pick the bitch up and drug her and bring her to you, I do it. What do you want, man? You got the girl. I got the money. I say nothing. We're all done here. It's all good.'

It's all good. A phrase I really despise. He was slick and polished and used to dealing with high-end customers who'd never buy 'party favors' from some slinger with prison ink and low riders. Most college kids and rich kids didn't like thinking what they did was criminal, really. They considered the goods he sold them just another arbitrarily outlawed delicacy, like Iranian caviar or unpasteurized Camembert. A man like Mauricio made the drug trade seem not unlawful but *exclusive*.

'For you I'd say it's pretty much all bad right now.'

On his bedside table was a Nokia cell phone. I grabbed it with my free hand and slipped it in my pocket.

Then I reached behind the headboard and found what felt a lot like a gun duct-taped back there. A very expensive STI pistol, I saw. I pocketed that too, then released my grip on his throat entirely. He drew a deep, rattling breath. His face was deep red, and he looked like he was on the verge of blacking out. Maybe I'd pushed it too far.

'All right,' I said, climbing off and standing beside the bed. 'Get up.'

He struggled to sit up, tangled up in the sheets and weak from oxygen deprivation. He was wearing only red Speedos. Weakly, he shifted his legs over the side of the bed. His fingernails and toenails were manicured to a high gloss. '*Jesus Cristo*,' he gasped, 'what you want from me, man?'

'You screwed up,' I said.

He shook his head, eyes terrified. 'I gave you – I gave it to – the guy.'

'Which guy?'

'The guy who gave me the phone. You – you guys? What the hell, man? You work for them, too?'

'Which one?' I said.

'No one give me names. What is this? Who are you, man?'

'*What was his name?*' I shouted.

'I don't know anyone's name, man! I can't talk. The guy got eyes on the back of his head!'

I was about to ask what he meant when I heard the thunder of footsteps on the stairs outside. He heard it too. His face was tight with fear. 'Oh, *Jesus Cristo*, that's them! That's them! He said they kill me if I talk to anyone. I didn't tell you *nothing*, man!'

Then came a crash and the splintering sound of his door being broken down with a metal ram.

The men who burst into the room were wearing green uniforms

with green ballistic vests and black Kevlar helmets and goggles that made them look like giant insects from some bad science-fiction flick. Right behind the breachers came the assaulters with their H&K MP5 submachine guns. The ones with shields carried Glocks. They all had FBI patches on their shoulders and chests.

When he saw who they were, the expression on his face changed. He looked relieved.

FORTY-ONE

The man was slowly crossing the bare earthen field toward the farm-house when the sat phone on his belt began to trill. The morning was cold and brisk and the sky was blue glass.

He knew who it was, because only one person had this number, and he knew what the caller wanted.

As he answered the phone, he stopped at the exact center of the hump of earth and made a mental note to take another run at it with the pneumatic backfill tamper. Or just a few passes with the backhoe tires: that should do it.

Not that the girl was going anywhere, ten feet down.

But here in rural New Hampshire, neighbors sometimes got curious, or too friendly.

'Yes?' Dragomir said.

'Nothing yet,' said the man who called himself Kirill. They spoke in Russian.

Maybe that was his real name, maybe not. Dragomir didn't care. Kirill was nothing more than an intermediary, an errand boy who passed messages back and forth between Dragomir and the very rich man Kirill called only the Client. Never a name. This was fine with Dragomir. The less he and the Client knew about each other, the better.

But Kirill fretted and hovered and yammered like a frightened old *babushka*. He worried that some detail might go awry. He seemed to think that his constant monitoring, the daily check-ins, would keep everything running smoothly.

He didn't know that Dragomir rarely made mistakes.

'It's only been a few hours,' Dragomir said.

'What do you think, the father went back to sleep? He should have sent the file immediately. His daughter—'

'Patience,' Dragomir said.

A plane roared overhead, and the line went staticky. Jets flew by every hour or so, mostly at night, from the air base in Bangor, Maine. They had that big lumbering sound of military cargo transport planes. It reminded him of Afghanistan, the Ilyushin 76s that were always blasting by overhead.

'—hostage is in good health?' Kirill was saying when the static cleared.

The Iridium sat phone was encrypted, so Kirill spoke fairly openly, even though Dragomir never did. He never trusted technology. His reply was curt: 'Is there anything else?'

'Nothing.'

He disconnected the call. The setting sun gave a golden cast to the freshly raked soil. His boots sank into the soft earth, the tread leaving precise impressions, like a plaster-of-Paris cast. Some of his footsteps crossed the deep tread of the backhoe loader's tires.

He had a fleeting memory of the hard dirt prison yard, where sunlight never entered and no grass could grow. He'd liked lawns ever since.

Dragomir mounted the porch, past the air compressor on its long yellow extension cord, and pulled the screen door open. There were holes in the screen, so he opened and closed the wooden back door swiftly to keep out the bugs. The whole damned farmhouse was falling down. But he had no right to complain. The house and the land it sat on, nearly three hundred acres of forest in a remote part of New Hampshire, were owned by an old man who'd moved to Florida. The property hadn't had a visitor in four years. Not even a caretaker.

So Dragomir had appointed himself the caretaker.

Even though the family trust had no idea.

As he went through the converted sunroom, he could hear the girl's pathetic mewling over the computer speakers. On the monitor she twisted and clawed and screamed and writhed like some eerie green apparition.

The noise irritated him, so he hit a key to mute it.

FORTY-TWO

An hour later I was on the sixth floor of One Center Plaza with Diana, who looked exhausted, her eyes red-rimmed and bleary. The corkscrew tendrils of her hair were even more Medusan than usual. Yet she was still the most beautiful woman I'd ever seen.

She waited for them to hand me my visitor badge, then escorted me in.

'So how'd that happen?' I said quietly as we walked.

Not until we'd passed the row of offices belonging to the assistant special agents in charge did she reply. Gordon Snyder's door was open, I noticed, but it was angled in such a way that I couldn't see whether he was there.

'All I was told was, a CI tipped them off.'

A confidential informant. 'Whose?'

No reply. We reached a warren of cubicles, most of them empty. It was still early.

Her cubicle was unmistakable.

It was the grade-school photos taped to the cubicle walls that marked it as her workspace: sweet-looking kids who obviously weren't relatives of hers. And the curling clips from the *Stowe* (Vermont) *Reporter* and the *Biddeford* (Maine) *Journal Tribune* and the *Boston Herald* with headlines like SEX OFFENDER CHARGED IN

GIRL'S DISAPPEARANCE. A close-up photo of a paisley-patterned bedspread. A photocopy of a note scrawled in block letters, a barely literate hand:

HI HONEY I BEEN WATCHING YOU I AM THE SAME PERSON THAT KIDNAPPED AN RAPE AN KILL ARDEN . . .

Things a normal person couldn't bear to look at even once hung before her eyes every minute she sat at her desk.

'I have no idea,' she said. 'I'm not cleared at that level.'

I could hear the annoying little snap of someone clipping fingernails at a nearby cubicle. 'So who gave the order to roll the SWAT team?'

'The only person who can mobilize tactical is the SAC. But how did *you* know where to find Perreira?'

'I put a tracker on Taylor Armstrong.'

She smiled, nodded. 'Nice.'

'Whoever did this just screwed up our best chance to find Alexa,' I said. 'Where is he?'

'Downstairs in a locked interview room.'

'I want to talk to him.'

'You can't.'

'Because I'm a private citizen?'

'That's not the only reason. He's not talking to anybody.'

'He's lawyering up?'

'He's invoking diplomatic immunity.'

'Who's with him now?'

'Nobody. We're in talks with Main Justice on how to handle this.'

'I know how to handle it.'

She smiled again. 'No doubt.'

'Can you sneak me in there?'

'You serious?'

'Completely.'

'The answer is no. A legal attaché from the Brazilian consulate in Boston is on his way in. A man named . . .' She glanced at a scrawl on a Post-it pad next to her desk phone. 'Cláudio Duarte Carvalho Barboza. Until he's finished consulting with Perreira, no one can even *enter* the interview room.'

I stood up.

'Do me a favor and show me where he is,' I said.

'Why?'

'Just curious,' I said.

Diana led me down a flight of stairs to a closed, windowless room. A plain white door with a metal knob. No one standing around outside keeping watch.

'Any cameras or one-way mirrors?'

'Never. It's against Bureau policy.'

'Huh. You know, I'd love a cup of coffee.'

'Don't do anything to screw me up, Nick.'

'I won't. Take your time with that coffee.'

Her face was impassive but there was a glint in her eyes. 'I may need to brew a fresh pot. Might take me a while.'

Mauricio was leaning back in a metal chair behind a Formica-topped table, looking bored. When he recognized me, he slowly grinned a broad smile of victory.

'I'm not talking, man. I got the . . . the *imunidade diplomática.*'

'So as soon as the legal attaché from the Brazilian consulate shows up, you're a free man. You go home. That it?'

'That's how it works, man. It's all good.'

'Excellent,' I said. 'I like that.'

He found this amusing. 'You like that, huh?' He laughed.

I did too. 'Oh, yeah. Definitely. Because out there, you don't have any diplomatic immunity.'

His smile dimmed a few clicks.

'As soon as they let you go,' I said, 'it's going to be like tossing a handful of chum into a shark tank. Gonna be a feeding frenzy out there. The water's going to be churning and the sharks are going to be circling.'

'Don't try to threaten me.'

'Think about this. The guys that hired you? They're going to assume you told us everything.'

A quick headshake. 'I don't cooperate with FBI.'

'You're far too modest about all the help you've given us.'

'I don't say nothing to the FBI. I don't say nothing to nobody.'

'Sure you did.' I pulled out his Nokia mobile phone and showed it to him. 'You gave us a phone number, for one. And the US government is extremely grateful to you. In fact, I'm going to personally see to it that we issue you a commendation for all your help to US law enforcement.'

'No one believe I talk,' he said. But he didn't sound so confident anymore. He'd assumed I was with the FBI, and I didn't plan to correct the impression.

'Yeah? I wonder what they'll think when I leave a message on your voice mail giving you the name of your regular contact here at the Bureau. Telling you how to arrange our next meeting. Maybe talking about how you'll be wearing a wire next time you meet with your Colombian friends.'

I could see the blood drain from his face.

'I hope you know they've got your line tapped,' I said. 'They probably cloned your cell phone too.'

He shook his head, jutted his lower lip, feigning skepticism, but I could see I'd gotten to him.

'Ever hear what they do to people who betray them?'

'They not gonna kill me.'

'True,' I said. 'They like to torture and mutilate first. They like to drag it out. You'll *wish* they'd kill you, what I hear. They have a saying, "You can't get a positive identification of a body from a torso."' I paused for effect. 'That's why they like to cut off the hands and feet and head. Of course, they're wrong. You *can* get a positive identification from a torso. It just takes a little longer.'

Mauricio's brown eyes had gone flat and dull, and terror was contorting his facial muscles.

'Maybe your daddy can pull in some favors and get them to go easy on you, hmm?'

His larynx worked up and down. He was trying to swallow, but his mouth had gone dry. It looked like a sock was stuck in his throat.

'But you know what?' I said. 'Today's your lucky day. Because I'm prepared to offer you a special deal. Great terms too. You tell us what we want to know, and you'll never hear from us again. No thank-you notes. No friendly calls. You might even live.' I waited a beat. 'It's all good.'

'What do you want?' he whispered, his voice cracking.

'A name. The name of the guy who hired you to pick up the girl.'

'I told you—'

'A full description. Height. Eye color. How he contacted you in the first place. Where you delivered the . . . "package" . . . to them.'

'I don't *know* the name, man,' he whispered. 'He was some big dude, real strong. Real scary.'

He was telling the truth now, I was convinced. His terror had yanked away his habitual scrim of dishonesty. He had just one objective, which was to stay alive. Not to protect his employers. He wasn't going to hold anything back from me.

'Did he tell you why he wanted the girl?'

'He just told me to pick her up and give her this drug and hand her over—'

I heard what sounded like footsteps approaching, voices becoming louder. Mauricio heard it too. He froze, looked at the door.

'Where did he take her?' I said.

'The guy's got eyes on the back of his head,' he whispered. 'I can't say nothing.'

'What do you mean, eyes on the back of his head?'

But then the door came open, and a squat, hulking man in a gray suit with a gleaming bald head stared in.

'What the hell are you doing in here?' came the rumbling voice of Gordon Snyder.

FORTY-THREE

'Hello, Spike,' I said.

'What's your game, Heller?' Snyder said. 'Trying to coach the witness? Or buy his silence?'

Before I could reply, a loud voice came from behind him: 'No one is allowed to talk to my client! I made that eminently clear on the phone.'

Someone shoved his way past Snyder into the interview room: a large, elegant man, probably six foot two, broad shoulders. He had long gray hair almost to his shirt collar, deep-set eyes, and acne-gouged cheeks. He was wearing a dark nailhead suit and a burgundy foulard tie and an air of imperious authority. The fabric of his bespoke suit draped snugly along his broad shoulders.

The legal attaché from the Brazilian consulate, of course. 'Remove this person at once,' he said, his English impeccable, with barely a trace of an accent. 'You may *not* question this man. And if there is any recording equipment in here, it must be switched off at once. My discussions with my client must be absolutely privileged.'

'Understood, Mr Barboza,' Snyder said. His eyes flashed with fury at me, and he leveled a stubby finger, then swiveled it smoothly toward the doorway like a magician wielding a wand.

'Get the hell out of here,' he said.

FORTY-FOUR

A dog was barking in the yard.

Dragomir's first thought was of hunters. It wasn't hunting season, but that didn't deter some people. He'd posted NO TRESPASSING/NO HUNTING signs every fifty feet in the wooded part of the property, but not everyone could read, or chose to.

Hunters meant intruders, and intruders meant scrutiny.

People in rural areas were always getting involved in their neighbors' business. Especially a stranger who showed up one day with no introduction.

Are you the new owner? Are you an Alderson?

What's with the Caterpillar backhoe loader out back? Are you doing construction? All by yourself, no crew? Really? Huh. Whatcha building?

He'd bought all the equipment with cash. The backhoe came from a farm supply store in Biddeford, the air compressor from the Home Depot in Plaistow.

The casket he'd picked out at a wholesale casket company in Dover. He'd said something about the family burial plot, double deep, his sadly departed uncle the first one in. At a depth of twelve feet, he'd explained, he wanted to make absolute certain it was crushproof.

The sturdiest one they had was sixteen-gauge carbon steel, painted Triton Gray, in the Generous Dimensions line. Americans were increasingly obese, so oversized caskets were strong sellers, and he'd had to settle for a floor model.

Groundwater seepage was always a problem, even in the most well-made caskets, which might cause the girl to drown slowly, before they were done with her, and that wouldn't do either. Fortunately, the model he'd purchased was equipped with a water-resistant gasket. You turned a crank at the end of the box to seal it tight. A steel bar rolled across the top to lock it down. All of this was standard equipment, as if grave robbers were still a problem in the twenty-first century.

The refitting was quick work, the sort of mechanical job he'd always enjoyed. Using a cobalt drill bit he drilled a hole through the carbon steel at the end where the girl's head would be. There he welded a quarter-inch brass connector plug in place and attached it to a crushproof hose that ran several hundred feet to the air compressor on the porch. Air would flow in here every time the air compressor went on, which was a couple of minutes each hour, night and day, since it was on a timer switch. He trenched the hose into the ground along with the Ethernet cable.

At the other end of the casket he cut a much larger opening with a hole saw. There he welded the brass bushing to attach a four-inch exhaust line. Now the gray PVC pipe stuck out of the ground in the middle of the dirt field like a solitary sapling. Its end curved down like an umbrella handle. It was the sort of thing used at a landfill to vent the methane gas that built up underground.

So the girl would get a steady supply of fresh air, which was more than his father had when he'd been trapped in the coal mine in Tomsk.

As a young boy, Dragomir used to enjoy watching his father and the other miners ride backwards in the mantrip, descending hundreds of meters into the depths. Dragomir was forever asking to ride too, but his father always refused.

Each night his father came home caked in black dust so thick you could see only his eyes. His coughing kept Dragomir up many a night. He spat black and left the sputum floating in the toilet bowl.

Coal mining, he told once told Dragomir, was the only job where you had to dig your own grave.

Dragomir listened, rapt, to his father's grim tales. How he'd seen a roof bolter come down on a friend of his and crush his face. Or watched a guy cut in half by the coal car. Someone was once caught between the drums of the coal crusher and smashed into pieces between its teeth.

His mother, Dusya, raged at his father for filling a young boy's head with such frightening stories. But Dragomir always wanted to hear more.

The bedtime stories stopped when Dragomir was almost ten.

A knock at the door to their communal apartment in the middle of the night. His mother's high thin scream.

She brought him to the mine to join the crowds gathered there, pleading for any sort of news, even bad news.

He was fascinated. He wanted to know what had happened, but no one would tell him. He overheard only fragments. Something about how the miners had accidentally dug into an abandoned, flooded shaft. How the water rushed in and trapped them like rats.

But Dragomir wanted to know more. His thirst was unslakable. He wanted details.

He imagined his father and the other men, dozens or even hundreds of them, struggling to keep their heads above the rising black water, fighting over a few inches of air space that dwindled by the minute. He imagined them grappling in the black water, pushing each other's heads down into the water, old friends and even brothers, trying to survive a few minutes longer, all the while knowing that none of them would ever come out.

He wanted to know what it felt like to realize with absolute certainty that you were about to die and to be powerless to do anything about it. His mind returned to this again and again, the way a child fingers a wound. He was fascinated by the unknown, lured to what repelled others, because it allowed him to draw close to his father, to know what his father knew in those last moments of his life.

He'd always felt cheated somehow not to have witnessed the last seconds of his father's life.

All he had was his imagination.

The damned dog would not stop barking. Now he could hear it pawing at the screen door out back. He looked out a window and saw a dirt-covered mongrel, leaping and snarling at the screen. Feral, maybe, though it was hard to tell for sure.

He opened the wooden door, his Wasp gas injection knife at the ready, his new toy. Just the screen between him and the cur.

Startled, the dog backed away, bared its teeth, gave a low snarl.

He called to it softly in Russian, 'Here, pooch,' and opened the screen door. The dog lunged at him, and he plunged the blade into the beast's abdomen.

With his thumb he slid the button to shoot out a frozen basketball of compressed air.

The explosion was instantaneous and satisfying, but he realized at once he'd done it wrong. He was spattered by the animal's viscera, red and glistening, slimy scraps of skin and fur, a rainburst of offal.

Once in a while he did make mistakes. Next time he would make sure to plunge the knife in to the hilt before flicking the gas release.

It took him half an hour to sweep the ruined carcass into a trash bag and haul it into the woods to be buried later, and then hose down the blood-slick porch and screen door.

He took a shower in the small pre-fab fiberglass stall on the second floor and got into clean jeans and a flannel shirt, and then he heard the doorbell ring. He looked out the bedroom window, saw a Lexus SUV parked in the dirt road out front. He put on a baseball cap, backward, to conceal the tattoo, and casually came down the stairs and opened the front door.

'Sorry to disturb you,' said a middle-aged man with no chin and thick wire-rim glasses. 'My dog ran off and I was wondering if you might have seen it.'

'Dog?' Dragomir said through the front screen.

'Oh, now, where's my manners,' the man said. 'I'm Sam Dupuis, from across the road.'

Then the man paused expectantly.

'Andros,' Dragomir said. 'Caretaker.'

Andros was a Polish name, but it also sounded Greek.

'Good to know you, Andros,' the neighbor said. 'I thought I saw Hercules run down your driveway, but maybe I was wrong.'

'Very sorry,' Dragomir said with a smile. 'Wish I could help. Hope you find him soon.'

FORTY-FIVE

I found Diana in a break room, sitting by herself, the *Boston Globe* spread out on a round table before her. It didn't look like she'd cracked it, though. The sections were arrayed but unopened. She was just waiting.

'Your coffee,' she said, holding out a cup. 'Walk with me.'

I followed her out. 'They found Alexa's purse under his bed,' she said. 'He'd taken all her cash but was probably afraid to use her credit cards. The stolen Jaguar was found in a Tufts University garage.'

'That give up any location information?'

'It's too old to have air bags let alone a nav system. But they did find trace quantities of a white powder.'

'Coke?'

'*Burundanga* powder. It's an extract of the *borrachio* plant – also known as Colombian devil's breath. A naturally occurring source of scopolamine.'

'An herbal date-rape drug.'

She nodded. 'I've heard that half the admissions to Bogotá's emergency rooms are caused by *burundanga*. Criminals spike their victims' drinks with the stuff at nightclubs and brothels. It's tasteless, odorless, and water-soluble. And it turns the victims into zombies, basically. Lucid, but totally submissive. A complete loss of will. So their victims will do what they're told – they'll withdraw cash from their ATMs and hand it over without arguing. And when it wears off, they have no recollection of what happened.'

On the way to the stairs we passed the legal attaché from the Brazilian consulate, the guy with the long gray hair and the expensive suit. Black curly chest hair sprouted out of his open shirt collar. He was walking briskly but seemed lost in thought, his head down.

As we climbed the stairs, I said, 'Any phone records in his apartment, cell phone records, any of that stuff?'

'They've collected everything and they're working it. Nothing so far.'

As she opened the door to the seventh floor, I stopped. 'Wasn't that guy wearing a tie?'

She looked at me in the dim light of the stairwell, then whirled around, and we went back down the stairs at a fairly good clip.

When we reached the interview room where I'd talked to Perreira, Diana opened the door, and she gasped.

I can't say I was entirely surprised by what I saw, but it was grotesque all the same.

Mauricio Perreira's body was twisted unnaturally, his face horribly contorted, frozen in a silent, agonized shriek. His lips were blue and his eyes bulged, the sclera mottled with blood from the burst capillaries. The classic signs of petechial hemorrhaging.

Fastened tightly around his neck like a tourniquet, like some kinky fashion statement, was the legal attaché's burgundy silk necktie. It was only slightly darker than the bruising on his throat above and below the ligature.

'He's probably still in the building,' Diana said. 'On his way out.'

'Check the tie,' I said. 'I doubt it's from Brooks Brothers.'

FORTY-SIX

I raced down the five flights of stairs to Cambridge Street, hoping I'd catch the Brazilian on his way out, but by the time I reached the street, there was no sign of him. There were at least a dozen ways he could have gone. I circled back to the lobby, hoping that he'd taken one of the glacially slow elevators, but he didn't appear. I took the stairs down to the parking garage underneath One Center Plaza, but once I got down there I saw it was hopeless, far too big and mazelike. And since he'd obviously come here to kill a man in FBI custody, he must have planned his getaway in advance.

I'd failed at catching the man who'd just snuffed out my only lead to Alexa Marcus.

Diana greeted me in the sixth-floor lobby and didn't even ask. 'You never had a chance,' she said.

A loud, blatting alarm was sounding throughout the floor, clogging the aisles with a lot of confused FBI agents and clerical staff who didn't know what they were supposed to do. Outside the interview room where Perreira had been detained, a small crowd had gathered. FBI crime-scene techs were already at work inside, gathering prints and hair and fiber. They'd probably never had to travel such a short distance to do a job. A couple of important-looking men and women in business suits stood outside the threshold of the room in tense conversation.

'You were wrong,' she said.

'About what?'

'The tie. It *was* Brooks Brothers.'

'My bad.'

'Only it had something like fishing line stitched inside.'

'Probably eighty-pound high-tensile-strength, braided line. It makes a very effective garrote. Works like a cheese slicer. He could easily have decapitated Perreira if he chose to, only he probably didn't want to get arterial blood all over his expensive suit.'

She looked horrified, said nothing.

'Who cleared him in?' I said.

'See, that's the problem. There is no clearance procedure. Everyone assumed someone else had vetted him. He presented ID at the desk, claiming to be Cláudio Barboza from the Brazilian consulate, and who's going to question him?'

'Someone should call the consulate to check whether there's anyone there with that name.'

'I just did.'

'And?'

'They don't even have a legal attaché in Boston.'

I just groaned. 'It's probably too much to expect that the guy left any prints.'

'Didn't you notice those very expensive-looking black lambskin gloves he wore?'

'No,' I admitted. 'But at least you guys have surveillance video.'

'That we do,' she said. 'Cameras all over the place.'

'Except in the interview room, where it might have done us some good.'

'The video's not going to tell us anything we don't know.'

'Well,' I said, 'I hope you have better facial recognition than the Pentagon had when I was there. Which was crap.' People sometimes forgot that facial *recognition* isn't the same as facial *identification*. It works by matching a face with a photo of someone who's already been identified. Unless you had a good high-resolution image to match it against, the software couldn't tell the difference between Lillian Hellman and Scarlett Johansson.

'No better. The guy's obviously a pro. He wouldn't have been sloppy enough to show his face here unless he felt secure we wouldn't catch him.'

'Right,' I said. 'He knew he'd have no problem getting in – or out. So why was that?'

She shrugged. 'Way above my pay grade.'

'Have you ever heard of anyone being killed in FBI custody before – *inside* an FBI field office?'

'Never.'

'A couple of guys break into my loft to put a local intercept on my Internet. The SWAT team shows up in Medford just minutes after I do. They grab a key witness, who's later murdered in a secure interview room within FBI headquarters. Obviously someone didn't want me talking to Perreira.'

'Don't tell me you're accusing Gordon Snyder.'

'I'd happily blame Gordon Snyder for the BP oil spill, cancer, and global warming if I could. But not this. He's too obsessed with bringing Marshall Marcus down.'

She smiled. 'Exactly.'

'But it's someone in the government. Someone at a high level. Someone who doesn't want me finding out who kidnapped Alexa.'

'Come on, Nico. That's conspiracy theory stuff.'

'As the saying goes, not every conspiracy is a theory.'

'I guess that means you don't trust me either.'

'I trust you absolutely. Totally. Without reservation. I just need to keep in mind that anything I tell you might end up in Gordon Snyder's in-box.'

She looked wounded. 'So you *don't* trust me?'

'Put it this way: if you learned something germane to your

investigation and you *didn't* pass it along to him, you wouldn't be doing your job, would you?'

After a moment, she nodded slowly. 'True.'

'So you see, I'd never lie to you, but I can't tell you everything.'

'Okay. Fair enough. So if someone's really trying to stop you from finding Alexa, what's the reason?'

I shrugged. 'No idea. But I feel like they're sending me a message.'

'Which is?'

'That I'm on the right track.'

FORTY-SEVEN

My old friend George Devlin – Romeo, as we called him in the Special Forces – was the handsomest man you ever saw.

Not only was he the best-looking, most popular guy in his high school class, as well as the class president, but he was also the star of the school's hockey team. In a hockey-crazed town like Grand Rapids, Michigan, that was saying something. He had a great voice too and starred in his high school musical senior year. He was a whiz at computers and an avid gamer.

He could have done anything, but the Devlins had no money to send him to college, so he enlisted in the army. There he qualified for the Special Forces, of course, because he was just that kind of guy. After some specialized computer training he was made a communications sergeant. That's how I first got to know George: he was the comms sergeant in my detachment. I don't know who first came up with the nickname 'Romeo', but it stuck.

After he was wounded in Afghanistan, and his VA therapy ended, however, he told us to stop calling him Romeo and start calling him George.

I met him in the enormous white RV, bristling with antennas, that served as his combination home and mobile office. He'd parked it in an underground garage in a Holiday Inn in Dedham. That was typical for him. He preferred to meet in out-of-the-way locations. He seemed to live his life on the lam. As if someone were out to get him.

I opened the van door and entered the dimly lit interior.

'Heller.' His voice came out of the darkness. As my eyes adjusted, I could see him sitting on a stool, his back to me, before a bank of computer monitors and such.

'Hey, George. Thanks for meeting me on such short notice.'

'I take it the GPS tracker was successful.'

'Absolutely. It was brilliant. Thank you.'

'Next time please remember to check your e-mail.'

I nodded, held out the Nokia cell phone I'd taken from Mauricio's apartment. He swiveled and turned his face toward me.

What was left of his face.

I'd never gotten used to seeing it, so each time it gave me a jolt. It was a horrible welter of ropy scar tissue, some strands paste-white, others an inflamed red. He had nostrils and a slash of a mouth, and eyelids the army surgeons had crafted from patches of skin taken from his inner thigh. The stitch marks were still prominent.

Fortunately, Devlin was able to breathe without too much pain now. He was able to see out of one eye.

But he was not easy to look at. He'd become a monster. I suppose there was some sort of irony in the fact that his physical appearance, which had defined him for so long, defined him still.

'I assume you know how to retrieve numbers from the call log,' he said. He spoke in a raspy whisper, his vocal cords ruined, and his mouth often made a wet clicking noise, the sound of tissue in the wrong place.

'Even I know how to do that.'

'Then what do you want from me?'

'The only phone number on here, dialed or retrieved, is for a mobile phone. That's probably his contact – whoever hired him to abduct the girl. If anyone can locate the bad guy from his phone, it's you.'

'Why didn't you ask the FBI for help?'

'Because I'm not sure who I can trust there.'

'The answer is no one. Why are you working with them, anyway? I thought you left all that government crap behind.'

'Because I need them. Whatever it takes to get Alexa back.'

He breathed in and out noisily. 'No comment.'

He despised all government agencies and viewed them with extreme paranoia. They were the enemy. They were all too powerful and malevolent and I think he blamed every one of them for the Iraqi IED that had detonated his Humvee's gas tank. He didn't seem to credit the heroic army plastic surgeons who'd saved his life and given him at least some semblance of a face, grotesque though it was. But who could blame him for being angry?

He tilted his head in a funny way to inspect the phone. He preferred to work in low light, even near-darkness, because his eye had become hypersensitive to the light. 'Ah, a Nokla 8800. This is no ordinary burner.'

'You mean Nokia.'

He showed it to me. 'Can you read, Nick? It says nokla.'

He was right. It said nokla. 'A knockoff?'

He punched out a few numbers on the phone. 'Yep, the IMEI confirms it.'

'The what?'

'The serial number.' He slid off the back cover and popped the battery out. 'A Shenzhen Special,' he said, holding it up. I leaned close. The battery had Chinese characters all over it. 'Ever look on eBay and see a special sale on Nokia phones – brand-new, half price? They're all made in China.'

I nodded. 'If you order mobile phones over the Internet, you don't have to risk going into Walmart or Target and having your face show up on a surveillance camera,' I said. I immediately regretted the choice of words. What he'd give to be able to walk into a Walmart without encountering the averted looks, the squeamishness, the screams of children.

Devlin abruptly turned to look at one of his screens. A green dot was flashing.

'Speaking of tracking devices, do you have one on you?'

'None that I know of.'

'Didn't I tell you to take precautions coming here?'

'I did.'

'May I see your handheld?'

I handed him my BlackBerry. He peered at it, set it down on the narrow counter, popped open its battery compartment. Lifted out the battery, then wriggled something loose with a pair of tweezers. Held it up and looked at it aslant. Devlin was no longer capable of facial expressions, but if he were, he'd probably have displayed triumph.

'Someone's been tracking your every move, Heller,' he said. 'Any idea how long?'

FORTY-EIGHT

I had no idea, of course, how long I'd been followed. But at least now I knew how they were able to track me to Mauricio Perreira's apartment in Medford. Some 'confidential informant'.

'Looks like the FBI put a tail on you. And I thought you were cooperating. Did anyone have an opportunity to meddle with your BlackBerry without you noticing?'

I nodded. I remembered checking my BlackBerry at the FBI's reception desk in Boston, not once but twice.

'Now even *I'm* starting to get paranoid,' I said.

He turned to look at me. Instinctively I wanted to look away from that face, so I made a point of meeting his eyes.

'Just because you're paranoid doesn't mean they're not out to get you,' he said. In the dark still interior of his van, his whisper gave me goose bumps. 'I believe I'm quoting Nick Heller.'

'Not original to me.'

'In any case, you're absolutely correct about the Chinese knockoffs. Buying them over the Internet reduces their risk of exposure, yes. But there's an even better reason. Something only the best bad guys know about.'

'Okay.'

'The IMEI. The electronic serial number. Every mobile phone has one, even the cheapest disposables.'

'Even Noklas?'

'Yes, even Noklas. But by using Shenzhen Specials, your bad guys make it much, *much* harder to be caught by traditional means.'

'How so?'

'Put it this way. If the FBI has the serial number of a *real* Nokia phone, all they have to do is call Finland and Nokia's going to tell them where the phone was sold. Bad guys don't want that. But this baby, on the other hand – who're you gonna call, some factory in Shenzhen? They won't speak English and they sure as hell don't keep records and they probably don't even answer the phone. Good luck with that.'

'So these guys are pros,' I said.

He didn't reply. He was leaning over the shallow ledge with a magnifying glass and a pair of tweezers trying to pry something out of the back of the phone. Finally he succeeded and held up a little orange cardboard rectangle.

'The SIM card,' I said. 'Chinese too?'

'Uzbek. These guys are *really* smart.'

'The SIM card's from *Uzbekistan*?'

'They probably buy 'em in bulk online, get them shipped to some drop box, end of the trail. Wow. A Chinese knockoff phone with an untraceable serial number and an untraceable SIM card. Know any FBI agents who speak Uzbek?'

'Then what do you suggest?'

'Some deep digging.'

'Of what sort?'

'Why don't you leave that part to me,' he said.

'Because my puny mortal mind cannot possibly hope to comprehend?'

'Here's your BlackBerry. Clean as a whistle.'

'I appreciate it,' I said. 'But I'd like you to put the GPS bug back in.'

'That's . . . foolish.'

'No doubt,' I said. 'But first I'd like you to drain the battery on the tracking bug. Can you do that?'

'It doesn't draw from your BlackBerry's battery, so sure, that's not a problem.'

'Good. I want it to die a natural death in about, oh, fifteen or twenty minutes.'

He nodded. 'So they'll never know that you discovered it.'

'Right. I much prefer being underestimated.'

If he could have smiled, he would have. But I heard it in his voice. 'You know something, Heller?' he said. 'I think *I've* underestimated you. You're really quite an impressive guy.'

'Do me a favor,' I said, 'and keep it to yourself.'

As I returned to the Defender, my BlackBerry was ringing.

'I thought I'd have heard from you by now,' Diana said.

'My BlackBerry was temporarily offline.'

'You didn't see what I sent you?'

'What did you send me?'

'A photograph of our kidnapper,' she said.

FORTY-NINE

The town of Pine Ridge, New Hampshire (population 1,260), had a police force that consisted of two full-time officers, two part-time officers, and one police chief.

Walter Nowitzki had been the police chief in Pine Ridge for twelve years. He'd been on the force in Concord before that and grabbed the chief's job when it opened up. He and Delia wanted to move to a small town, and he wanted more time to hunt. The work here was routine and uneventful, and when it wasn't hunting season, it was downright slow.

Jason Kent, the rookie, entered his office hesitantly. His cheeks and his jug ears were red, as they always got when he was nervous.

'Chief?' Jason said.

'Sam Dupuis keeps calling,' Chief Nowitzki said. 'Got a bug up his ass about the Alderson property.'

'What's the deal? No one lives there.'

Nowitzki shook his head. 'Something about how his dog ran off, I didn't quite get it. But now he says he thinks they're doing work without a permit and who knows what else.'

'You want me to drive out and talk to Mr Dupuis?'

'Just head on over to the Alderson property, would you? Go out there and introduce yourself and see what's up.'

'I didn't know any of the Aldersons even came here anymore. I thought the old man was just, like, an absentee owner.'

'Sam says it's a caretaker or a contractor or something, works for the family.'

'Okay.' Jason rose and was out the door when Chief Nowitzki said, 'But keep it polite, would you? Don't go ruffling any feathers.'

FIFTY

I clicked on Diana's e-mail and waited impatiently as the attachment opened.

A photograph, muddy and low-contrast. The back of a man's head and shoulders. The picture looked like it had been taken at night. A surveillance photo, maybe?

So why was Diana so sure this was the guy?

I studied it more closely, though on the BlackBerry's screen it wasn't easy. I saw what might have been the headrest of a car. The photo had been taken from the back seat.

The man's shoulders rose well above the headrest. He was tall. His head appeared to be shaved. But something was obscuring a large area of his head and neck: a shirt with a high collar? No, maybe it was just a dark blotch, a flaw in the photo. As I looked closer, it seemed like the entire back of his head and neck was covered with some sort of hideous birthmark.

But then, as I continued to study it, I realized it wasn't a birthmark at all. It was a design, an illustration. It looked like a tattoo, but no one got tattoos on their scalp, did they?

Wrong.

It was a tattoo of the head of a large bird, maybe an eagle or a vulture. A line drawing in black or dark blue, highly detailed if crudely executed. Stylized feathers, a sharp beak, erect ears. An owl, maybe, with large, fierce staring eyes. Huge blank circles with much smaller circles at their center, representing the irises.

They stared at you. They stared at whoever had taken the picture.

The guy got eyes on the back of his head.

When Mauricio Perreira had babbled that to me, I'd paid it no attention. It was a figure of speech, part of a long desperate rant by a terrified man, nothing more. I assumed he meant to say, in his broken English, *He's got eyes in the back of his head.* Meaning: This man hears and sees everything, has sources everywhere, I can't give you his name, I'm scared of him.

He *was* scared. But it wasn't a metaphor. He meant it literally, almost. There were eyes on the back of the man's head.

Diana answered on the first ring.

'Who took the picture?' I said.

'Alexandra Marcus. This came from her iPhone, taken the night she disappeared.'

'When?'

'At 2:36 A.M. Apparently all iPhone photos are encoded with metadata that tell you the date and time. And something called a geotag, which gives you the GPS coordinates of the phone at the time the picture was taken.'

'Leominster?'

'Straight down the road about a mile from where you found it.'

'That's an owl.'

'Right. I wasn't sure whether you'd be able to make it out on your BlackBerry. But if you enlarge the photo it appears that the tattoo covers his head and neck and probably a good portion of his upper back as well.'

'You already searched NCIC?'

'Sure. One of the fields in the database is for scars and marks and tattoos. No hits.'

'Did you send it to your Gang Intelligence Center?'

'Sure. But no luck.'

'Isn't there some central database of criminal tattoos?'

'There should be, but there isn't.'

I thought a moment. 'Ever see the Latin Kings tattoos?' The Latin Kings were the biggest Hispanic street gang in the country.

'It's a five-pointed crown or something?'

'That's one of them. There's also a tattoo of a lion wearing a crown. Sharp teeth, big eyes. Some gang members get it tattooed on their backs. It's huge.'

'You think he's part of a Latino gang?'

'Some kind of gang, anyway.'

'I've sent the photo to our seventy-five legal attachés around the world. Asking them to run it by local law enforcement. Maybe we'll get lucky.'

'Yeah, maybe,' I said dubiously. 'You'd think a guy with an owl on his head and neck would be fairly memorable. People aren't likely to forget a sight like that.'

'That's not smart. Owls are supposed to be smart.'

'Your average street pigeon is ten times smarter than the smartest owl. It's not about smart. It's about scary. In some cultures, an owl is a symbol of death,' I said. 'A bad omen. A prophecy of death.'

'Where? Which countries?'

I thought for a moment. 'Mexico. Japan. Romania, I think. Maybe Russia. Ever see an owl hunt?' I said.

'Oddly enough, I haven't.'

'It moves its head side to side and up and down, looking and listening, triangulating on its prey. You really can't find a more perfect, more ruthless killer.'

FIFTY-ONE

'Hi, Mr Heller,' Jillian Alperin said as I entered the office. 'Dorothy's looking for you.'

'You're allowed to call me Nick,' I said, for what must have been the twentieth time since she'd started working for me.

'Thank you, Mr Heller, but I'm not comfortable with that.'

'Right,' I said. 'Then just call me El Jefe.'

'Excuse me?'

I noticed the butterfly tattoo on her right shoulder. She was wearing some kind of lacy tank top that bared a few inches of her midriff. Her navel was pierced. 'What does that mean, the butterfly?' I asked.

'It's a symbol of freedom and metamorphosis. I got it when I stopped eating flesh.'

'You used to be a cannibal? I didn't see that on your job application.'

'*What?* I mean, I used to eat meat. I have a "meat is murder" tattoo on my lower back, want to see it?' She stood up and turned around.

Dorothy's voice rang out as she approached. 'Jillian, you can show your tramp stamps after work and on your own time. Also, you and I need to have a talk about appropriate office attire.'

'You said I didn't have to wear high heels.'

Dorothy shook her head. 'I got that picture you sent,' she said to me. 'I've been Googling tattoos, but no luck so far.'

'My brother worked in a tattoo parlor in Saugus,' Jillian said.

'How about you replace the toner cartridge like I asked,' Dorothy said.

In my office, I said, 'Remind me why you hired Jillian again.'

'She's a very, very smart young woman.'

'That escaped me.'

'I admit she's taking a little longer to catch on to the clerical stuff than I expected—'

'Isn't her job all *about* the clerical stuff?'

'Give her a chance,' she told me sternly, 'or you can hire her replacement. Now, if we can please move on. I found spyware on our network.'

'What kind of spyware?'

'Well, a molar virus. It burrowed into our intranet, injected code, and opened a back door. For a couple of days now it's been scanning all volumes for protected files and then sending them out.'

'That's how they got my security system codes,' I said. 'Where did it send to?'

She shook her head. 'Proxy servers so many times removed that it's just about impossible to find. But I rooted it out. It should be gone.'

'How did it get onto our system in the first place?'

'I'm working on that. I—'

My intercom buzzed, and Jillian said, 'You have a visitor.'

I looked at Dorothy, who shrugged. 'Name?' I said.

'Belinda Marcus,' Jillian said.

FIFTY-TWO

'I'm worried sick about Marshall,' Belinda said. 'I think he's going to have a heart attack.' She was wearing a light brown scoop-neck linen top with sequins around the neckline. It sort of belled out at the midriff. She threw out her thin arms and embraced me. Her perfume smelled like bathroom deodorizer.

'I'm sorry, Belinda, did we have an appointment?'

She sat and folded her legs. 'No, we did not, Nick, but we need to talk.'

'Give me one quick second.' I turned my chair and typed out an instant message to Dorothy:

> Need bkgd on Belinda Marcus ASAP.
> How soon?
> Immediately. Whatever you can get.

'I'm all yours,' I said. 'Can I get you a Coke?'

'The only soda I drink is Diet Pepsi, but I don't need the caffeine. Nick, I know I should have called first, but Marshall had to go in to the office, and I got a ride with him. I told him I wanted to meet a girlfriend for coffee in the Back Bay.'

'Why did he have to go to the office?'

She shook her head. 'I'm sure it's about Alexa. It has to be. Nick, I've been wanting to talk to y'all privately, without Marshall, since this whole nightmare began.'

I nodded.

'I feel like I'm being disloyal, and he'd probably kill me if he knew I was telling y'all this. But I – I'm just at my wit's end, and *someone* needs to say something. I know Marshall's your old and dear friend, and you barely know me, I understand that, but can you *please* promise me Marshall will never find out we spoke?' She bit her lower lip and held her breath and waited for my response.

I paused a moment. 'Okay.'

She let out a sigh. 'Thank you, thank you, thank you. Nick, you need to know that Marshall is . . . he's under a great deal of pressure. All he wants is to get his beloved daughter back, but they . . . they won't let him hand over what they want, and it's tearing him up inside.'

'Who won't let him?'

She looked at me anxiously. 'David Schechter.'

'How do you know this? Does he talk to you about it?'

'Never. I've . . . just heard them arguing. I've heard Marshall pleading with him, it would break your heart.'

'So you must know what Mercury is?'

She shook her head violently. 'I don't. I really don't. I mean, it's a file of some sort, but I have no idea what it's about. I don't care if it's the answers to next Sunday's *New York Times* crossword puzzle or the nuclear codes. We've got to give it to them. We've got to get that girl free.'

'So why are you telling me?'

She studied her fingernails. It looked like a brand-new manicure. The polish matched her blouse. 'Marshall is so deep in some kind of trouble, and I don't know who to turn to.'

I looked at my computer screen. An instant message had popped up from Dorothy. A few lines of text.

'I'm sure he trusts you,' I said. 'You've been married for, what, three years, right?'

She nodded.

'You were a flight attendant when you met Marshall?'

She nodded, smiled. Her smile was abashed and ruefully embarrassed and pleased, all at once. 'He saved me,' she said. 'I've always hated flying.'

'That's got to be a Georgia accent.'

'Very good,' she said. 'A little town called Barnesville.'

'Are you serious? Barnesville, Georgia? I love Barnesville!'

'Have you been there? Really?'

'Are you kidding, I dated a girl from Barnesville. Went down there a bunch, met her parents and her brothers and sisters.'

Belinda didn't look terribly interested. 'What's her name? Everyone knows everyone down there.'

'Purcell. Cindy Purcell?'

Belinda shook her head. 'She must be a lot younger.'

'But I'm sure you've eaten at her parents' restaurant, Brownie's.'

'Oh, sure. But Nick—'

'I've never had anything like their low-country boil.'

'Never had that dish, but I'm sure it's good. Southern cooking is the best, isn't it? I miss it so.'

'Well,' I said, standing. 'I'm glad you came in. I'm sure it wasn't easy, but it sure was helpful.'

She remained seated. 'I know what people call me. I know some people think I'm a gold digger because I happened to marry a wealthy man. But I didn't marry Marshall for his money. I just want what's best for him. And I want that girl back, Nick. Whatever it takes.'

After she'd left, I called Dorothy in.

'You ever meet a Georgian who preferred Pepsi to Coke?' I said.

'I'm sure they exist. But no, I haven't. And I've certainly never met a Georgian who uses the word "soda". Every soft drink is always "Coke". You didn't really date a woman from Barnesville, did you?'

'No. And there's no Brownie's.'

'A good one about the low-country boil, Nick. If you've never had that, you're not from Georgia. What tipped you off in the first place?'

'Her accent's wrong. Words like "square" and "here", she drops her *R*'s. Georgians don't talk like that. And then there's the way she keeps calling me "y'all".'

'Good point. "Y'all" is always plural. She's not from Georgia, is she?'

'I don't even think she's southern.'

'Then why's she faking it?'

'That's what I want to find out. Can you do a little digging—?'

'Already started,' Dorothy said. 'As soon as she said "Pepsi".'

FIFTY-THREE

Unlike Belinda Marcus, Francine Heller never wanted to be a rich man's wife.

My mother had gone to the same small-town high school in upstate New York as my father. She was the class beauty. In her old photos she looked like Grace Kelly. Whereas my father, to put it delicately, was no Gregory Peck.

From the moment Victor Heller saw her, he launched an all-out campaign to win her over. My father was a live wire, a charmer, a wheedler. He was a force of nature. And when he wanted something he invariably got it.

Eventually he got Francine, of course, then kept her in a gilded cage for decades.

It was pretty clear what he saw in her – that sylphlike grace and almost regal presence, accompanied by an appealing frankness – but it was less clear what she saw in him besides the fact that he wanted her with a relentless, outsize ambition. Maybe that was all it took to win over an insecure girl. She needed to be needed. Her parents were divorced – her mother had moved to the Boston area, and the girls stayed behind with Dad, not wanting to change schools. They shuttled between parents. Maybe she craved stability.

Money certainly wasn't part of the bargain, and I don't think she ever fully understood Victor's hunger for it. Her father, a lawyer for the State of New York, would reuse teabags to save a dime.

It was hardly a match made in heaven. Being married to the Dark Prince of Wall Street turned out to be a full-time job. She had to attend endless galas and cocktail parties. At every charity event the names of Mr and Mrs Heller invariably appeared in the printed program, in the shortest list of the biggest donors. Not merely the Patrons or Sponsors or, God forbid, the coupon-clipping Friends. Always the Benefactors, the President's Circle, the Chairman's Council, the Century Society.

When all she really wanted to do was stay home with her two little boys, me and Roger.

My father vanished when I was thirteen, a fugitive from justice with thirty-seven charges of financial misconduct trailing him like a pack of hounds. He traveled around Europe, eventually landing in Switzerland. All of his assets were frozen, and our family went from high-living to hardscrabble. The loss of security, combined with the humiliation, was traumatic for her, as it was for the rest of us. But I always wondered whether, on some level, she wasn't relieved.

Relieved to be out of the golden bubble. Relieved to be free of command-performance hostess duties. Relieved to be away from his soul-destroying, oxygen-depleting narcissism.

When she'd found work as a personal assistant to Marshall Marcus, it was a lifesaver for her and for all of us. I guess it could have been demeaning – one day the guy's a guest at your dinner table, the next you're keeping his call list – but Marshall somehow made sure the situation didn't *feel* that way. He didn't make it feel like charity, either, though I suppose that's what it was. Instead, she once explained to me, he made it seem like he was running a family business, and she was family.

Eventually she moved on, got a job teaching in a local elementary school. Now she was ostensibly retired, but she kept busy as a volunteer school librarian. She also took care of the old ladies in her condo complex. Need a ride to your eye doctor's appointment? Call

Frankie. Confused by the fine print of your prescription-drug benefit? Ask Frankie. She knew everything or knew how to find it out. I don't know why she pretended to be retired, when she was busier than any medical resident.

And ever since she'd been liberated from the gilded cage, she spoke her mind. She took no crap from anybody. My sweet, soft-spoken mom had evolved into a plainspoken, peppery older woman.

It was delightful.

She lived on the bottom half of a 'townhome' in a retirement community in Newton overlooking the reservoir. All the townhomes, set among winding paths and landscaped gardens, were identical. I could never tell them apart; I always got lost. It was like the Village in that old TV show *The Prisoner*, only with bingo.

The door flew open almost as soon as I pushed the buzzer. My mother was wearing turquoise pants and a white top under a flowing knitted caftan of rainbow hues and a necklace of big jade-colored glass beads. A few minimum touches of makeup, but she'd never needed much. In her sixties she was a gorgeous woman, with sapphire blue eyes and dark eyelashes and a milky complexion, which she really shouldn't have had, given how much she smoked. When my father first met her she must have been a knockout.

She was holding a cigarette, as always. A nimbus of smoke swirled around her. Even before she had a chance to say hello, a large dark projectile launched itself at me from behind her like a cruise missile.

I tried to sidestep, but her dog was on me, baring its glistening fangs, snarling and barking in a rabid frenzy, its sharp toenails raking my chest and arms through my pullover. I tried to knee it down, but the hound from hell was far too wiry and nimble and that only made it come at me more furiously.

'Down, Lilly,' my mother said in a matter-of-fact tone. Her voice had gotten lower and huskier from decades of smoking. The beast promptly dropped to the tiled entry hall, head resting on its paws. But it continued staring at me menacingly, growling softly.

'I'm glad she obeys you,' I said. 'I think I was about to lose an eye.'

'Nah, she's a love pooch, aren't you, Lilly-willie? Come here.' She reached out one arm to hug me. The other one she kept splayed backward, daintily holding her cigarette away from me in two long curved fingers as if she were channeling Bette Davis.

As I entered, the beast got up to follow us, nails clacking on the wooden floor. It stayed so close it kept bumping against my legs. This seemed deliberate, a warning: it could rip out my throat at any time. It was just waiting for its Master to leave the room for a few seconds.

'Gabe here?' I said.

'In his room playing some computer game where you're a soldier and you kill a lot of people. There's a lot of bombs and explosions. I told him to put on his headphones. The noise was starting to bug me.'

That was just as well. I didn't want him overhearing what I had to say. 'Do you really want Gabe breathing all this secondhand smoke?' I said.

She squinted at me through slitted eyes as a plume of smoke snaked around between us. 'Have you ever *seen* "Call of Duty: Modern Warfare"? I think cigarette smoke is the least of his problems.'

'Fair enough.' I tried never to argue with my mother.

'Listen, honey, I know you're awfully busy, but do you think you could make some time to teach him to drive?'

'He wants to drive?'

'He just got his learner's permit.'

'What about driving school?'

She scowled at me. 'Oh, for God's sake, Nick, you're the only father figure in the kid's life. You're his godfather. Don't you remember how disappointed you were when you had to learn from me because your father was gone?'

'I wasn't disappointed.'

'Lord knows he doesn't want me to teach him.'

'You're absolutely right. I'll do it. Though the thought of Gabe on the Beltway . . .'

'And what kind of foolishness are you putting in his head about how he shouldn't look in Lilly's eyes or he'll drop dead?'

I shrugged. 'Busted. You can also blame me for that vegetarian kick he's on now. He picked that up from my new office manager.' I smiled, shook my head. 'I think he's trying to impress her.'

'Honey, as long as he's eating, what do I care. You want me to remind you of some of the things you did to impress girls? How about when you tried to grow a goatee when you were fourteen so Jennie Watson would think you were manly?'

I groaned.

'Are you getting any sleep?'

'I had to work late last night.'

Her condo was very IKEA: comfortable but unstylish. Plexiglas stools around the apartment's 'kitchen nook'. An armchair in some sort of maroon chintz floral pattern next to a matching couch. On the counter was a *Boston Globe* folded to the crossword puzzle, and a copy of *Modern Maturity* that looked like she'd actually read it.

I sat in the chintz armchair and she sat at the end of the couch, put out her cigarette in an immaculate stone ashtray.

'Nicky, my book group is meeting in a few minutes, so can we make this quick?'

'Just a couple of questions. When was the last time you talked to Alexa?'

She lighted another cigarette with a cheap Bic lighter and inhaled deeply. 'Couple, three days ago. Yesterday Marshall called me to ask if she was here. She's acting up again, isn't she?'

I shook my head.

'Gabe tells me she spent the night at her friend Taylor's house on Beacon Hill – you know her father's Dick Armstrong, the senator? – but I think we know what that really means. She's a beautiful girl, and—'

'It's nothing like that.'

She looked up. 'Did she run away?'

'No.'

She studied my face. 'Something happened to her,' she said.

I hesitated.

'Tell me what happened to her, Nick.'

I did.

FIFTY-FOUR

I expected her to be upset.

But I wasn't prepared for the magnitude of her reaction.

She seemed to crumple, to collapse in on herself in a way I'd never seen before. She gave a terrible anguished cry, and tears spilled from her eyes. I hugged her, and it was several minutes before she was able to talk.

'I know you care for her—'

'*Care* for her? Oh, honey, I love that girl.' Her voice trembled.

'I know.'

She couldn't talk for a while. Then she said, 'How much are they demanding?'

'They must have given her a script. She said they want something called Mercury. Marshall says he has no idea what that referred to.'

'Mercury?'

'You worked for him for years. You must have come across that name in a file or a letter or something.'

'My memory's still sharp, thank God. That doesn't ring any bells. But if Marshall has the slightest idea what Mercury is, he'll give it to them in a heartbeat. He'd give up his fortune to get his daughter back.'

'If he had a fortune left.'

'I never heard anything about this. He didn't mention his troubles at all. But he and I don't talk much anymore. How widely known is it that he's . . . what?'

'Ruined. So far he's somehow managed to contain it. But I'm sure the word will get out any day now. He doesn't confide in you?'

'Not since Belinda moved in.'

'That's quite a change.'

'Honey, Marshall used to check in with me before he used the john. That's the difference between him and your father. One of the many differences. Marshall actually respected my judgment.' This was painful to hear, but my mother was always allergic to self-pity, and she said it lightly.

'You think she's deliberately cutting you off from him?'

She inhaled deeply. The red ember at the tip of the cigarette flared and crackled and hissed. 'They've had me over to dinner twice, and she's always hugging me and telling me in that Georgia peach accent that "We just *have* to go shopping on Newbury Street, me and you," and "Why don't we see more of you?" But whenever I call Marshall at home, she answers the phone and says she'll pass along a message, and I doubt he ever gets it.'

'What about e-mail?'

'She changed his e-mail address, and I never got the new one. She says he has to be much more careful, much less accessible. So I have to e-mail Belinda, and she actually answers for him.'

'Well, Alexa doesn't get along with her either.'

She shook her head, blew out a lungful of smoke. 'Oh, that woman is toxic. Alexa was always complaining about her, and I kept urging her to give Belinda a chance, it's not easy being a stepmother. Until I met the woman and understood. I think Belinda actually hates her stepdaughter. I've never seen anything like it.'

'She talks about how much she adores Alexa.'

'In front of others. With Alexa, she doesn't bother concealing it.'

'Maybe that's not the only thing she's concealing. You haven't complained to Marshall about being cut off?'

'Sure I did. At the beginning. He'd just shrug and say, "I've learned not to argue."'

'Strange.'

'I see this sort of thing happen to a lot of married men as they get older. Their wives start taking charge of their social lives, then their friendships. The husbands abdicate all responsibility because they're too busy or they'd just as soon not take the initiative, and before you know it they're wholly owned subsidiaries of their ladies. Even rich and powerful men like Marshall . . . used to be. I think the only person he sees outside the office besides Belinda is David Schechter.'

'How long has Schechter been his lawyer?'

'Schecky? He's not Marshall's lawyer.'

'Then what is he?'

'You know how Mafia dons always have an adviser?'

'A consigliere?'

'That's it. Schecky is Marshall's consigliere.'

'Advising him on what?'

'I just think he's someone whose judgment Marshall trusts.'

'Do you?'

'I don't know him. But Marshall once told me he has the most extensive files he's ever seen. Reminded him of J. Edgar Hoover.'

I nodded, thought for a moment. 'Why did Marshall hire you in the first place?'

She smiled. 'You mean, why would he hire a woman with no particular skills to run his office?'

'That's not what I meant.'

'Yes, it is,' she said kindly. 'You don't want to hurt my feelings. That's all right.' She smiled. 'Marshall is a good man. A good person. He saw what had happened to us after your father left. How the government took everything. Was there a part of him that thought, *There but for the grace of God go I*? Sure, probably.'

'You always said that he was a friend of Dad's, and that's why he wanted to help.'

'That's right.'

'But he didn't know you, did he?'

'Not really. He knew your father much better. But that's Marshall. He's the most generous person I know. He just loves to help people. And that was a time when I needed help, desperately. I was a mother with two teenage sons and no house and no money. We'd gone from that house in Bedford to sharing Mom's split-level ranch in Malden. I had no income and no foreseeable income. Imagine how I must have felt.'

In the scale of human misery, that barely registered, I knew. But at the same time I truly couldn't conceive of what it must have been like to be Francine Heller, ripped untimely from her chrysalis of immense gilded wealth, naked and shivering, lost and vulnerable, not knowing who to turn to.

'I can't,' I admitted. 'But you were a hero. That much I do know.'

She gripped my hand in her small soft warm one. 'Oh, for God's sake, not even *close*. But you need to understand how much it meant to me to have this man step in, someone I barely knew, and offer me not just an income, a way to keep food on the table, but an actual job. A way for me to do something useful.'

She looked so uncomfortable that I felt bad I'd raised the subject. She shifted in her seat, blew out a puff of smoke, stubbed out her cigarette, her face turned away.

'I'm sure you've heard the rumors that Marshall secretly cooperated with the SEC when they were building their case against Dad. In effect helped turn Dad in.' If they were true, though, then Marcus would have hired my mother for one very simple reason: guilt.

'Never. Not Marshall.'

'Well, you know him as well as anyone.'

'I did, anyway. So let me ask *you* something.'

'Sure.'

'Do you think these kidnappers will let her go if they get what they want?' She asked this with such hushed desperation that I had no choice but to give her, dishonestly, the assurance that she, like Marcus, seemed to crave so badly.

'Yes.'

'Why are you saying that?'

'Why? Because the typical pattern in a kidnap-for-ransom situation—'

'That's not what I'm asking. I mean, why do you think I can't hear the truth? I know when you're not being honest, Nick. I'm your mother.'

I'd always thought that I'd gotten my talent at reading people from her. She was, like me, what Sigmund Freud called a *Menschenkenner*. Loosely translated, that meant a 'good judge of character'. But it went beyond that. She and I both had an unusual ability to read faces and expressions and intuit whether people were telling us the truth. It's certainly not foolproof, and it's not at all like being a human polygraph. It's merely an innate talent, the way some people are natural painters or can tell stories or have perfect pitch. We were good at detecting lies. Though not perfect.

'No,' I said. 'I don't think they're going to let her go.'

FIFTY-FIVE

She was crying again, and I immediately regretted my candor.

'I'll do everything in my power to find her,' I said. 'I promise you.'

She held my right hand in both of hers. Her hands were bony yet soft. She leaned close, her eyes pleading. 'Get her back, Nick. Please? Will you please get her back?'

'All I can do is promise I'll do my best.'

'That's all I ask,' she said, and she squeezed my hand again.

As I got up, the hound from hell growled at me without even bothering to move. As if to remind me that if I disappointed its Master, I'd be facing the wrath of the beast.

On the way out I stopped at Gabe's room. Stacked in tall heaps everywhere were his favorite graphic novels, including multiple copies of *Watchmen*, the collected comics of Will Eisner, Brian Azzarello's *Joker*.

It was remarkable how much his temporary quarters here had acquired exactly the same funky odor as his room back home in Washington. It smelled like a monkey house: that teenage-boy smell of sweat and dirty laundry and who knows what else.

He sat on his bed, headphones on, drawing in his sketchbook. He was wearing a red T-shirt – a rare departure from his habitual black 'emo' attire – with a drawing on the front of a stylized, boxy computer exploding and the word KABLAAM! superimposed over it in a comic font. I took a chair next to his desk, which was dwarfed by a big monitor – probably a gift from my mother – and an Xbox 360 video game module and wireless controller. When he felt the bed move he took off his headphones. I could hear some loud, repetitive electric guitar riff and a screaming vocal.

'Nice,' I said. 'What are you listening to?'

'It's an old band called Rage Against the Machine. They were totally awesome and brilliant. They were all about Western cultural imperialism and the abuses of corporate America.'

'Huh. Sounds fun. Let me guess. Did Jillian turn you on to this?'

He gave me an evasive look. 'Yeah.'

'Which song is this?'

'"Killing in the Name". I don't think you'd like it.'

'No?'

'You wouldn't get it.'

'Is that the song that uses the F-word twenty times in, let's see, five lines of lyrics?'

He looked at me, startled.

'You're right,' I said. 'Not my kind of thing.'

'There you go.'

'I'm not a big fan of drop D tuning. But see what your Nana thinks.'

'Nana's a lot cooler than you give her credit for.'

'I've known her longer,' I teased.

He hesitated. 'Nick, I – I heard what you were saying to her.'

'You shouldn't have been listening.'

'She was *screaming*, Uncle Nick. I could hear her through my headphones, okay? I mean, what am I supposed to do, ignore that? Why'd you have to make her cry?'

I doubted he could actually hear anything through that music. He was eavesdropping, plain and simple.

'Okay,' I said. 'Listen.'

But he interrupted: 'Where's Alexa?'

'We don't know yet.'

'She got kidnapped, right?'

I nodded. 'Listen to me, Gabe. You have a special role here. You need to be strong. Okay? This is going to be really hard on your Nana.'

He compressed his lips, his oversized Adam's apple bobbing up and down. 'Yeah? How about me?'

'It's hard on all of us.'

'So who's behind it?'

'We're not sure yet.'

'Do you know she once got kidnapped for a couple hours?'

I nodded.

'You think it's the same people?'

'I don't know, Gabe. We just found out. We still don't know anything. We've seen a video of her talking, but that's pretty much all we have so far.'

'You don't know where she is?'

'Not yet. I'm working on it.'

'Can I see the video?'

'No.'

'Why not?'

I gave him the answer that has infuriated teenagers since the beginning of time: 'Just because.'

He reacted exactly the way I expected, with a tight-lipped glower.

'Hey, how about when this is over I teach you to drive.'

He shrugged. 'I guess,' he said glumly. But I could see he was trying not to show how pleased he was.

My phone rang. I glanced at it: Dorothy.

I picked up. 'Hey, hold on a second.'

'Who's that?' Gabe said. 'Is that about Alexa?'

'Yeah,' I said. 'I think it is.'

I gave him a quick hug and walked out toward my car. 'What do you have?' I said.

'I talked to Delta Air Lines. Belinda never worked for them.'

I stopped in the middle of the parking lot. 'Why would she lie about that?'

'Because Marshall Marcus would never have married her if he knew her real employment background.'

'Which is?'

She paused. 'She was a call girl.'

FIFTY-SIX

'Why does that not surprise me?' I said.

'I ran her Social Security number. She's a failed actress, looks like. Took acting classes for a while in Lincoln Park, but dropped out. Employed as an escort' – I could hear the scare quotes – 'with VIP Exxxecutive Service, based out of Trenton. That's three X's in Exxxecutive.'

'Let me guess. A *high-priced* escort service.'

'Are there any other kinds?'

'Well, she did good for herself. Married up. She's not southern, is she?'

'Southern Jersey. Woodbine.'

My BlackBerry emitted two beeps, its text-message alert sound. I glanced at it.

A brief text message. It said only, '15 minutes,' and gave the precise polar coordinates of what looked like a 7-Eleven parking lot .73 miles away.

The message was sent by '18E'. No name, no phone number.

But he didn't need to use his name. An 18E was US Army occupation code for a communications sergeant in the Special Forces.

George Devlin was an 18E.

'Excuse me,' I said. 'I have to see an old friend.'

'How did you know I was close enough to make it here in fifteen minutes?' I said. 'You knew where I was?'

George Devlin ignored my question. Like it was either too complicated or too obvious to explain. He had his ways, leave it at that. He was preoccupied with angling a computer monitor so I could see it. The screen glowed in the dim interior of his mobile home/office and momentarily illuminated the canyons and rivulets and dimpling of his scarred face, the striated muscle fibers and the train-track stitches. There was a vinegary smell in there, probably from the salve he regularly applied.

A greenish topographical map of Massachusetts appeared on the screen. A flashing red circle appeared, about fifteen miles northwest of Boston. Then three squiggly lines popped up – white, blue, and orange – each emanating from the flashing red circle. One from Boston, two from the north.

'I don't get it,' I said.

'If you look closely,' he said, 'you'll see each line is made up of dots. The dots represent cell tower hits from the three mobile phones belonging to Alexa Marcus, Mauricio Perreira, and an unknown person we'll call Mr X.'

'Who's what color?'

'Blue is for Mauricio, as we'll call him. White is for Alexa. Orange is for Mr X.'

'So Mr X came down from close to the New Hampshire border, it looks like.'

'Right.'

'Mind if I ask where you got this data?'

He inhaled slowly, making a rattling sound. 'You can ask all you want.'

I leaned forward. 'So they all met fifteen miles northwest of Boston in . . . is it Lincoln?'

'That's right.'

'Were they all there at the same time?'

'Yes. For only five minutes. Mauricio and the abducted girl arrived together, of course. They were there for seventeen minutes. Mr X stayed for only four or five minutes.'

They'd met in a wooded area, I saw. Near Sandy Pond, which was marked as conservation land. Remote, isolated after midnight: a good place for a rendezvous. So Alexa's iPhone went from Boston to Lincoln and then north to Leominster. Which was where it was discarded.

Now I could see the pattern. Mauricio took her from the hotel to Lincoln, twenty minutes from Boston, where he handed her off to 'Mr X'.

While Mauricio went back to Boston – actually, to his apartment in Medford, just north of Boston – Mr X was driving Alexa north. He tossed her phone out as they passed through Leominster. Presumably she stayed in the vehicle with him.

Then they crossed the border into New Hampshire.

'So the route stops in southern New Hampshire,' I said. 'Nashua.'

'No, Mr X's mobile phone goes off the grid in Nashua. That could mean that he shut it off. Or it lost reception, and then he shut it off. Whatever, he hasn't used it since.'

'Sloppy for him to keep his cell phone on,' I said.

'Well, to be fair, he assumed it was untraceable.'

'Is it?'

'No, actually. But there's a difference between untraceable and untrackable. It's like following a black box on the back of a truck. We don't know what's inside the box, but we know where it is. So we can't determine his identity, but maybe we can find his location. Understand?'

'He's in New Hampshire. Which means she probably is too. Maybe in or near Nashua.'

'I wouldn't assume that. Mr X might have passed through New Hampshire on his way to Canada.'

'That's not a logical route if you're driving all the way to Canada.'

He nodded in agreement.

'They're in New Hampshire,' I said.

FIFTY-SEVEN

The offices of Marcus Capital Management were on the sixth floor of Rowes Wharf. I gave the receptionist my name and waited in the luxuriously appointed lobby, on a gray suede couch. The floors were chocolate-brown hardwood and the walls were mahogany. An enormous flat-screen monitor on the wall showed the weather on one half of a split screen and financial news on the other, with a stock crawl at the bottom.

I didn't have to wait even a minute before Marcus's personal assistant appeared. She was a willowy redhead named Smoki Bacon, a stunningly beautiful, elegant young woman. This didn't surprise me. Marcus had a reputation for hiring only beautiful women as admins, beauty contest winners, former Miss Whatevers. My mother, who'd been lovely and attractive in her prime, was the sole exception. She never looked like a runway model. She was more beautiful than that.

The curvaceous Smoki gave me a dazzling smile and asked if I wanted coffee or water. I said no.

'Marshall's in a meeting right now, but he wants to see you as soon as it's over. It might be a while, though. Would you like to come back a little later?'

'I'll wait.'

'At least let me take you to a conference room, where you can use the phone and the computer.'

She showed me down a corridor. 'It's so nice to meet you,' she said as we rounded a bend and passed by what was once the trading floor. There were thirty or forty workstations, all empty. All the computers were off. The place was as quiet as a tomb. 'I just can't tell you how worried sick we've all been about Alexa.'

'Well,' I said, not knowing how to reply, 'keep the faith.'

'Your mom used to babysit for her sometimes, you know. She told me that.'

'I know.'

'Frankie's the best.'

'I agree.'

'She calls me every once in a while just to check up on things. She really cares about Mr Marcus.'

At the threshold to an empty conference room she put a hand on my shoulder. She leaned close and said through gritted teeth, 'Please get that girl back, Mr Heller.'

'I'll do my best,' I said.

But instead of waiting, I decided to wander down to Marcus's office.

His assistant, Smoki, sat guard at her desk outside his office, I remembered. I also remembered that Marcus had a private dining room next to his office. When I'd had lunch with him there once, the waitstaff came and went through a back hallway.

It didn't take long to find the service hallway. One entrance was next to the men's room. It connected a small prep kitchen to the boardroom and Marcus's dining room.

His dining room was dark and tidy and bare. It looked like it hadn't seen much use in quite a while.

The door to his office was closed. But when I stood next to it I could hear voices raised in argument.

At first I could make out only fragments. Two men speaking, I was sure. One, of course, was Marcus. His voice was the louder, more emotional one. Easier to make out.

The other was soft-spoken and calm and barely audible.

VISITOR: '. . . to go all soft now.'

MARCUS: 'Wasn't that the point?'

VISITOR: '. . . pretty much to be expected . . .'

MARCUS: 'If she dies, it'll be your doing, you understand me? It'll be on your conscience! You used to have one of those, didn't you?'

VISITOR: '. . . damnedest to keep you alive.'

MARCUS: 'I don't care what you people do to me now. My life is over. My daughter is the only—'

VISITOR: (a *lot of mumbling*) '. . . years you've been the guy with all the solutions . . . they decide now you're the problem? . . . what their solution will be.'

MARCUS: '. . . on my side!'

VISITOR: '. . . want to be on your side. But I can't be unless you're on mine . . .'

MARCUS: (*voice growing steadily louder*) '. . . you wanted, I did. *Everything!*'

VISITOR: '. . . have to spell this out for you, Marshall? "Grieving financier kills self at Manchester residence"?'

I pushed the door open and entered the office. Marcus was sitting behind a long glass desk heaped with papers.

Leaning back in the visitor chair was David Schechter.

FIFTY-EIGHT

'Nickeleh!' Marcus exclaimed. 'What are you – didn't Smoki take you to a conference room to—'

'He was eavesdropping,' Schechter said. 'Isn't that right, Mr Heller?'

'Absolutely. I heard everything you said.'

Schechter blinked at me. 'As of this moment, your services are no longer required.'

'You didn't hire me,' I said.

'Schecky, let me talk to him,' Marcus said. 'He's a *mensch*, he really is.'

Schechter rose, straightened his tweed blazer, and said to Marcus, 'I'll expect your call.'

I watched him leave, then sat in the chair he had just vacated. It was still warm.

Behind Marcus was a glittering picture-postcard view of the Atlantic, red ochre in the dying light.

'What kind of hold does he have over you?' I said.

'Hold . . . ?'

I nodded. 'You hired me to find Alexa, and I can't do that unless you level with me. If you don't, you know what's going to happen to her.'

His eyes were bloodshot and glassy, with heavy pouches beneath them.

'Nicky, you need to stay out of this. It's . . . personal business.'

'I know how much you love Alexa—'

'That girl means everything in the world to me.' Tears came to his eyes.

'It took me a while to understand why in the world you'd withhold the one thing that could get her back. Schechter is blackmailing you. He's keeping you from cooperating with the kidnappers. And I think I know why you hired me.'

He turned around in his chair and stared out the window, as if he were looking to the sea for answers. Or at least avoiding my eyes.

'I hired you because I thought you were the only one who could find her.'

'No,' I said quietly. 'You hired me because that was the only way you could get her back without giving in to their demands. Right?'

He wheeled slowly back around. 'Does that offend you?'

'I've been offended worse. But that's not the point. From the beginning you've been sandbagging me. You lied about calling the police. You didn't tell me how you were forced to take money from criminals, and you didn't tell me you'd lost it all. Now they want the Mercury files – they are files, aren't they? – and you pretend you don't know what they are. So let me ask you this: Do you think David Schechter really cares if Alexa dies?'

He looked stricken, but he didn't reply.

'Whatever he has on you, is it worth your daughter's life?'

His face crumpled, and he covered his eyes like a child as he wept silently.

'You need to tell me what Mercury is,' I went on. 'Then we'll figure something out. We'll come up with a way for you to give these kidnappers what they want without facing . . . whatever it is you're afraid of.'

He kept sobbing.

I got up and walked toward the door, but then I stopped and turned back. 'Did you ever do a background check on Belinda before you married her?'

He lowered his hands. His face was red and wet with tears. 'Belinda? What does Belinda have to do with anything?'

'I've come across some information in the course of my investigation, and I'm not sure how much you want to know.'

'Like . . . what?'

'I'm sorry to have to tell you this,' I said. 'But she was never a flight attendant. She never worked for Delta.'

'Oh, Nickeleh.'

'She's not from Georgia either. She's from New Jersey.'

He sighed. Shook his head slowly. Was it disbelief? An unwillingness to accept so painful a truth, that he'd been deceived by the woman he loved?

'She was a call girl, Marshall. An escort. Whether that makes a difference to you or not, I think you should know.'

But Marcus rolled his eyes. 'Nickeleh, boychik. Grow up.' He shrugged, his palms open. 'She's a sensitive girl. For some *meshugge* reason she's kinda touchy about people knowing too much about our first date.'

A smile slowly spread across my face as I headed again for the door. The old bastard.

From behind me I heard him call out, 'Please don't quit.'

I kept going and didn't look back. 'Don't worry about it. You can't get rid of me. Though you might wish you had.'

FIFTY-NINE

Dragomir was sitting at the computer in the musty sunroom at the back of the house when he heard the girl's cries.

Strange. He'd muted the computer's speakers. The screams were remote and barely audible, but they were definitely hers. He didn't understand how he could be hearing them. She was ten feet underground. He wondered whether the solitude was making him imagine things.

He rose and scraped the old railback dining chair along the floorboards and went to the back door. There he listened some more. The cries were coming from outside. Faint and distant and small, like the buzz of a greenhead fly.

On the porch he cocked his head. The sounds were coming from the yard, maybe the woods beyond. Maybe it wasn't the girl at all. Then he saw the gray PVC pipe standing in the middle of the field. That was where it was coming from. The vent pipe carried not just the girl's exhalations but her cries as well.

She had a set of lungs on her. By now you'd think she would have given up.

He was grateful she was buried so deep.

When Dragomir had first come up with the idea of putting her in the ground, it seemed a stroke of pure genius. After all, the Client's intelligence had turned up a psychiatrist's file indicating the target was afflicted with a debilitating claustrophobia.

Of course, the terror of being buried alive was deep-seated and universal and held a coercive power far beyond any conventional kidnapping technique.

But that wasn't his real reason.

Buried ten feet down she was safely beyond his reach.

If the girl had been under his direct control and easily accessible, like some irresistible pastry in the refrigerator, he wouldn't have been able to restrain himself from doing things to her. He would rape her and kill her as he'd done to so many other pretty young women. He'd never have been able to stop the impulse. That wouldn't do at all.

He recalled the puppy he'd been given as a boy, how much he loved its softness, its fragility. But how could you truly appreciate such fragility without crushing its tiny bones? Very nearly impossible to resist.

Burying her deep was like putting a lock on the refrigerator.

He was listening so hard, with such fascination, to the mewling, faint as a radio station that hadn't been fully tuned in, that he almost didn't hear the far louder crunch of a car's tires on the dirt road out front. If that was the neighbor again, still looking for his damned mongrel, he would have to do something about it finally.

Back in the house, he strode to the front and looked out the window. A police cruiser, dark blue with white lettering: PINE RIDGE POLICE.

He didn't know the town even had its own police force.

A gawky young man got out and gazed at the house with apprehension. He couldn't have been more than twenty-five. He was tall and scrawny with ears that stuck out like jug handles.

By the time the policeman rang the door buzzer, Dragomir was wearing a long brown mullet wig.

He suspected the policeman was here about the dog. He stood on the front porch, shifting his weight from foot to foot, his long spindly arms hanging awkwardly at his side.

'How're you doing?' he said. 'I'm Officer Kent. Could I ask you a few questions?'

SIXTY

In the late afternoon, when I returned to the office, Jillian was on the floor packing boxes for some reason. I didn't want to get involved. She looked up as I entered. Her face was red and sticky with tears.

'Goodbye, Mr Heller.'

It took me a moment. I had my mind on other things. 'What's going on?' I said.

'Before I leave, I wanted to apologize.'

'About the clothing? Don't be silly.'

'That e-card.'

'What are you talking about?'

'Someone e-mailed me a greeting card and I opened it at work.'

'That's why you're leaving?'

'Dorothy didn't tell you?'

'Did she fire you?'

'No, I'm leaving.' She lifted her chin in pride, or maybe defiance. 'And I was even starting to think that, like, for corporate America, this really wasn't too sucky a job.'

'Nice of you to say. Now you want to tell me what happened?'

'I guess that e-card had some kind of software bug in it, like spyware or something? Dorothy says that's how people got into our

234

server and your personal files and got the codes to your home security system?'

'It was you?'

'I – thought she told you,' Jillian stammered.

'Well, Jillian, I'm sorry, but you picked a bad time to quit, so you can't. Unpack your boxes and get back to answering phones, please.'

She looked at me questioningly.

'Let's go,' I said. 'Back to work.'

As I was headed over to Dorothy's office, she called after me. 'Um, Mr Heller?'

'Yes?'

'I heard you guys talking about that owl tattoo?'

'Yeah?'

'I might be able to help. My brother used to work—'

'In a tattoo parlor,' I said. 'Yes, I remember. You know what would be a really big help?'

She looked at me eagerly.

'How about reading the office phone system manual?'

SIXTY-ONE

The more I thought about Marshall and Belinda Marcus, the more I was sure something wasn't right.

I knew a cyber-investigator in New Jersey named Mo Gandle who was very good – when I was with Stoddard Associates in DC, I had used him on a couple of cases – and I gave him a call.

'I want you to check on the dates of her employment by VIP Exxxecutive Service in Trenton,' I said. 'And I want you to trace her back as far as you can.'

I found Dorothy sitting at her desk, chin resting on the palms of her hands, staring at her computer screen.

On the monitor, Alexa was speaking, her eyes sunken, her hair matted. '*I don't want to be here anymore, Daddy!*'

The image froze, then broke up into thousands of tiny colored squares, like a Chuck Close painting. They scattered and clumped irregularly.

And then as the image redrew, she went on: '*. . . They want Mercury, Daddy, okay? You have to give them Mercury in the raw. I – I don't know what that means. They said—*'

'I unfired Jillian,' I said.

She hit a key without glancing at the keyboard, and the same few seconds of video played again: Alexa speaking, the picture freezing and then breaking up into jagged geometric detritus, and then reforming into a coherent image.

Dorothy murmured distractedly, 'I didn't fire her.'

'Well, I told her she can't quit. What are you doing?'

'Cracking my head against a brick wall, that's what I'm doing.'

'Anything I can do?'

'Yeah. Fire my ass.'

'You too? Nope.'

'Then I quit.'

'You're not allowed to quit either. No one's allowed to quit. Now tell me what's up.'

Dorothy replied quietly and slowly, and I saw she was baring a part of herself she'd never shown before. 'I'm not going to quit, you know that. I never quit. But I'm not earning my salary. I'm not doing what you pay me to do. I'm failing at the most important job anyone's ever given me.'

Tears gleamed in her eyes.

Placing my hand on top of hers, I said, 'Oh, come on. Whatever happened to the good old arrogant Dorothy I know and love?'

'She saw the light.'

'Dorothy,' I said. 'You're frustrated. I get that. But I need you on this full throttle. And I thought you never give up. Remind me what your father says about you?'

'Stubborn as a mule on ice,' she said in a small voice.

'Why "on ice" anyway?'

'How the hell do I know? Nick, do you know how often I think of that girl and what she must be going through? I pray for her, and I keep asking myself who would do something like this to an innocent girl, and I just feel . . . powerless.'

'It's not your job to save her.'

Her eyes shone, fierce and haunted. 'In the Gospel of John it says, "We know that we are children of God and the whole world is under the control of the evil one." I never got that before. Like, what's that supposed to mean? That Satan's in charge of the whole show? But now I'm starting to get it. Maybe there's just . . . evil in the world that even God is powerless to do anything about. And that's the real point.'

'Why do bad things happen to good people?' I said softly. 'I've stopped asking the big questions like that. I just keep my head down and do my job.'

'I'm sorry, Nick. I promised myself never to bring my religion to the office.'

'I never expected you to leave it at home. So tell me what you're stuck on.'

She hesitated only briefly. 'Okay, listen to this.'

She tapped a key, moved the mouse and clicked it, and we were back to that same loop of Alexa speaking. Dorothy raised the volume. Under Alexa's words a hum grew steadily louder. Then the image froze and broke up into tiny bits.

'You hear the noise, right?'

'A car or truck, like we said. So?'

She shook her head. 'Notice the noise is always followed by the picture breaking up? Every single time.'

'Okay.'

'Thing is, a car or a truck or a train, they're not going to interrupt the video transmission like that.'

'So?'

She gave me the Look: she widened her eyes, lowered her brows, and glowered. The Look could turn a lesser being into stone or a pillar of salt. Our old boss, Jay Stoddard, found the Look so unsettling that he refused to deal with her directly unless forced to. Staring back was pointless. It was like a staring contest with the sun. One of you was going to go blind, and it wasn't not likely to be the sun.

'"*So*"?' she said. 'It's going to tell us where Alexa Marcus is.'

SIXTY-TWO

'There is some problem, Officer?'

Dragomir had learned that American policemen liked it when you used the honorific 'Officer'. They craved respect and so rarely got it.

'Well, no big deal, sir. We just like to introduce ourselves, just so's you know who to call in case you ever need any help.'

The young man's ears and cheeks had gone crimson. When he smiled, his gums showed.

'Is good to know.' Exaggerating his bad English was disarming to most people. It made him seem more hapless. Dragomir had made a habit of studying other people as a butterfly collector examines a specimen.

The policeman shifted his weight from foot to foot again. The porch floorboards creaked. He drummed his fingertips against his thighs and said, 'So you, ah, work for the Aldersons?'

Dragomir shook his head, a modest grin. 'Just caretaker. I do work for family. Fix up.'

'Oh, okay, right. So I guess one of your neighbors kinda noticed some construction equipment?'

'Yes?'

'Just want to make sure there's no, um, infractions of the building code? You know, like, if you're building an extension without a permit?'

The youngster projected no authority whatsoever. He was almost apologetic for being here. Not like the police in Russia, who treated everyone like a criminal.

'Just landscape.'

'Is that – you're not doing construction here, or . . . ?'

'No construction,' Dragomir said. 'Owner wants terraced gardens.'

'Mind if I take a quick look out back?'

This was going too far. If Dragomir insisted on a search warrant, the boy would be back in an hour with two other policemen and a court order, and they'd search the house too, just to show they could.

He shrugged, said hospitably, 'Please.'

Officer Kent seemed relieved. 'You know, just so I can tell the chief I did my job, right?'

'We all have to do our jobs.'

He followed the policeman around the back, onto the field of bare earth. The officer seemed to be looking at the tracks in the hard soil, then the gray vent pipe in the middle of the field, and he approached it.

'That a septic tank, um, Andros?'

Dragomir went still. He hadn't told the cop his name. Obviously the neighbor had.

This concerned him.

'Is to vent the soil,' Dragomir said as they stood next to the pipe. 'From the landfill, the . . . compost pile.' An improvisation, the best he could do.

'Like for methane buildup or something?'

Dragomir shrugged. He didn't understand English. He just did what he was told. He was a simple laborer.

'Because you do need a permit if you're putting in a septic tank, you know.'

The cop's cheeks and ears were the color of cold borscht.

Dragomir smiled. 'No septic tank.'

Tiny muffled cries from the vent pipe.

The policeman cocked his head. His ridiculous ears seemed to twitch. 'You hear something?' he said.

Dragomir shook his head slowly. 'No . . .'

The girl's cries had become louder and more distinct.

'HELP GOD HELP SAVE ME PLEASE OH GOD . . .'

'That sounds like it's coming from down there,' the policeman said. 'How weird is that?'

SIXTY-THREE

'I'm listening,' I said.

Dorothy sighed. 'Let's start with the basic question: How are they getting on the Internet, okay? And I don't think it's your standard high-speed connection.'

'Why not?'

She leaned back, folded her arms. 'My parents live in North Carolina, right? So a couple of years ago they decided they wanted to get cable TV so they could watch all those movies. Only there wasn't any cable available, so they had to put one of those satellite dishes on their roof.'

I nodded.

'Once I tried to watch a movie at their house, and the picture kept fuzzing out. Drove me crazy. So I asked them what the problem was, you know, was it always like this, did they call the satellite company to get it fixed, right? And Momma said, oh, that happens a lot, every time a plane flies by overhead. You get used to it. Nothing to do about it. See, they live close to the Charlotte/Douglas airport. Right in the flight path. I mean, the planes are *loud*. And then I began to notice that, yeah, every time I heard a plane overhead the TV would crap out.'

'Okay,' I said. 'If our kidnappers are deep in the woods somewhere, or in some rural area where they don't even *have* high-speed Internet, satellite is probably their only way to get online,' I said. 'And you think a plane can break up the signal?'

'Easy. A bad rainstorm can do it too. Satellite works by line-of-sight, so if something gets between the dish and the big old satellite up there in the sky, the signal's gonna break up. You got a big enough plane, flying low enough, that thing can interrupt the signal. Might only be a fraction of a second, but that'll screw up the video stream.'

'This is good,' I said. 'That noise we're hearing could well come from a jet engine. So let's say they're near an airport. How near, do you think?'

'Hard to calculate. But close enough so when a plane lands or takes off, it's low enough to the ground to block the path to the satellite. So it depends on how big the plane is and how fast it's going and all that.'

'There are a hell of a lot of airports in the US,' I pointed out.

'That right?' she said dryly. 'Hadn't thought about that. But if we can narrow down the search, it gets a whole lot easier.'

'I think we can.'

'You do?'

'New Hampshire.' I explained about George Devlin's cell phone mapping. How we knew that 'Mr X' took Alexa across the Massachusetts border into New Hampshire.

She listened, staring into space. After twenty seconds of silence, she said, 'That helps a lot. I don't know how many airports there are in New Hampshire, but we've just narrowed it down to a manageable number.'

'Maybe we can narrow it down more than that,' I said. 'Does that creepy website CamFriendz stream in real time?'

'They claim to. I'd say yes, within a few seconds. You have to account for slow connections and server lag time and so on. Maybe the times are five seconds off.'

'So we match up those times with the exact flight times in the FAA's flight database.'

'They have such a thing?'

'Of course they do. We're looking for airports in New Hampshire – hell, let's broaden the search, make it Massachusetts and Maine and New Hampshire, just to be safe – with a flight schedule matching the times of our four interruptions.'

She nodded vigorously.

'And we can narrow it down a lot more,' I said. 'Aren't there two separate interruptions during one of those broadcasts?'

'You're right.'

'So we have an exact interval between two flights.'

Her smile widened slowly. 'Not bad, boss.'

I shrugged. 'Your idea.' One of the few things I've learned since going into business for myself: the boss should never take credit for anything. 'Can you hack into the Federal Aviation Administration's secure electronic database?'

'No.'

'Well, the FBI will be able to get it through channels. I'll give Diana a call.'

'Excuse me?'

Jillian Alperin was standing there hesitantly.

'We're in a meeting,' Dorothy said. 'Is there a problem?'

'I forgot to take this out of the printer.' She held up a large glossy color photograph. It was an enlargement of the photograph from Alexa's iPhone of her kidnapper's tattoo.

'Thank you,' Dorothy said, taking it from her.

'I think I know what it is,' Jillian said.

'That's an owl,' I said. 'But thanks anyway.'

Then she held up something else, which she'd been holding in her other hand. A slim white paperback. On the front cover was a black-and-white line drawing of an owl.

It was identical to the owl tattoo in the photo.

'What's that?' I said.

'It's a book of tattoos my brother found?'
She handed me the book. It was titled *Criminal Tattoos of Russia*.
'Dorothy,' I said. 'What time is it in Russia right now?'

SIXTY-FOUR

One of my best sources in Russia was a former KGB major general. Anatoly Vasilenko was a whippet-thin man in his late sixties with an aquiline profile and the demeanor of a Cambridge don. By the time the Soviet Union collapsed, he was already cashing in on his access and connections.

I couldn't say I liked him very much – he was one of the most mercenary men I'd ever met – but he could be affable and charming, and he did have an amazing Rolodex. For the right price he could get you almost any piece of intelligence you wanted.

Tolya always knew who to call, who to bribe, and who to throw a scare into. If a client of mine suspected the local manager of their Muscow plant was embezzling, Tolya could take care of the problem with one quick phone call. He'd have the guy hauled in and interrogated and so terrified he'd be scared to steal a paper clip from his own desk.

I reached him at dinner. From the background noise I could tell he wasn't at home.

'Have I never taken you to Turandot, Nicholas?' he said. 'Hold on, let me move someplace quieter.'

'Twice,' I said. 'Shark-fin soup, I think.'

Turandot was a restaurant a few blocks from the Kremlin, on

Tverskoy Boulevard, which was allegedly the favored dining spot of oligarchs and criminals and high government officials (many of them all three). It was a vast gilded reproduction of a Baroque palace with a Venetian marble courtyard and statues of Roman gods and Aubusson tapestries and an enormous crystal chandelier. Burly security guards gathered out front to smoke and keep a watch over their employers' Bentleys.

When he got back on the phone, the background clamor gone, he said, 'There, that's much better. Nothing worse than a table full of drunken Tatars.' His English was better than that of most Americans. I didn't know where he'd acquired his plummy British accent, unless they taught it at KGB school. 'That's quite a picture you sent.'

'Tell me.'

'That tattoo? It's Sova.'

'Who?'

'Not "who". Sova is – well, *sova* means owl, of course. It's a criminal gang, you might say.'

'Russian mafia?'

'Mafia? No, nothing that organized,' he said. 'Sova is more like a loose confederation of men who've all done time at the same prison.'

'Which one?'

'Prison Number One, in Kopeisk. Quite the nasty place.'

'Do you have a list of all known Sova members?'

'Of all Sova members?' He gave a low chortle. 'If only I had such a list. I would be either very rich or very dead.'

'You must have *some* names.'

'Why is this of interest to you?'

I told him.

Then he said, 'This is not a good situation for you. Or for your client's daughter, more to the point.'

'Why's that?'

'These are very bad people, Nicholas. Hardened criminals of the very worst sort.'

'So I understand.'

'No, I'm not so sure you do. They don't operate by normal rules. They're . . . untroubled, shall we say, by conventional standards of morality.'

'How bad?'

'I think you had a very unpleasant incident in the States not so long ago. Do you remember a brutal home invasion in Connecticut?'

He pronounced the hard C in the middle of 'Connecticut'. A rare slip.

'Not offhand.'

'Oh, dear. Some wealthy bedroom community in Connecticut – Darien, maybe? Truly a nightmare. A doctor and his wife and three daughters were at home one night when a couple of burglars broke in. They beat the doctor with a baseball bat, tied him up, and tossed him down the basement stairs. Then they tied the girls to their beds and proceeded to rape them for seven hours. After which, they poured gasoline on the women and lit them afire—'

'All right,' I said, unable to hear any more. 'These were Sova members?'

'Correct. One of them was killed during an attempted arrest, I seem to recall. The other one escaped.'

'A burglary?'

'Entertainment.'

'Excuse me?' I felt something cold and hard form in my stomach.

'You heard me. Just fun and games. These Sova people will do things a normal person cannot begin to imagine. You couldn't ask for better enforcers.'

'Enforcers?'

'They hire themselves out. If you need outside talent for a really dirty job, something violent and extremely bloody, you might hire a couple of Sova gang members.'

'Who hires them? Russian mafia groups?'

'Usually not. The mafia have some pretty brutal talent of their own.'

'Then who?'

'Certain oligarchs. Our newly minted Russian billionaires. They're often in need of hard men. A few in particular are known to use Sova members.'

'Which ones?'

He laughed. 'Nicholas, we haven't even discussed a fee yet! First things first.'

He told me his fee, and after I stifled the impulse to tell him where to stuff his hard currency, I agreed to his usurious terms.

Then he said, 'Excellent. Let me make some calls.'

SIXTY-FIVE

Dragomir was a fast learner.

This time he used the Wasp knife correctly. The young police officer didn't even have time to turn around before the blade went into his side, lightning-fast, right up to the hilt.

He thumbed the button and heard the hiss and the pop.

Officer Kent sagged to the ground. It looked like he'd suddenly decided to sit right there in the middle of the yard, except that his legs sprawled awkwardly in a way that would be unbearably painful if he were alive.

But he died instantly, or close to it. His internal organs had expanded and frozen at the same time. His abdomen was swollen as if he'd suddenly developed a beer belly.

As Dragomir hoisted the body over his shoulders, he could hear the crackle of Officer Kent's handheld radio.

SIXTY-SIX

Diana and I met at the Sheep's Head Tavern, a sorta-kinda Irish pub in Government Center right next to FBI headquarters. She'd told me she had to grab a quick dinner and then get back up to work. That was fine with me: I had a very long night ahead.

The outside tables were all full, so we sat in a booth inside. I saw a lot of old-looking wood, or new wood made to look old with random gouges and a lot of dark varnish. There were old pub signs on the wall and a carved wooden bar with Celtic lettering on the front and reproductions of old Guinness ads. There were a lot of fancy beers on tap, mostly American microbrews, some German. She was wearing a turquoise silk top and black jeans that somehow managed to emphasize her curves without looking totally unprofessional.

'I'm afraid I don't have anything for you,' she said. 'We didn't turn up anything in the FAA's flight log database.'

'How often is it updated?'

'Constantly. In real time.'

'And it's complete?'

She nodded. 'Private airports as well as public ones.'

'Well, it was a brilliant idea,' I said. 'But not all brilliant ideas work out. Thanks for trying. Now I have something for *you*.'

'Bad news?'

'No. But I don't think you're going to like it.' I handed her Mauricio's mobile phone in a ziplock bag.

'I don't understand,' she said after looking at it for a few seconds. 'What is it?'

I told her.

'You took that from his apartment?'

I nodded.

'Without telling me?'

'I'm sorry. I didn't trust Snyder.'

Her mouth tightened and her nostrils flared.

'It was wrong to withhold it from you,' I said. 'I know that.'

She didn't say anything. She just looked down at the table, face flushed.

'Talk to me,' I said.

Finally she looked up. 'So was it worth it, Nick? You know we can never use that as evidence in court, right? Since you disrupted the chain of custody?'

'I don't think the Bureau is going to be prosecuting a dead guy.'

'I'm talking about whoever's behind this thing. There's a reason we have procedures.'

'You always colored within the lines.'

'I'm a rules girl, Nico. Whereas you were never big on the chain of command, as I recall. You're not an organization man.'

'The last organization I joined sent me to Iraq.'

'We both want the same thing. We just have different ways to get there. But as long as you're working with me and the FBI, you have to respect the rules we play by.'

'I understand.'

She looked at me hard. 'Don't ever do this to me again.'

'I won't.'

'Good. Now, at least tell me you got something useful out of it.'

I nodded. 'His phone number and the only number on his call

log, presumably the guy who hired him to abduct Alexa. One of my sources plotted those numbers along with Alexa's phone number on a map of cell phone towers and was able to chart the route they traveled.'

She shook her head in disbelief. 'How the hell did he get a map of cell phone towers?'

'Don't ask. Bottom line, the path seems to point up north to New Hampshire.'

'Meaning what? The kidnapper came down from New Hampshire?'

'Yes, but more important, it means he's probably got her up there now.'

'Where, specifically?'

'That's all we know – New Hampshire. Somewhere in New Hampshire.'

'Well, that helps, I guess,' Diana said. 'But we're going to need more data points than that. Otherwise it's a lost cause.'

'How about the tattoo?'

She shook her head. 'Nothing came back on that from any of our legats.'

'Well, I've got an excellent source in Moscow who's making some calls for me right now.'

'Moscow?'

'That owl is Russian prison ink.'

'Who's your source on that?'

'Actually, my twenty-four-year-old militant-vegan office manager.'

She gave me a look.

'I'm serious. It's complicated. That owl tattoo identifies members of Sova, a gang of former Russian prison inmates.'

She took out a small notepad and jotted something down. 'If Alexa's kidnapper is Russian, does that mean he's working for Russians?'

'Not for sure. But I'd put money on it. My source in Moscow

says Sova members are often hired by Russian oligarchs to do dirty work when they need plausible deniability. He's helping me narrow down the pool of suspects. Meanwhile, I want to find out what David Schechter's role in all this really is.'

'How's that going to help find Alexa?'

I told her about the exchange I'd overheard between David Schechter and Marshall Marcus.

'You think Schechter is controlling Marcus?' she said.

'Clearly.'

'How?'

'I don't know yet. Maybe his wife's shady past has something to do with it.'

She cocked a brow, and I explained what I'd found out about Belinda Marcus's last profession. 'I have a PI digging into it right now,' I said. 'To see what else he can find. But I don't think that's it. It's too recent and too trivial.'

'Then what's the hold Schechter has over him?'

'That's what I plan to find out.'

'How?'

I told her.

'That's illegal,' she said.

'Then you didn't hear it from me.'

'It doesn't bother you that you'd be committing a crime?'

I shrugged. 'As a great man once said, in certain extreme situations, the law is inadequate. In order to shame its inadequacy, it is necessary to act outside the law.'

'Martin Luther King?'

'Close. The Punisher.'

She looked confused.

'I guess you don't read comic books,' I said.

SIXTY-SEVEN

Dragomir drove out to the main road, relieved to pass only a lumber truck. Not someone from the town who might notice a police squad car coming out of the Alderson property and gossip about it later, maybe ask questions.

He knew where to go. Earlier, he'd driven around the area, scouting escape routes in case it came to that, until he'd discovered a deserted stretch of narrow road that would do well. A place where the road curved sharply on the lip of a ravine.

Of course there was a guardrail. But not on the long straight stretch leading into it, where the plunge was just as steep.

He pulled over at a point where he could see the traffic in both directions. There wasn't any. Then he drove a bit further down the road until he was about twenty feet or so from an edge where there was no guardrail.

Glancing around again, he opened the trunk of the police cruiser, lifted Officer Kent's body out, and quickly carried it around to the open driver's door. There he carefully positioned the body. Then he lifted the black plastic trash bags from the floor of the trunk.

An autopsy wasn't likely. Mostly likely they'd see a police officer killed in a tragic car crash and it would end there. Anyway, by the time any autopsy was done, he'd be long gone. He only cared about what might be found in the next twenty-four hours.

Before he pushed the car into the ravine he put it in drive. If the gear selector were in neutral when the crash was discovered, any skilled investigator would immediately figure out what had really happened.

He didn't make that kind of mistake.

SIXTY-EIGHT

At a few minutes after nine at night, the John Hancock Tower, the tallest building in Boston, was an obsidian monolith. A few lighted windows scattered here and there like a corncob with not many kernels remaining. Some of the building's tenants were open round the clock.

But not the law offices of Batten Schechter, on the forty-eighth floor. No paralegals toiling frantically through the night to meet a filing deadline or a court date. Batten Schechter's attorneys rarely soiled their hands with anything so vulgar as a public trial. This was a sedate, dignified firm that specialized in trusts and estates and the occasional litigation, always resolved in quietly vicious backroom negotiations, perhaps a word whispered in the ear of the right judge or official. It was like growing mushrooms: they preferred to work out of the light of day.

I drove the white Ford panel truck down Trinity Place along the back of the Hancock Tower, and up to the loading dock. A row of five steel pylons blocked my way. I got out, saw the warning signs – DO NOT SOUND HORN FOR ENTRY and PUSH BUTTON & USE INTERCOM FOR ACCESS WHEN DOOR IS CLOSED – and I hit the big black button.

The steel overhead door rolled up, and a little fireplug of a man stood there, looking annoyed at the interruption. It was 9:16 P.M.

257

Stitched in script on his blue shirt, above the name of his company, was CARLOS. He glanced at the logo on the side of the van – DERDERIAN FINE ORIENTAL RUGS – nodded, hit a switch, and the steel columns sank into the pavement. He pointed to a space inside the loading dock where a few other service vehicles were parked.

He insisted on guiding me in as if I couldn't park by myself, waving me in closer and closer to the dock until the van's front end nudged the black rubber bumpers.

'You here for Batten Schechter?' Carlos said.

I nodded, striking a balance between cordial and aloof.

All he knew was that the law firm of Batten Schechter had called the Hancock's property management office and told them that a carpet cleaner would be working in their offices some time after nine o'clock. He didn't need to know that the 'facilities manager' of Batten Schechter was actually Dorothy.

Couldn't have been easier. All I had to do was promise Mr Derderian I'd buy one of his overpriced, though elegant, rugs for my office. In exchange he was happy to lend me one of his vans. None of them were in use at night anyway.

'How's it going there, Carlos?'

He gave the standard Boston answer: 'Doin' good, doin' good.' A Boston accent with a Latin flavor. 'Got a lotta carpets to clean, up there?'

'Just one.'

He grunted.

I pulled open the van's rear doors and wrestled with the big bulky commercial carpet extractor/shampooer. He helped me lower it to the floor, even though it wasn't his job, then pointed a thumb toward a bank of freight elevators.

The elevator was slow to arrive. It had scuffed steel walls and aluminum diamond-tread-plate floors. I hit the button for forty-eight. As it rose, I adjusted Mauricio's STI pistol in my waistband. I'd been storing it in the Defender's glove box ever since I'd grabbed it from his apartment.

I didn't see any security cameras inside the elevator, but I couldn't be sure, so I didn't take it out.

A moment later, the steel doors opened slowly on a small fluorescent-lit service lobby on the forty-eighth floor. Obviously not where the firm's clients or partners entered. I wheeled out the rug shampooer and saw four doors. Each was the service entrance to a different firm, each labeled with a black embossed plastic nameplate.

The one for Batten Schechter had an electronic digital keypad mounted next to it. David Schechter's firm probably had reason to take extra security measures.

From my duffle bag I drew a long flexible metal rod, bent at a ninety-degree angle, a hook at one end. This was a special tool called a Leverlock, sold only to security professionals and government agencies.

I knelt down and pushed the rod underneath the door and twisted it around and up until it caught the lever handle on the inside, then yanked it down. Thirteen seconds later I was in.

So much for the fancy digital keypad.

Now I found myself in some back corridor where the firm stored office supplies and cleaning equipment and such. I pushed the rug shampooer against a wall and made my way by the dim emergency lighting.

It was like going from steerage to a stateroom on the *Queen Mary*. Soft carpeting, mahogany doors with brass nameplates, antique furnishings.

David Schechter, as a name partner, got the corner office. In an alcove before the mahogany double doors to his inner sanctum was a secretary's desk and a small couch with coffee table. The double doors were locked.

Then I saw another digital keypad, mounted unobtrusively by the doorframe at eye level. Strange. It meant that Schechter's office probably wasn't cleaned by the crew that did the rest of the building.

It also meant there was something inside worth protecting.

The odds were, the combination to the digital lock was scrawled on some Post-it pad in his secretary's desk drawer. But faster than looking for it would be to use the Leverlock.

The whole thing felt almost too easy.

From the duffle bag I removed a black carrying case. Inside, a flexible fiberscope lay coiled in the form-fitted foam padding like a metallic snake. A tungsten-braided sheath encased a fiber-optic cable two meters long and less than six millimeters in diameter. Bomb-disposal teams used these in Iraq to look for concealed explosives.

I bent the scope into an angle, screwed on the eyepiece, and attached an external metal-halide light source, then fished it under the door. A lever on the handle allowed me to move the probe around like an elephant's trunk. Now I could see what was on the other side of the door. Angling it upward, I inspected the wall on the far side of the doorframe. Nothing appeared to be mounted there.

When I swiveled the scope over to the other side of the door frame, I saw a red pinpoint light, steady and unblinking.

A motion detector.

A passive infrared sensor. It would detect minute changes in room temperature, caused by the heat given off by a human body. A common device, but not easy to defeat.

A solid red light meant the sensor was armed and ready.

I cursed aloud.

There were ways to get by these things. I tried to recall the tricks I'd heard about, though this wasn't my expertise. Not at all. The best I could do was guess. I considered abandoning the operation.

But I'd come too far to turn back.

SIXTY-NINE

So I gathered a few items from the Batten Schechter offices. The first was easy. Arrayed on the console behind Schechter's assistant's desk was an assortment of pictures. I slid the rectangle of glass out of a framed photograph of a panicked-looking little girl sitting on a shopping-mall Santa's lap.

In a storeroom among the shelves of packing and mailing supplies I found a carton of polystyrene sheets, used to line boxes or protect rolled documents, and a roll of packing tape.

When I returned to Schechter's office, I slid the Leverlock flat against the carpet under the double doors and had them open in ten seconds.

Then came the tricky part.

Holding the polystyrene square in front of me like a shield, I advanced toward the motion sensor, moving slowly through the eerie twilit interior, palely illuminated by the city lights below and the stars above. If I was remembering correctly, the foam would block my heat signature from being detected.

It took an agonizingly long time to reach the wall where the sensor was mounted. I held the sheet of foam a few inches from the sensor's lens. Not too close, though. If I blocked it entirely, that would set it off too.

Like most state-of-the art infrared sensors, this one had a built-in flaw. It was equipped with what's called 'creep zone' coverage: if someone tried to slither on the floor underneath it, its lens would detect it right away.

But it couldn't see above.

From behind the polystyrene scrim I took the small square of glass, taped to my belt, lifted it slowly, then placed it against the sensor's lens. The strip of packing tape kept it securely in place.

Then I let the foam sheet drop to the floor.

The red light remained steady. I hadn't triggered it.

I exhaled slowly.

Glass is opaque to infrared light. The sensor couldn't see through it, yet didn't perceive the glass as an obstruction.

I switched on the overhead lights. Two walls were paneled in mahogany. The other two were glass, nearly floor to ceiling, with breathtaking views of Boston: the Back Bay, the Charles River, Bunker Hill, the harbor. The lights twinkled like a starlit canopy fallen to earth. If this was the view from your office every day, you might start to believe you ruled the land below.

His desk was a small, delicate antique: honeyed mahogany, tooled bottle-green leather top, fluted legs. The only object on it was a phone.

There was a time once when the more powerful an executive was, the bigger his desk. You'd see CEOs with desks big as tramp steamers. But now the more important you were, the smaller and more fragile your work surface. As if to show the world you exerted power by mind control. Paperwork was for peons. There was no computer anywhere in sight. How someone could conduct business these days without a computer baffled me. Clearly it was good to be king.

Priceless-looking antiques were everywhere – spindly Regency chairs, dusky mirrors, parchment waste cans and credenzas and pedestal tables. A finely knotted antique silk rug in pale olive green flecked with muted yellows and reds that Mr Derderian would drool over.

I knew bank CEOs who'd been fired for spending this kind of money on their office décor. They'd forgotten that if you decorated like an eighteenth-century French aristocrat, you were likely to die like one, at the guillotine. The smart CEOs ordered from Office Liquidators.

But David Schechter had no shareholders to answer to. His clients didn't care that their billable hours paid for expensive furniture. A rich lawyer is a successful one.

Then I noticed a second set of mahogany double doors.

They were unlocked. As I pulled them open the overhead lights came on.

Schechter's personal filing cabinets. The ones that held documents too sensitive to be kept in his firm's central files where anyone could access them.

Each steel file cabinet was secured with a Kaba Mas high-security lock. An X-09, electromechanical, developed to meet the US government's most stringent security standards and generally considered unpickable.

The locks were unpickable, but not the cabinets themselves. These were commercial steel four-drawer file cabinets, not GSA-approved Class 6 Security file cabinets. It was like putting a thousand-dollar lockset on a hollow-core door a kid could kick in.

I chose the one marked H–O, hoping to find Marshall Marcus's file. Kneeling, I inserted a metal shim between the bottom drawer and the frame, and sure enough, the locking bar slid up.

Then I pulled open the top drawer and scanned the file tabs. At first they looked like client files, past and present.

But these were no ordinary clients. It was a Who's Who of the Rich and Powerful. There were files here for some of the most influential public officials in the US in the last three or four decades. The names of the men (mostly, and a few women) who ran America. Not all of them were famous. Some – former directors of the NSA and the CIA, secretaries of State and Treasury, certain Supreme Court justices, White House chiefs of staff, senators and congressmen – were dimly remembered if at all.

But it wasn't possible that David Schechter could have represented even a fraction of them. And what kind of legal service could he have provided anyway? So why were these files here?

As I tried to puzzle out the connection among them, one name caught my eye.

MARK WARREN HOOD, LTG, USA.

Lieutenant General Mark Hood. The man who'd run the covert operations unit of the Defense Intelligence Agency I once worked for.

I pulled out the brown file folder. It was an inch thick. For some reason my heart began to thud, as if I had a premonition.

Most of the documents were tawny with age. I rifled through quickly, not sure what these papers were doing here.

Until I noticed one word stamped in blue ink at the top of each page: MERCURY.

So here it was.

And somehow it was connected, through my old boss, to me.

The explanation was here, if only I could make sense of the columns of figures, the cryptic abbreviations or maybe codes. I kept turning the pages, trying to find a phrase or a word that might bring it all into focus.

I stopped at a photograph clipped to a page of card stock. At the top of the card were the words CERTIFICATE OF RELEASE OR DISCHARGE FROM ACTIVE DUTY. A military discharge form, DD-214. The man in the photograph had a buzz cut and was a few pounds lighter than he was now.

It actually took a second before I recognized myself.

The shock was so profound that I didn't hear the tiny scuffling on the carpet behind me until it was too late, and then I felt a hard crack against the side of my head. A sharp, crippling pain shot through my cranium, and in the moment before everything went black I tasted blood.

SEVENTY

When I came to and my eyes were finally able to focus, I found myself in a paneled conference room, seated at one end of an immense coffin-shaped conference table.

My head throbbed painfully, especially my right temple. When I tried to move my hands, I realized my wrists were secured with flex-cuffs to the steel arms of a high-end office chair. The nylon straps cut into the skin. My ankles were bound to the center stem of the chair.

I had a dim memory of being dragged somewhere, trussed upright, cursed at. Hell, maybe waterboarded for good measure. I wondered how long I'd been slumped in this chair.

At the far end of the table, peering at me curiously, was David Schechter. He was wearing a bright yellow V-neck sweater and gave me an owlish look behind his round horn-rimmed glasses. I half expected him to start speaking in the voice of Dr Evil, pinkie extended, demanding *one million dollars* for my release.

But I spoke first. 'I suppose you're wondering why I've called you here today.'

Schechter gave what was apparently his rendition of a smile. The corners of his nearly lipless mouth turned down into a perfect inverted arch, like a frog's, tugged downward by dozens of vertical wrinkles. It looked like smiling was hard work for him and something he rarely practiced.

'Did you know,' he said, 'that breaking and entering at night with intent to commit felony can land you in prison for twenty years?'

'I knew I should have gone to law school.'

'And that doing so with an unregistered dangerous weapon can get you life behind bars? There's not a judge in the Commonwealth of Massachusetts who wouldn't give you at least ten years. Oh, and there's the matter of your private investigator's license. That's as good as revoked.'

'I assume the police are on the way.'

'I see no reason why we can't settle this man to man without the police.'

I couldn't help but smile. He wasn't going to call the police. 'I find it hard to think clearly when I'm losing circulation in my lower extremities.'

A slight motion in my peripheral vision. Skulking on either side of me were a couple of wide-bodied thugs. Security guards, probably. Or bodyguards. Each held a Glock at his side. One of them was blond with no neck and a vacant face with a steroid-ravaged complexion.

The other one I recognized.

He had a black crew cut and a muscle-bound physique even more extreme than the blond guy's. It was one of the two men who'd broken into my loft. Over his left eye just below the brow was a thin white bandage. A much bigger one was plastered next to his left ear. I remembered throwing an electric shaver into his face and drawing blood.

Schechter looked at me for a few seconds, blinked slowly like an old iguana, and nodded. 'Cut the man free.'

Mongo threw his employer a look of protest but fished a yellow-handled strap cutter from a pocket of his ambush jacket. He approached me cautiously like he was a bomb disposal expert, I was an armed nuclear weapon, and he was about ten seconds too late.

Silently, sullenly, he jabbed his cutters at the nylon loop that held my wrist to the chair's right arm, while his moon-faced colleague fixed me with a beady vacant stare, his pistol leveled.

As Mongo worked, he leaned close and muttered under his breath, through clenched teeth, 'How's George Devlin doing?'

I stayed very still.

He took his time. He was enjoying the chance to taunt me. Almost inaudibly, he went on, 'I caught a glimpse of Scarface on one of our surveillance cams. Broke the lens.'

He gave me a furtive smile, met my cold stare.

'Gotta be tough looking like a monster.' He snipped the other loop, freeing my hands from the arms of the chair but still leaving them cuffed together. 'One day every girl you meet wants to get into your pants, next day you couldn't *pay* a skank to get near y—'

With one quick upward thrust I slammed my fists under his chin, shutting his jaw so violently I could hear his molars crack. Then, as he reeled, I smashed down on the bridge of his nose. There wasn't much room to maneuver, but I put a lot of force into it.

Something snapped loudly. The gout of blood from his nostrils indicated I'd probably broken his nose. He roared in pain and rage.

Schechter rose from his chair and said something quick and sharp to the other guard, who racked the slide on his pistol to chamber a round. Bad form. His weapon should have been loaded already.

'Heller, for God's sake,' Schechter said, exasperated.

Mongo reared back and took a wild swing at me, which I easily dodged. When Schechter shouted, 'That's enough, Garrett,' he stopped short like a well-trained Doberman.

'Now, please finish cutting him loose,' Schechter said. 'And keep your mouth shut while you're doing it.'

Garrett, or Mongo, as I preferred to think of him, snipped the remaining cuffs, his eyes boring holes into mine. Twin rivulets of blood trickled down the lower half of his face. When he was done, he wiped the blood off with his sleeve.

'Much better,' I said to Schechter. 'Now, if we're going to have a candid conversation, please tell these two amateur muscleheads to leave.'

Schechter nodded. 'Semashko, Garrett, please.'

The guards looked at him.

'You can stand right outside. There won't be a problem, I'm sure. Mr Heller and I need to speak privately.'

On his way out, Mongo brandished his pistol at me threateningly as he once again wiped his bloody nose with his sleeve.

When the door closed, Schechter said, 'Now, was there something you wanted to find out?'

'Yes,' I said. 'Does Marshall Marcus know you arranged the kidnapping of his daughter?'

SEVENTY-ONE

He expelled a puff of air, a scoff. 'Nothing could be further from the truth.'

'Given your association with both Marcus and Senator Armstrong – the father of the kidnapped girl and the father of a girl who assisted in that kidnapping – don't try to pretend it's a coincidence.'

'Did it ever occur to you that we're all on the same side?'

'When you ordered me to stay away from the senator and his daughter, and when you announced that my services were no longer needed, it kinda made me wonder. Me, I'm on the side that wants to get Alexa Marcus released.'

'And you think I don't?'

I shrugged.

'Look at it statistically,' he said. 'What are the odds, truly, of Alexa coming home alive? She's as good as dead, and I think Marshall already understands this.'

'I'd say you tilted the odds against her considerably by refusing to let Marcus hand over the Mercury files.'

Schechter went silent.

'Are they really worth two lives?' I said.

'You have no idea.'

'Why don't you enlighten me.'

'They are worth far, far more. They are worth the lives of the one million Americans who have died defending our country. But I think you already know that. Isn't that why you had to leave the Defense Department?'

'I left because of a disagreement.'

'A disagreement with General Hood, your boss.'

I nodded.

'Because you refused to call a halt to an investigation that you were explicitly ordered to drop. An investigation that would have warned off certain parties who were unaware they were targets of the greatest corruption probe in history.'

'Is that right,' I said sardonically. 'Funny no one said anything about that back then.'

'No one could. Not then. But now we have to trust your discretion and your judgment and your patriotism. And I know we can.'

'You know nothing about me,' I said.

'I know plenty about you. I know all about your remarkable record of service to this country. Not just on the battlefield, but the clandestine work you did for DOD. General Hood says you were probably the brightest, and certainly the most fearless, operative he ever had the good fortune to work with.'

'I'm flattered,' I said sourly. 'And what got you so interested in my military record?'

He folded his arms, leaned forward, and said heatedly, 'Because if *you* had been in charge of Marshall's security, this would never have happened.'

'There's no guarantee of that.'

'You know damned well I'm right. You are an extraordinary talent. Yes, of course I have your file. Yes, of course I've checked you out.'

'For what?' I said.

He paused for ten, fifteen seconds. 'I'm sure you know about that "missing" two-point-six *trillion* dollars that an auditor discovered at the Pentagon a few years ago?'

I nodded. I remembered reading about it, then kicking it around with some friends. The story didn't get the kind of play in the so-called mainstream media you'd have expected. Maybe Americans had gotten blasé about corruption, but it's not like we're Somalia. Maybe such a sum of money was just too big to conceive of, like the weight of planet Earth.

'That's what happens when you have a government agency with a budget of three-quarters of a trillion dollars and barely any internal controls,' he said.

'The money was never found, right?'

He shrugged. 'Not my concern, and not my point. I'm just saying that the Pentagon is a black hole. Everyone inside the intelligence community knows that.'

'How would you know? You're not on the inside.'

He tipped his head to one side. 'It's all in how you define the term. A half century of CIA proprietaries might argue with you.'

'What, so Batten Schechter is a CIA front?'

He shook his head. 'CIA? Please. Have you seen how far down they are on the org chart these days? Somewhere just below the Bureau of Labor Statistics. The CIA used to run the intelligence community. Now they report to the director of national intelligence, and the knee bone's connected to the thigh bone—'

'All right, then what the hell are you?'

'A middleman, nothing more. A conduit. Just a lawyer who's helping make sure that no one "misplaces" three trillion dollars again.'

'Could you possibly be any more vague?'

'Let me get a bit more specific. Who paid your salary when you worked for the DOD in Washington?'

'Black budget,' I said. That was the top-secret funding, buried in the US government budget, for clandestine operations and classified research and weapons research, and so on. All the stuff that officially doesn't exist. It's so well hidden in the tangled mess of a budget that no one's ever sure how much there is or what it's paying for.

'Bingo.'

' "Mercury" refers to US black-budget funding?'

'Close enough for government work, as they say. Any idea how big the black budget is?'

'Sixty billion dollars or so.'

He snorted. 'Sure. If you believe what you read in the *Washington Post*. Let's just say that's the figure that's leaked for public consumption.'

'So you're . . .' and I stopped.

Suddenly it all seemed clear. 'You're telling me that Marshall Marcus has been investing and managing the *black budget of the United States*? Sorry, I don't buy it.'

'Not all of it, by any means. But a good healthy chunk.'

'How much are we talking?'

'It's not important how much. Quite a few years ago some very wise men took a look at the ebbs and flows of defense spending and realized that we were putting our national security at the mercy of public whims and political fads. One year it's "kill all the terrorists", the next it's "why are we violating civil liberties?" We lurch from Cold War to "peace dividend". Look at how the CIA was gutted in the 1990s – by both Republican and Democratic presidents. Then 9/11 happens, and everyone's outraged – Where was the CIA? How could this have happened? Well, you *eviscerated* the CIA, folks, that's what happened.'

'And . . . ?'

'So the decision was reached at a very high level to set aside funds from the fat years to take care of the lean years.'

'And give it to Marshall Marcus to invest.'

He nodded. 'A few hundred million here, a billion or two there, and pretty soon Marshall had *quadrupled* our covert funds.'

'Brilliant,' I said. 'And now it's all gone. Talk about a black hole. Doesn't sound like you did a whole lot better than the green eyeshades at the Pentagon.'

'Fair enough. But no one expected Marshall to be targeted the way he was.'

'So Alexa's kidnappers aren't after money at all, are they? "Mercury in the raw" – that refers to the investment records?'

'Let's be clear. They want some of our most sensitive operational secrets. This is a direct assault on American national security protocols. And frankly it wouldn't surprise me if Putin's people have a hand in this.'

'So you think it's the Russians?'

'Absolutely.'

That would explain why the kidnapper was Russian. Tolya had said members of the Sova gang were often hired by Russian oligarchs. But now I wondered whether the Russian *government* might instead be behind it all.

'You're given access to security-classified information above top secret?'

'Look, it's no longer possible for the Pentagon to sluice money directly into false-front entities like they used to. You know all those anti-money-laundering laws aimed at global terror – they just give far too many bureaucrats in too many countries around the world the ability to do track-backs. Private funding has to originate in the private sector or else it's going to be unearthed by some corporate auditor running the financials.'

'I get that. So what?'

'If the wrong people got hold of the transfer codes, they'd be able to identify all sorts of cutaways and shell companies – and figure out who's doing what for us where. To hand all that over would be nothing less than a body blow to our national security. I can't allow it. And if Marshall were in his right mind, he wouldn't either.'

'I wouldn't be so sure of that.'

'Believe me,' Schechter said, 'nothing would make me happier than if you could find Alexa Marcus and somehow free her. But that's just about impossible now, from everything I'm told. We don't have the names of her captors. We don't have the slightest idea where she is.'

I didn't correct him. 'Are we done here?'

'Not quite. You've seen some highly classified files, and I want your assurance that it goes no further. Do we have an under-standing?'

'I really don't care what's in your files. My only interest is in finding Marshall Marcus's daughter. And as long as you stay out of my way, then yes, we have an understanding.'

My head began thudding again as I got to my feet. I turned and walked out the door. His goons attempted to block my way, but I pushed past them. They scowled at me menacingly. I smiled back.

'Nick,' Schechter called out.

I stopped. 'Yes?'

'I know you'll do the right thing.'

'Oh,' I said, 'you can count on it.'

SEVENTY-TWO

It was almost ten thirty by the time I returned to Mr Derderian's van. I powered on my BlackBerry and it began to load up e-mails and emitted a voice-mail-alert sound.

One of the calls was from Mo Gandle, the PI in New Jersey looking into Belinda Marcus's past.

I listened to his message with astonishment. Her employment as a call girl was by far the least interesting part of her history.

I was about to call him back when I noticed that four of the calls I'd received were from Moscow. I checked my watch. It was twenty minutes past six in the morning, Moscow time. Far too early to call. He would certainly be asleep.

So I called and woke him up.

'I've been leaving messages for you,' he said.

'I was temporarily offline,' I said. 'Do you have names for me?'

'Yes, Nicholas, I do. I didn't think it prudent to leave this information on your voice mail.'

'Let me pull over and get something to write with.'

'Surely you can remember one name.'

'Let's hear it,' I said.

Then he told me.

* * *

It was too late to catch a shuttle flight from Boston to New York's LaGuardia Airport.

But there was always a way. An old friend flew cargo planes for FedEx. He was based out of Memphis, but he got me on the eleven o'clock run from Boston to New York. In a little over an hour I was walking into an 'adult entertainment club' called Gentry on West Forty-fifth street in Manhattan.

This was what used to be known as a strip club. Or a jiggle joint. But in polite circles it was called a 'gentleman's club' until that term became politically incorrect too.

I guess the tittie-bar owners didn't want to offend feminists.

The mirrored lobby was lined with the requisite bouncers from New Jersey in black blazers too short at the sleeves over black shirts with white pinstripes. The carpeting inside was garish red. The railings and banisters were so shiny they didn't even try to look like brass. The music was bad and loud. There were swoopy red vinyl lounge chairs, red vinyl banquettes and booths, half of them empty. The other half were filled with conventioneers and mid-level executives entertaining clients. Bachelor parties from Connecticut. Japanese businessmen on expense accounts. Spotlights swiveled and disco strobe lights spun overhead and there were mirrors everywhere.

The girls – excuse me, 'entertainers' – were pretty and stacked and spray-tanned. Most of them looked cosmetically enhanced. When they danced, nothing jiggled. There was enough silicone in the place to grout every hotel bathroom in Manhattan. They wore thongs and garters, skimpy black brassieres and heels so high I was amazed they could keep their balance without pitching forward head first.

On the main stage, a shallow half-moon with a brass railing, an embarrassed-looking young guy with bad skin was getting a 'stage dance' in the bright spotlights with a slinky black woman doing acrobatic moves an Ashtanga yoga master wouldn't attempt.

A collage of huge 'art' photos of selected female body parts lined the stairs. I found the 'VIP Room', according to the red neon sign on the door, upstairs just past the cigar bar and a line of private 'rooms' with red velvet curtains that served as walls. A generously proportioned woman with pasties on her nipples held the door open for me.

Here the music was more traditional. Justin Timberlake was singing about bringing sexy back, which segued into Katy Perry confessing she'd kissed a girl and liked it. The walls were lined with white drapes illuminated from below with purple spotlights. A slightly higher class of clientele sat here, in tan suede clamshell banquettes that faced the stage. More scantily clad fembots tottered around with trays of drinks. A Brazilian-looking beauty was giving a lap dance to a corpulent Middle Eastern businessman.

The guy I was looking for was sitting at a banquette with burly bodyguards on either side of him. Each wore a cheap black leather jacket and was as big as a linebacker. One had a crew cut; the other had black Julius Caesar bangs. You could tell they were Russian a mile away.

The boy was tall and skinny, with a pasty complexion and a patchy goatee. He wore a foppish black velvet jacket with skinny, beaded lapels that would have looked fruity on Liberace. Under it he wore a black shirt with a tiny collar and a skinny black tie. He was drinking a glass of brown liquid and holding court for five or six equally scruffy-looking guys his age who were doing shots and ogling the entertainers and laughing too loudly and generally acting obnoxious.

Arkady Navrozov looked fourteen, though he was almost twenty. Even if you didn't know that his father, Roman Navrozov, was obscenely rich, you could tell by the kid's entitled demeanor.

Roman Navrozov was said to be worth over twenty-five billion dollars. He was an exile from Russia, where he'd amassed a fortune as one of the newly minted oligarchs under Boris Yeltsin by seizing control of a few state-owned oil and gas companies and then taking them private. When Vladimir Putin took over, he threw Navrozov in jail on grounds of corruption.

He served five years in the notorious prison Kopeisk.

But he must have struck a deal with Putin, because he was quietly released from prison and went into exile, much of his fortune still intact. He had homes in Moscow, London, New York, Paris, Monaco, St Bart's . . . he'd probably lost track himself. He owned a football club in west London. His yacht, the biggest and most expensive in the world, was usually docked off the French Riviera. It was equipped with a French-made missile defense system.

Because Roman Navrozov lived in fear. He'd survived two publicly reported assassination attempts and probably countless others, thanks to his private army of some fifty bodyguards. He'd made the mistake of speaking out against the government and apparently they didn't like it.

His only son, Arkady, had been thrown out of Switzerland the year before for raping a sixteen-year-old Latvian chambermaid at the Beau-Rivage Palace in Lausanne. His father had spread around quite a bit of money to make the charges go away.

He feared his son might be kidnapped and made sure that Arkady never went anywhere without his own matched set of bodyguards.

But Arkady was a modern kid, and he posted things on Facebook and some social-media site called Foursquare where apparently you tell all your friends your whereabouts every moment of the day.

Earlier in the day he'd posted:

> Arkady N. in New York, NY:
> wrote a tip @ Gentry: Rocking VIP Rm tonight!

When he arrived, he posted:

> Arkady N. @ Gentry
> w. 45th St.

Not long afterward, I arrived at Gentry too, only I wasn't rocking it and I didn't post it anywhere.

I don't like people to know where I'm going before I get there. It spoils the surprise.

My table was across the room but within view. I glanced at my watch.

Exactly on time the best-looking woman in the room sidled up to Arkady. His bodyguards shifted in their seats but didn't consider Cristal to be a mortal threat. She whispered something in the kid's ear and slithered onto his lap. One hand stroked his crotch.

His friends sniggered. He got up bashfully and followed her through the purple-lighted drapes to one of the private areas on the other side.

Arkady's bodyguards hustled over, but he waved them away.

As I'd expected.

Before they returned to the banquette I was gone.

The curtained-off private-dance area where Cristal had led Arkady looked like a fake Victorian boudoir in a Nevada brothel. It had red velvet tufted walls, a shaggy red carpet, and a large red velvet bed with gold fringe. The lights were low.

From behind the red curtains I could see the two of them enter.

'—to make yourself nice and comfortable while I fetch us some champagne, all righty? You like Dom?'

She settled him down on the bed and put her tongue in his ear and whispered, 'I'll be back in two shakes.'

'Hey, where the hell you going?' the kid said. He had a flat, over-Americanized Russian accent.

'Honey, when I get back I'm gonna take the top of your head off,' she said, slipping out through the curtains. Then I handed her a wad of bills, the second half of what I'd promised her.

Arkady smiled contentedly, stretched like a cat, and called after her, 'That a promise?'

He didn't notice me sidling up to the bed from the other side. I lunged, quick as a cobra, clapped a hand over his mouth and jammed my revolver against the side of his head. I cocked the trigger.

'You ever see the top of a man's head come off, Arkady?' I whispered. 'I have. You never forget it.'

SEVENTY-THREE

Roman Navrozov owned the penthouse condominium in the Mandarin Oriental, with one of the great views of the city. He had been spending a lot of time in the city recently. He was trying to buy the New York Mets, whose owner had been hit pretty hard by the Bernard Madoff fraud.

He felt safe in the Mandarin, according to my KGB friend Tolya. There were multiple layers of protection and several entrances and egresses. The vigilant staff were only his first line of defense.

I was met in the lobby of the Residences by a slim, elegant, silver-haired man of around sixty. He wore an expensive navy pinstriped suit with a gold pocket square, perfectly folded.

He introduced himself as Eugene, no last name: an 'associate' of Mr Navrozov.

He reminded me of an English butler. Even though it was after midnight, and he knew I had just kidnapped his boss's son, his demeanor was cordial. He knew I was here to transact business.

As he led me toward Navrozov's private elevator, I said, 'I'm afraid there's been a slight change in plans.'

He turned around, arched his brows.

'We won't be meeting in his condo. I've reserved a room in the hotel, a few floors below.'

'I'm quite sure Mr Navrozov will not agree to that . . .'

'If he ever wants to see his son again, he might want to be flexible,' I said. 'But it's up to him.'

SEVENTY-FOUR

Fifteen minutes later, the elevator on the thirty-eighth floor opened, and five men emerged.

Roman Navrozov and his small army of bodyguards moved with a military precision: one in front, one behind, and two on either side. These bodyguards seemed to be of a higher caliber than the cretiris he assigned to his son. They wore good suits and curly earpieces like Secret Service agents wear. They were all armed and appeared to be wearing body armor. Their eyes briskly surveyed all angles of approach as they escorted their boss down the hallway.

Roman Navrozov was a portly man, not tall, but he exuded authority. He could have been a Vatican cardinal emerging on the balcony of St Peter's Basilica to proclaim, '*Habemus papam.*' He had hawkish eyebrows and an unnaturally black fringe of hair around a great bald dome. He reminded me a little of the actor who played Hercule Poirot on the British TV series.

His thin lips were cruelly pursed in a regal glower. He wore a black blazer with one tail of his crisp white shirt untucked, as if he'd just thrown it on and was annoyed to be skulking around the halls of the hotel in the middle of the night.

When they were halfway down the corridor, the lead guard made a quick hand gesture, and Navrozov stopped, flanked by the rest of his entourage. Meanwhile, the first guard approached the door, weapon out.

He saw at once that the door was ajar, propped open on the latch of the security lock.

He flicked his hand again, and a second guard joined him, then the two moved swiftly into position on either side of the door. The first one kicked the door open, and they burst in, weapons drawn, in classic 'slicing the pie' formation.

Maybe they were expecting an ambush. But since I was watching through the peephole in the room across the hall, they didn't find anyone inside.

Then I hit a number on my phone. 'Moving into position one,' I said when it was picked up.

'Roger that,' a voice replied.

The voice belonged to a member of my Special Forces detachment named Darryl Amos. While I was in flight, Darryl had driven into the city from Fort Dix, New Jersey, where he worked as a convoy operations instructor. He'd checked into a true fleabag on West Forty-third called the Hotel Conroy. If you look it up on one of the travel websites, you'll find it described as the filthiest hotel in the city. Not long ago a maid had discovered a body under a bed wrapped in a bedsheet. The sheet was reused, though they did launder it first.

Then he waited for me, and Arkady Navrozov, in the alley behind the strip club.

Right now Darryl was babysitting Roman Navrozov's son at the Hotel Conroy. I was fairly certain the oligarch's son had never seen its likes before.

Satisfied that Navrozov's men were simply doing their job – making sure their boss didn't walk into a trap and not attempting anything more – I opened the door and crossed the hall.

SEVENTY-FIVE

A minute later I was standing at the window a few feet away from the man who had masterminded Alexa Marcus's kidnapping.

We were alone in the room. He sat in a chair, legs crossed, looking imperious. 'You're a very trusting man,' he said.

'Because I'm unarmed?'

We both were. He rarely carried a weapon, and I'd surrendered mine. His guards were stationed in the hall right outside the door, which had been left propped open, by mutual agreement. I was sure they were prepared to burst in if their boss so much as coughed.

He replied without even looking at me. 'You say you have my son. Maybe you do, maybe you don't. In any case, now we have you.' He shrugged. Very matter-of-fact; very casual. 'Now we have all the leverage we need.' He grinned. 'So you see: you haven't played this very well.'

'You see that building?' I said.

Directly across the street, looming like a great gleaming black monolith, was the Trump International Hotel and Tower.

'A fine hotel, the Trump Tower,' Navrozov said. 'I wanted to invest in Mr Trump's SoHo project, but your government blocked me.'

'See that row of rooms right there?'

I pointed again, this time to a line of dark windows. Offices, not hotel rooms, though he probably didn't know that.

Then I raised my hand, as if to wave, and a single window in the long dark row lit up.

'Hello,' I said. 'We're right here.'

I raised my hand again, and the window across the street went dark.

'My friend over there is a world-class sniper,' I said.

Navrozov shifted his body to one side, away from what he probably thought was the line of fire.

'An army buddy?'

'Actually, no. He's from Newfoundland. Did you know some of the best sharpshooters in the world are Canadian?'

'Perhaps, but at this distance—'

'My Canadian friend holds the record for the longest confirmed combat sniper-shot kill. He hit a Taliban fighter in Afghanistan from two and a half kilometers away. Now, do you think we're even one kilometer away from the Trump Tower?'

He smiled uncomfortably.

'Try four hundred feet. You might as well have a bull's-eye painted on your forehead. To my Canadian friend, you're such a big fat easy target it's not even fun.'

His smile faded.

'He's using an American Tac-50 sniper rifle made in Phoenix. And fifty-caliber rounds made in Nebraska. It's a hot round – ultra-low-drag tip and a flat trajectory.'

'Your point?' he snapped.

'The second any of your men approaches me, my friend across the street will drop you without a second's hesitation. And did you know that this room connects with the two on either side? Yep. The doors between them are unlocked. The hotel management really couldn't have been more accommodating to a group of old college buddies in town for a reunion.'

He just stared. His eyelids drooped.

'So am I trusting?' I said. 'Not so much.'

To my surprise, Navrozov laughed. 'Well done, Mr Heller.'

'Thank you.'

'Have you ever read O. Henry?'

'It's been a while.'

'O. Henry was very popular in the Soviet Union when I was a child. My favorite was his story "The Ransom of Red Chief".'

'And I thought we were here to discuss your son.'

'We are. In O. Henry's story, a rich man's son is kidnapped and held for ransom. But the boy is such a little terror that the kidnappers, who can't stand him, keep dropping their ransom price. Until finally the father offers to take him off their hands if they pay *him*.'

'Maybe you'd like to tell your son you don't care what happens to him.' I turned to the laptop I'd set up on the desk and tapped at the keys to open a video chat window.

'Here's Red Chief,' I said.

On the laptop screen was a live video feed of Arkady Navrozov, hair matted, against a grimy white plaster wall, a wide strip of duct tape over his mouth.

He wasn't wearing his black velvet jacket anymore.

Instead, Darryl had put him in a medical restraint garment borrowed from the hospital at Fort Dix, used to immobilize and transport violent prisoners. It was an off-white cotton duck Posey straitjacket, with long sleeves that crossed in front and buckled in the back.

The Posey wasn't strictly necessary – Darryl probably could have duct-taped him to the chair – but it was an effective restraint. More important, it had its effect on Roman Navrozov. In the bad old days, Soviet 'psychiatric prison hospitals' used them on political dissidents.

I knew the sight would strike fear into Navrozov's granite heart.

His son was cowering. You could see the corner of a bed next to him, its coverlet a hideous shade of orange.

Then you could see the barrel of a gun, with a long sound suppressor screwed onto the end, move into the frame and touch the side of the guy's head. His eyes started moving wildly. He was trying to shout, but nothing was coming out except high, screeching, muffled sounds.

His father glanced at the screen, then away, as if someone tiresome were trying to show him an unfunny YouTube clip.

He sighed. 'What do you want?' he said.

SEVENTY-SIX

'Simple,' I said. 'I want Alexa Marcus released immediately.'

Navrozov breathed softly in and out a few times. His eyes had gone hard.

A few minutes ago he'd regarded me with something approaching admiration. Now he recognized me as a threat. I could see the predator instinct come out. He looked at me the way a wolf stalks his prey by staring it down, his body rigid.

'Is this a name I should recognize?'

I sighed, disappointed. 'Neither one of us has time for games.'

He smiled mirthlessly, a flash of long sharp teeth.

'Where is she?' I said. 'I want exact coordinates.'

'When I hire a man to do a job, I don't look over his shoulder.'

'Somehow I doubt that. Guy like you, I bet you know exactly where she is and what they're doing to her.'

'They don't know who I am, and I don't know who they are. Much safer this way.'

'Then how do you communicate with them.'

'Through an intermediary. A cutout, I think is the term, yes?'

'But you have some idea where they are.'

A shrug. 'I think New Hampshire. This is all I know.'

'And where is your cutout located? Don't tell me you don't know that.'

'In Maine.'

'And how do you reach him?'

He replied by pulling out his mobile phone. Wagged it at me. Put it back in his pocket.

'Call him, please,' I said, 'and tell him the operation is over.'

His nostrils flared and his mouth tightened. It rankled him, I could see, to be spoken to that way. He wasn't used to it.

'It's far too late for that,' he said.

'Tell your men to close the door,' I said. 'Tell them you want privacy.'

He blinked, didn't move.

'*Now*,' I said.

Maybe he saw something in my eyes. Whatever the reason, he gave me a dour glance and rose from the chair. He walked to the door, spoke in Russian, quickly and quietly. Then, pulling the security latch back, he let the door shut and returned to his chair.

'Cancel the operation,' I said.

He smiled. 'You are wasting my time,' he said.

Now I tapped a few keys on the laptop, and the video image began to move. Then, hitting another key to turn on the computer's built-in microphone, I said, 'Shoot him.'

Navrozov looked at me, blinked. A slight furrow of the brow, a tentative smile.

He didn't believe me.

On the laptop screen there was sudden movement. A scuffle.

The camera jerked as if someone had bumped against the laptop on the other end. Now you could see only half of the kid's body, his shoulder and arm in the white duck fabric of his Posey straitjacket.

And the black cylinder of the sound suppressor screwed onto the end of Darryl's Heckler & Koch .45.

Navrozov was staring now. 'You don't think I will possibly believe—'

Darryl's hand gripped the pistol. His forefinger slipped into the trigger guard.

Navrozov's eyes widened, raptly watching the image on the screen.

Darryl's finger squeezed the trigger.

The loud pop of a silenced round. A slight muzzle flash as the pistol recoiled.

Navrozov made a strange, strangled shout.

His son's scream was muted by the duct tape. His right arm jerked and a hole opened in his upper arm, a spray of blood, a blotch of red on the white canvas.

Arkady Navrozov's arm twisted back and forth, his agony apparent, the chair rocking, and then I clicked off the feed.

'*Svoloch!*' Navrozov thundered, his fist slamming the desk. '*Proklyaty sukin syn!*'

A pounding at the door. His guards.

'Tell them to stand down,' I said, 'if you'd like to discuss how to save your son's life.'

Enraged, face purpling, he staggered out of his chair and over to the door and gasped, '*Vsyo v poryadke.*'

He came back, stood with folded arms. Just stared at me.

'All right,' I said. 'Call your cutout and tell him the operation is over.'

He stared for a few seconds. Then he took out his mobile phone, punched a single button, and put it to his ear.

After a few seconds, he spoke in Russian, quickly and softly.

'*Izmeneniya v planakh.*' He paused, and then: '*Nyet, ya ochen' seryozno. Seichas. Osvobodit' dyevushku. Da, konyeshno, svyazat' vsye kontsy.*'

He punched another button to end the call.

He lowered the phone to his side, then sank down in the chair. The power and menace seemed to have seeped out of the man, leaving a mere Madame Tussaud waxwork: a lifelike model of a once terrifying figure.

In a monotone, he said, 'It is done.'

'And how long after he makes the call before Alexa is free?'

'He must do this in person.'

'You haven't heard of encrypted phones?'

'There are loose ends to tie up. This can only be done in person.'

'You mean, he's going to eliminate the contractor.'

'Operational security,' Navrozov said.

'But he has to drive from Maine?'

He glowered at me. 'It will take thirty minutes, no more. So. We are done here.'

'Not until I speak to Alexa.'

'This will take time.'

'I'm sure.'

'My son needs immediate medical treatment.'

'The sooner she's free, the sooner your son will be treated.'

He exhaled, his nostrils flaring like a bull's. 'Fine. We have concluded our business here. Marcus will get his daughter, and I will get my son.'

'Actually, no.'

'No . . . what?'

'No, we're not done here.'

'Oh?'

'We have more to talk about.'

He squinted at me.

'Just a few questions about Anya Afanasyeva.'

He drew breath. I knew then I had him.

'Where did she pick up such a lousy Georgia accent?'

SEVENTY-SEVEN

Roman Navrozov took from his breast pocket a slim black box with a gold eagle on the front. Sobranie Black Russians. He carefully withdrew a black cigarette with a gold filter and put it in his mouth.

'This is a no-smoking room, yes?'

I nodded.

He pulled a box of matches from his front jacket pocket. He took out a match and lit it with his thumbnail. He put the match to the end of the cigarette and inhaled. Then he let out a long, luxuriant plume of smoke between his rounded lips.

Navrozov didn't just smoke Russian cigarettes; he smoked like a Russian too. Russians, especially older Russians, hold cigarettes the way Westerners hold a joint: between the thumb and forefinger. Habits like that never go away.

'Anya Ivanovna really was not a bad actress at all,' he said. 'But she was not, shall we say, Meryl Streep. Clearly she needed to do more research into the State of Georgia.'

I had no reason to think that Marshall Marcus was lying about how he met the woman who called herself Belinda Jackson. He was the victim, after all. And when he'd met her at the Ritz-Carlton bar in Atlanta, he must have known she was an escort. A horny old goat like Marcus could tell, the way a spaniel can smell game.

He just didn't know that she was no longer employed in that capacity by VIP Exxxecutive Service.

She was employed by Roman Navrozov.

My cyber-investigator had checked on the dates of her employment by the escort service and confirmed my gut instinct. Then, as he traced her background, he was able to dig much deeper than Dorothy ever could, since he had access to certain archives and records in New Jersey that she didn't.

The woman who changed her name to Belinda Jackson, who'd dropped out of the School for the Performing Arts in Lincoln Park, New Jersey, had in fact enrolled under her real name. The name on her birth certificate: Anya Ivanovna Afanasyeva. She'd grown up in a Russian enclave in Woodbine, New Jersey, the daughter of Russian émigrés. Her father had been an engineer in the Soviet Union but could only get some low-level desk job at an insurance company here.

That was about the sum total of the facts I knew. Everything else was informed guesswork. I imagined that Anya sought work as a call girl only when she couldn't get work as an actress. Or maybe out of some sort of rebellion against her old-fashioned émigré parents.

'I assume you provided Anya with a complete dossier on Marshall Marcus,' I said. 'His likes and dislikes, his tastes in movies and music. Maybe even his sexual peccadilloes.'

Navrozov burst out laughing. 'Do you really think an attractive and sexually talented woman like Anya needs a dossier to capture the heart of such a foolish old man? It takes very little. Most men have very simple needs. And Anya more than met those needs.'

'Your needs were simple too,' I said. 'His account numbers and passwords, the way his fund was structured, where the critical vulnerabilities were.'

He gave a snort of derision that I assumed was meant to be a denial.

'Look, I'm familiar with the history of your career. The way you secretly seized control of the second-largest bank in Russia, then used it to take over the aluminum industry. It was clever.'

He blinked, nodded, unwilling to show me how much he enjoyed the blandishment. But men like that were unusually susceptible to flattery. It was often their greatest vulnerability. And I could see that it was working.

'The way you stole Marcus Capital Management was nothing short of brilliant. You seized control of the bank that handled all of Marcus's trades. You actually bought the Banco Transnacional de Panamá. Their broker-dealer. It was . . . genius.'

I waited a few seconds.

Strategic deception, in war or in espionage, is just another form of applied psychology. The thing is, you never actually deceive your target – you induce him to deceive himself. You reinforce beliefs he already has.

Roman Navrozov lived in a state of paranoia and suspicion. So he was automatically inclined to believe that I actually had a shooter positioned in an empty office across the street – not just a remote-controlled light switch that I could turn on and off by hitting a pre-programmed key on my cell phone. George Devlin, of course, had designed it for me and had a colleague in New York set it up: that kind of technology was far beyond my capabilities.

And he had no reason to doubt that I had people in the adjoining rooms. Why not? He'd do it too.

Same for the staged video that Darryl had taped earlier, with the help of a buddy of his who'd agreed to wear a straitjacket wired with a squib and a condom full of blood. A buddy who trusted Darryl's assurance that his H&K was loaded with blanks, not real rounds.

Roman Navrozov believed the whole charade was real. After all, he'd done far worse to the spouses and children of his opponents; such cruelty came naturally to him.

But what I was attempting now – to pull information out of him by convincing him I knew more than I did – was much riskier. Because at any moment I might slip and say something that would tip him off that I was just plain lying.

He watched me for a few seconds through the haze of his cigarette smoke. I saw the subtle change in his eyes, a softening of his features, a relaxing of his facial muscles.

'Well,' he said, and there it was, the proud smile that I'd been hoping to provoke.

In truth, it was sort of genius, in a twisted way.

If there's some hedge fund you want to loot, all you have to do is buy the bank that controls its portfolio. Obviously that's not going to happen with most normal hedge funds, which use the big investment banks in the US. But Marcus Capital wasn't a normal hedge fund.

'So tell me something,' I said. 'Why did you need to kidnap Marshall's daughter?'

'It was a salvage operation. A desperation move. Because the original plan didn't work at all.'

'And the original plan . . . ?'

He sucked in a lungful of smoke, let it out even more slowly. Then fell silent.

'You wanted the Mercury files,' I said.

'Obviously.'

It made sense. Roman Navrozov was a businessman, and certain businessmen at the highest levels traffic in the most valuable commodities. And was there any commodity more rare than the deepest darkest intelligence secrets of the world's sole remaining superpower?

'So were you planning on selling the black-budget files to the Russian government?'

'Black budget?'

'Maybe that's a term you're not familiar with.'

'Please. I know what black budget is. But you think the Mercury files have something to do with America's secret military budget? I am a businessman, not an information broker.'

'They contain the operational details of our most classified intelligence operations.'

He looked at me in surprise. 'Is that what you were told? Next you will tell me you believe in Santa Claus and the Tooth Fairy as well.'

Then his mobile phone rang, emitting that annoying default Nokia ringtone you used to hear everywhere until people figured out how to select a different one.

He glanced at the display. 'The cutout,' he said.

My heart began to thud.

SEVENTY-EIGHT

Kirill Aleksandrovich Chuzhoi drove up the long dirt road, chest tight with anticipation.

He didn't enjoy wet work, but sometimes he had no choice, and he did it efficiently and without hesitation. Roman Navrozov paid him extremely well, and if he wanted loose ends tied up, Chuzhoi would do whatever it took. For God's sake, he'd even gone down to Boston to take out a low-level drug dealer inside FBI headquarters! He had attracted too much attention and would very soon have to leave the country. He could work for Navrozov elsewhere in the world.

No, he didn't much enjoy that kind of job. Whereas the contractor – the zek, the convict who'd done time in Kopeisk, was reputed to enjoy killing so much that he preferred to draw out the process, in order to make it last.

In this man's line of work, such a disturbing streak of sadism was a qualification. Maybe even necessary. He was capable of doing anything.

He made Chuzhoi extremely uncomfortable.

Chuzhoi knew very little about the *zek* beyond this. And of course the owl tattoo that disfigured the back of his head and neck. He knew that the Sova gang recruited the most brutal inmates at Kopeisk.

Chuzhoi, who had trained in the old KGB and later climbed the greasy rungs of its main successor, the FSB, had encountered this type on a few occasions and had put a few in prison. The most successful serial killers were like that, but they rarely got caught.

With his shaved head and his staring eyes and his grotesque tattoo and his bad teeth, the contractor knew he frightened people, and he surely enjoyed that. He viewed all others with contempt. He considered himself a more highly evolved species.

So he would never imagine that a washed-up old *silovik*, a former KGB agent, a lousy petty bureaucrat, could possibly attempt what Chuzhoi was about to do.

The element of surprise was Chuzhoi's only advantage against this sociopathic monster.

An overgrown lawn came into view: wild, almost jungle-like. In the midst sat a small clapboard house. He parked his black Audi on the gravel driveway and approached the front door. It had started to rain.

Chuzhoi wore the same nailhead suit he'd worn in Boston, tailored to fit his broad physique. He moved with his accustomed air of authority. His long gray hair spilled over his shirt collar.

His trusty Makarov .380 was concealed in a holster at the small of his back.

The green-painted door swung open suddenly, and a face came out of the darkness. The shaved head, the intense stare, the deeply etched forehead: Chuzhoi had forgotten how fearsome the man was.

Something about his amber eyes: the eyes of a wolf, wild and feral and ruthless. Yet at the same time the eyes were cold and disciplined and ever calculating. They studied his acne-pitted cheeks.

'The rain has started,' Chuzhoi said. 'It's supposed to be a bad storm.'

The *zek* said nothing. He glared and turned around, and Chuzhoi followed him into the shadowed recesses. The house had the stale smell of a place long closed up.

Was the girl here?

'You have no electricity?' Chuzhoi said.

'Sit.' The *zek* pointed to an armchair with a high back. It was upholstered in little flowers and looked like something chosen by an old lady.

Of course, the *zek* had no right to speak to him this way, but Chuzhoi allowed him his impertinence. 'The girl is here?' he said, shifting uncomfortably in the chair. It was so dark he could barely see the sociopath's face.

'No.' The *zek* remained standing. 'Why is this meeting necessary?'

Chuzhoi decided to meet brevity with brevity.

'The operation has been terminated,' he said. 'The girl is to be released at once.'

'It's too late,' the *zek* said.

Chuzhoi pulled a sheaf of papers from his breast pocket. 'I will see to it that you are wired your completion fee immediately. All you have to do is sign these forms, as we've already discussed. Also, in consideration of your excellent service, you will receive a bonus of one hundred thousand dollars in cash as soon as the girl is handed over.'

'But "terminated" is not the same as "concluded",' the *zek* said. 'Was the ransom not paid? Or were other arrangements made?'

Chuzhoi shrugged. 'I am only a messenger. I pass along what the Client tells me. But I believe other arrangements have been reached.'

The *zek* stared at him, and Chuzhoi, hardly a delicate man, felt a sudden chill. 'Do you need a pen?' he said.

The *zek* came near. Chuzhoi could smell the cigarettes on his breath.

The *zek* gave a hideous grimace. 'You know, we can go into business for ourselves,' he said. 'The girl's father is a billionaire. We can demand a ransom that will set us up for life.'

'The father has nothing anymore.'

'Men like that are never without money.'

A sudden gust of wind lashed the small window with rain. There was a rumble of distant thunder.

But why not offer him whatever he asked? It was all irrelevant anyway. He'd never get a cent.

The *zek* put his arm around Chuzhoi's shoulder in a comradely fashion. 'We could be partners. Think of how much we can make, you and I.'

His hand ran smoothly down Chuzhoi's back until it lightly grasped the butt of his pistol. As if he knew precisely what he would find and where.

'Last time you came unarmed.'

'The weapon is for my protection.'

'Do you know what this is?' the *zek* said.

Chuzhoi saw the wink of a steel blade, a thick black handle.

Of course he knew what the thing was.

In the calmest voice he could muster, he said, 'I am always happy to discuss new business opportunities.'

He felt the nip of the blade against his side.

The *zek*'s left hand slid back up his spine to his left shoulder, the long fingers gripping the shoulder blade at the front. Suddenly he felt a deep twinge and his left arm went dead. Chuzhoi sensed the man's hot breath on his neck.

'I know the Client's ransom demands have still not been met,' the *zek* said. 'I also know he has made a deal to give me up.'

Chuzhoi opened his mouth to deny it, but the blade penetrated a little more, then pulled back. The pain was so intense it made him gasp.

'If we are to do business together, we need to trust each other,' the monster said.

'Of course,' Chuzhoi whispered, eyes closed.

'You need to earn my trust.'

'Yes. Of course. *Please*.'

A tear rolled down his cheek. He wasn't sure if it was from the physical pain of the *zek*'s pressure point or simple fear.

'I think you have some idea where the girl is located,' the *zek* said.

Chuzhoi hesitated, not wanting to admit he'd had the man followed after their last meeting. That would only enrage him.

Chuzhoi had ordered the follower to keep the surveillance discreet. In fact, he'd stayed back so far he'd lost him.

But . . . was it possible the *zek* had detected the surveillance?

Even so, Chuzhoi had only an approximate location of the burial site. He didn't know the name of the town. The county, yes. Hundreds of square miles. So what? That was as good as nothing.

Before he could think how to reply, the *zek* spoke. 'A man with your experience should hire better eyes.'

Chuzhoi felt the blade again, white hot, but this time the *zek* didn't pull back, and the pain shot up to the top of his head and down to the very soles of his feet. Heat spread throughout his body, or so he thought, until he realized that in fact his sphincter had given way.

In desperation he cried, '*Think of the money*—*!*'

But the knife had gone in deep into his stomach. He struggled against the *zek*'s iron embrace, retched something hot, which burned his throat.

Outside the wind whistled. Rain spattered the clapboard sides of the house. It had become a downpour.

'I am,' the *zek* said.

'What do you want?' he screamed. 'My God, what do you *want* from me?'

'May I borrow your mobile?' the *zek* said. 'I'd like to make a phone call.'

SEVENTY-NINE

'Put it on speaker,' I told Navrozov.

This was it. The call that told us either that the kidnapping had been successfully called off, or . . .

Navrozov answered it abruptly: '*Da?*'

'Speaker,' I said again.

To me he said, 'I don't know how to do this.'

I took it from him and punched the speaker button, and I heard something strange, something unexpected.

A scream.

And then a man's voice, speaking in Russian.

I could make out only intonation and cadence, of course, but the man sounded calm and professional.

In the background was a continuous whimpering, a rush of words that sounded like pleading. I set the phone down on the desk, looked at Navrozov, whose face registered puzzlement.

He leaned over the phone, not fully understanding the concept of a speakerphone, and said, '*Kto eto?*'

The calm voice on the other end: '*Vy menya nye znayete.*'

'*Shto proiskhodit?*' Navrozov said.

'Who's that?' I said.

'He says the contractor is not available to speak but he can pass along a message—'

The whimpering in the background abruptly got louder, turned into a high, almost feminine shriek that prickled the hairs on the back of my neck. A peculiar gargling sound, then a rush of words: '*Ostanovitye!* . . . *Ya proshu* . . . *pazhaluista prekratitye! Shto ty khochish?* . . . *Bozhe moi!*'

Navrozov looked stricken. His face was flushed, his features gone slack as he listened.

'*Nye magu* . . . *nye* . . . *magu* . . .'

The pleading voice in the background grew fainter.

'Who is it?' I demanded.

Then the calm voice was back on speaker. 'Someone is there with you?' the man said, this time in English. 'Tell Mr Navrozov that his employee will no longer be reporting back to him. Goodbye.'

A few seconds of silence passed before I realized that the connection had been severed.

I had a sick feeling. I knew the worst had happened. So did Navrozov. He hurled the phone across the room. It hit a bedside lamp, knocking it to the carpeted floor. His face was dark, mottled. He let loose a string of Russian obscenities.

'The bastard thinks he can defy me!' Navrozov said, spittle flying.

The door to the room came open, and his security guards burst in. The one in front had a weapon in his right hand, a keycard in his left. They'd managed to get one from the front desk.

'This bastard murders my employee!'

The security men did a quick assessment, assured themselves that I wasn't doing harm to their boss. They muttered hasty apologies, I guessed, and retreated from the room.

'Who was that?' I said.

'This is the whole point of cutouts!' he shouted. 'I don't *know* who it is.'

'*Where* is he, then?'

'I told you, somewhere in New Hampshire!'

'Within a thirty-minute drive from the Maine border,' I said. 'Right? We know that much. But do you know if he was based in the north part of the state, or the south, or what? You have no idea?'

He didn't answer, and I could tell that he didn't know. That he was experiencing something he rarely felt: defeat.

'Wait,' he said, his voice hoarse. 'I do have something. A photograph.'

I looked at him, waited.

'The cutout was able to take a covert photograph of the contractor. For insurance purposes.'

'A face?'

He nodded. 'But no name.'

'I want it.'

'But this man's face is not in any of your law-enforcement databases. It will not be easy to find him.'

'I want it,' I repeated. 'And I want one more thing.'

Navrozov just looked at me.

'I want to know what Mercury really is.'

He told me.

Thirty minutes later, still numb with shock, I found my way to the street and into a cab.

Part Three

If you shut up truth and bury it under the ground,
it will but grow, and gather to itself
such explosive power that the day it bursts
through it will blow up everything in its way.
                                            – Émile Zola

EIGHTY

Just before six in the morning, the FedEx cargo flight landed in Boston.

I desperately needed sleep.

If I was to have any hope of locating Alexa Marcus, I needed a little rest. Just a few hours of downtime so I could think clearly again. I was at the point where I could be mainlining caffeine and it still wouldn't keep me awake.

My phone rang as I was parking the Defender.

It was Tolya Vasilenko. 'The picture you just sent me,' he said. 'I am very sorry for you. This is a particularly bad egg.'

'Tell me.'

'You remember this terrible murder of the family in Connecticut I told you about?' He was still pronouncing it wrong.

'He was the one who survived? The one who escaped?'

'So I am told.'

'Name?'

'We still haven't discussed a price.'

'How much do you want?' I said wearily.

'It's not money I want. It's . . . let's call it a swap of intelligence.'

He told me his demand, and I agreed to it without a moment's hesitation.

Then he said: 'Dragomir Vladimirovich Zhukov.'

I mulled over the name, tried to connect it to the snapshot that Navrozov's security chief, Eugene, had e-mailed me: the hard-looking man with the shaven head and the fierce expression. Dragomir, I mentally rehearsed. *Dragomir Zhukov.* A hard-sounding name.

'An unusual name for a Russian,' I said.

'Uncommon. His mother's a Serb.'

'What else do you have on him?'

'Besides the fact that he is a sociopath and a monster and an extremely clever man? There is maybe more you need to know?'

'Specifics about his background. His childhood, his family.'

'You have decided to become a psychoanalyst in your spare time?'

'It's how I work. The more I know about a target's personal life, the more effective I can be.'

'Unfortunately we have very little, Nicholas, apart from the arrest files and his military records and a few interviews with family members and witnesses.'

'Witnesses?'

'You don't think this home invasion in Connecticut was his first murder, do you? When he served in Chechnya with the Russian ground forces, he was disciplined for excess zeal.'

'What kind of "zeal"?'

'He took part in a *zachistka* – a "cleansing operation" – in Grozny, and did certain things that even his commanders couldn't bring themselves to talk about, and these are not sensitive souls. Acts of torture. I know of only a few things. He captured three Chechen brothers and dismembered them so thoroughly that nothing remained but a pile of bones and gristle.'

'Is that why he was sent to prison?'

'No, no. He was jailed for a crime he committed after he returned from the war.'

'Another murder, I assume.'

'Well, no, not exactly. He was sentenced to five years for theft of property. He'd gotten work on one of the oil pipeline projects in Tomsk, operating excavation equipment, and apparently he "borrowed" one of the excavators for his own personal use.'

'Like getting Al Capone for not paying taxes.'

'That was all they could get him on. The Tomsk regional police were unable to definitively connect him to something far worse that they were sure he did. The reason he borrowed the excavation equipment. For more than a year the police investigated the disappearance of a family, a husband and wife and their teenage son who vanished overnight. They questioned Zhukov extensively but got nothing. They had nothing more than unfounded rumors that Zhukov had been hired by a fellow prison inmate to do a hit.'

'A hit on a family?'

'The man owned several auto dealerships in Tomsk. He had been warned that if he didn't sell his dealerships to a friend of Zhukov's, his entire family would suffer. It seems these threats were not hollow.'

'So the family's bodies were never found.'

'They were found. A year after their disappearance. And purely by coincidence. An abandoned parcel of land outside the city was being developed for a housing project, and when they dug the foundation, three bodies were unearthed. A middle-aged couple and their teenage son. The police forensic examiners found large quantities of dirt in their lungs. They were buried alive.'

'Which was why Zhukov borrowed the excavation equipment.'

'So it seems. But the case could never be proven in the courts. You see, he is very, very good. He covered his tracks expertly. I can see why Roman Navrozov hired him. But if you are looking for a psycho-history, Nicholas, you might be interested to know that when Zhukov was a boy his father died in a coal-mining accident.'

'Also buried alive?'

'Maybe "drowned" is more accurate. The father worked in an underground mine, and when some of the miners accidentally dug into an abandoned shaft that was filled with water, the tunnels were flooded. Thirty-seven miners drowned.'

'How old was Zhukov?'

'Nine or ten. You can imagine how traumatic this must have been for the families. Especially for the young children who were left fatherless.'

'I don't see a connection between some childhood trauma and—'

'His mother, Dusya, told our interviewer years ago that her son's chief complaint at the time was that he never saw it happen. She says that was when she first realized that Dragomir wasn't like the other little boys.'

Suddenly I didn't feel sleepy. 'He's not doing this for the money, is he?'

'I'm sure the money will come in handy for his escape and buying new identities and such. But no, I imagine he took this job because it offered him a rare opportunity. I'm just guessing, of course.'

'Opportunity?'

'To watch someone drown before his eyes.'

EIGHTY-ONE

Alexa sang as loud as she could: songs she liked to dance to, songs she loved listening to. Or just scraps of songs, when she couldn't remember the rest.

Anything to keep her mind off where she was.

Lady Gaga's 'Bad Romance'. She tried to remember the French lyrics near the end of the song. Something about revenge. That distracted her briefly. Then 'Poker Face'. She sang so loud she was almost yelling. But that one was too easy. She imagined being Lady Gaga herself and wearing a skintight outfit made entirely of duct tape.

Black Eyed Peas next. 'Imma Be' worked for a little while. She moved on to Ludacris: lots of lyrics there to try to remember. Too many. She tried MC Hammer's 'Can't Touch This' for a while but that was too hard and she soon gave up.

When she stopped, bored with it and discouraged, her throat hurting, she remembered where she was, and she began to shudder uncontrollably again. It felt like something was raking her nerve endings. She felt chills deep down, her entire body cringing. The way the mere *thought* of rubbing Styrofoam against cardboard set her teeth on edge.

But the physiological reaction was nothing compared to the deep horror that came over her now, the cold black cloud of fear, as it had done over and over again throughout this nightmare. That realization that there really was something worse than death, and this was it.

She screamed, long and loud, and it became a hopeless sob. She felt her tears scald her cheeks.

She screamed, clawed at the lining of her coffin. Her fingertips hit a hard square object mounted on the lid, and she knew it had to be the video camera.

She could feel the tiny lens and she put her thumb on it.

Held it there for a while.

Now he couldn't see her.

She had the power to blind the Owl.

She held her thumb over the lens until her hand began to tremble.

Then the Owl's voice bleated through the speakers and she jumped. 'If you are playing a joke, Alexa, this is not a very good idea.'

She didn't reply. Why should she? *She didn't have to answer him.*

Then she thought of something so monumental that her heart began racing from excitement instead of terror.

She could rip the damned camera off its mounting.

She could blind the Owl forever.

Without his camera, he had no power over her!

Grabbing the camera's casing, she tugged, wiggling it back and forth like a loose tooth to dislodge it from its mounting.

This was genius. The videocam was the key to his whole plot. This was how he made his demands, using her, coaching her, having her recite his bizarre demands over video so Dad would totally freak out.

So she'd get rid of it.

Cut off his access to her, his surveillance. Cripple his scheme, where he couldn't do anything about it.

Without the video, the Owl's plan couldn't work. No camera, no ransom.

Tear down the camera, he'd get desperate. He'd have to improvise.

He'd have to dig her up.

He'd have to fix his damned camera, because that was the key to the whole thing.

Why the hell had it taken her so long to figure this out?

She felt a little warm pulse of pleasure. Her father, who probably did love her after all but totally didn't respect her, would be proud of her now, wouldn't he? He'd be amazed at her cleverness, her resourcefulness. He'd say, 'My Lexie, you got the *saichel*, you got the head of a Marcus.'

She gripped the little metal box so hard her whole arm shook. She tugged at it, twisted it, and finally she felt something start to give way.

A tiny piece of something dropped onto her face. She felt it with her left hand. A little metal screw. Must be part of the mounting.

She was doing it. She was ripping out the Owl's eyes.

She smiled to herself, crazy with triumph, felt the camera thing began to wobble ever so slightly.

A sudden blare: 'Another bad idea.'

She didn't reply.

Of course he didn't want her to rip the damned thing down. *Of course* he didn't want that.

'You know, Alexa, I am your only means of communication with the world,' the voice said. Not angry, but patient.

She gritted her teeth and kept twisting, hand shaking with exertion, the sharp metal corners cutting into her palm.

'If you disable the camera,' the Owl said, 'you will be cut off from the rest of the world, you know.'

She stopped twisting for a moment.

'They will think you have died,' the voice said. 'Why else would the video stream stop, yes?'

Her hand was frozen in a grip just above her face. A few more minutes of this and she'd be able to snap off the other screws or posts or whatever it was that kept the camera stuck to the lid of the . . .

'Maybe your father will cry. Maybe he feels relief. But at least he knows this is over. There's nothing he can do. He never wanted to give us what we ask anyway, and now he thinks, *I don't need to do this.* What is the point, yes? His daughter is dead.'

She said, in a guttural animal growl, 'He'll know you *failed.*'

'He will give up. Believe me. Or don't believe me. I don't care.'

The muscles in her forearm and wrist were aching. She had to lower her hand.

'Yes,' said the Owl. 'You prefer to get out of this box, isn't that right?'

She began to sob.

'Yes,' he said again. 'This camera is your only hope of getting out of there alive.'

EIGHTY-TWO

As badly as I needed sleep, I needed to talk to Diana Madigan even more, to tell her what I'd found out.

Six in the morning. She was an early riser. Odds were she was awake and having coffee and reading e-mail or whatever FBI agents do before they go to work in the morning, those who aren't married and don't have kids.

So instead of going straight home, I drove a few minutes out of my way, looped around to the South End, down Columbus Avenue and a left up Pembroke Street.

Her apartment lights were on.

'How about coffee?' she said warily.

'I think I'm past the point of no return,' I said. 'Any more caffeine's just going to put me into a coma.'

'Ice water, then?'

I nodded. I sat on her couch, and she sat on the chair next to it. Exactly where we'd sat last time. She was wearing a white T-shirt and sweatpants and was barefoot.

She went to her little kitchen and filled one of her funky hand-blown drinking glasses with ice water. She handed it to me and sat down again.

Then I told her as much of what I'd just learned as I could. It wasn't exactly a coherent presentation. My brain was much too fried. But I managed to set out the basic facts. 'Now I've got Dorothy checking on every place in New Hampshire that rents excavation equipment, but she's not going to find anything until nine or ten when the places open.'

'Okay,' she said. 'Meanwhile, I've looked at the case files on that Connecticut home invasion.'

'Already? But how did you know . . . ?'

She smiled ruefully. 'Nico, you need sleep. Badly. You told me about that last night.'

I shook my head, embarrassed.

'The husband survived. I wanted to see whether he might recall anything more about the attackers. But . . . well, he's not going to be talking to anyone. Zhukov left him seriously brain damaged.'

I nodded.

'No latent prints were found at the scene. Neither Zhukov nor his associate. I was hoping that the locals might have submitted any unidentified fingerprints to the unsolved latent file at IAFIS. Maybe those same prints turned up somewhere else . . . But nothing.'

'And that's it?' I stood up. I was exhausted and cranky and desperate to do something. I started pacing around her living room.

'What's that supposed to mean?'

'What's the FBI's budget again? Like almost ten billion dollars, right? And every single law-enforcement officer in the country on tap. More databases than you know what to do with. And you still haven't found a damned thing more than me and Dorothy.'

'Oh, and what have you found? Last I heard, that girl is still in the ground.'

I turned away, headed toward the door. 'I've got to get back to the office.'

'No,' she said, 'you need sleep. You're just about at the breaking point. There's not a damned thing you can do right now until one of our leads comes in. Or one of *your* leads. Or until the business day starts. So go to sleep, Nick.'

'After.'

She came in close, put a hand on my shoulder. 'If you don't give your brain and your body a rest, you're going to start screwing up, and then what?'

I whirled around. 'Don't worry about that,' I said. 'I don't screw up.'

'Now I know you're sleep deprived,' she said with a laugh.

And before I knew it, my lips were on hers.

Her mouth was warm and tasted of mint. I held her face in my hands and stroked her hair. Her eyes were closed. Her smooth hands slid underneath my shirt and pressed flat against my chest, her fingernails lightly raking my chest hair. Then I was caressing her breasts and kissing her throat, and I heard the clink of her fingers at my belt.

'Diana,' I said.

She silenced me with her mouth on mine, and her legs wrapped tightly around my waist.

'I know we can't go back to the way things were,' she said.

'I wasn't thinking this was a do-over.'

She smiled, but her eyes were wet. She reached for me, and I held her for a long time. It felt wonderful. Almost enough.

My phone rang, and I glanced at it. Marshall Marcus.

'Nick,' he whispered, 'I just got a message.'

A beep indicated a call coming in on the other line. Dorothy.

'Message from whom?'

'*Them*. I have until the end of the day and then they'll—'

'Hold on.' I clicked on Dorothy's call.

'Nick, Marcus just got an e-mail from the kidnappers.'

'I know, he's on the other line, he was just telling me.'

'It's not good,' she said.

I felt my mouth go dry.

'Are you near your computer?'

I hesitated. 'I'm near *a* computer.'

'I'm going to send you an e-mail right now.'

I signaled to Diana, who brought her laptop over, and I signed on to my e-mail. Meanwhile, I clicked back to the other line. 'Hold on, Marshall, I'm just opening it right now.'

'How can you do that?'

I didn't reply. I was too busy reading the text on another anonymous e-mail.

> The rules are all change now
> Now demand is very simple for you to save your daughter
> Five hundred 500 $ US mil must be wired into account
> listed below by close of business 5:00 pm 1700 hours
> Boston time today
>
> This is not open of negotiation
> This is final offer.
>
> If $$$ received satisfactory by 5:00 pm 1700 hours Boston
> time today your daughter Alexa will be released. You will
> be notified of her public place location and can pick her up
> then.
> No further negotiation possible.
> If $$$ not received by 5:00 pm 1700 hours Boston time
> today you will get one last opportunity to watch your
> daughter Alexa on internet
> You will watch when coffin is flood with water.
> You will watch your daughter drown before your eyes
> You will watch last minutes of your daughters life

Then followed the name and address of a bank in Belize, bank codes, and an account number.

'Jesus,' I said.

'Nicky,' Marshall Marcus said, his voice high, quavering. 'Dear God in heaven, please, Nick, help.'

'That's all we're doing,' I said. 'Round the clock.'

'Five hundred million dollars? I don't have that kind of money anymore, thanks to those bastards, and they damned well know it.'

'Where's Belinda?'

'Belinda? She's right here beside me. Like always. Why?'

'Let me get off the phone,' I said. 'Maybe there's a way to pull this off.'

'How?'

But I just hung up.

I leaned over and gave Diana a kiss.

'Call me as soon as you know anything,' she said.

EIGHTY-THREE

I arrived at the office with a Box o' Joe from Dunkin' Donuts and a dozen assorted donuts.

Half an hour later, after repeated calls to Belize City, I was on the phone with the Honorable Oliver Lindo, minister of national security in Belize.

'Nick!' he said. 'Have you been trying to call me? I'm so sorry. I was at the gym. I have a personal trainer now. Someday I may even look like you, my man.'

'And how's Peter?'

'Did you know he's in his second year at Oxford, Nick?'

'I had no idea. Congratulations. Have you remarried, by any chance?'

He chuckled. 'We have a saying here: Why buy the cow if the milk is free?'

'I may have heard that before,' I said.

No need to get explicit with Oliver Lindo. When I was working at Stoddard Associates in DC, I'd helped him out with a sticky problem involving a boat, a rum factory, one of his ex-wives, and a lot of angry Cubans. Later he asked me to extricate his son, who was then at the Lawrenceville School in New Jersey, from a situation involving gang-bangers in Trenton.

'Do you happen to know anyone at the Belize Bank and Trust Limited?'

'If you are thinking about hiding money, well, I can recommend – actually, this is not a conversation we should be having on the mobile phone.'

'If I ever have enough money to hide away somewhere, you'll be the first person I'll call,' I said. 'But I'm calling about something else. I need a favor.'

'Anything you want, Nick. You know that.'

EIGHTY-FOUR

'You want to explain to me how this is going to work?' Dorothy said.

'Just before the bank in Belize closes, Dragomir Zhukov is going to get a confirmation that five hundred million dollars has been deposited into his account,' I said.

She took a long sip of coffee from a mug that said JESUS SAVES – I SPEND. 'And your friend in Belize can get this done?'

'He'll pay a visit to the bank's president himself. I'm guessing that this bank might not want to be complicit in the abduction of a teenage girl. Or maybe he has other means of persuasion. I don't know, and I don't care.'

'But it's all a trick, right? The bank is going to confirm a deposit that was never made?'

'Of course.'

'But what's the point? If this Zhukov guy has gone rogue, he doesn't answer to anyone. It doesn't make any difference whether he gets the money or not, he's never going to let Alexa go.'

'Not if he thinks he doesn't have to. That's why the timing is crucial. There's going to be a last-minute complication. Some screwup in the number of his bank account that requires him to make a call.'

'And you'll be on the other end of that call.'

I shrugged. 'I'm going to let him know that he gets the five hundred million only after he releases Alexa.'

She looked at her computer, looked at me. Looked down at the floor and then back up at me. 'Nick, you're delusional. You have no leverage. None. He'll just refuse, he'll say it's my way or the highway, and then he'll kill her.'

'You're probably right.'

'So what am I missing here?'

'He'll want to keep her alive until five o'clock. So he can show that she's still alive. He'll want to keep his options open.'

'Okay, but then at five, whether he gets the money or not, whether there's a last-minute hitch or not, he'll kill her anyway.'

'I agree.'

'So what's the *point*, Nick?'

'To give me until five o'clock today to find Alexa,' I said. 'Now I want you to go back to your idea about locating him based on the schedule of plane flights, the interruptions in the satellite signal.'

'What's to go back to? That's a dead end. Didn't you tell me the FBI didn't find any matches in the FAA database?'

'Yes, I did.'

'And you think they're wrong?'

'Not at all. I think they searched all flights in the FAA database. But I don't think they searched *all* flights.'

'You don't? Why not?'

'Because the one thing I know is the US military. And I know that they don't like to share information on military flights with pencil-neck civilian geeks in the federal government.'

'Military flights?'

'There are military air bases in Maine and Vermont and New Hampshire. They each keep their own flight logs.'

'Online?'

'Never.'

'Then how do we get to them?'

I picked up the phone and handed it to her. 'The old-fashioned way,' I said.

EIGHTY-FIVE

Dorothy assigned Jillian to pull up a list of all companies in New Hampshire that rented or leased construction equipment.

There were almost nine hundred.

Even after narrowing it down to just 'earth-moving equipment' and 'heavy construction equipment', we had close to a hundred. It was just about hopeless. We'd have to get extremely lucky.

Meanwhile Dorothy spent two hours on the phone with military air bases and Air National Guard air traffic controllers. I had to get on a few times and throw around names of generals in the Pentagon who probably didn't remember me. But when she walked into my office with a wide grin on her face, I knew she had something for me.

'What's a KC-135?' she asked.

'Ah. The Stratotanker. Made by Boeing. Mostly aerial refueling tankers, though some of them have been reconfigured as airborne command posts. Let's hear it.'

'We got a hit. Each one of those interruptions in the video signal coincides exactly with a KC-135 flight out of the Pease Air National Guard Base.'

'Meaning what? They're in Portsmouth, New Hampshire.'

'No, no,' she said. 'Not that simple. The kidnap site could be anywhere from about five miles to forty miles away.'

'You can't narrow it down? Like by triangulating or something? Don't you digital forensic techs always triangulate stuff?'

'Not enough data points to do that. All I have is three cutouts on the video, about ten seconds after three KC-135s take off.'

'You've got plenty,' I said. 'You know the direction the planes took off toward, right?'

'True.'

'You probably know the speed the planes generally take off at, right?'

'Maybe.'

'You should be able to get within ten miles, I'd say. Do I have to do all your work for you?'

I tried to head off the Look with what I thought was a disarming smile. But it didn't work. I got the Look anyway.

Then my BlackBerry rang. I glanced at it, saw it was Diana.

'Hey,' I said. 'You got the photo I sent.'

'More than that, Nick,' she said. 'I think we found him.'

EIGHTY-SIX

I didn't say anything for a long moment.

'Nick?'

'You found Zhukov?'

Diana's voice was taut, louder than normal. 'We got a hit on his phone.'

'New Hampshire?'

'Right. Just west of Nashna.'

'He must have switched it on.'

'Listen, I have to go. We're deploying up north.'

'Where?'

'A forward staging area in a parking lot a couple of miles away from the target site.'

'You're deploying with the SWAT team?'

'They're calling in all assets, operational or not. They want me at a surveillance point outside the SWAT perimeter.'

'Give me the exact location.'

'You can't be there. You know that. It's a Bureau operation. You're a civilian.'

I inhaled slowly. 'Diana, listen. I don't want her to die in the middle of some big noisy SWAT team operation. I want her alive.'

'So do they, Nick. Their number-one priority is always victim recovery.'

'I'm not talking about intention. I'm talking about technique.'

'Our SWAT guys are as good as you get.'

'I'm not arguing.'

'So what are you suggesting?'

I closed my eyes, tried to focus. 'What's the location?'

'A house on a country road. It looks deserted, from the satellite imagery.'

'Is there land?'

'It's a farmhouse.'

'Secluded?'

'What's your point, Nick?'

'Is it just him, hiding out there? Or is that where he has Alexa buried? It makes all the difference in how you approach him.'

'We don't know if she's there or not.'

'As soon as he hears the snap of a twig, or he sees guys in ghillie suits coming through the woods, he's not going to wait to be shot. He's going to kill her. He's already threatened to flood the grave, and it wouldn't surprise me if he's set up to do it remotely. As simple as pulling a lever on an irrigation system in the house. And no matter how fast you guys can dig, you're not going to save her in time.'

'That doesn't make sense. She's his bargaining chip. He wants her alive. If he floods the grave and kills her, he has no leverage.'

'Diana, this guy doesn't operate by normal rules. To assume he does would be a dangerous miscalculation. He wants to flood the grave or shut off her air supply and he wants to watch it on his computer screen. He wants to watch her gasping and struggling and trying to scream. He wants to watch her die.'

'Then why the ransom demand?'

'He figures he'll collect a load of money and kill her anyway. Tell your squad commander he wants me there on scene. Tell him I'm the only one who knows anything about Dragomir Zhukov.'

EIGHTY-SEVEN

As I drove north on 93, it started to rain, first a few ominous drops from a steel sky, then a full-fledged torrential downpour. It came down with the sort of force that almost always tells you it's going to be short-lived, that it can't possibly last.

But this one kept going. Out of nowhere, the wind began to gust, driving the rain nearly sideways. My windshield wipers were flipping at maximum speed but I could still barely see the road. The other cars began to skid, then slowed to a crawl, and a few pulled over to wait it out.

Normally I enjoy dramatic weather, but not then. It seemed to echo the strange, unaccustomed feeling of anxiety that had come over me.

My instinct told me that this was not going to end well.

So I blasted music. Few tunes pump me up like the twangy guitar licks and huge, booming, diesel-fueled rockabilly sound of Bill Kirchen, the Titan of the Telecaster, the guy who did 'Hot Rod Lincoln' years ago. I played 'Hammer of the Honky-Tonk Gods' and then his live version of 'Too Much Fun'. By the time I reached the New Hampshire border, I was feeling like my old self.

Then I had to hit MUTE to answer the phone.

It was Diana, with directions to the SWAT staging area. 'We're mustering at a parking lot two miles from the house,' she said. 'You're going to join me on the perimeter surveillance team. But that means staying outside the hard perimeter.'

The highway had gotten narrower, down to a two-lane road with steel guardrails on either side. I passed a BRAKE FOR MOOSE sign.

'Works for me. Are we going to be in a vehicle or on foot?'

'In one of their SUVs, thank God. I'd hate to be standing around in weather like this. Is it raining where you are?'

'Pouring. I'm maybe thirty miles away, no more.'

'Drive safe, Nico.'

EIGHTY-EIGHT

Forty-five minutes later I was sitting in the passenger's seat of a black Suburban. It had been specially modified for the SWAT team with roof rails and side rungs, though it wasn't armored. We were outside the crisis area. We weren't supposed to get hit.

Diana was behind the wheel. Under her FBI sweatshirt she was wearing a level III trauma vest, a concealable ballistic garment fitted with a trauma plate.

Rain sheeted down. The windshield wipers whipped back and forth like a metronome at top speed.

We were parked at the end of the woods, just off a narrow winding asphalt road, stationed at what the SWAT team called 'phase line yellow', the last cover-and-conceal position before the action started. Phase line green was the imaginary line around the house. Phase line green meant game on.

Supposedly we were part of the perimeter team, at the point of egress, but in truth we were nothing more than observers. My role was limited and quite clear: if they were able to take the Russian alive, and if he resisted cooperation, I was to be put on the radio to communicate directly with him. Not in person, on the radio.

Surrounding us were various American-made SUVs – Ford Explorers and Blazers and Suburbans, also fitted with roof rails and side rungs. SWAT operators hung off the side, wearing two-piece olive drab suits with armor that was supposed to withstand a rifle round, ceramic trauma plates inside. They wore ballistic helmets and eye protection and FBI signage everywhere. They carried M4 carbine rifles equipped with red-dot optical sights. In their side holsters they had pistols, to be used only if their machine guns jammed. Snipers in ghillie suits were secreted in the woods, in the shadows cast by the trees, within range of the house.

For a long while we sat in silence, listening to the exchange on the dash-mounted radio.

We waited. Everyone out there seemed to be waiting for a signal. The air was charged with tension.

I said, 'If he shows his face—'

'The snipers will take him out. Deadly force has been pre-authorized.'

'Is that FBI protocol?'

'Only in circumstances where we believe the target has the means and the probable intention to kill his victim, yeah, killing him is considered legally justified.'

'And if he doesn't show his face?'

'They'll attempt a silent breach of the house from two points and go into hostage-rescue mode.'

After sitting in silence a while longer, Diana said, 'You want to be up there, don't you? Admit it.'

I didn't reply. I was still mulling things over. Something seemed somehow *off* about the whole situation.

She looked at me. I said, 'Can I borrow your binoculars?' I hadn't grabbed mine from the Land Rover. I didn't think I'd need them.

She handed me a pair of army-green Steiners, standard SWAT-team issue, full-size, a PROPERTY OF FBI SWAT sticker on one side. I dialed in the focus until the house came into view: a small, neat, white-painted clapboard house with dark green shutters. It wasn't a farmhouse at all but a house in the woods. The land surrounding it was surprisingly small, given the size of the property. The grass was overgrown and wild, probably waist-high, as if no one had been looking after it for a year or more.

It was dark. No car or truck in the driveway that I could see.

Then I handed the binoculars back to her. 'I don't think we're in the right place,' I said.

'How so? It's his phone number that came up, no question about it.'

'Look at the egress. Only one way in or out, and we're sitting at it. The woods in back of his house are overgrown, choked with underbrush and vine. He can't walk for two minutes through that without getting stuck in thorn bushes.'

'You saw all that?'

'Good binoculars.'

'Good eyes.'

'He's trapped. This isn't the sort of property he'd ever pick.'

'Maybe he didn't pick it. Maybe Navrozov's people chose it for him. It's been abandoned for a year and a half.'

'I don't think he'd ever let someone else make that kind of decision for him. He doesn't like to rely on anyone.'

'That's your assessment, based on a third-hand evaluation in some old KGB file.'

I ignored that. 'Did anyone check the utility bills on this place?'

'It's been empty for eighteen months.'

'I don't see any generators, do you? So how the hell does he get on the Internet?'

She shook her head slowly, considering.

'Or a satellite dish,' I said.

She continued to shake her head.

'Also, it's sloppy,' I said.

'What's sloppy?'

'Using his mobile phone. He shouldn't be using it again.'

'He doesn't know we have his phone number.'

'This guy never underestimates anyone. That's why he's still alive.'

I took out my cell phone and hit the speed-dial for Dorothy.

'Where are you, Heller?'

'New Hampshire.'

'Right. Where?'

'In the middle of what's beginning to feel a lot like a diversion,' I said. 'West of Nashua.'

'Nashua? That's . . . something like forty miles south of the flight path area.'

'Can you send me the GPS coordinates?' I said.

'Done.'

'How large an area are you vectoring in on? I wonder if we can narrow down the possibilities. Look at terrain and available properties and—'

'I may have one more data point.'

'Let's hear it.'

'I've been combing NCIC for anything coming out of New Hampshire, and I came across a possible homicide.'

The National Crime Information Center was the computerized database of crimes maintained by the FBI and used by every police force and other law-enforcement agency in the country.

'How is that connected?'

'The code on the report was 908. A premeditated homicide of a police officer by means of a weapon.'

'And?'

'So a rookie police officer was found in his car at the bottom of a ravine in New Hampshire. At first it looked like he drove off the road. But the local police chief strongly suspects homicide.'

'Why?'

'Because of the victim's injuries. According to the county coroner, they're nothing like what you'd expect to see in a car accident. For one thing, all the internal organs in his chest cavity were destroyed. Like someone detonated a depth charge down there.'

My pulse started to race. 'Where was this?'

'Within the flight path radius. Town of Pine Ridge, New Hampshire. Forty miles away, like I said.'

EIGHTY-NINE

'We're in the wrong place,' I said.

'What makes you so sure?'

'His phone's probably in there. But he's not. This is a diversion, maybe even a setup.'

'How so?'

'He knows Navrozov is trying to shut him down. Maybe he wants to lure Navrozov's guys to the wrong site to conceal his true whereabouts.' I took the handset from the dash-mounted radio, pressed the communicator button, and said, 'Break – Zulu One, this is Victor Eight.'

'Nick, what are you doing?' Diana said.

'We need to stand down,' I said to her. 'And head north.'

The SWAT team leader's voice came over the speaker, crisp and loud: 'Go ahead, Victor Eight.'

'Zulu One, I have some new intel I need to pass to you. What's your location for a meet?'

Diana stared, aghast.

A pause. 'Say again, Victor Eight?'

'Zulu One, I have urgent intel I need to pass on. Request a meet ASAP. How copy?'

'That's a negative, Victor Eight,' the voice came back.

But I wasn't going to give up. 'Zulu One, urgently request meeting.'

The team leader's voice came back immediately: 'Received, Victor Eight, and that's a negative. Get off the radio. Out.'

I shrugged, replaced the handset on the hook.

'Wow, Nick,' Diana said. 'Just . . . wow.'

'What?'

'We're about to launch an assault.'

'Which means that the FBI's best people are tied up forty miles away while our guy finishes the job. Come on, let's go.'

'I can't just leave the scene, you know that. You don't leave your position without permission.'

'They don't need you here. You're a spectator. This is a waste of your time and your talents.'

She looked agonized, wracked with indecision.

'Come on,' I said, opening the Suburban's door.

'Heller!'

'Sorry,' I said, getting out.

'Nick, wait.'

I turned back.

'Don't do it, Nick. Not by yourself.'

For a moment I looked at her: those amazing green eyes, the crazy hair. I felt something inside me tighten. 'I've got to go,' I said.

'Don't, Nick.'

I gently pushed the door closed.

NINETY

The walk back to the parking lot where I'd left my car, a mile away, was arduous and slow, along narrow country roads and then a heavily trafficked highway. The rain had become a downpour of biblical proportions. By the time I reached the Defender, my clothes were soaked through, ever despite the rain slicker.

Then I cranked the heat all the way up and headed north toward Pine Ridge. Dusk rapidly turned into night, and still the rain didn't let up.

Three hundred and twenty days a year the Land Rover was an overpowered beast, a curiosity, an M1 Abrams tank in the city streets. That night, the driving treacherous, it was king of the road. I passed countless beached cars, washed up along the side of the road, their drivers waiting out the storm.

About fifteen minutes after I'd set out, Diana called.

'They found a body.'

'Any ID?' I asked.

'Yes. The name is Kirill Chuzhoi. In the US on a green card, residing in East Rutherford, New Jersey. Born in Moscow. He's on the payroll of Roman Navrozov's holding company, RosInvest.'

'And in his pocket you found a knockoff Nokia cell phone,' I said.

'Right. Probably Zhukov's.'

'No, more likely his own phone, with Zhukov's SIM card inside.'

'Huh?'

'He knew if he put his SIM card in the other guy's phone, his phone number would pop up in your search and you'd think you finally found him. And he was right.'

'I don't get it. Why not just swap phones?'

'Look, the guy's smart. He didn't want to take the chance that Chuzhoi's phone had some sort of tracking software encoded in it. Now, can you send me a photo of the body?'

'Hold on,' she said. A minute or so later she got back on. 'You should have it now.'

I put the call on hold, looked at my e-mail, and found the picture.

The bogus legal attaché from the Brazilian consulate. The one who'd killed the drug dealer at the FBI office in Boston. Roman Navrozov had probably sent him to make sure Mauricio Perreira didn't give up any information that might tie him to Alexa's abduction.

When I got back on the call, I told Diana, 'Send this picture to Gordon Snyder, okay?'

'Why?'

'Because it ties Navrozov to the murder at FBI headquarters.'

'Got it. Will do.'

'Where are you now?' I said.

'Headed back to the staging area. You?'

'Twenty-two miles away. But the driving is really slow. Can you get the team redeployed up here?'

'Where?'

I read off the GPS coordinates.

'Is that the exact location where you think he is?'

'No. That's the center of the town of Pine Ridge. Which covers thirty-five square miles.'

'What makes you so sure you have the right place?'

'I'm not sure. Dorothy's cross-checking property records against Google Earth satellite views.'

'Looking for what?'

'Land that's big enough and private enough. Multiple points of egress. Unoccupied, abandoned, foreclosed, whatever. Absentee owner goes to the top of the list.'

'What about utility bills?'

'We don't have your resources. We're sort of running blind here. So try to get SWAT up here as soon as possible.'

'I'll do my best,' she said. 'See you up there.'

'I hope so.'

A minute or so after I hung up, I had an idea. I reached Dorothy on her cell. 'Can you get me the home number of the chief of police in Pine Ridge?' I said.

NINETY-ONE

'Oh, believe me,' the police chief's wife said, 'you're not interrupting dinner. Walter's out there sandbagging, and I don't know *when* to expect him home. They're all out there, the part-timers and every volunteer they can rustle up. It's a mess. The river's swollen and there's mudslides just all over the place. Can I help you with anything?'

'Think he can use one more volunteer?' I said.

'Head out there.'

'What's his cell phone?'

Chief Walter Nowitzki answered on the first ring.

'Chief,' I said, 'I'm sorry to bother you during such a difficult time, but I'm calling about one of your officers—'

'That's gonna have to wait,' he said. 'I'm up to my neck in alligators here.'

'It's about Jason Kent. He was on your force, reported as a homicide?'

'*Who's this?*' he said sharply.

'FBI,' I said. 'CJIS.'

He knew the jargon. Any cop would. CJIS was the FBI's Criminal Justice Information Services Division, which maintained the central NCIC database of all reported crimes.

'How can I help you?'

'You reported this as a 908, a premeditated homicide on a police officer, and I was following up on that.'

'All right, I – you know, this is probably not the best time to talk, we've got some real bad flooding up here in New Hampshire and we've got people stuck in their cars and the river's swelling its banks, and—'

'Understood,' I replied. 'But this is a matter of some urgency. We've got a homicide in Massachusetts that seems to fit some of the basic parameters of the one you reported, so if you could answer just a couple of real quick questions . . .'

'Let me get into my vehicle so's I can hear you. Can't even hear myself think out here.'

I could hear him fumbling with the phone, then the door slam.

'Tell me what you wanna know,' he said.

'Do you have any suspects?'

'Suspects? No, sir. I'm sure it was someone from out of town.'

'Was he investigating a crime or anything of that sort before he was killed?'

'We don't get a lot of crime in these parts. Mostly speeders, but they're usually not from around here. He made some routine rounds, checked up on a noise complaint, but . . .'

'Did he make a traffic stop near where he was killed?'

'Not so far's I know. That was my theory, but he didn't call anything in.'

'No run-ins with anyone?'

'Not that he mentioned.'

'Any theory at all what might have happened to him?'

'No, sir. I wish I did. That kid – they didn't make 'em any better than that one—' He seemed to swallow his words, and he went quiet for a moment.

'I'm very sorry.'

'If that kid met Satan himself he'd offer him the shirt off his back. Only bad thing I can say about him is he probably wasn't cut out to be a cop. That's on me. I shouldn't never have hired him.'

'The day he was killed, what were his duties?'

'The usual. I mean, I asked him to look into a sort of, well, I call 'em nuisance calls. We got a fella called Dupuis who's sort of a fussy sort, you know? Kept calling to complain about one of his neighbors, and I asked Jason to go check it out. And I'll bet you Jason didn't even—'

'What sort of complaint?'

'Oh, I dunno, Dupuis said he thought the guy down the road stole his dog, like anyone would want that mangy mutt, and he said the guy mighta been doing work without a permit.'

I was about to steer him into another line of questioning when I had a thought. 'What kind of work?'

'Construction maybe? All I know is, there hasn't been no one living on the Alderson farm for years, not since Ray Alderson's wife died and he moved down to Delray Beach. I figured maybe Ray had a caretaker getting the place ready to sell, because they had your, whatcha call it, earth-moving equipment delivered a week or so back.'

I'd stopped listening. I was less than ten miles away. The rain was drumming the roof of the car and the hood, though it seemed finally to be letting up. The visibility wasn't great. Ten miles in weather like this could take twenty minutes.

Then a couple of words jumped out at me.

Caretaker.

Moved down to Delray Beach.

That meant the owner didn't live there.

'This caretaker,' I said. 'Has he been there a while?'

'Well, of course, I'd have no way of knowing that. I've never met the fella. Foreigner, maybe, but they all are these days, right? Can't get an American to do manual labor worth a damn. Far as I know he just showed up one day, but we keep to ourselves up here, try to stay out of other people's business for the most part.'

'Do you have a street address?'

'We don't really go by numbers so much around here. Ray's farm is a nice piece of land, more than two hundred acres, but the main house is a wreck, you know? Doesn't show well, which is why—'

'Where is it?' I cut in sharply.

'It's on Goddard just past Hubbard Farm Road. You thinking the caretaker had something to do with this?'

'No,' I said quickly.

The last thing I wanted was for the local police chief to show up and start asking questions.

'Because I would be more than happy to take a run over there. Take the four-by-four – that's a summer road, and it's surely a swamp by now.'

'No hurry,' I said. 'Next couple of days would be fine.'

'You wanna talk to the owner, I can probably rustle up Ray's number down in Florida, give me a couple minutes.'

'Don't bother. I know you've got your hands full. This is for the database. Routine data entry. It's what I spend my life doing.'

'Well, it's important work,' the police chief said kindly. 'Somebody's got to do it. I'm just glad it's someone who speaks the language.'

I thanked him and I hung up before he could ask anything else.

'Dorothy,' I said fifteen seconds later. 'I need directions.'

NINETY-TWO

By the time I drove into Pine Ridge, the rain had slowed to a drizzle. The main highway looked recently built. Its asphalt surface was as smooth as glass, the road crowned, the drainage good. I passed Pine Ridge Quality Auto, which was nothing more than a glorified gas station, and then the Pine Ridge Memorial School, a modern brick structure built in the architectural style best described as Modern High School Ugly. Then a post office. At the first major intersection was a gas station on one side next to a twenty-four-hour convenience store that was dark. At the next light I took a left.

I passed farmhouses and modest split-level ranches built too close to the road. There were unmarked curb cuts, narrow lanes sliced through the woods, most of the roads dirt, a few paved. The only landmarks were mailboxes, most of them big, names painted on, occasionally press-on letters.

About three miles down a narrow tree-choked road I came to a roadblock. Hastily improvised: a couple of wooden saw-horses lined with red reflector discs.

This was Goddard Road. About two miles down this way was the Alderson farm.

If I'd guessed right, it was also where Alexa Marcus was buried in the ground.

And where I might find Dragomir Zhukov.

I nosed the car right up to the saw-horses, clicked the high beams.

The road was rutted, deep mud. Walking the two miles, especially down a road like this, would be tortuously slow, time I couldn't afford.

I got out, dragged a saw-horse out of the way, got back in the Defender, and plowed ahead.

It was like driving across a marsh. The tires sank deep into the muck, and a curtain of water sprayed into the air. I kept it in third gear and drove at a steady pace. Not too fast, not too slow. You don't want to be in too low a gear when moving through mud. Drive too slowly and you risk water seeping into the exhaust pipe and flooding the engine.

Gradually the road became a narrow dark lane choked with tall pines and birches. The only illumination came from my headlights, which skimmed over the river of mud.

The car performed like an amphibious vehicle, though, and soon I was halfway there.

Then the tires sank in a few more inches and I was finally stuck.

A mile to go.

I knew better than to rev it. Instead, I lifted my foot off the accelerator pedal, gave it some gas.

And I was still stuck.

A quick burst of gas, just a tap of the pedal, and it started rocking back and forth, and after a few minutes of this the car climbed out of the gulley and back through the brown soup.

Then my high beams lit up a rusty metal mailbox that said ALDERSON.

An absentee owner, a caretaker recently arrived. Earth-moving equipment: might that include a backhoe?

Everything was pure speculation at this point.

But I had no other possibilities.

NINETY-THREE

The driveway to the Alderson property was the main access road. If this was indeed the right place – and I had to assume for now that it was – Zhukov was likely to have surveillance equipment in place: cameras, infrared beams, some sort of early-warning system.

Then again, it's not easy to set up equipment like that outdoors and have it work effectively. Not without advance preparation.

But, it was safer to assume the driveway was being monitored.

So I drove on ahead, past the entrance, plowing through the muddy river another half mile or so until it came to an abrupt stop. There I drove up the steep bank as deep into the woods as I could.

According to the map Dorothy had sent to my phone, this was the far end of the property. The farm was two hundred and forty acres of land with a half mile of frontage on a paved road and a mile of frontage along this dirt path.

The house was easily a quarter mile from here. Given the topography, the road couldn't be seen from the house.

The owner had for years permitted hunters to come through his land. Dorothy had looked at the state's online hunting records.

This wasn't unusual in New Hampshire. You were allowed to hunt on state or even private lands as long as they hadn't been 'posted' – in other words, unless the property owner put up NO HUNTING signs.

But I'd been concentrating so hard on trudging through the muck that I hadn't until now noticed the NO TRESPASSING/NO HUNTING signs posted to trees every fifty feet or so.

They looked brand-new. Someone had put them up recently to keep anyone from approaching the house.

I had some decent overhead satellite photos of the Alderson property, but nothing recent. The photos could have been three years old, for all I knew. I was at a real disadvantage.

At least I had a good weapon: a SIG-Sauer P250 semiautomatic. The SIG P250 was a beautiful gun: compact and lightweight, smooth, perfectly engineered. Mine was matte black, with an aluminum frame. I'd installed a Tritium night sight and an excellent internal laser sight, a LaserMax. I'd also had a gunsmith in Manassas, Virginia, add stippling and checkering on the metal grips, round all the sharp angles for an unhindered draw, and funnel the grip for easier reloading. He tuned it like a Stradivarius, adjusting the trigger pull down to a zero sear, meaning that I hardly had to touch the trigger to fire.

There's an elegance to a well-made gun, like any finely engineered machine. I like the precision engineering, the honed finish, the smooth pull of the trigger, the smell of gun oil and smoke and gunpowder and nitroglycerin.

I loaded several magazines with hollow-point bullets. They're designed to do a lot of damage to a person: when they hit soft tissue they deform and expand and create a large crater. Cops prefer them because they won't pass through walls – or the target, for that matter.

My Defender was painted Coniston Green, also known as British Racing Green, but it was so mud-spattered that it looked as if I'd sprayed it with camouflage paint. I stashed it in a copse of birch trees, where it couldn't be seen from the road, and took some equipment out of the back. My binoculars: an excellent pair of

Leicas. A pair of boots, still crusted with mud from the last time I'd worn them. I strapped on a side holster and jammed in the SIG, then clipped a few extra magazine holsters to my belt.

At the last minute I remembered something under the rear seat that I might need. It was an old military-spec Interceptor ballistic vest made of aramid fiber. It wasn't bulletproof – no such thing, really – but it was the most effective soft armor you could get. It was supposed to stop nine-millimeter machine-gun rounds. I put it on, adjusted the Velcro straps.

If I'd come to the right place, I needed to be prepared.

Compass in hand, I set off through the woods.

NINETY-FOUR

The ground was sodden, even spongy, and so slick in places I nearly lost my footing. Low branches and thorn bushes whipped and scratched my face and neck. The land rose steeply and then plateaued until, standing atop a knoll, I spotted in a clearing in the distance a small building.

I peered through the binoculars and saw a large, windowless structure: a barn.

A few hundred yards beyond it, according to the aerial photo, was the farmhouse.

I came closer and finally saw the house. But it was dark. That wasn't promising. Either this was the wrong place, or Zhukov had already left.

Meaning that Alexa was dead.

I drew closer, weaving through the forest, keeping to the shadows, until the barn was close enough to see with the naked eye. Then I circled around. From there I could see the long expanse of yard leading up to the house. The sky had begun to clear, and there was enough moonlight to make out a patchy lawn, with more bald spots than grass.

And midway between the barn and the darkened house a neat

oblong had been cut into the sorry-looking lawn. A rectangle about ten feet long by three feet wide.

Like a freshly dug grave.

But instead of the sort of earthen heap you see in a new grave, the ground was flat, crisscrossed with tire tracks, as if someone had driven a car or a truck back and forth on top of it, and the rain had later softened the marks.

I felt a tingle of apprehension.

At one end of the rectangular patch of dirt a gray PVC pipe stuck up like the sawn-off trunk of a sapling.

I dropped the binoculars, let them dangle on their strap around my neck, and I approached the edge of the woods.

The house was an old brown tumbledown wreck, its clapboard weathered and cracked, several roof shingles missing.

Mounted to the roof of the house was a white satellite dish.

It looked new.

In the shadows behind the barn I began to discern the contours of a tall piece of equipment. It loomed like an enormous, geometric bird, a seagull, a whooping crane.

I looked closer and saw that it was a Caterpillar backhoe loader.

NINETY-FIVE

Peering through the binoculars, I focused on the house. Two floors, a sharply canted roof, small windows. No light inside. On the low wooden porch was another piece of equipment. An air compressor?

Yes. That made sense. This was how he kept air flowing into her box, or crypt, or whatever it was.

This had to be the right place.

For a minute or two I watched carefully, looking for some kind of movement in the darkness, a glint of reflected moonlight. I estimated I was about three hundred yards from the house, beyond the range of accuracy of my pistol.

But if someone was inside with a rifle, three hundred yards was no problem.

The moment I stepped into the clearing, I was a target.

I got on the cell phone and called Diana. In a whisper, I said, 'I think she's here.'

'You've seen her?' Diana said.

'No, I'm looking at what may be a burial site. A vent pipe in the ground. Signs of recently excavated earth.'

'Zhukov?'

'House is dark. I can't be sure if he's there. Tell your bosses that there's not much doubt this is the place. They need to get up here right away. And bring shovels.'

I hit END. Checked to make sure the ringer was off.

Then I took a few more steps, emerging from the shadows. Walked across the barren lawn toward what had to be the burial site.

Something caught the moonlight, something near my feet, and suddenly the entire yard lit up, and I was blinded by the blaze of spotlights from two directions.

NINETY-SIX

I flattened myself against the ground. I could smell the rich loamy odor of the dirt. Gripping the SIG, the safety off, I felt for the trigger, careful not to apply any pressure. The slightest squeeze would fire a round.

In one quick motion I rolled over so I was facing up. The lights came from two directions: from the barn on my left and from the house on my right. I inhaled slowly, over the thudding of my heart, and listened hard.

Nothing.

I knew what had happened. I'd hit an invisible tripwire at ankle level.

Zhukov had served with the Russian army in Chechnya, where he must have learned all the standard army techniques, like how to string tripwire to detonate a mine or detect the enemy's approach. The stuff we'd used was black and as thin as dental floss, made from a polyethylene fiber called Spectra. You could get fishing line made from the same thing. It was low-stretch and had high tensile strength. And you wouldn't spot it in the dark unless you had a flashlight and knew where to look. He'd probably strung the filament around at least part of the perimeter, from tree trunk to tree trunk, rigged up to a microswitch to set off the beams. A low-tech motion detector.

So was he here, or not? Was he waiting for me to get up so he could take aim?

I listened for footsteps, for the scuff of shoes on dirt or gravel.

Nothing.

After two minutes, the spotlights went off and everything was black.

No shot was fired. No crack of twigs. Just the ambient noise of the forest: the rustle of leaves in the wind, the distant chirruping of a nocturnal bird, the skittering of a ground squirrel or a chipmunk.

The vent pipe was roughly a hundred feet from me. Would she hear me if I spoke into it?

Then I realized what a mistake that would be. If Zhukov was hiding in the house, monitoring Alexa over a remote connection, then whatever she heard he'd hear too.

Of course, if he was in the house, it was only a matter of time before he saw me.

So I had to take him out first.

Holster the weapon? Or keep it handy? I needed both hands. Jamming it into the holster, I rolled and spun into a crouch. Sprang to my feet.

And started toward the house.

NINETY-SEVEN

But I didn't run.

I didn't want to trip another wire. As I walked, I looked around for fence posts, stakes, anything a wire might be strung around.

Maybe I was walking right into a trap. Maybe he was waiting for me in the dark with a high-powered rifle.

Around to the side, past a set of wooden bulkhead doors, the wooden frame rotting, the paint blistering and peeling. No padlock.

Enter the basement? No. Maybe it wasn't a basement but a root cellar: dirt floor, accessible only from the outside, no internal door to the upstairs.

On this side of the house was a door, behind a screen with a large hole in it. But I kept going around to the front. Past an oval of bare earth where cars probably parked and turned around. No vehicles there, though. None in the front of the house either.

He couldn't be inside, or I'd be dead by now.

But what if Zhukov had simply abandoned the farmhouse? After all, he knew from Navrozov's cutout that he was being actively hunted. Why stay here? Leave his victim in the ground, let her die.

A path had been worn across a scrubby lawn to the front door, though how recently it was impossible to say. I detected no movement in any of the windows, so I pulled open the screen door and tried the front door.

It came right open.

Someone had been here very recently.

NINETY-EIGHT

The smell of food that had been cooked not long ago: maybe sausage or eggs, something fried in grease.

A small entryway, low ceilings, a musty odor under the cooking grease. Cigarettes too, though fainter here, as if he smoked in another part of the house. I moved stealthily, the SIG in a two-handed grip, pivoted abruptly to my left, weapon pointed, ready to fire. Then to my right.

Nothing. The floorboards creaked.

Now I faced a choice. There were three ways to go. A doorway on my right led to a small front room. On my left was a steep staircase, the wooden treads worn and bowed. Straight ahead was another doorway, which I guessed led to a kitchen and the back of the house.

The stairwell was a potential hiding place. I listened closely, heard nothing.

I pivoted again, tracing an arc right to left. Then I lunged toward the dark stairwell.

I said, 'Freeze.'

No response.

And then I heard a voice.

Not from upstairs, though. From the back of the house. A

woman's voice, muffled, indistinct, its cadence irregular, the tone rising and falling.

A TV had been left on.

I stepped through the threshold, searching the dim corners, my body a coiled spring. My finger caressed the trigger. I scanned the room, slicing with the pistol left to right, then toward the corners.

The kitchen was windowless, carved out of an interior space, an afterthought. The floor was dark red linoleum, a swirly white pattern running through it, the tiles chipped and cracked. An old white GE stove, vintage 1940 or so. A Formica counter edged with a metal band. A white porcelain sink with two separate spouts, one for hot water and one for cold. It was stacked high with plates and bowls that were crusted with food. An empty box of Jimmy Dean breakfast sausages lay discarded in the middle of a tin-topped kitchen table.

I heard the woman's voice again, much clearer now, coming from the next room. From the back of the house.

Not from a TV.

The voice was Alexa's.

NINETY-NINE

Amped with adrenaline, I burst into the adjoining room, gun extended.

'—Bastard!' she was saying. 'You goddamned bastard!'

Then her tone changed abruptly, her voice wheedling, high-pitched. 'Please, oh God, please let me out of here, please oh God please oh God what do you goddamn *want*? I can't stand it I can't stand it please oh God.'

And I saw that Alexa wasn't in here.

Her voice was coming from computer speakers. A black Dell computer on a long wooden workbench that ran the length of one wall. In the monitor I saw that same strange close-up of Alexa's face, with a greenish cast, that I'd seen in the streaming video.

But she looked so bad I almost didn't recognize her. Her face was gaunt, her eyes swollen to slits, deep purple hollows beneath them. She was speaking out of one side of her mouth, as if she'd had a stroke. Her face shone with sweat. Her eyes were wild, unfocused.

In front of the monitor was a keyboard. To the left of it was a small, cheap-looking microphone on a little plastic tripod. Like something you'd find in a discount bin at RadioShack.

For an instant Alexa seemed to be looking at me, but then her eyes meandered somewhere else. She fell silent, then started whimpering, all her words rushing together. I could make out only 'please' and 'God' and 'out of here'.

I spoke into the microphone: 'Alexa?'

But she went on, uninterrupted. On the stem of the microphone was a little black on/off switch. I slid it down to on. Said, 'Alexa?' again. This time she stopped. Her mouth came open. She began to sob.

'Alexa?' I said. 'It's Nick.'

'Who – who is this?'

'It's Nick Heller. You're going to be okay. I'm at the house. Right nearby. Listen, Alexa, help is coming, but I need you to stay quiet and keep calm, all right? Can you do that for me? Just for a little while. You're going to be okay. I promise.'

For a second I thought I saw a flash of light in the backyard coming through the window.

'Nick? Where are you? Oh my God, where are you?'

The light again. A car's headlights. I heard the rumble of a car's engine, then a door slamming.

Zhukov was here. It could be no one else.

But I couldn't see him. He'd parked on the side of the house that had no windows.

'Nick, answer me! Get me out of here please oh God get me out of here, Nick!' She started screaming.

'You're going to be okay, Alexa. You're going to be okay.'

Finally she seemed be listening. 'Don't leave me here,' she moaned.

'He's back,' I whispered. 'Can you hear me?'

She stared up, her lips parted, and as she nodded she began sobbing again.

'Everything will be fine,' I said. 'Really. As long as you don't say a word. Okay? Not a word.'

I gripped the SIG in both hands.

But what if it wasn't Zhukov who'd just arrived? What if it was the police? It was far too soon for the FBI's SWAT team. They were driving, since getting a helicopter there and loading it and all that, would take even more time, and would also deprive them of the heavy armaments.

Zhukov, if it was him, would enter the house through the front door, as I had. The worn path told me that. Yet he wouldn't expect anyone to be here. That would give me a temporary advantage. If I positioned myself correctly I might be able to get a jump on him.

Heart thudding now. Time had slowed. I went into that strange calm place I so often did when faced with grave danger: senses heightened, reactions quickened.

A door opened somewhere.

But not the front door. Which one?

The side door I'd noticed earlier.

I needed to conceal myself, but where?

No time to hesitate.

A door next to the kitchen entrance. A closet, probably, with a wooden kitchen chair next to it. I slid the chair a few inches out of the way.

Opened the door with my left hand, stepped into the darkness—

And dropped into space.

Not a closet, but the basement stairs. I reached out and grabbed something to arrest my fall. My boots landed with a muffled thud.

A wooden banister. Swiveled myself around, pulled the door shut behind me. My hand on the knob, keeping it turned so the latch wouldn't click.

Silently eased it shut. Lowering myself to my knees on the first step, I peered out through the keyhole.

Waited for him to appear.

ONE HUNDRED

Dragomir Zhukov had parked at the side of the house just to vary the pattern. Never be predictable.

It was for the same reason that he'd shut off the satellite Internet connection. It was predictable that he'd want to stay connected. It was also a needless risk. There were ways to trace an Internet signal.

Of course he had left one cable in place: the one connecting his computer to the casket.

Before he opened the door, he glanced down at the baseboard and saw the tiny strip of transparent tape he'd placed between the door and the jamb. It was still in place. That meant no one had entered here.

Or probably not, anyway. Nothing was ever certain.

Long ago Dragomir had learned the importance of leaving nothing to chance. This was one of the many lessons he'd learned at the University of Hell, also known as Prison Number One, in Kopeisk.

The money transfer had been received in his account. The cutout had been eliminated.

Some time ago he had made provisions for a quick escape in the event the operation did not go to plan. In a steel box he'd buried in the Acadia National Park in Maine was a Ukrainian passport and wads of cash, in US dollars and euros. The passport didn't expire for another two years.

With a new identity, crossing the Canadian border would be quick and easy, and there were plenty of international flights out of Montreal.

The only chore that remained was hardly a chore at all.

It was his reward for all the long tedious days of vigilance and patience and restraint.

He knew how it would go: he had rehearsed it countless times, savoring the prospect. He'd tell the young girl what was about to happen, because there was nothing as delicious as a victim's foreknowledge. Hour after hour he'd seen her fear, but when she learned, in precise and clinical detail, what was imminent, her terror would reach a whole new physical state.

Then he'd go about the business methodically: he'd disconnect the air hose from the compressor and attach it to the garden hose with the brass coupler. Once he pulled up the lever on the farmer's hydrant, the water would start to flow. It would take a few seconds before the water began to trickle into the casket.

He had drowned small animals – mice, chipmunks and rabbits, a stray cat – in a trash barrel. But the squeals and the frantic scrambling of a dumb animal were ultimately not satisfying. They lacked *apprehension*.

She would hear the trickle, and then she would know.

Would she scream, or plead, or both?

As the water level grew higher and the air pocket grew smaller, she would flail and pound and most of all beg.

He had done some calculations. The interior volume of the casket was 230 gallons. Given the water pressure in the house and the diameter of the hose and the distance from the spigot to the burial site and then the nine feet down through the soil into the casket itself, it would take just short of half an hour to fill to capacity.

Then the water would reach her chin and she would have to

struggle to keep her head above water, gasping her last precious breaths, her neck trembling from the exertion, her lips pursed like a fish.

He would watch in hypnotized fascination.

She would attempt to scream as her lungs filled with water; she'd flail and plead, and when she was entirely submerged, she would hold her breath until she couldn't take it anymore and she was forced to expel the air from her lungs. And like a child in utero she would be forced to breathe liquid.

She would drown before his eyes.

It was a terrible way to die. The way his father died. For years he could only imagine it.

But now he would *know*.

Dragomir knew he was not like other people. He understood his own psychology, the way he drew sustenance from the fear of others.

As he entered the house, he paused.

Something was different here. A shift in the air? A vibration? He had the finely tuned senses of a wild animal.

Now that the cutout was dead, he wondered how long it would take for the Client to realize what had happened. They had some idea where he was based, but he was sure he hadn't been followed after the last rendezvous.

Still, he wondered. Something was *off*.

He moved quietly through the parlor to the front door, where he'd placed another tell, a barely visible slice of Scotch tape at the bottom of the door next to the jamb, both inside and out.

A minuscule ribbon of tape lay on the floor. No one who wasn't looking for it would see it.

But now he knew for certain: someone was here.

ONE HUNDRED
AND ONE

I could hear footfalls, the creaking of the wooden floor, the sounds becoming louder, closer. Grasping the pistol in my right hand, the banister in my left, I squatted and looked through the keyhole and saw only the ice-blue light from the computer monitor.

Alexa on the screen. Such advanced technology in the service of such primitive depravity.

He had entered the room.

I saw a leg, clad in jeans, but just for an instant. Walking toward the computer, or at least in that direction. Then he came to a stop.

The man was standing a few feet away. I could see his back: large torso, broad shoulders, a dark sweatshirt.

Did he suspect anything? But his body language didn't indicate suspicion.

He was standing at the window, I saw now, casually looking outside, a black knit watch cap on his head.

And the hideous pattern on the back of his neck.

The bottom half of an owl's face.

ONE HUNDRED
AND TWO

Dragomir Zhukov entered the back room, peering around at the filthy windowsills and the peeling yellow paint on the walls and the uneven floorboards.

A voice crackled from the small computer speaker. The girl was speaking.

'Nick!' she screamed. 'Please don't go away!'

The pistol was in his right hand even before he'd made the conscious decision to draw it.

Zhukov turned swiftly, holding a weapon, an enormous steel semiautomatic with a barrel like a cannon.

I recognized it at once. An Israeli-made .50 caliber Desert Eagle. Made by the same folks who gave the world the Uzi. It was the sort of thing you were far more likely to see in a movie or a video game than in reality. It was too large and unwieldy, so unnecessarily powerful. When Clint Eastwood declared, in *Dirty Harry*, that his .44 Magnum was the most powerful handgun in the world, he was right. In 1971. But since then, that title had been claimed by the Desert Eagle.

I saw his wide angry stare, his strong nose, a sharp jaw, a cauliflower ear.

'Nick, where'd you go? I thought you were here! When are the others coming? Nick, please, get me out of here, oh God, please, Nick, don't leave me—'

Zhukov turned slowly.

He knew.

ONE HUNDRED
AND THREE

Zhukov knew I was here somewhere.

Alexa's voice, steadily more frantic: 'Please, Nick, answer me! Don't leave me stuck here. Don't you *goddamn* go away!'

Zhukov moved with the taut, coiled grace of a cat. His eyes scanned the room, up and then down, ticking slowly and methodically in a grid.

I breathed noiselessly in and out on the other side of the heavy wooden door. Watching through the keyhole.

I'd come to rescue Alexa. But now it was a simple matter of survival.

The hollow-point ammo I was using might have had unequaled stopping power, but the rounds wouldn't penetrate the thick old wooden door between us. The instant they hit wood they'd start to fragment. If they actually passed through the door, they'd be traveling at such a reduced velocity that they'd no longer kill.

I was all but defenseless.

Nor was my body armor meant to stop the .50 caliber Magnum rounds fired by the Desert Eagle. I didn't know whether the rounds would penetrate the ballistic vest; they might. But even if they didn't, the blunt-force trauma alone would probably kill me.

So I watched him through the keyhole and held my breath and waited for him to move on to another part of the house.

Zhukov scanned the room again. He seemed to be satisfied I wasn't hiding here. I saw his eyes shift toward the kitchen. He took a few steps in that direction.

Slowly I let out my breath. As soon as I was sure he'd moved into the kitchen, I'd turn the knob silently, and step out as noiselessly as I could.

If I got the jump on him I might be able to drop him with one well-aimed shot.

Reaching out slowly, I placed my left hand on the doorknob. Ready to turn it once he was safely out of the room.

I continued watching.

Drew breath. Waited patiently. A few seconds more.

Then he swiveled around, back toward me. His gaze dropped to the floor, as if he'd just discovered something. I saw what he was looking at.

The railback chair I'd just moved out of the way of the basement door.

It was out of place. Not exactly where he'd left it.

His gaze rose slowly. He smiled, baring teeth that were brown and belonged in a beaver's mouth.

He raised the Desert Eagle and pointed it right at the basement door, directly at me, as if he had X-ray vision and could see through the wood, and he squeezed the trigger—

blam blam blam

—and I lurched out of the way and everything was happening in slow motion, the thunderous explosions and the muzzle flash, fireballs that lit up the entire room, the splintering of the door, and as I let go of the doorknob and the banister and leaped backward I felt a bullet slam into my chest, the pain staggering, and everything went black.

ONE HUNDRED
AND FOUR

When I came to, a few seconds later, my body was wracked with excruciating pain. Like something had exploded inside my chest while my rib cage was being crushed in some enormous vise. The pain in my left leg was even worse, sharp and throbbing, the nerve endings shrieking and juddering. Everything moved in a sort of stroboscopic motion, like a rapid series of still images.

Where was I?

On my back, I knew, sprawled on a hard cold floor in the near darkness, surrounded by the dank odor of mold and old concrete and the stench of urine. As my eyes adjusted, I saw snowdrifts of what looked like shredded newspaper all around me, and a lot of rat droppings.

Something scurried by, made a *scree* sound, and I lurched.

A large shaggy Brown Norway rat, its long scaly tail writhing, stopped a few feet away. It gazed with beady brown eyes, maybe curious, or maybe resentful that I'd disturbed its den. It twitched its whiskers and scuttled away into the darkness.

Pale moonlight filtered in from above, through a gaping hole in the underside of a wooden staircase.

In an instant I realized what had just happened.

A bullet had struck me, slamming into the left side of my ballistic vest, but it hadn't penetrated my body. I was alive only because two inches of solid oak had slowed the round's velocity. But I'd been knocked off balance, shoved backward down the stairs. Then I'd crashed feet first through the termite-damaged, rotten planks and broken through, landing on the concrete floor below.

I tried to breathe, but each time I inhaled it felt like daggers piercing my lungs. I sensed warm blood seeping down my left leg. I reached down to feel the bullet wound.

But there wasn't any.

Instead, the jagged end of a broken plank a foot long was sunk several inches into my left calf, through tough denim.

I grabbed the board and wrenched it out of my flesh. A couple of long rusty nails protruded from the wood. As painful as it had been lodged in my calf, it was far worse coming out.

I tried to recall the number of shots he'd fired at me. The .50 caliber Desert Eagle's magazine held only seven rounds. Had he fired four or five? Maybe even six.

Maybe he didn't have any rounds left. Maybe he had one.

I was short of breath and dazed and numb. A creak somewhere overhead, then heavy footsteps on the top steps. Zhukov was coming down the stairs.

Maybe he thought he'd killed me but wanted to make sure. Maybe he thought he could just finish me off. I had to move before he fired straight down as I lay here gasping.

I felt for my weapon but it wasn't in the holster. I'd been holding it when the bullets struck me. Maybe I'd dropped it when I took a tumble. Now I felt for it on the cold floor, my hands sweeping over the concrete and the debris and the rat droppings. But it was nowhere within reach.

A light came on: a bare bulb mounted to one of the rafters about ten feet away. The ceiling was low. The basement was small: maybe thirty feet by twenty.

Wooden shelves were screwed on to the cinder block walls, lined with old canning jars. Rickety children's bookcases, painted with clowns and dancers, were heaped with newspapers and magazines that had been chewed through, cobwebbed, littered with rat droppings. In one corner, in a square hole cut into the concrete floor, a rusty sump pump was planted in gravel, collecting dust and cobwebs. Here and there were folding tables stacked with old toasters and kitchen implements and assorted junk.

He took another step. I lay absolutely still, held my breath. Lay flat, looking up.

If I made a sound, he'd locate me, and he'd get a direct, unimpeded shot straight down. The vest wouldn't protect me.

He knew I was here. He'd heard me stumble down the steps. Surely he'd seen the broken boards, the gaping hole, the missing treads. But did he know I was directly below him?

As soon as he looked down, he'd know. Once he did, it was all over.

I looked over at the bare light bulb again, and then I noticed the splintered two-by-four on the ground, the blood-spattered plank whose jagged end had sunk into my leg.

I grabbed it, and in one hard swift throw I hurled it, smashing the bare light bulb, and everything went dark again.

In the dark I stood a chance.

But a few seconds later, a flashlight beam shone down the stairs. The cone of light swept slowly back and forth over the floor and the walls, into the dark corners. I could hear him coming down the stairs, slowly and deliberately.

Then the beam went off. The only light was the faint trapezoid cast by the open door above. Maybe he'd stuffed the flashlight in a pocket. He needed two hands to hold the Desert Eagle.

Now it was all a matter of seconds. I had to get to my feet to be ready to pounce, but do it silently. The slightest scrape would announce my location like a beacon.

The timing was crucial. I could move only when he did, when

the sound of his tread and the creaking and groaning of the old wood masked whatever slight noise I made getting up.

Lying flat, I listened.

A dry whisking. The rat had come out of its hiding place, alarmed by yet another disturbance, maybe fearful that a second human being was about to come crashing down into its nest. It pattered across the floor toward me. Paused to make a decision, surveying the terrain with shrewd eyes.

Directly overhead another step creaked. Startled, the rat came at me, skittered across over my neck, the sharp nails of its paws scratching my skin, its dry hard tail whisking my face, tickling my ear canal. I shuddered.

Yet somehow I stayed absolutely still.

Abruptly clapping both hands over the thing, I grabbed its squirmy shaggy body . . . and hurled it across the room.

Suddenly there was a shot, followed by the clatter of metal objects crashing to the floor.

My ears rang.

Zhukov had heard the rat's scuffling and assumed it was me.

But now he knew he hadn't hit me. No one can get shot with a .50 caliber round without giving a scream or groan or cry.

So was that his last shot? Was that number six or seven? I couldn't be sure.

Maybe he had one round left.

Or maybe he was on a new cartridge.

He took another step down, and I knew what I had to do.

ONE HUNDRED
AND FIVE

I had to grab his gun.

Through one of the missing risers in the decrepit staircase I could see the heels of his boots.

Then I heard the unmistakable metallic *clackclack* of the pistol's magazine being ejected. The weapon was directly above me, close enough to seize, wrench out of his hands. If I moved fast enough, took him by surprise.

Now.

I shoved down against the floor with both hands, using the strength in my arms to rise into a high push-up. Favoring my right foot, I levered myself up until I was standing.

Then, reaching out both hands, I grabbed his right boot and yanked it toward me. He lost his footing, stumbled down the steps, yelled out in surprise and anger. The staircase groaned and creaked and scattered chunks of wood. Something heavy and metal clattered near my feet.

The Desert Eagle?

Go for the weapon, or launch myself at him, try to immobilize him before he could get back up?

I went for the gun on the floor.

But it wasn't the gun. It was his flashlight: a long black Maglite. Heavy aircraft-grade aluminum with a knurled barrel, heavy as a police baton.

I leaned over and grabbed it, and when I spun around, he was standing maybe six feet away, pistol in a two-handed grip. Aiming two feet to my left.

In the dark, he couldn't see me. I couldn't see much either, but for the moment I could see more than he could.

I arced the Maglite at his head. He didn't see it coming. It struck him on the bridge of his nose, and he roared in pain. Blood trickled from his eyes and gushed from his nostrils.

He staggered, and I lunged, knocking him to the floor, driving a knee into his stomach, my right fist aiming for his larynx, but he'd twisted his body so that I ended up delivering a powerhouse uppercut to the side of his jaw.

He dropped the weapon.

I landed on top of him, pinioned him to the floor with my right knee and my left hand. His blood was sticky on my fist. But he had unexpected reserves of strength, like an afterburne. As if the pain only provoked and enraged him and fueled him. As if he enjoyed the violence.

He levered his torso up off the floor and slammed a fist at my left ear. I turned my head but he still managed to cuff me hard just behind the ear. I swung for his face, but then something large and steel came at me and I whipped my head to one side though not quite in time, and I realized he'd retrieved his weapon.

Holding the Desert Eagle by its long barrel, he swung the butt against my temple, like a five-pound steel blackjack.

My head exploded.

For a second I saw only bright fireworks. I tasted coppers blood. My hands grabbed the air and I careened to one side and he was on top of me and cracked the butt of the gun on the center of my forehead.

I was woozy and out of breath. His face loomed over me. His eyes were an unnerving amber, like a wolf's.

'Do you believe there is light at end of tunnel when you die?' he asked. His voice was higher pitched than I remembered from the videos and had the grit of sandpaper.

I didn't reply. It was a rhetorical question anyway.

He flipped the gun around, then ground the barrel into the skin of my forehead, one-handed, twisting it back and forth as if putting out a cigarette.

'Go ahead,' I panted. 'Pull the trigger.'

His face showed no reaction. As if he hadn't heard me.

I stared into his eyes. 'Come on, are you weak?'

His pupils seemed to flash.

'Pull the trigger!' I said.

I saw the hesitation in his face. Annoyance. He was debating what to do next.

I knew then he had no more rounds left. And that he knew it too. He'd ejected the magazine but hadn't had the chance to pop in a new one.

Blood from his nostrils seeped over his beaver teeth, dripping steadily onto my face. He grimaced, and with his left hand he pulled something from his boot.

A flash of steel: a five-inch blade, a black handle. A round steel button at the hilt. He whipped it at my face and its blade sliced my ear. It felt cold and then hot and extremely painful, and I swung at him with my right fist, but the tip of the blade was now under my left eye.

At the base of my eyeball, actually. Slicing into the delicate skin. He shoved the handle and the point of the blade pierced the tissue.

I wanted to close my eyes but I kept them open, staring at him defiantly.

'Do you know what this is?' he said.

My KGB friend had told me about the Wasp knife.

'Dusya,' I said.

A microsecond pause. His mother's name seemed to jolt him.

'I spoke to her. Do you know what she said?'

He blinked, his eyes narrowed a bit, and his nostrils flared.

That second or so was enough.

I scissored my left leg over his right, behind his knee, pulling him toward me while I shoved my right knee into his abdomen. Two opposing forces twisted him around as I grabbed his left hand at the wrist.

In an instant I'd flipped him over onto the ground.

Jamming my right elbow into his right ear, I tucked my head in so it was protected by my right shoulder. My right knee trapped his leg. He pummeled me with his right fist, clipped the top of my head a few times, but I was guarding all the sensitive areas. I gripped his left wrist, pushing against his fingers, which were wrapped around the knife handle. I kept pushing at them, trying to break his grip and strip the knife from his hand.

But I had underestimated Zhukov's endurance, his almost inhuman strength. As we grappled over the knife, he jammed his knee into my groin, sending shockwaves of dull nauseating pain deep into my abdomen, and once again he was on me, the point of his knife inches from my left eyeball.

I gripped his hand, trying to shove the Wasp knife away, but all I managed to do was keep it where it was, poised to sink in. His hand trembled with exertion.

'If you kill me,' I gasped, 'it won't make any difference. The others are on their way.'

With a lopsided sneer, he said, 'And it will be too late. The casket will be flooded. And I will be gone. By the time they dig her up, she will already be dead.'

The knife came in closer, and I tried to push it back. It shook but continued touching my eye.

'I think you know this girl,' he said.

'I do.'

'Let me tell you what she did to me,' he said. 'She was a very dirty little girl.'

I roared in fury and gave one final, mighty shove with all the strength I had left. He flipped onto his side, but he still didn't loosen his grip on the handle.

I drove my knee into his abdomen and shoved his right arm backward. The knife, still grasped tightly in his fist, sank into his throat, into the soft flesh underneath his chin.

Only later did I understand what happened in the next instant.

The palm of his hand must have slid inward a fraction of an inch, nudging the raised metal injector button.

Causing his Wasp knife to expel a large frozen ball of gas into his trachea.

There was a loud pop and a hissing explosion.

A terrible hot shower of blood and gobbets spat against my face, and in his bulging amber eyes I saw what looked like disbelief.

ONE HUNDRED
AND SIX

I was able to hold out until shortly after the casket came out of the ground.

It took five members of the FBI's SWAT team two hours of digging by hand, using shovels borrowed from the Pine Ridge police. The casket was almost ten feet down and the earth was sodden and heavy from the recent deluge. They hoisted it out on slings of black nylon webbing, two men on one side, three on the other. It lifted right up. The casket didn't weigh more than a few hundred pounds.

It was dented in several places and had a half-inch yellow hose coming out of one end. The hose had been trenched into the ground for two hundred feet or so and was connected to the air compressor on the back porch. A much thicker, rigid PVC tube came out of the other end, the pipe sticking out of the ground.

The team didn't believe my assurances that the casket wasn't booby-trapped. I didn't blame them, of course. They hadn't looked into the monster's eyes.

If Zhukov had placed a booby trap in the casket, he would not have denied himself the opportunity to taunt me with it.

But he hadn't. There was none.

Two of their bomb techs inspected the compressor hose and the vent pipe and the exterior of the casket, looking for triggering mechanisms.

Somehow they were able to ignore all the thumping and pounding and muffled screams from within. I wasn't.

Diana had her arm around me. She was supporting me, and I mean that in a physical sense. My legs had turned to rubber. Everything before my eyes was moving in and out of focus, though I didn't understand why. The blood loss was minimal. True, the pain in my chest had grown steadily worse. The blunt-force trauma had been bad, but I'd thought the worst had passed.

I was wrong. The escalating pain should have been the first sign. But I was preoccupied with getting Alexa out of her coffin.

'Nico,' she said, 'you weren't wearing trauma plates.'

'Hey, I was lucky I had a plain old vest with me,' I said between sharp gasps. 'Trauma plates aren't exactly standard equipment.' Breathing was getting more difficult. I couldn't fill my lungs. That should have been the second sign.

'You should have waited for us.'

I looked at her, tried to smile.

'Okay,' she conceded, nuzzling me on the neck. 'I'm glad you didn't wait. But do you always have to be the first one on the battlefield and the last one to leave?'

'No. I'll leave as soon as I see her.'

The hollow thumps, the remote anguished cries that could have been half a mile away. I couldn't stand listening to it. Yet the bomb techs continued their methodical inspection.

'There are no explosive devices,' I said. I staggered across the marshy field. 'He would have boasted about it.'

'Where are you going?'

'To get her out of there.'

'You don't know how.'

But I did. I knew something about caskets. The Department of

Defense provided standard-issue metal or wooden caskets to the families of soldiers killed in the line of duty, if they were wanted. A few times I'd had the solemn and terrible duty of accompanying the body of a friend on the plane home.

When I got to Alexa's casket I shoved aside one of the guys in their bulky blast-resistant space suits. He protested, and the other one tried to block me. Someone yelled, 'Back away!'

The other guys on the SWAT team stayed back as per standard procedure. I shouted to them, 'One of you must have a hex key set, right?'

Someone threw me a folding tool with a bunch of Allen keys on it. I found the right one and inserted it in the hole at the foot of the casket and turned the crank counterclockwise four or five turns to unlock the lid.

The rubber gasket had been mashed in places where the steel casket had begun to cave in under ten feet of dirt, but I managed to pry it up.

A terrible odor escaped, like from an open sewer.

Alexa had been lying in her own excrement, or just a few inches above it. She stared up, but not at me. Her hair was matted, her face chalk white, her eyes sunken in deep pits.

She was wearing blue medical scrubs and was covered in vomit. Her hands were curled in loose fists that kept jerking outward. She couldn't stop pounding the sides of her coffin. Her bare feet twitched.

She didn't understand she was free.

I knelt over and kissed her forehead and said, 'Hey.'

Her eyes searched the sky. She didn't see me. Then she did. She looked directly at me, uncomprehendingly.

I smiled at her and she started to cry.

That was about the last thing I remembered for a long while.

ONE HUNDRED
AND SEVEN

I hate hospitals.

Unfortunately I had to spend a few days at the Beth Israel Hospital in Boston, where my FBI friends were kind enough to helicopter me from New Hampshire. The ER doc told me I'd developed a tension pneumothorax as a result of the blunt-force trauma. That my entire chest cavity had filled up with air, my lungs had collapsed, and I'd gone into respiratory distress. That it was a life-threatening condition and if one of the SWAT guys hadn't done what he did, I'd surely be dead.

I asked him what had been done.

'I don't think you want to know,' he said.

'Try me.'

'Someone with medic training stuck a large-bore needle in your chest to let the air out,' he said delicately.

'You mean like a Cook kit?'

He looked surprised.

'In the army we called that a needle thoracostomy. Every field medic carries a Cook pneumothorax kit in their aid bag.'

He looked relieved.

He ordered up a lot of X-rays and put a chest tube in me, had the wound in my calf cleaned out and bandaged, gave me a tetanus shot, and sent me to another ward to recover. After three days they let me go.

Diana was there to give me a ride home.

Even though I could now walk just fine, the nurse insisted on rolling me to the hospital entrance in a wheelchair while Diana got the car.

She pulled up in my Defender. Nice and shiny and newly washed.

'Look familiar?' she said as I got in.

'Not really. It looks almost new. Someone find it in the woods up in New Hampshire?'

'One of the snipers. He drove it back to Boston and decided he liked it better than his Chevy Malibu. It wasn't easy to pry it out of his sweaty little hands. But at least he washed it for you.'

'I want to see Alexa. Is she still in the hospital?'

'Actually, she got out a lot faster than you. She was treated for dehydration, they checked her out, and she's fine.'

'I doubt that.'

'You're right. I've dealt with plenty of kids who've gone through traumatic experiences. I know some good therapists. Maybe you can convince her to see one.'

'Is she at home?'

'Yeah. In Manchester. I don't think she's happy about it, but it's home.' As we headed down Comm Ave toward Mass Ave, she said, 'How about I cook dinner for you tonight? As a celebration.'

'A celebration of what?'

She gave me a sideways glance and pursed her lips. 'I don't know, maybe the fact you saved that girl's life?'

'If anything was a team effort—'

'You're doing that thing again.'

'Thing?'

'Where you give everyone else credit except yourself. You don't have to do that with me.'

I was too tapped out to argue.

'Let's make it my place,' she said. 'I don't want to be the first person to turn on your oven. Does it even work?'

'I'm not sure. Let me go home and get changed and take a shower. Or a sponge bath.'

'It's just dinner, you know.'

'Not a date. Of course.'

'Like the thought never occurred to you.'

'Never,' I said.

'You know something, Nico? For a guy who's so good at recognizing a lie, you're a really bad liar.'

I just shrugged. She wasn't so good at it either.

ONE HUNDRED
AND EIGHT

One week later

The waves crashed loudly on the rocks below, and the wind howled along the point. The sky looked heavy, a mournful gray, as if any moment it might begin to pour.

No more armed guards, I saw. The guardhouse was empty. I parked in the circular drive and crossed the porch, the floorboards creaking underfoot.

I rang the bell and waited almost a minute, then rang again. After another minute the door opened, and Marshall Marcus stood there.

He was wearing a gray cardigan and a rumpled white dress shirt that looked like it hadn't been pressed.

'Nickeleh,' he said, and he smiled, but it was not a happy smile. He was weary and defeated. His face seemed to have sunk and his teeth seemed too big for his mouth and far too white. His face was creased and his reddish hair stuck out in crazy tufts. It looked like he'd been napping.

'Sorry to wake you,' I said. 'Want me to come back?'

'No, no, don't be silly, come on in.' He gave me a big hug. 'Thank you for coming.'

I followed him to the front of the house where you could watch the sea. His shoulders slumped as he walked. The front room was gloomy, the only light coming from the fading late-afternoon sky. Crumpled on one of the couches was a cheap synthetic Red Sox blanket, the kind they sell at Fenway.

'She's still not talking?' I said.

Marcus heaved a long sigh as he sank into a chair. 'She hardly even comes out of her room. It's like she's not even here. She sleeps all the time.'

'After what she's been through, she needs to see someone. It doesn't have to be one of the trauma specialists Diana's recommending. But someone, at least.'

'I know, Nick. I know. Maybe you can change her mind. Lexie always seems to listen to you. You feeling better?'

'Totally,' I said.

'Good thing you were wearing a vest, huh?'

'Yeah. Lucky break. You're doing the right thing.'

He gave me a questioning look.

'Meeting with the FBI.'

'Oh. Yeah, well, only because Schecky says he can get me a deal.'

'Give Gordon Snyder what he wants,' I said, 'and you'll have the FBI on your side. They have a lot of influence with the US Attorney's Office.'

'But what does that mean? They're gonna put me in prison? My little girl, look what's she's already been through – now she has to lose her daddy?'

'Depending on how much you cooperate, you might even walk,' I said.

'You really think so?'

'It depends on how much you give them. You're going to have to tell them about Mercury. They know a lot already.'

'Schecky says I have nothing to worry about if I just do what he says.'

'How well has that worked out for you?' I said.

He looked uneasy and said nothing for a long while.

Finally I broke the silence. 'Where's Belinda?'

'That's why I asked you to come here,' Marcus said. 'She's gone.'

ONE HUNDRED
AND NINE

He handed me a pale blue correspondence card with BELINDA JACKSON
MARCUS on the top in small navy blue copperplate. The script was
big and loopy and feminine, but a few of the letters – the *H*'s and
the *A*'s and the *W*'s – looked Cyrillic. Like they'd come from the
hand of someone who'd learned to write in Russian as a child. The
note said:

> *Darling —*
> *I think it's better this way. Someday we'll talk.*
> *I'm so happy Alexa is home.*
> *I really did love you.*
> *Belinda*

'She said she was going out to meet a girlfriend in the city, and
when I got up I found this propped up against the coffeemaker.
What does it mean?'

It meant she'd been warned the FBI was about to close in on her.
Though in truth, it would have been difficult to prove Anya
Afanasyeva guilty of any serious crime.

'Sometimes it takes a crisis to find out who a person really is,' I said.

I doubt he knew who I was really talking about.

Marcus shook his head, as if he were trying to dodge a pesky fly, or a thought. 'Nick, I need you to find her for me.'

'I don't think she wants to be found.'

'What are you talking about? She's my wife. She loves me!'

'Maybe she loved your money more.'

'She knew I was broke for months. It never changed anything with us.'

'Well, Marcus, there's broke and there's *broke*, right?'

A long pause.

He then turned away.

'Come on, Marshall. Did you really think you could move forty-five million dollars offshore without anyone finding out? It's not so easy anymore.'

Marcus flushed. 'Okay, so there was a little nest egg,' he said. 'Money I wasn't going to touch. Money I'll need if I'm ever going to get back in the game.' He sounded defensive, almost indignant. 'Look, I'm not going to apologize for what I've got.'

'Apologize? What do you have to apologize for?' I said.

'Exactly.'

He didn't notice my caustic tone. 'I mean, you've been consistent from the beginning – you've never stopped lying to me. Even back when Alexa was kidnapped the first time and you told me you had no idea who was behind it. You knew it was David Schechter's people, cracking the whip. Making sure you did what you were told. I'm guessing Annelise had her suspicions, though. Maybe it had something to do with why she couldn't live with you anymore.'

He hesitated a few seconds, apparently deciding not to deny it. 'Look, if this is about money, then fine. I'll pay your bill in full.' The ends of his mouth twitched as if trying to conceal a tiny smile.

I laughed. 'Like I said, Marcus, there's broke and there's broke. As of nine o'clock this morning, you're wiped out for real. Check with the Royal Cayman Bank and Trust. The entire forty-five million dollars was withdrawn this morning.'

'It's *gone*?' Marcus sank into the sofa and started to rock back and forth. Like he was either about to pray or about to weep. 'How could this happen to me *again*?'

'Well,' I said, 'maybe it wasn't the smartest idea to put it all in Belinda's name.'

ONE HUNDRED
AND TEN

David Schechter wanted to meet with me before the FBI arrived at his office. He said it was a matter of some urgency.

'I wanted to apologize to you,' he said. He sat in his rickety antique chair behind the tiny antique desk.

'For what?'

'I overreacted, I'll be the first to admit it. I should have been up-front with you from the get-go. You're a reasonable man. More than that, you're a true American hero.'

He fixed me with a look of the deepest admiration, as if I were some great statesman, like Winston Churchill. Or maybe Bono.

'You're too kind,' I said. 'Apology accepted.'

'You of all people understand that our national security must never be compromised.'

'No question,' I said.

'I've already impressed upon Marshall the importance of not divulging to the FBI anything about Mercury that's not germane to their investigation.'

'Why keep it secret from the FBI?'

'Nick, you know how Washington works. If it ever gets out that ten billion dollars in military black-budget funds has been lost because it was being privately invested – dear Lord, we'd be throwing buckets of chum upon the water. The sharks will come for miles. You were a soldier. Can you imagine what damage such a revelation would do to our nation's defense?'

'Not really.'

He blinked owlishly behind his horn-rimmed glasses. 'You don't understand what a huge scandal would result?'

'Oh, sure. It'll be huge, all right. Lots of people are going to wonder how you stole all that money from the Pentagon.'

He smiled uneasily.

ONE HUNDRED
AND ELEVEN

Because I'd finally learned the real story in a hotel suite at the Mandarin.

'You must realize,' Roman Navrozov had said, 'how frustrating it is to sit on the sidelines with billions of dollars and billions of euros at my disposal, ready to invest in American industry, and yet every single one of my deals is blocked by the US government. While America sells itself off to every country in the world. Including its sworn enemies.'

'I think that's a bit of an exaggeration,' I'd said.

'Ten per cent of America is owned by the Saudis, do you know this? The Communist Chinese own most of your Treasury bonds. Some of your biggest defense contractors are owned by foreign conglomerates. But when I try to buy an American steel company or an energy company or a computer company, your government refuses. Some anonymous bureaucrats in the Treasury Department say it would harm national security.'

'So you wanted the Mercury files for leverage? To force the US government to rubber-stamp all of your deals?'

He shrugged.

'Then there must be something in the Mercury files that a lot of powerful people want kept secret.'

He shrugged.

'Let's hear it,' I said.

Now, I leaned back in my fragile antique wooden chair. It creaked alarmingly. Schechter winced.

'Turning a slush fund into a hedge fund to funnel secret payments to some of the most powerful people in America for three decades,' I said. 'That's genius.'

I glanced pointedly at his ego wall. At all those photographs of him doing the grip-and-grin with former secretaries of Defense and secretaries of State and four former vice presidents and even a few former presidents. 'But what was the point? Your own self-aggrandizement? What could you possibly have wanted? How much influence did you need to buy? For what?'

'You don't have the slightest idea, do you?'

'About what?'

He paused for a long time, examined his immaculate desktop, looked back up. 'You're probably too young to remember that there once was a time when the best and the brightest went into government work because it was the right thing to do.'

'Camelot, right?'

'Now where do the graduates of our top colleges end up? Law schools and investment banks. They go where the money is.'

'Can you blame them?'

'Precisely. The CEO of Merrill Lynch pockets a hundred million dollars for driving his company into the ground. The guy who almost destroyed Home Depot gets two hundred and ten million dollars just to go away. Yet a hard-working public servant who helps run the fifteen-*trillion*-dollar enterprise called the United States of America can't afford to send his kids to college? A general who's fought all his life to keep our country safe and strong spends his retirement in tract housing in Rockville, Maryland, scraping by on a pension of a hundred thousand bucks a year?'

'This is good,' I said. 'I don't think I've ever heard a better rationalization for graft.'

'Graft?' Schechter said, red-faced, eyes glittering. 'You call it graft? How about calling it retention pay? Stock options in America? The whole point of Mercury is to make sure that the best and the brightest aren't punished for being patriots. Yes, Nick, we diverted the money and built a goddamn moat. We guaranteed that our greatest public servants would never have to worry about money. So they could lead lives of genuine public service. This sure as hell is about national security. It's about rewarding heroes and statesmen and patriots – instead of bankers and swindlers who'd sell out their country for two basis points.'

I could see the veins on his neck pulsing.

'Well,' I said softly, 'you make a good argument. And I'm sure you'll have the opportunity to make it before a jury of your peers.'

'I'll deny we ever spoke about it,' he said with a cruel smile.

'Don't bother,' I said. I got up and opened the door to his office. Gordon Snyder and Diana Madigan were standing there, flanking Marshall Marcus. Behind them were six guys in FBI windbreakers. 'Marshall is cooperating.'

He shook his head. 'You son of a bitch.' He pulled open his desk drawer and one of the FBI guys shouted, 'Freeze!'

But it wasn't a gun Schechter was after. It was a breath mint, which he popped in his mouth.

'Gentlemen,' he said with a beatific smile. 'Please enter.'

He didn't rise, though, which wasn't like him.

'David, I'm sorry,' Marcus said.

I turned and saw that Schechter was staring at me, his eyes fixed. His mouth was foaming. I could smell almonds.

I shouted, 'Anyone have a medical kit?'

A couple of the FBI agents rushed in. One of them checked Schechter's pulse, at his wrist and on his neck. Then he shook his head.

David Schechter liked to brag that he always had all the angles figured out.

I guess he was right after all.

ONE HUNDRED
AND TWELVE

Early in the fall I took Diana out for a drive. She wanted to see the New England foliage. I've never cared much about foliage, though the fiery red maples were impressive.

She had no itinerary in mind; she just wanted to drive. I suggested New Hampshire, where the leaves were further along.

Neither one of us spoke about the last time we'd been in New Hampshire together.

After we were on the road a while, I said, 'I have something for you.'

'Uh-oh.'

'Look in the glove box.'

She gave me a puzzled look, then popped open the glove compartment and took out a small box, badly gift-wrapped.

She held it up and pretended to admire the wrapping job. 'Aren't you a regular Martha Stewart,' she teased.

'Not my skill set,' I said. 'Obviously.'

She tore it open, gasped.

'I don't believe it,' she said, staring at the octagonal black perfume bottle. 'Where the hell did you get Nombre Noir? And a full ounce? And sealed? Are you out of your *mind*?'

'I meant to give it to you years ago,' I said.

She reached over and gave me a kiss. 'I'm almost out, too. I thought I'd never have it again. Last time I checked eBay, a half-ounce of Nombre Noir was selling for more than seven hundred dollars. Where'd you *get* this?'

'Remember my friend the Jordanian arms dealer?'

'Samir?'

'Right. Sammy found it for me. One of his clients is a sheikh in Abu Dhabi who had a stockpile in an air-conditioned storeroom.'

'Thank Samir for me.'

'Oh, I did. Believe me, I did. You'd have thought I asked him for a nuclear warhead. But by the time he handed it to me, you were gone.'

'You could have sent it.'

'I don't trust the mail,' I lied.

Diana once explained to me that Nombre Noir was one of the greatest perfumes ever created. But it was impossible to find now. Apparently the company that made it ended up losing money on each bottle. Then the European Union, in its infinite wisdom, decided to ban one of its main ingredients, something called damascone, because it causes sun sensitivity in some tiny percentage of people. The company recalled every bottle they could and then destroyed each one by running a steamroller over them.

As soon as she told me it was impossible to find, of course, I made a point of tracking some down.

'Well, that serves me right for leaving without letting you know,' she said.

'Yeah, so there.'

'So, um, speaking of which? They've offered me a supervisory special agent job in Miami,' she said.

'Hey, that's a big deal,' I said with all the enthusiasm I could muster. 'Congratulations. Miami could be great.'

'Thanks.'

'Hard to turn down a job like that,' I said.

The awkward silence seemed to go on forever.

'What about Gordon Snyder's job?'

Snyder's superiors weren't so happy about his planting an unapproved, off-the-books tracking device in my BlackBerry and then trying to cover his tracks by claiming that a confidential informant had tipped him off to Mauricio Perreira's location. He'd been demoted and transferred to Anchorage.

I'd heard he could see Russia from his desk.

'Nah, they're looking for an organized crime specialist for that slot. So, Nico. Mind if I ask you something about Roman Navrozov?'

'Okay.'

'That helicopter crash in Marbella? A bit too convenient, don't you think?'

I shrugged. A deal was a deal.

'Let me guess. Putin's guys have been trying to get him for years. But he never made it easy for them. So you struck a bargain with one of your ex-KGB sources. Some sort of trade for information. It isn't like what happened to Navrozov was a tragedy. Some might even call it justice. You probably figured it was win–win.'

'Or maybe it was just a cracked rotor blade, like they say.'

She gave me a look. 'Sure. Let's go with that.'

After a long moment, I said, 'Sometimes, stuff just happens.'

'Hmph.'

'You see that story in the *Globe* a couple days ago about the accountant who was crushed to death by a falling filing cabinet? There's no safe place. No guarantees.'

'I didn't mean what I said about marrying a CPA.'

'No?'

'No. I'd settle for a database administrator.'

'I mean it. You can swathe yourself in five layers of security, but your luxury helicopter is still going to come down over Marbella. I don't know about you, but I'd much rather *see* the bullet that's coming for me.'

We both stared straight ahead for a while.

'You know,' she said, 'I probably shouldn't tell you this, but we're about to make an arrest in the Mercury case.'

'I was wondering if that would ever happen.'

The weeks had turned into months, and not a single one of Marshall Marcus's 'investors' had even been brought in for questioning. None of their names had surfaced in the press.

Marshall Marcus remained at liberty, since he'd cooperated fully with the FBI – and his new lawyers were still negotiating with the SEC. There were a lot of investors out there howling for his head. He'd certainly face some kind of prison time.

But apart from that, it was like nothing had happened.

Call me cynical, but I couldn't help but wonder whether a quiet call had been placed to the attorney general. Maybe a whispered aside over steaks at Charlie Palmer's in DC.

'It's complicated,' she said. 'We're talking about some extremely prominent individuals – senior government officials, elder statesmen. As the saying goes, if you shoot at a king, you must kill him.'

'But you have names and account numbers . . .'

'Suddenly there are a whole lot of very nervous people at the top of the Justice Department who insist on signing off on everything. They want us to cross every *t* and dot every *i*. They want everything completely nailed down before they'll go ahead with such a high-profile corruption sweep. Something like this will destroy careers and reputations and, you know, shake the faith of the country in our elected officials.'

'Sure wouldn't want to do that,' I said dryly.

'The Criminal Division is insisting on all sorts of bank records from around the world, including from offshore banks that won't cooperate in a hundred years.'

'In other words, nothing's going to happen.'

She was silent. 'Like I said, it's complicated.'

'You don't find this frustrating?'

'I just keep my head down and do the best job I can.'

'So who are you about to arrest?'

'General Mark Hood.'

I gave her a sideways glance, then looked back at the road. 'On what grounds?'

'Embezzlement, fraud . . . It's a long charge sheet. He was the one who supervised the illegal transfer of covert funds out of the Pentagon's black budget.'

I nodded. 'I figured as much.'

'You were on to him, weren't you? Before he fired you?'

'I guess so. Though I didn't know it at the time.'

For several miles neither of us spoke.

Maybe, I thought, the only true justice was karma.

Take Taylor Armstrong. She claimed that when Mauricio Perreira pressured her into setting him up with her BFF, Alexa, she really had no idea what was going to happen. I believed her. Not that it made her any less narcissistic, sleazy, and underhanded.

Shortly after we last talked, Taylor was pulled out of school and sent to a place in western Massachusetts that specialized in 'novel treatments' for students with severe behavioral problems, controversial for its use of electric shock as an 'aversive'. It made the Marston-Lee Academy look like the Canyon Ranch Spa.

The place also required weekly counseling sessions with parents, which wasn't going to be a problem, since her father, Senator Armstrong, had announced he was leaving public service in order to spend more time with his family.

I saw the exit sign and hit the turn signal.

'Where are we going?'

'Ever seen the Exeter campus?'

'No. Why would I . . .' Then, realizing, she said, 'You think she's ready to see you?'

'I guess we'll find out.'

* * *

Diana waited for me in the car. She thought it was best for me to have some time alone with Alexa.

The girls' field hockey team was practicing on the dazzling green artificial turf field in the football stadium at the far end of the campus. I knew nothing about field hockey, but it looked like a scrimmage. It was a cluttery game, hard to understand at first. The whistle was constantly sounding. A few of the girls really stood out, one in particular, and when she turned I saw it was Alexa.

She was wearing a headband, her hair tied back. Her arms were tan and muscular, her legs long and lean.

Her blue mouth guard gave her a fierce appearance, but she looked healthy and happy.

The coach blew her whistle and shouted, 'Let's get some water,' and the girls all popped out their mouth guards: a precise, automatic gesture. Some tucked the mouthpieces under the tops of their sports bras; some slipped them into their shin guards. They shouted and talked loudly and squealed as they straggled toward the drinking fountain. A couple of them hugged Alexa – I'd forgotten how much more affectionate girls are than guys at that age – and laughed about something.

Then she turned, as if she'd sensed my presence, and caught my eye. She spoke quickly to one of her teammates and approached reluctantly.

'Hey, Nick.'

'You're really good, you know that?'

'I'm okay. I like it. That's the main thing.'

'You play hard. You're tough. Fearless, even.'

She gave a quick, nervous laugh. 'Gift of fear, right?'

'Right. So I just wanted to say hi and make sure everything's okay.'

'Oh, um, okay, thanks. Yeah, everything's cool. It's good. I'm . . .' She looked longingly over at her teammates. 'It's kinda not the best time, is that . . . that okay?'

'No problem.'

'I mean, like, you didn't drive all the way up here just to see me or anything, right? Like, I hope not.'

'Not at all. I was in the area.'

'Business or something?'

'Yeah.'

'So, yeah. Um . . .' She gave me a little wave. 'I gotta go. Thanks for coming by. Nice to see you.'

'Yeah,' I said. 'You too.'

I understood: just seeing me brought on all kinds of dark and troubling emotions. I'd forever be associated with a nightmare. I made her uncomfortable. There were things in the subbasement of her mind she couldn't yet deal with. Her way of recovering was to try to forget.

We all have our ways of coping.

As she returned to the field, her stride got looser. I could see the tension leave her body. One of her friends made a crack, and she gave a quick grin, and the coach blew her whistle again.

I stood there watching for a few minutes longer. She played with a fluid grace, almost balletic. Once I began to understand how the game worked, it was sort of exciting. She charged down the field, dished it off to another player in a give-and-go, and kept on going. Suddenly everything was happening too fast to follow of. Just as she entered the striking circle she somehow got the ball back, and then I could see what all of her teammates saw: that the goalkeeper had been fooled and Alexa had a clear shot, and she smiled as she flicked the ball up in the air and it soared toward the goal.

She'd take it from here.

ACKNOWLEDGMENTS

I wish I could quote the late Spike Milligan: 'I am not going to thank anybody – because I did it all myself.' Unfortunately, in my case, this is not accurate.

I just did the hard part.

But I did turn repeatedly to a small group of victims – er, technical advisers. My varsity squad of sources: Jeff Fischbach, amazing forensic technologist and real-life character out of *The Matrix* who knows a scary amount about electronic evidence and cell-phone tracking; Stuart Allen, preeminent forensic audio expert who shares my taste in good wine and bad jokes; and, again, Dick Rogers, founder of the FBI's Hostage Rescue Squad and fount of wisdom about kidnapping and rescue strategy, field ops, and weaponry.

A lot of people in the FBI's Boston Field Office helped me get the details right, particularly Supervisory Special Agent Randy Jarvis, a real-life action hero who runs the violent crimes task force; Kevin Swindon in digital forensics; Ed Kappler in firearms; Steve Vienneau in crimes against children; and S.A. Tamara Harty of the CARD team in Providence. Thanks especially to Special Agent Gail Marcinkiewicz, for introductions and guidance.

A few hedge-fund titans generously took time with me to explain the intricacies of their business – time they could have spent trading

406

and making millions. Yes, I feel guilty about that. But also grateful, to Jon Jacobson of Highfields Capital Management, Richard Leibovitch of Gottex Funds (whose son, Jeremy, demonstrated 'Call of Duty'), Bill Ackman of Pershing Square Capital Management, and Seth Klarman of the Baupost Group. Kristin Marcus at Highfields explained how funds are structured, as did Steve Alperin of the Harvard Management Company.

Once again, Nick Heller was backstopped by a team of 'private spies': Skip Brandon and Gene Smith of Smith Brandon International, Terry Lenzner of the Investigative Group International, and Jack Devine of the Arkin Group.

Lawyers, guns, and money: deepest thanks to Jay Shapiro for legal advice; Dr Ed Nawotka, Jr., on guns and ammo; Jack Blum, expert in offshore banking, shell companies, and money laundering, for help figuring out the big swindle; and to my old friend and unindicted co-conspirator, Giles McNamee, owner of Nick's Land Rover Defender 110, Coniston green.

For background on computer forensics, thanks to Anish Dhanda and Rich Person of DNS Enterprise, Inc., Simson Garfinkel, Mark Spencer of Arsenal Consulting, and Larry Daniel of Guardian Digital Forensics. For eavesdropping detection, Kevin D. Murray of Murray Associates; for satellite communications, Wolf Vogel; and for covert entry and security, Marc W. Tobias, Michael Huebler, and Jeffrey Dingle of Lockmasters Security Institute. Thanks as well to Randy Milch, general counsel at Verizon; Michael Sielicki, chief of police, Rindge, New Hampshire; Maj. Greg Heilshorn of the New Hampshire Air National Guard; Kevin O'Brien; Justin Sullivan of RegentJet; Mercy Carbonell of Phillips Exeter Academy; and Kevin Roche of the US Marshals Service. Raja Ramani of Pennsylvania State University, Brian Prosser of Mine Ventilation Services, and Kray Luxbacher of Virginia Tech all provided important logistical details about Alexa Marcus's underground ordeal. And Dennis Sweeney of Dennis Sweeney Funeral Home in Quincy, Massachusetts, kindly gave me a taste of what Alexa

Marcus went through. I really hope never to do it again as long as I'm alive.

Domo arigato to Nick Heller's personal trainer, Jack Hoban, ethical warrior and musician. Christopher Rogers of Grubb & Ellis found me Nick Heller's 'steampunk' office in downtown Boston, and Diane Kaneb graciously let me move Marshall and Belinda Marcus into her family's graceful waterfront house in Manchester. Hilary Gabrieli and Beth Ketterson told me a bit about Louisburg Square. Lucy Baldwin was Alexa Marcus's fashion consultant. Vivian Wyler and Anna Buarque of my Brazilian publisher, Rocco, helped with the Portuguese. Liz Berry gave me some wonderful tips on how to tell a real Georgia native. Thanks to Sean Reardon of the Liberty Hotel, Ali Khalid of the Four Seasons Hotel, and Mike Arnett of the Mandarin Oriental, for hotel security details; and to my brother, Dr Jonathan Finder, and Dr Tom Workman, for medical information.

The perfume that Nick gives Diana, Nombre Noir, is real (though discontinued and almost impossible to find). It was suggested to me by two remarkable perfume experts, the biophysicist (and 'emperor of scent') Luca Turin, and his wife, the writer Tania Sanchez.

With all these experts in my corner, if I've made any mistakes, obviously one of them must have left something out.

There's no better literary agent than Molly Friedrich. At the Friedrich Agency, thanks as well to Paul Cirone, and – for some extremely astute editorial insight – Lucy Carson. I've got a terrific web manager, Karen Louie-Joyce, and a top-notch editor and researcher in Clair Lamb.

Without Claire Baldwin, my assistant, I wouldn't get a damned thing done. You're the best.

To my brilliant editor, Keith Kahla: I know I drove you crazy writing this book . . . but you got me back good.

Henry Finder, editorial director of *The New Yorker*, was an invaluable contributor at every stage, and yes, he's my *younger* brother.

Since the age of two, when she poured a sippy cup of water over the keyboard of my laptop, my daughter, Emma, has been an astute critic of my work. With *Buried Secrets* she turned her acute editorial eye to some crucial scenes and saved me from some embarrassing gaffes. I'd say you rock, Em, but then you'd say I'm just some pathetic old guy trying to sound cool.

My wife, Michele Souda, had the hardest job of all: being married to a writer. Thanks for standing by me all this time. I know it ain't easy to keep dancing.

— JOSEPH FINDER
Boston, Massachusetts